SHERIFF ADONAI

"The Encounter at Rock Pointe"

D. Keith Jones

BOOK ONE IN THE SHERIFF ADONAI SERIES

SHERIFF ADONAI, The Encounter at Rock Pointe
Copyright © 2015 by D. Keith Jones

All rights reserved. No part of this book may be reproduced or transmitted in any form or by any means without written permission from the author.

This novel is a work of fiction. Names, descriptions, entities, and incidents included in this story are products of the author's imagination. Any resemblance to actual persons, events, and entities is entirely coincidental.

ISBN (978-0-692-32856-9)

Printed in USA by 48HrBooks (www.48HrBooks.com)

Dedication

I dedicate this book, first and foremost, to You, my Heavenly Father. It is only by You and because of You that all things exist. You gave me this story in the middle of the night, and anything good that might come from the words I type, are only because of You, God, who gave me the talent, the wisdom, and the resources to make this book a possibility. I thank you for all those who have been won to You because of this story and I pray that countless others will find You as they follow the story of Misief Stone. You are my strength, my Redeemer, and my personal friend!

To my lovely wife, Nancy, who is my greatest supporter and has always believed in me. This series of books would not be a reality without your input and guidance. I love you very much! K.J. + N.J. = T.F.!

To my Mother and Father, who raised me in a godly home and provided me with a Christian heritage. Mom, you are now at home with Jesus and I cannot wait until I get to see you again someday. Dad, thank you for your support of this book ministry! You are my #1 salesman! Keep showing people God's love as you do each day of your life and keep selling books for Jesus!

To my son, Josh Jones, thank you for your creative work on the cover design. You have a gift and I thank you for sharing your talent with me. I will always cherish the time we spent working on this project together!

To Kristin Vrieswyk, you were sent to help me on this book project at the perfect time! You were an answer to prayer and I thank you for your hours of work to help form this book into what it has become!

To each one who reads this story, I pray that the message inside this story will speak to your heart, enrich your life and change your eternal destiny! May you be blessed as you sit back and enjoy this book!

D. Keith Jones

Foreword

We've all read books and watched movies where two people fall in love and live happily ever after. They have this perfect love, and it lasts forever. We call that a fairytale. What about in the real world? Does unconditional love really exist? Have you ever been the recipient of it? I am talking about a no strings attached, no fine print, all out, kind of love. A love that is unmerited, unrestrained and unending. We humans don't tend to love that way. We love for a little while, until we get hurt or tired, and then we just walk away.

But, I have good news for you; there is someone who truly loves unconditionally. His love for us compels him to pursue us relentlessly. His love never fails, never gives up and never grows weary. To experience his love is indescribable. His love cannot be earned or purchased. His love is freely given. But, there is one string attached....you must be willing to accept his love. You have to open your heart and let him embrace you. It's your choice.

When you hear him knocking, let him in. I encourage you to allow yourself to become the beneficiary of a love like nothing you've ever experienced or could ever imagine. He loves you, period. He loves you just the way you are. He could have anything he wanted, but what he wants most is you. And he has gone to great lengths to show you just how much he loves you.

So, who is this I speak of? Well, you'll meet him in the pages to come. As you read this story, I pray that you begin to see how he has been chasing after you throughout your entire life. I pray that you hear him speaking to you, and I urge you to accept his offer. It will absolutely change your life.

Be blessed as you read these pages. I pray that this story speaks to your heart as it has to mine.

Kristin Vrieswyk

Introduction

Diary entry dated April 16, 1845 –

"The wagon is loaded and the horses are ready. We are leaving the East Coast this morning headed to make a new life in the Western Frontier. I am not sure what we will experience, but we are looking for a new life. My boyfriend, Barak, is going to pursue a new opportunity and has promised a better life for me. I'm leaving my family and going with him. There are two other couples going with us; Davis Williams & his girlfriend, Tammy Sue, along with Misty Lou & Jeno Stephens."

Signed,
Bett Stone

Diary entry dated June 3, 1845 –

"We've been on the trail for six weeks. We arrived in Independence, Missouri, late this evening. We've gathered a few supplies and then decided to give the horses a day or two to rest. While we were here, Barak surprised me by asking me to marry him! He found a local reverend and we got hitched yesterday afternoon. I'm now a married woman! There was a man in the saloon that had a camera so we went inside and he took our picture! Tammy Sue and Davis got in on the act and got married too. I am so excited!!"

Signed,
Bett Stone

Diary entry dated June 5, 1845 –

"It's time to get moving again. We finished loading up the supplies and prepared the horses for the final half of the journey. My husband, Barak, is still excited about his great idea. It seems strange to call him my husband. Anyway, he keeps telling me we are going to be rich. He purchased a leather satchel today and is wearing it around his neck. He says he is going to put all his great ideas in this leather bag."

Signed,
Bett Stone

Diary entry dated July 22, 1845 –

"We've been on the trail for over three months. We are all tired and weary. Supplies are running low and the travel is much slower than we anticipated. We will need to pick up the pace to reach our destination of Fort Hall, Idaho before bad weather sets in."

Signed,
Bett Stone

Diary entry dated August 9, 1845 –

"We stopped at a Trading Post to pick up much needed supplies. Grasslands for the animals have been plentiful but water is sometimes hard to find. The man who ran the Trading Post told my husband about a nice place to live, just a few days journey from here. We are thinking about a change of plans."

Signed,
Bett Stone

Diary entry dated August 21, 1845 –

"We jumped off the Oregon Trail a day or so ago and arrived in Rock Springs, Wyoming this afternoon. We are going in to the Land Grant office to see if we can get a piece of land to start our new life. The Williams and the Stephens are still with us. We think we can all get a nice section of land within a few miles of each other. It is not what we had planned, but this seems to be a nice place to raise a family."

Signed,
Bett Stone

Diary entry dated August 26, 1845 –

"We were quite surprised to find a piece of land with an old cabin already standing on it. It is only eleven miles outside of Rock Springs. The property sits at the base of a mountain and has a creek that runs along the back of it. It also has an old stable that will work well to keep our animals and a nice place to plant a garden. The cabin needs a little work but Barak promised to fix it up for me."

The Williams and the Stephens also found some land, but their new property does not have any buildings on it yet. They will be staying with us through the winter until the men can work together to get homes built on their homesteads.

It feels great to be off the trail and settling in our new home!

Signed,
Bett Stone

Chapter 1

"A Man Called Lucas"

June 2, 1857

It sounded like a thunderstorm rumbling in the west, but as he peeked over the ledge of the small frame window in the kitchen, the cloudless blue sky made it obvious that the noise Misief (*mee-suf*) was hearing was not coming from Mother Nature. Without wasting time, his father sprang up from the head of the table and grabbed his gun belt. Being that Misief's father lived most of his life outside the long arm of the law, his trusty .45 caliber revolvers were never more than an arm's length away. The family rule required all guns to be removed and hung on the wall beside the fireplace before sitting down at the family dinner table.

As the sound grew increasingly closer, Misief watched his mother grab his baby sister and dash away from the kitchen table. "Misief! Quick, we gotta get out of here!" his mother shouted.

In an instant, Misief spun around and followed his mother to the safety of the bedroom, which was on the back side of their small cabin. With his sister in her arms, his mother kicked the bedroom door open and he trailed in behind her.

As the three of them scrambled to take cover in the tiny bedroom, Misief accidently stumbled into a wooden crate that was sitting beside his parent's iron bed. The old crate served as a nightstand on which an oil lamp and several pictures were sitting. Reaching up, Misief caught the oil lamp as it began to tip over, but he couldn't catch the pictures that had been carefully placed around the lamp. One of the pictures crashed to the floor, and the glass shattered into tiny pieces. This particular picture was very special to his parents. It captured the moment in June of 1845 when Barak and Bett became husband and wife.

Misief was never sure of the exact location where his parents wedding took place; however, in the background of the picture there appeared to be a wooden player piano, barstools and multiple round card tables. Based on this photo, he always assumed they got married in a saloon; but whenever he asked, his parents wouldn't confirm either way. As he stared at the shattered glass that had once served to protect the precious photo, his eye caught an inscription on the back of the picture that read "Bett, I love you always, Barak."

Misief's understanding of his father's past was sketchy at best. He didn't know all the details, but gathering from the bits and pieces he'd overheard through the years, something drastic occurred that changed his father from a loving and devoted husband to a man who stayed in trouble with the law.

****

Barak Stone married Bett when she was 17 years old. Bett grew up on the East Coast with her family but agreed to run off and go west with Barak, so he could pursue his dreams of becoming a rich man. Barak told Bett he'd developed a new way to send communications to the towns across the Western Frontier by using a network of flux wire. According to Barak, his idea had been reviewed by the Midwest Communication Company, and the owner of the company had verbally promised him they would buy the rights to his idea if he could finish the testing to prove his concept would work properly. Barak was convinced the flux wire idea was going to be the ticket to allow him to give his bride the life she deserved. All he needed was $250 to finish testing his idea, and then he could sell the rights to the company and enjoy the rich life he'd promised to Bett.

In addition to the verbal commitment of the company President, The Midwest Communication Company had also issued Barak a *'Letter of Intent to Purchase'*, pending the successful completion of the final testing. Barak kept this *'Intent to Purchase'* letter, along with the detailed drawings of the flux wire concept in an old, brown leather bag. On the outside of the leather bag he'd taken a Cross Pointe knife and inscribed the letters *'S.F.F.'* which stood for *'Stone Family Fortune'*. He carried this leather bag with him everywhere he went, guarding it with his life.

The year was 1845 when Barak and Bett settled in a cabin eleven miles outside the small western town of Rock Springs, Wyoming. The cabin was a five room, log home that was about thirty-five years old. The main room sported a rock fireplace with a hand carved mantel made from a chestnut tree. On each side of the fireplace was a window which provided views of the mountains. In the right front corner was a modest kitchen with a wood burning stove. Along the back of the cabin were three bedrooms; one much larger than the other two. A single front door opened up to a long wood plank front porch, which extended the length of the cabin. To the left of the cabin was a well where the family drew water for drinking, bathing and washing clothes. Life at the cabin was tolerable, but Barak always talked of his plans to move his family from the small cabin to a large ranch with a big white house, just as soon as he collected on the flux wire concept.

****

Most every Friday evening Barak Stone could be seen heading into town to meet his drinking buddies for a night of poker. The saloon on the outside edge of Rock Springs served as the perfect place to host their weekly event. Bett and the children hated this weekly tradition and often begged him not to go, but Barak was determined to do things his own way.

On one hot, summer, Friday night, Barak found himself at his usual place, seated at the poker table with his two closest friends, Jeno Stephens and Davis Williams. Barak, Davis and Jeno had been the best of friends for many years.

On this particular night they were short a player. Glancing around the room, they spotted a stranger at the bar finishing off a glass of bourbon. The man had a slender build with a pencil thin mustache. He was well dressed in a charcoal colored Callahan Frock Coat and sported a Victorian Top Hat. Jeno, Davis and Barak agreed he was new in town and most likely just passing through. Barak, who was an above average poker player, was always looking for a sucker of whom he could take advantage. He thought this could be the night he could win the $250 he so desperately needed to finish testing his flux wire concept. So, after mulling it over, he decided to invite the well-dressed man to their table to join them for a 'friendly' game of poker.

Approaching the stranger from his blind side, Barak tapped him on the shoulder and asked, "How about a game of poker? We're short a player over here at our table."

The distinguished man turned around and said, "I'm afraid I don't know too much about card games. You're probably looking for someone that knows a little more about it than me."

Barak immediately perceived this man was the perfect target. "Oh come on and join us. It's just a game of poker between friends, and we'll take it easy on you. We might even teach you a thing or two," Barak said as he laughed.

Then Barak added, "I'll even buy you another shot of bourbon just to show you I'm a good guy."

That was all it took to convince the stranger to join them. Stretching his arm across the table and firmly gripping Jeno's hand, then Davis's, he introduced himself as Lucas Benson.

Jeno greeted him and said, "Pleased to make your acquaintance, Mr. Benson, won't you have a seat."

"Lucas. Call me Lucas," he replied, between sips of his fresh glass of bourbon.

Davis began shuffling the cards as Jeno reminded everyone of the rules. Barak sat there struggling to remain calm, as in his mind he was already celebrating a victory, convinced he had found the perfect pigeon. What Barak didn't know was that while Lucas Benson was a newcomer to Rock Springs, he was certainly no stranger to the poker table. In fact, Mr. Lucas Benson had won numerous poker tournaments all over the Western Frontier.

Soon after the cards were dealt, Barak began winning, and his confidence grew. After just a few hands, Barak had a sizeable stack of money piled in front of him. He wasn't certain, but he believed he was close to winning the $250 he so desperately needed to finish testing the flux wire project.

Then something peculiar began to happen. Lucas Benson began a winning streak like nothing Barak had ever experienced. Within an hour, Lucas had laid claim to all the cash Barak had won, along with all the money Davis and Jeno had with them.

Knowing when to quit, Davis and Jeno folded and were ready to leave for the night, but Barak always believed the next hand would be the 'big one' that would turn his luck around. His problem was the whiskey hindered his judgment. There were many

Friday nights when Barak gambled away the resources allocated to provide food for his family and to pay the mortgage on his land.

As Barak sat there with no more money left to gamble, he remembered the old leather bag hanging on the back of his chair. Jeno's eyes grew large, and Davis shook his head in disbelief as Barak took another swig of whiskey, dangled the brown leather bag in the air, and then deposited it on the center of the old wooden card table.

Curious, Lucas raised his eyebrows with an inquisitive look and asked, "What's that? You got more money in the bag?"

Barak leaned back in his chair and bragged, "Mr. Lucas, this bag contains the plans that's gonna make me a mighty rich man."

Barak went on to explain to Lucas that he'd discovered a way to revolutionize communication between all the towns on the Western Frontier using a new type of flux wire.

It was obvious Barak had sparked Lucas' interest. Both Jeno and Davis feared what Barak was about to do and pleaded with him to not be so foolish, but he wouldn't listen. The alcohol was now in control, and Barak looked square at Lucas and said, "Let's go one more hand! Five cards! No draw! I'll bet this here leather bag and all my rights to the flux wire concept against your entire stack of money."

Lucas swallowed a sip of bourbon, paused for a moment, then laughed wickedly as he shook his head in agreement and answered, "Mr. Barak, you got yourself a deal."

Lucas pushed his large stack of money forward until it rested right beside the leather bag.

At first, Davis refused to become involved in this ordeal, but Barak was insistent and asked him to deal the cards. To appease his life-long friend, Davis took a deep breath and picked up the cards. He slowly shuffled as he prayed Barak would change his mind.

Barak and Lucas stared directly at the playing cards as they floated neatly back and forth lying directly on top of each other. With the deck thoroughly shuffled, one by one Davis dealt the cards to Lucas and Barak until each man had five cards. The tension was as thick as the smoke in the room as each player picked up their cards one at a time and held them tightly against their chest.

Lucas peeked at his cards. His first card was a ten of hearts, followed by a seven of the same suit.

Barak squinted as he surveyed his cards through the smoke and dim light. His first card was an ace of spades. His second was an ace of clubs. With two aces in hand, he put on his best poker face and kept his lips tightly pressed together.

Lucas took a glance at his third card which was a nine of hearts.

Barak looked at his third card and to his surprised he saw an ace of hearts. With three aces in hand, Barak was feeling confident.

Lucas then slipped his fourth card out from behind the third to reveal a six of hearts.

Barak's wishes came true when he realized his fourth card was the final ace, the ace of Diamonds.

All of a sudden, Lucas began coughing as if he was choking on something. In the commotion, one of Lucas' cards slipped from his hands and dropped to the dusty saloon floor. Catching his breath, Lucas leaned down to pick up the card and sat back up at the table. Barak then noticed one of Lucas' hands was slightly under the edge of the table, and he immediately growled, "Hey, what are you doing? Get your hand back up here so I can see it."

Lucas obliged and with order restored, Barak took a quick look at his fifth and final card which was a two of clubs. With four aces, Barak glanced at the stack of money piled in the middle of the table that he believed he was now certain to win.

With their cards in hand, Lucas and Barak glared at each other for a minute. Then Barak glanced over at Davis, winked at him, and began laying down his cards. One by one, the aces made their way to the table. Barak cracked a slight grin and sat up with his head held high, confident that his four aces would be all but impossible to beat.

Lucas was not fazed and stared directly at Barak. Slowly, Lucas shifted his eyes from Barak to the cards in his own hand. Then, Lucas slowly laid them down one by one. The first card was the ten of hearts, then the nine of hearts, followed by the seven of hearts and then the six of hearts. Barak's heart began to pound as he realized Lucas was one card away from a 'Straight Flush' which would beat his 'Four of a Kind'. Lucas slowly flipped the last card around and sure enough, an eight of hearts revealed itself to all those who had gathered around the poker table to witness this historic, late night showdown.

Barak immediately thought back to just a few moments earlier when Lucas bent down under the table. "You nasty cheater," he shouted. "I know you cheated when you reached under the table! You slipped in a card, didn't ya! I know you did! You cheated me!"

Barak went crazy, shouting profanities as he continued to accuse Lucas of cheating. Grabbing his sidearm, Barak aimed the barrel directly at Lucas' forehead and pulled back the hammer. Davis hollered, "Don't do it Barak, just let it go!"

In a split second, Jeno jumped in and wrestled the pistol away from Barak. It took both Jeno and Davis to restrain Barak, as Lucas claimed the brown leather bag from the table and stuffed all the cash into it. He then draped the bag over his right shoulder and stood up.

"Nice doing business with you gentlemen, I must be on my way," Lucas said with a smirk on his face.

Lucas took his last swig of bourbon and began backing his way out of the saloon, as Barak struggled to break free from the grip of Jeno and Davis. He wanted one shot, one punch, just one swing at Lucas. It was more than he could take, to watch Lucas Benson walk away with his dreams. With a single swing of the rusty café doors, Lucas disappeared into the dark of the night. The leather bag had slipped away from Barak without a fight. Once Lucas was out of sight, Jeno and Davis led their intoxicated friend out of the saloon and helped him up on his horse.

With that final card, Barak lost the rights to his flux wire idea. His hopes and dreams dissipated like the smoke from a lit match in a western storm. He truly believed in his heart that Lucas had cheated him, and he dreaded facing Bett with the bad news. This night became a pivotal moment in Barak's life. All he had ever wanted was to give Bett a wonderful life, but that dream seemed to be lost forever.

The moment Lucas Benson strolled out of the saloon with the brown leather bag, Barak Stone became a changed man. His motivation dissipated, his self-esteem plummeted and his involvement in criminal activity escalated. He never held an honest job from that night forward, but somehow always had a little money in his pocket. Bett knew her husband was leading a life of crime, but he would never be honest with her or disclose the details of his actions. Many times he would be gone for days, and she suspected he was involved in some type of illegal activity. There were even rumors among the locals in Rock Springs of Barak's connection to the Mexican army.

Misief never questioned what his father did at night when he was away from home. He learned as a young boy the volatility of his father and the rage that would ensue whenever anyone questioned him about the private matters of his life. Late at night, when his parents thought he was asleep, Misief would overhear his mother crying as she begged Barak to give up the lifestyle he had chosen. Misief didn't know all the details, but he clearly understood whatever this Lucas guy had stolen from his father had forever changed him. Misief vowed that someday he would track down Lucas Benson and re-claim the brown leather bag that meant so much to his father. Even though he was just a young boy when the infamous poker game with Lucas occurred, Misief inherited his father's deep hatred for Lucas Benson and his thirst for revenge.

****

Crouched down on the bedroom floor with his mother and sister, Misief wondered if what happened years earlier with Lucas was somehow connected to the ruckus he was hearing outside the cabin. Sensing her children's fear, Bett wrapped her arms around Misief and his sister. As the noise outside the cabin intensified, Bett ripped the tattered quilt from the iron bed and covered both of her children. Misief was unsure exactly what was happening, but he suspected his mom knew something dangerous lurked on the horizon.

Bett was a beautiful woman with long, chestnut brown hair. She had big brown eyes and a smile that sparkled when she laughed. It was easy to see why Barak fell in love with her. Not only was she stunning to the eye, but she was also a beautiful person on the inside. She was full of patience and kindness and had a heart of gold. There was a time when she loved Barak more than anything in the world and privately, she dreamed of getting their marriage back to the romantic days when they were first married. From time to time, Bett would insist on Barak changing his ways, but her words seem to fall on the deaf ears of a stubborn man.

Tucked under the quilt, Misief looked directly into the eyes of his mother. Bett was a strong woman and had put herself between impending danger and her children many times before. This night would be no different, and the comfort of her embrace made him feel safe.

"Everything is going to be okay," Bett whispered, even though she feared deeply for her children's safety.

Misief found a small gap in the quilt which allowed him to peek out to see what was happening. Through the tiny gap he could see his father in the front room. Barak stood beside one of the windows and was frantically working to load his Remington rifle.

The uproar outside was now deafening, and Misief realized what he was hearing was the rumble of horses hooves. Barak shouted toward the bedroom, "Bett, stay down, keep the kids with you, and don't none of ya' come out for any reason, you hear?"

"What's going on Barak? Who is it?" she demanded.

He didn't respond. Through the hole in the blanket, Misief could see the irritation on his father's face and knew he was in no mood for a lengthy discussion.

All of a sudden the rumbling of the horses came to a halt, and for a moment it became eerily quiet outside the cabin. From his vantage point under the blanket, Misief could hear the breath of the horses as they labored to recover from the eleven mile ride from Rock Springs. He listened to what sounded like footsteps outside the window, indicating to him that people were running around all sides of the cabin. He watched intensely as his father positioned his rifle out the front window. What Misief did not know was their little cabin was now completely surrounded by a posse of over thirty men. The group was made up of lawmen from the local sheriff's office as well as citizens of Rock Springs, each one with a single motive in mind.

The silence was broken as one of the lawmen shouted, "Barak Stone, this is Sheriff Samuel Anderson. Come out with your hands up!"

Without hesitation Barak yelled back, "NEVER!"

Bett pressed her body closer to her children to protect them from what she anticipated might be coming next. As Bett shielded her children from the trouble brewing outside, Misief's little sister, Ashel, started to cry.

"Shh…. Mama is right here," Bett whispered as she kissed Ashel's tender cheeks. Her mother's embrace and words of comfort soon brought his baby sister's crying under control.

Misief was nine years old when his sister was born, and he helped watch after Ashel while his mother cooked, cleaned and worked outside in the garden. Now eleven years old, Misief loved his baby sister very much and was very close to her, despite the nine year difference in their ages.

With Ashel calmed a bit, Misief turned his attention back to the action taking place outside the shadows of the quilt. Once again he snuck a quick peek through the tiny hole. Much to his surprise, he caught a glimpse of a large male figure standing in the corner of the bedroom. He wondered if one of the men from outside the cabin had ventured into the room through the window.

As Misief stared at the image, trying to determine if it was real or just a figment of his imagination, he was immediately captivated by this individual. The man wore cowboy boots made of shiny white leather with gold studs on the outer side of each boot. He appeared to be well over six feet tall and had broad shoulders with a thin waist. Overwhelming anxiety overtook Misief as he whipped around and yanked the quilt back over his head. He was hoping this was just his imagination playing tricks on him. His body trembled as he silently panicked. He wondered, "Should I tell mama?"

Not wanting to alarm her, Misief decided to keep quiet, but his curiosity was getting the best of him. After a few moments, he mustered up the courage to take a second peek. He paused for a moment, took a deep breath and looked through the hole once again.

Hoping it was all a bad dream, Misief's worst fears were realized as he saw the stranger still quietly standing in the corner.

Misief wanted desperately to get a better look at the man. Bravely, he reached down and lifted up the blanket. As Misief's eyes shifted back toward the corner of the room, to his surprise the man was looking right at him. Their eyes locked on each other! Frozen in place, Misief watched the man place his index finger over his closed mouth indicating he wanted him to keep quiet. The man did not seem to be interested in hurting him, but rather wanted to communicate a message to him. The man then slipped his hand into his right hip pocket and pulled out a single gold bullet. Twirling the bullet between his index finger and his thumb, it was apparent he wanted Misief to see what he was going to do with it. The stranger took the bullet and placed it on top of the wardrobe. He then made a motion indicating to Misief he was leaving it for him.

Misief's fixation on the strange man in the corner of the bedroom was interrupted by a single gunshot which rang through the cabin. The sound of the gunshot echoed like a single burst of thunder on a hot summer night. Misief jerked his head toward the front room to see his father reloading his rifle. He realized his father had fired a shot at the men outside the cabin.

Sheriff Anderson shouted, "Barak, we're gonna give you one chance to end this peaceful like…..then we are gonna come in and get ya! There's no reason for anybody to get hurt tonight. We just need you to come out here so we can talk to you about something. Now drop your weapon and come out with your hands…."

Before the Sheriff finished speaking, Barak fired a second shot in the direction of Sheriff Anderson's voice.

The sound of the blast echoed in the cabin so loud it frightened Ashel. She buried her head into her mother's chest and began to cry again.

Bett pleaded, "Barak, do what they tell you! Please, Barak, they are serious and will kill you and could harm the children."

Barak didn't respond verbally to Bett but looked back at her and the children with a stone faced glare. It was as if he was looking at them for the first time and the last time all in one glance. You could tell he was contemplating a plan, but no one could have predicted what he was about to do. Over time, Bett had learned to endure his temper and his strong will. He always did whatever he wanted and wouldn't accept instruction from anyone. This night would prove to be no different; Barak was determined to handle this his own way.

The next thirty seconds forever changed the future of the Stone family. A plan was brewing in Barak's mind and the wheels turning in his head could be seen as he stared at his family. The evidence would later show his actions were based on his own twisted way of showing love to them. Barak was not a man who expressed his emotions unless it was his anger. It seemed he wanted to show his family there was a side to him that truly loved them more than anything else.

Barak made two decisions regarding how this night was going down. First, he made up his mind he was not going to surrender to the authorities. He knew the crimes he'd committed, and he knew they would hang him if he surrendered. Second, he was not going to let this become a gun battle inside his home where stray bullets could harm his children or his beloved Bett. Without warning, Barak bolted toward the front door and burst out onto the front porch of the cabin.

Who shot first will forever remain unknown. None of the lawmen would ever admit they were the one who pulled the trigger. What was certain was that for the next minute or so, deafening gunfire rang out from all sides of the cabin. The smell of gunpowder filled the air, and when the dust settled, Barak Stone lay mortally wounded on his own front porch.

Silence replaced the sound of gunfire as Bett began screaming for Barak, but there was no response. The silence seemed as loud to her as the gunfire itself. She placed Ashel into Misief's arms, and then left them in the safety of the bedroom. As fast as her weakened legs would carry her, she ran screaming through the cabin to the front porch.

Horrified at the scene, she fell to her knees and began to caress the body of her bleeding husband. His blood ran out from multiple gunshot wounds staining her beautiful yellow dress. Nervously patting his cheeks and running her fingers through his hair, she whispered, "No…Please… No!" It was as if time had stopped.

A few minutes later, Misief picked up his sister and tiptoed to the front room. The two children were met by a group of lawmen who were roaming through the cabin as if they were looking for something. The lawmen instructed him to stay inside, but he was determined to see his father. Ignoring their instructions, Misief made his way through the crowd of rifle bearing lawmen and witnessed a scene no child should ever behold. His father was lying on the front porch struggling to breathe. A tear came to Misief's eye as he saw the blood pour out of his dying father.

Panting, Barak looked up at Bett, Misief and Ashel and said, "I'm so sorry for all the pain I've caused you. If only Lucas hadn't cheated me things could have been so different…….."

At that moment Barak took his final breath and died in Bett's arms. Tears flowed down her cheeks, splashing onto his battered body, as she whispered, "I love you Barak."

It was obvious the last thing on Barak's mind was his regret for the pain he had caused his family and his hatred for the man named, Lucas Benson.

Chapter 2

"Saying Goodbye"

June 3, 1857

    A beautiful, 80 year old maple tree stood fifteen feet to the left of an aging horse stable. The stable was about 100 feet directly behind the wooden cabin where Barak, Bett and the children lived. The stable was on the property when Barak and Bett purchased the place and was in need of minor repair. The wood on the side of the stable had grayed and the old tin roof had rusted from the years of exposure to the intense summer sunlight and harsh winter weather. It was primarily used as a place for Barak to keep his horses, but it also served as a hang-out for his outlaw friends when they came to visit. Bett did not approve of Barak's criminal partners and wouldn't even consider allowing any of them inside the cabin or around her children.

    The maple tree and the horse stable were favorite places for Misief to play. Each branch on the tree extended directly horizontal and was perfect for climbing. The limbs of the tree hovered over the stable and provided much needed shade in the hot summer months. The stable had a loft filled with hay for the horses and several small individual stalls. Many times when his father's associates came to visit, Misief would hide in the loft and eavesdrop on their conversations. Though Barak was not a role model for any young boy, Misief idolized his father and would fantasize of following in his father's footsteps.

Misief spent much of his childhood scaling up the maple tree and hiding in the horse stable, pretending to be an outlaw on the run from the authorities. He would take the toy gun his father had given him and emulate the stories he'd overheard him tell of barroom brawls, gunfights and wild poker games.

"Bang, bang, ya got me," Misief would shout, as he toppled from the top wall of the loft falling onto a pile of hay nestled below. However, the events that had occurred in the last twenty four hours were not make-believe. The days of pretend gunfights and shootouts had played out for real, bringing a tragic end to his father's life.

Before Sheriff Anderson and the other lawmen left, they carried Barak's lifeless body from the front porch and laid him inside the cabin on the floor next to the fireplace. As Bett cried in disbelief, Sheriff Anderson pulled her aside and informed her that Barak was wanted for questioning in relation to a recent murder at the local train station in Rock Springs. The Sheriff told Bett that two men had robbed a train engineer at gunpoint, killing the man in cold blood. Barak had been identified as a possible suspect by one of the locals. Bett did not want to believe the accusation, but she knew in her heart Barak was secretive and had developed a dark side since his encounter with Lucas Benson. The Sheriff gave his condolences to Bett and reached out to shake Misief's hand, but Misief was not interested in his kind words and refused to shake his hand or speak to him. In his young mind, he believed this sheriff and his cohorts were responsible for killing his father, and he despised them all.

As the lawmen rode off on their horses, a river of tears began flowing down Bett's cheeks. The realization that she was going to be a widow for the rest of her life began to settle on her like the evening fog. She paused to reminisce about all the nights Barak chose to head off on his horse to engage in foolish and violent behavior, leaving her all alone with the children. She never knew if he would return alive or not. He didn't seem to care about her feelings or the children and always chose to involve himself in activities that made him happy. Her resentment toward Barak had grown over the years, and her deep love for her husband had faded. They basically co-existed in their cabin, and Barak no longer seemed to notice Bett or even care about her feelings. What she feared most had finally come to pass; she only wished Misief and Ashel hadn't been present to personally witness the demise of their father firsthand.

Although the children were still full of nervous energy from the events of the night, Bett managed to corral them to the bedroom. As she tucked them into bed, she kissed each of them on the cheek, placed her hands on their shoulders and prayed a prayer. She remained seated on the bedside and softly hummed lullabies as they drifted off to sleep. When she was certain they were both fast asleep, Bett retreated to the front room to be alone with her thoughts.

The cabin sat in utter silence as she prepared herself a place to rest on the sofa. She took an old quilt made by her mother and draped it over her body, pulling it to her chin. As Bett lie in the stillness, she glanced over at Barak's motionless body. She reached down and stroked the lines of his face with her index finger. After a little while, she blew out the oil lantern and turned over to face the back of the sofa.

Sleep did not come to Bett during the long night. As she lay sobbing on the sofa, with Barak's lifeless body lying beside her on the floor, she wrestled with her emotions. She was angry with Barak for allowing something like this to happen. Why couldn't he have stayed the man she fell in love with, instead of turning into a man full of hatred and revenge? Then she thought back to what he had said just before he died; he apologized for all the pain he had caused her.

Was this Barak's way of telling her that he still loved her?

At that moment, Bett realized she still loved Barak and wished their lives had not ventured down such a broken path. She clutched her tear stained pillow wishing this was all just a bad dream. The uncertainty of the future tormented her mind as she wondered how she would provide for her children. The Western Frontier was not an easy place to live, and without Barak, she knew her life was going to get extremely difficult.

****

The dark night, which seemed like a never-ending nightmare, finally gave way to the flicker of sunlight. As the bright rays beamed through the front windows of the cabin, Bett heard the soothing sound of the familiar voices of Jeno Stephens and Davis Williams. The two men heard of Barak's demise and rode out to the cabin to see what they could do to help.

Jeno and Davis were different from all of Barak's other friends. In their younger days, Jeno, Davis and Barak participated in some minor illegal activity and enjoyed their Friday night saloon activities. Soon after Barak's confrontation with Lucas Benson, Davis and Jeno drifted away from criminal activity and chose honest lifestyles working in Rock Springs. Davis built scales to weigh corn, grain and livestock; Jeno was a painter, mostly hand crafting signs for local businesses and lettering stage coaches. Jeno and Davis were not squeaky clean, but they had made the choice to settle down, raise a family and provide for them by earning an honest wage.

That was not the path Barak had taken with his life. He never matured like his friends and wouldn't listen when they advised him to change his ways. Despite different lifestyles, they remained connected over the years and continued to meet in Rock Springs for Friday night poker games. The three friends had much in common. They all supported families with children; lived on farms and were rugged cowboys.

In her grief stricken state, Bett ran out to meet the two men, and with tears still moist on her face, she recounted in great detail the entire saga between Barak, Sheriff Anderson and his men. Davis took off his hat, looked at Bett and said, "Bett, I really don't know what to say….I'm so sorry."

Jeno noticed the blood stains on the porch and admitted, "I was afraid something like this would happen if Barak didn't change his ways. I tried to tell 'em."

"I know you did. We all did. I begged him time after time. He was just stubborn and had to do things his way," Bett replied.

She invited the two men into the cabin. Once inside, they immediately spotted Barak's body lying on the floor in the front room. Taken aback, they paused a moment to absorb the reality of their friend's demise.

Clearing his throat, Davis asked, "What can we do to help you Bett?"

Bett replied, "I want his body buried out back, under the maple tree beside the horse stable. Would the two of you be willing to help me?"

Jeno quickly stepped up and said, "It would be our honor, Bett. Don't worry; we'll take care of it."

Bett led Jeno and Davis around the cabin to the horse stable. She pointed to a nice grassy spot and said, "I'd like to bury him right here."

Bett turned to go back into the cabin, and Davis made his way into the stable to retrieve a couple of shovels and a mallet.

Jeno and Davis labored in the blazing summer sun for the next few hours. The sound of the metal mallet hitting stone rang through the air, and into the cabin, as the two men fought to break through the rock filled clay that was native to the territory. It took them the better part of the day to dig the hole that would serve as a final resting place for Barak's body, but right before sunset, Jeno made his way up on the porch of the cabin and knocked on the front door.

Sticking his head inside, he called for Bett. "We're ready, now," he said.

While Jeno and Davis had been outside digging the grave, Bett had been drawing buckets of water from the well and giving Barak's body a final bath. Even though it wouldn't change the outcome, she had applied an ointment salve solution over the gunshot wounds and carefully bandaged each of them. On many occasions, she'd tended to wounds and mended broken bones for Barak when he'd come in after a fight or skirmish, but this time was different. The wounds were fatal, and the care she was giving couldn't possibly help. This time, there would not be a quick healing or a miraculous rising from the dead. It was final! These tender moments would be the last ones she would ever spend with her beloved Barak.

Her hands trembled as she struggled to dress his body in clean clothes and covered him in a quilt she had made the first year they were married. She'd learn to quilt from her mother, and she wanted her first quilt to be buried with him. She reminisced about the times they snuggled together under this very quilt when they were first married and deeply in love. Covering her lifeless husband in this sentimental quilt was the hardest thing she had ever done. In a strange way, she found comfort in knowing Barak would be wrapped and laid to rest in its warm memories.

Jeno and Davis walked into the front room of the cabin. As they entered, they removed their hats, out of respect, and asked Bett if they could take time to wash off the dirt and sweat that covered their bodies. Bett obliged and soon walked back into the room with washcloths, a couple of towels, and a bar of soap.

Jeno nodded his head and said, "Thank you Bett, we'll just be a few minutes."

Jeno and Davis went back outside, walked over to the well and retrieved a bucket filled with cool, clear water. Through his bedroom window, Misief watched as the men washed the dirt from their arms, faces and hands. Against his will, he hadn't been allowed to help them dig the grave. From various vantage points inside the cabin, he had watched them work all afternoon and wanted so desperately to help in some way with the burial of his father.

Now a bit cleaner, Davis and Jeno stepped back up on the porch and placed the towels over the handrail to dry. Bett met them at the door and stepped out onto the porch. She immediately burst into tears, sobbing uncontrollably. She had done her best to be strong for Misief and Ashel, but she knew the end was now approaching. Even though Barak was deceased, and had been dead for almost twenty-four hours, having his body in the house gave her some level of comfort. As unpractical as it might seem, in her mind she wished she could keep his body in the house, but the time had come to say goodbye.

Davis and Jeno watched in silence as Bett leaned against the porch rail holding tightly to it as she cried. She was so distraught, and weak from lack of eating, that she found it difficult to stand on her own. Dropping to her knees, she used the splintery rail that lined the edge of the porch for support. Jeno and Davis glanced back and forth at each other and then at Bett, not knowing what to say or do. They had all been friends for so many years, and the next few minutes were going to be extremely difficult for all of them. Jeno swallowed, paused a moment, then walked over to her. He gently placed his hand on Bett's shoulder and asked her to go back inside. Bett regained her composure as the men helped her to her feet and led her back into the front room.

Bett slowly walked over to Barak's body. At first, she knelt in silence, as if stalling might keep her from facing the inevitable. Finally, from her kneeling position, she gently pulled back the quilt to see Barak's face one last time. She bent over, gave him a kiss on the cheek and whispered that she loved him. Misief joined his mom beside his father's body while Ashel lay sleeping in her mother's bedroom. Bett then stretched the quilt back over her deceased husband's face and stepped back across the room.

Jeno and Davis moved forward and carefully lifted Barak's body from the cabin floor. Misief ran to the front door and held it open as he tried to be the man he knew his father would want him to be. During the last twenty-four hours he had only shed one tear, and this was something he felt his father would be proud of. This was Misief's chance to be the tough guy his father had raised him to be; which was to remain hard, cold, and always fearless.

The previous night, as Misief lay awake in the dark of his cabin bedroom, he vowed he would not shed another tear for the rest of his life. He was determined to be like his father. He made a declaration that he would get even with those who had killed his father, and someday, he was going to track down the man they call Lucas Benson-the scoundrel that had stolen his father's leather bag and with it, the plans that could have changed the direction of his family!

Jeno and Davis stepped off the front porch with Barak's stiff body in their arms. They made their way around the right side of the cabin and walked toward the back of the property, stopping at the grave they had prepared under the maple tree. Misief followed along right behind Jeno and Davis. Bett was a few steps behind them, as she had slipped into the bedroom to retrieve Ashel who had been napping. Ashel tucked her head under the cover of her mother's hair, as though she wanted no part of what was happening. Actually, she was too young to comprehend what was going on and was still sleepy from her unfinished nap.

There were no flowers to adorn the grave, no music to comfort the grieving souls and no minister present to officiate over the proceeding. They simply stared down at the open grave as the evening sun cast a peculiar shadow of Barak's body lying on the ground beside the grave. Bett's heart was breaking inside, but she fought back tears, as she was determined to be strong for the children. As the evening breeze blew through her long brown hair, she closed her eyes wishing she could simply wake up from this horrific nightmare. The warmth of the western sun on her delicate skin somehow served to comfort her as she nodded to Jeno and Davis, indicating she was ready to proceed. With Ashel in her right arm, she pulled Misief close to her left side. The three of them stood as one, while Jeno and Davis picked up Barak's body and lowered him into the ground. Suddenly, Misief jerked free from his mother's embrace and dashed toward the cabin.

Bett called out, "Misief, come back!"

Misief's pace was swift, and he'd already made his way around the corner of the cabin before she could stop him. Davis and Jeno waited a moment, wondering if he would return. They weren't sure if they should proceed with the burial or go check on him.

A moment later they all heard the sound of the cabin door squeaking. The door slammed shut, and Misief raced back around the corner of the cabin, heading directly toward them. As he approached, they noticed he was carrying his father's cowboy hat.

Misief looked into his mother's eyes and said, "I think we should bury 'em with his hat."

Tears streamed down Bett's face as she nodded in agreement. Davis took the hat from the young son and placed it over his father's face. As Barak's breathless body found its final resting place, Bett inched forward to the very edge of the grave.

Looking down at her deceased husband she said, "I will always love you. I will take good care of Misief and Ashel. Goodbye Barak."

With those words, Bett turned around, and with Ashel still in one arm, she grabbed Misief with her other hand and began walking back to the cabin. Misief pulled away from his mother and told her he wanted to help Davis and Jeno bury his father. At first Bett was hesitant, but understanding her son was trying to grow up, she allowed him to participate in the burial process.

With Bett and Ashel back inside the cabin, Jeno and Davis knew it was time to close the grave. Misief stood watching, but they could tell he was determined to get involved. Jeno and Davis only had two shovels, but they understood the importance of this young son participating in his father's burial. So, Davis turned to Misief and handed him his shovel.

Misief gripped the wooden handle and scooped up a shovel full of dirt from the mound piled up beside the grave. He stood there for a moment and stared down at his deceased father. Jeno and Davis weren't sure if this child would, or could, bring himself to toss the dirt onto his father's body. Finally, Misief's arms began moving as he gently tossed the first shovel of dirt onto the feet of his deceased father. It was the hardest thing Misief had ever done in his young life! Driven by the hatred he had toward those who had brought this tragedy to his family, he continued to place the dirt on his father's body. With each shovel filled with western soil, his anger grew, and his determination for revenge intensified.

Davis realized Misief's temperament was changing and his anger was increasing. He gently walked over to him and said, "Misief, let me give you a break."

But Misief was in a zone all of his own and didn't want to give up his shovel. Davis didn't push the issue and allowed the young son to continue filling the grave.

As the final slice of the evening sun was setting in the western sky, the three of them finished the task of burying Barak. Jeno took a rake and smoothed the dirt forming it with just a small rise in the center that would settle with time. Misief ran into the stable and soon returned with two small pieces of wood.

He looked at Davis and said, "I want to make a cross to mark my father's grave. Will you help me?"

Davis replied, "Sure, can you get me a hammer and a few nails?"

Misief darted back into the stable. He soon returned with a hammer in his left hand and opened his right hand to display a handful of rusty nails he'd found in an old jar. As Davis took the nails, he saw blisters covering the palms of Misief's hands. The fresh blisters were beginning to ooze and bleed. This proud son had labored with total disregarded of the toll the rough wooden shovel handle was having on the tender skin of his young hands. Jeno took the two of the pieces of wood and placed them in the form of a cross, as Davis hammered a couple of nails into the wood.

Jeno handed the cross to Misief. The young son walked to the head of his father's grave and placed the cross in the dirt. Davis hammered it into the ground as Misief held it tightly in his hands. It didn't take much effort to secure the cross in the loose dirt. When Misief took his hands off the cross, Davis noticed crimson red blood stains on the cross; blood that came from the battered and blistered hands of one tough young man!

Their work now complete, the three of them stood there staring at the grave. Jeno cleared his throat as he said, "Goodbye ole' buddy." He then picked up the mallet and shovels, and returned them to the horse barn. Davis placed his arm around Misief, and they turned to walk back to the cabin. Barak's life was over, and each one had paid their respects to their father and friend. The impact Barak had made on Misief's life was profound, however it was not necessarily positive.

Jeno and Davis kicked the dirt off their cowboy boots and went inside the cabin. They found Bett standing in front of a wood cook stove. She was busy putting the finishing touches on a meal that included beans, cornbread and pork ribs. "You guys get washed up, I've got supper ready," she said.

Davis was the first to resist, "Bett, we didn't come to eat....."

Bett interrupted, "It's the least I can do, now wash up."

Davis said no more and accepted Bett's hospitality.

Jeno and Davis sat at the table with Bett, Misief and Ashel. The sixth chair at the table, Barak's chair, was left empty. Bett stared at the empty chair and thought back to the events of the last twenty-four hours. Just the night before, about this same time, Barak was sitting in his chair eating. Their meal had started so peaceful, but then it was interrupted by the sound of horses and lawmen. Bett hadn't eaten a thing since and found she still wasn't very hungry. Her mind was still trying to process the day's events, and she wondered what the future might hold for her and her children.

Misief nibbled at the food on his plate. He was exhausted, and his hands were in intense pain from the blisters. Bett noticed the grimace on her son's face, and then spotted his bleeding hands. She went into the bedroom, retrieved her first aid supplies, and with the love that only a mother can provide, Bett gently applied ointment to relieve the burning sensation. Then she took a piece of white cloth and wrapped it around his hands, just like she had done for each of the wounds on Barak's body a few hours earlier. She bent over and kissed her son on the forehead and thanked him for all his help. "Your father would be very proud of you," she said.

After splitting the final piece of cornbread, Davis and Jeno thanked Bett for the meal and prepared to leave. They told her they would check on her from time to time. Jeno personally thanked Misief for his help, and the two men headed for the front door.

Misief stood in front of Bett as she stood holding Ashel. He was trying to be the man of the house, as the three of them stood on the front porch and watched Jeno and Davis mount their horses.

As Davis and Jeno headed back home, a deep sadness came over Bett. In the darkness, she couldn't see them as they rode off, but she listened intently to the sound of the horses' hooves as they galloped away. It took only a few minutes for the sound to dissipate into complete silence. Standing on the front porch of the cabin, Bett absorbed the realization that she was now a widow and would bear the responsibility of raising Misief and Ashel alone.

Chapter 3

"Life Without Barak"

June 7, 1857

Four long days had passed since Barak's death, and Bett was doing her best to move forward without him. There were numerous chores that demanded her attention, and this morning's assignment was to catch up on a growing pile of dirty laundry. Carrying a basket filled with laundered clothing, Bett made her way out the back door and headed toward the clothes line that ran beside the cabin.

The clothes line stretched from the far right side of the stable to an oak tree, then turned and ran to a pole that once supported an old dinner bell. The dinner bell was missing, and the pole was somewhat rotten. Bett always placed the heavier clothes on the section of the line that ran between the stable and the oak tree, leaving the lighter clothes to hang on the section supported by the rotten dinner bell pole.

As Bett passed the rotten, wooden pole she thought of how many times she'd ask Barak to replace it with a new one. His answer was always the same; "I will as soon as I get a minute." This was followed by him going on with whatever else was more important to him. Unfortunately, Barak never found, or made, time to take care of the needs around the aging cabin. The old dinner bell pole was just another reminder of the workload that always seemed to fall upon Bett's shoulders.

It was a gorgeous mid-summer morning and as Bett hung the last article of clothing on the line, her eyes glanced across the garden that was also in desperate need of attention. Weeds were beginning to take over, and Bett knew she needed to tend to it if she planned to feed her children during the cold winter months that would soon be approaching. The list of tasks needing Bett's attention was overwhelming; however she knew that keeping busy would help her deal with the grief and loneliness she was experiencing since Barak's death.

Misief had been a tremendous help since his father's passing. It was as if he had grown up overnight, as he tried his best to become the man around the house. The day after they buried Barak, Bett and Misief spent time tending to the horses, cleaning out the stable and making minor repairs to the fence surrounding the chicken coop. Since the moment Davis and Jeno left, Misief had worked non-stop. He hadn't talked about his father since his death, and Bett knew that staying busy was helping her young son cope with all the things that had happened in the last few days.

Even though Misief was only eleven years old, Bett knew she would need to lean heavily on him if they were to survive without Barak. Since the age of four, Misief had tagged along with his father on several hunting trips, and Bett knew she would be dependent on him to help provide meat for the family. She would also rely on him to help with critical tasks, such as hitching the horses to the wagon when they needed to go to Rock Springs to get supplies. For this family to survive without Barak, Bett knew it would take a total team effort from her and her two children.

****

Later that afternoon, Bett checked on the clothes she'd hung out on the line earlier. As she removed the laundry and placed it in the basket, she glanced over to look at the maple tree as its branches hung gracefully over the gravesite of her late husband. With all his faults and failures, Bett still loved Barak, and she missed him more than words could express.

Softly Bett whispered, "I love you Barak", as she pulled the last dried article of clothing from the line.

Over the last four days, Bett did her best to keep her mind from reflecting back to her life with Barak. While there were many happy moments she shared with her husband, there were also numerous occasions that were very painful to relive. So, whenever her mind would drift to days passed, Bett would immediately immerse herself back in her chores and her children.

When Misief saw his mother coming into the cabin with the basket of clothes, he jumped to his feet and asked, "Can I help you put the clothes away?"

Bett placed the basket on the table and said, "Sure son. I'll fold 'em, and then you can put them where they go."

Bett began folding the clothes, and Misief made quick work of putting them in their place. This particular basket of clothes was mostly bath and kitchen towels, as well as a few items Barak had worn before his death. Misief picked up the folded kitchen towels and placed them on the shelf above the wood burning stove. Then he picked up two of his father's shirts. He took the neatly folded shirts and marched into his mother's bedroom to put them in the wardrobe. As he stacked the shirts on top of the others on the shelf, his mind drifted back to the night his father was shot. This was his first visit to his mother's bedroom since that fateful night.

As he stared at the wardrobe, Misief recalled the tall stranger he'd seen the night his father was killed. A cold tingle ran up his spine as he thought about the strange man, and then he remembered the bullet. The stranger had shown him the bullet and Misief watched intently as the stranger purposefully placed it on top of the wardrobe. With his mind focused on helping his mom for the last four days, he had completely forgotten about the stranger and the bullet until now.

Determined to find out if what he saw was real or just some type of twisted hallucination, Misief raced into the kitchen and retrieved a three-step stool. Bett caught a glimpse of Misief, out of the corner of her eye, as he darted across the kitchen and back into the bedroom.

Bett asked, "What do you need a stool for son? The clothes don't stack up that high."

He replied, "Oh, it's not for the clothes, I just wanna see if I left something up on the wardrobe."

"Like what?" Bett asked, questioning him further.

Misief hadn't told his mom anything about the stranger or the bullet. He didn't want to scare her, and he wasn't even certain if what he saw was actually real or just his imagination playing tricks on him.

Misief didn't answer his mother's questions as he disappeared into the bedroom, and she did not push him further. He placed the stool beside the wardrobe and climbed the three steps. As he steadied himself on the stool, his heartbeat began to race. He had mixed emotions about what he might or might not find lying on top.

What if he found a bullet?

What if he didn't?

Where did the stranger come from?

How did he get out of the room?

Had he imagined the entire episode?

All the questions rolling around in his young mind settled like the dust in a summer rain when his eyes broke the surface of the top of the wardrobe. Right smack dab in the center lay a bright shiny gold bullet. It was the largest bullet Misief had ever seen!

He picked the bullet up and stepped down from the stool, so he could get a better look at it. Upon closer examination, he saw that the bullet had a single spot of blood on the top of it and that '.50' was engraved on the base of the bullet.

"Wow," Misief exclaimed, as he was momentarily awestruck!

Misief was familiar with .38 caliber and .45 caliber ammunition but never had he seen a .50 caliber bullet. "Whoever owns this bullet must have the best gun in the whole world," he thought.

Misief further inspected the bullet and noticed the letter 'J' beautifully engraved on the side of it. He was perplexed as to why the stranger had left it there for him. He also wondered about the identity of the stranger and was curious as to how the man got into their bedroom?

Was the stranger part of the posse?

As Misief stood there reflecting back, he remembered the incredible stature of the stranger and the width of his broad shoulders. He recalled his solid white boots with the gold studs. Most of all, it was impossible to forget the stranger's eyes and the peace he experienced when the stranger looked his way.

Quietly, Misief slid the large gold bullet into his pocket and picked up the stool to return it to the kitchen. As he walked in to join his mom, he noticed she had finished folding the clothes and had begun to prepare supper. She told him it would only take her a few minutes and the evening meal would be ready. Misief nodded absently as he wandered through the room and told his mom he was going outside.

Now alone in the front yard, Misief pulled the bullet out of his pocket to take a better look at it. He now knew the stranger in the bedroom was not a figment of his imagination and wondered if the man was somehow connected to his father's death. He wanted to know more about the stranger and began combing the front porch and the grassy areas around the cabin for clues. He hoped to find more spent .50 caliber shell casings or anything that might help him solve the mystery surrounding the strange man that had appeared on that dreadful night in his mother's bedroom.

Misief aimlessly roamed over to the woodpile, which was about seventy-five feet to the right of the front porch. He knew this stack of wood would be a great place to take cover in a gunfight and thought some of the posse might have used it during the shootout. Combing the grass on his knees, he found numerous spent shell casings littered all over the ground. Most of the shell casings appeared to come from a .25 caliber rifle. He also found a few that were somewhat larger than the .25 caliber and upon closer inspection, discovered '.38' etched on the bottom of them. He believed there had to be at least two men hiding behind the woodpile; one with a .25 caliber rifle and the other with a .38 caliber pistol. However, there was not one single .50 caliber shell casing anywhere to be found.

He continued searching around every tree, behind the well house, at each corner of the cabin, and anywhere he thought one of the lawmen might have taken cover during the shootout. Every place he looked he found empty shell casings, but none of them matched the caliber of the one in his pocket. As he scouted around the last corner of the cabin, he was met by his mother who had come out the back door to find him.

"What are you looking for?" she asked.

"Oh, I'm just lookin' around," he answered.

"Supper's ready. Wash up and come on in," she said in a gentle voice.

"Okay mama," he replied.

Misief wanted so desperately to tell his mother about the stranger and the .50 caliber bullet, but he decided it would be best to keep it his little secret. He knew she already had enough on her mind, and he did not want her to become concerned about some stranger that had been inside the bedroom of their cabin. Besides, he wondered if his mom would even believe his story about the strange man and the gold bullet.

****

The cabin was filled with the aroma of the evening meal. On the table was a pot of beef stew, an iron skillet steaming with fresh baked cornbread and milk. As Bett dipped out the stew and sliced the cornbread, Misief retrieved the butter from the icebox. The three of them enjoyed the meal together and discussed plans for the next day.

With his mouth full of cornbread, Misief stated, "Mom, tomorrow I am going to try and ride Coal."

Coal was a jet black stallion and had been Barak's pride and joy. Barak had promised a couple of weeks earlier to let Misief ride Coal, believing he was now old enough to handle the large animal. Misief had ridden several of the other horses in the stable, but he had never ridden Coal, who was a very temperamental stallion and only responded to Barak's commands.

With concern sketched all over Bett's face, she looked at Misief and said, "I don't know son, Coal is a big horse with a huge wild streak to boot. You know your father was the only one who was ever able to ride 'em. You might need to wait a spell before you think about riding him. Maybe you should just stick to riding the tamer horses for now."

"Mama, I can ride 'em! I know I can! Just give me a chance," Misief pleaded.

"Let's sleep on it tonight and talk about it in the morning," Bett replied.

Misief nodded in agreement as he ate the last bite of beef stew. With supper over, he immediately started helping his mom clean up the dishes. Bett knew her son was trying his best to do anything possible to win her favor, even if that meant helping clean up dirty dishes!

****

The following morning, Misief was up at dawn! Bett came from her bedroom to find her son already scurrying around in the kitchen. He had a fire going in the woodstove and a pot of coffee ready for her. She could tell he was excited and still had his mind set on trying to ride Coal. Even though Bett was extremely concerned about an eleven year old boy riding such a large horse, she knew he wanted to prove to her he could do it. Like his father, Misief had a will made of iron and was determined to do things his way.

"What's for breakfast?" Bett asked with a slight smile on her face.

"Oatmeal," he replied, as he placed the bowl in front of his mother. Then he picked up the pot off the stove, poured her a cup of coffee and asked, "Would you like some toast to go with your oatmeal?"

"Sure, why not?" she answered, as she took a sip of the coffee.

Her eyes widened as Bett did her best to swallow what was the hottest, blackest coffee she had ever tasted in her life. However, she said not a negative word about it and simply thanked her son for her early morning surprise.

"You're welcome Mama," Misief said proudly. Then he added, "Well Mama, can I go ride Coal this morning?"

Bett knew this was very important to her son. Taking a deep breath, she gave a hesitant reply, "Okay, if you will be careful, I guess you can ride 'em."

As soon as she gave her approval, Misief grabbed his hat and headed out the back door of the cabin.

Bett squeezed in one last bit of advice, "Misief, please be careful with 'em. He's a might stronger than the horses you've been riding."

"Yes ma'am, I'll be careful," he replied grinning ear to ear as he darted outside.

****

Misief was no stranger to horses. His father always had several, and he had played in and around the stable since he was old enough to walk. As a special gift on his sixth birthday, Misief received his first horse from his father. He named the horse Stony, and spent countless hours riding the animal in the yard, as his father held the reins. However, in a sad turn of events, Stony fell sick and died a couple of years after his father gave it to him. Since that time, he'd resigned to riding one of the other horses, and did not have a horse that was necessarily his own.

As Misief drew near the stable, he began to feel apprehensive about riding Coal. He was well aware of Coal's temperamental nature and knew the horse would buck furiously if he got a chance.

But his desire to ride the stallion trumped his fear. He desperately wanted to ride his father's personal horse, and believed that in some way the horse might connect him back to the time he spent in the stable with his father. Now, only a few feet from Coal's stall he looked up at the mighty stallion and sheepishly asked, "Hey Coal, how are you doing this morning?"

Misief really didn't expect an answer, but it would have been comforting if Coal would have responded, "I'm doing fine Misief, how about taking me for a ride."

But that didn't happen. Coal just looked down at him with those big black eyes and did not make a sound.

Misief located Coal's saddle and placed it on the wooden rail that surrounded his stall. He climbed up on the rail, and with a mighty heave, he threw the saddle across the back of the black stallion. Coal squirmed back and forth in the stall as Misief jumped down to finish securing the saddle. After successfully attaching the saddle, he retrieved a bridle and gently moved to the front of the animal. He spoke tenderly to Coal as he slipped the metal bit into his mouth. Then he softly pitched the reins over the stallion's head, and opened the door of the stable.

Misief walked close beside Coal and directed him toward the open door. He took a deep breath and placed his left foot in the stirrup as he reached up to grip the saddle horn. Next, he threw his right leg over the back of the horse, and before he could get completely situated, Coal bolted out of the stable into the open field. Misief's young body flailed back and forth on the animal, and he tried his best to get both feet in the stirrups. He thought for certain he would fall off, as the horse raced in a straight line away from the stable. Nobody but Barak had ever ridden on Coal, and the horse was not ready to begin a new relationship!

After about one-quarter mile, Misief finally gathered himself in the saddle and pulled back on the reins. Coal responded and actually slowed down to a fast trot. Misief began talking to Coal like he'd heard his father do, and within ten or fifteen minutes he had the horse walking at a steady pace.

With his confidence growing by the minute, Misief wanted to see if he could get Coal to follow a few basic commands. Bowing his back to get a deep voice, he gave the command for Coal to go left, and with a gentle pull on the reins and a slight nudge in his side, the stallion turned left. Next, he shouted the command to turn right, and the horse obeyed perfectly. After a series of left hand turns followed by right hand turns, he brought Coal to a complete stop.

After pausing for thirty seconds or so, Misief took a deep breath, gently nudged the horse and gave the command, "Giddy Up." Coal immediately accelerated like a speeding locomotive. He had never ridden a horse with such explosive power and held on for dear life!

After ridding Coal for at least an hour, and feeling like he was beginning to have him under his control, Misief directed the horse to the front of the cabin and led him right to the edge of the porch. Mounted proudly on the majestic stallion, he called out, "Hey Mama, come look!"

Bett walked out the front door of the cabin with Ashel in her arms. A tear came to her eye as she saw the beaming smile on her son's face. At that moment, Bett knew her son was going to grow up into a strong young man just like his father.

"What-cha think, Mama?" He asked.

She responded, "Misief, I am so proud of you, and your father would be proud of you too."

Misief jumped down from Coal and tied the end of the reins to the rail on the front porch. "You didn't think I could do it, did ya?" He asked.

Bett replied, "I knew it was important to you, and if there was any way at all, I knew you'd figure out how to do it."

"Do you wanna go for a ride with me?" he asked with a smile on his face.

"Oh no, not me," she replied.

Misief laughed as he walked back over to Coal. Coal stood perfectly still this time as he threw his leg across his back. Misief felt like a grown man as he backed Coal away from the porch.

As he rode to the stable, he pondered what his mother had just told him. Knowing his father would be proud of him was very important to him. Misief hadn't forgotten what Lucas Benson stole from his father and vowed someday he would find him and get even. He also wanted to know why the lawmen had surrounded the cabin and killed his father. He'd made a commitment to get revenge, and overcoming his fear of Coal was a critical first step.

As Misief led Coal to the door of his stall, he sprang off the horse and led him by the reins. Although this was his maiden ride, he felt an immediate bond with the animal. He could feel the spirit of his father with him while riding Coal. Once securely inside the stable, he removed the saddle and bridle and then took extra time to brush the horse's beautiful black coat.

Running the brush along the back of the animal, he began talking to Coal like he was his best friend in the world. With each stroke of the brush, it was as if he momentarily forgot about his problems. He felt a sense of serenity descend upon the stable as he focused his attention on caring for his father's prize horse. After a thorough brushing, he placed hay mixed with a small amount of oats into the trough and gave Coal a big hug.

Before leaving the stable, Misief made certain all the horses had plenty of food and water. As he walked toward the door, he felt the .50 caliber bullet in the front pocket of his trousers. He'd had the bullet in his pocket ever since he found it yesterday, and it was beginning to rub a sore spot on his leg. Removing the bullet from his pocket, he searched for a prominent place to keep it. Walking past Coal's saddle, he noticed a place right above the saddle horn that appeared it might make a perfect home for the bullet. Sure enough, the leather had just enough slack for him to wedge the bullet under it. It was tight enough to securely hold the bullet in place and still allow it to be on display whenever he rode Coal.

Happy with his new home for the special bullet, Misief headed toward the stable door. On his left was a shelf that was filled with rusty nails, horseshoes, and leather straps his father used to take care of the horses. Lying on the shelf beside the nails was an old three-blade knife his father used to cut the leather into smaller pieces. Misief picked up the knife and opened the smallest of the three blades. He slowly walked over to the stable door and began carving.

His first stroke with the knife came straight down vertically followed by a smaller horizontal stroke that connected at the bottom of the first one. As he carved the first letter, the shavings fell to the floor of the stable.

He skipped a small distance from the first letter and began making the second letter which was a "U" shaped form.

Following the "U" shape, the third letter was in the form of a circle that was not completely closed on the right side. Three letters down, two to go.

He skipped over and started making the fourth letter by making two strikes, which touched at the top and moved away from each other as they progressed downward. He connected these two strikes with a cross bar right in the middle.

Finally, he completed his inscription by making the fifth letter in the shape of a vertical serpent. The five letters that formed this piece of artwork were now forever etched on the back of the stable door. Misief stepped back a few steps to admire his handiwork. These five letters would forever remind him of his commitment to get revenge for his father's murder!

Chapter 4

"A Girl Named Nainsi"

June 14, 1863

Six years had passed since the night of Barak's death. Misief was now seventeen years old and had become the man of the house. Ashel had grown into a beautiful, eight year old girl with long brown hair just like her mother. Bett, Misief and Ashel had adjusted to life without Barak. Ashel rarely mentioned her father, and Misief often wondered if his little sister even remembered anything about him at all. Bett missed Barak for sure, but nobody missed the volatility of his temper, and the cabin now had an aura of peace that wasn't evident while Barak was living. Each member of the family had their own role; and knew what they needed to do to keep things running smoothly.

Misief had taken full control of all the chores related to caring for the horses and was doing a masterful job. He had also become quite the sportsman hunter, and the meat he brought home was butchered and smoked with help from Bett.

Ashel was very handy in the kitchen and helped outside, feeding the chickens as well as collecting eggs each morning. She had learned to help with the laundry and with the cleaning of the cabin.

Bett did her best to hold the family together. Money was tight without Barak, and she managed their finances with a prayerful heart, trusting there would be enough to keep a roof over their head and food on the table. Life was tough, but the threesome made a good team and for the last six years had worked together to scratch out a living.

****

Since Barak's death, Bett, Misief and Ashel had a routine of going into Rock Springs at least once a month for supplies. Misief would hitch the horses to the wagon, and they would load up young chicks, smoked venison and fresh vegetables, whenever they were in season. With the wagon loaded, the three of them would make the eleven mile journey down the beaten trail from their cabin to Rock Springs. Once in town, they would trade for items such as flour, sugar, spices, tools, cotton fabric for making clothing and gunpowder.

The trip, by wagon, to Rock Springs was a long, winding two-hour journey over rough, rugged terrain. Once in Rock Springs, their interaction with the locals was limited to dialogue necessary to sell and trade their wares. Bett didn't allow Misief or Ashel to make friends with anyone in town. On the night of Barak's death, the Sheriff had informed Bett that he was investigating the murder of a train engineer in Rock Springs and that Barak was a suspect. Since then, she'd learned from Jeno and Davis, that many of the people in Rock Springs believed her late husband was responsible for the murder. Supposedly, Barak was identified, by a couple of eyewitnesses at the scene, as one of the men present when the train engineer was robbed and murdered.

According to those who witnessed the crime, the robbery attempt was unsuccessful, and the train engineer was shot when he refused to comply with their demands. Bett felt in her heart that Barak might be involved in the train robbery, but she wanted to give him the benefit of the doubt since he was never actually convicted. However, in the court of public opinion, it seemed everyone believed that Barak was guilty. Not knowing for sure, Bett hoped and prayed Barak wasn't the one who actually killed the man; nonetheless, the local citizens of Rock Springs seemed to hold her and her children responsible for Barak's assumed guilt.

Nobody in Rock Springs had ever said anything to Bett about the murder, but she always felt an uneasy feeling every time she went into town. The townspeople would buy, sell and trade with her, but she believed it was partly out of pity for her and her children. Regardless, she never made friends with anyone in Rock Springs. Her conversations were always confined to small talk or answering questions about the items she and the kids were peddling.

Misief had a very different perspective about his father's demise. He wanted to talk about his father's death all the time, but Bett would rarely engage him in dialogue. Misief would beg his mother for permission to go into the saloon to see if he could find Lucas Benson, but Bett forbid him to do so. Finding out who pulled the trigger on that fateful night six years ago tormented him, but Bett always told him it did not matter. Her advice to her son was to simply let it go and forget it.

But something inside Misief's spirit would not let it go. He desperately sought answers to the questions bombarding his mind. Subsequently, since their positions were so different on the topic of Barak's death, Misief and Bett rarely broached the subject. The topic was not a sore spot between them; they simply understood each other's position and respected their differing opinions.

When they would travel to Rock Springs, Bett guarded Misief closely. She was concerned he would engage one of the townsfolk in conversation about the death of his father, which would stir up negative emotions buried inside of him. With each trip, Bett's goal was simple; she wanted to get into town and sell or trade their items for the supplies they needed and then head back to the cabin as quick as possible. Like clockwork, she timed the trips so they would arrive around mid-morning, and she always did her best to be headed back home by mid-afternoon.

As Misief grew older, his engagement with the locals in Rock Springs increased, much to the chagrin of his mother. He had an outgoing personality and tried to talk to everyone he met. Bett did her best to encourage her son to keep the dialogue focused on buying, selling or trading and would divert away from any conversation that seemed to be headed toward questions regarding her late husband. Sometimes she was successful, but there were other occasions when she would have to confess that Barak was the father of her children and that he had died after a bloody shootout with the local sheriff's office. However, as soon as they sold their goods, and she had collected what she needed from the local merchants, Bett would swiftly gather her children up in the wagon and begin the two hour journey back to the cabin.

****

One evening, after returning from Rock Springs, Bett, Misief and Ashel were busy unloading the supplies from the wagon, when suddenly, Bett turned to Misief and said, "Oh no! I forgot to stop by Doc Lynch's office to get Ashel's medicine. How could I have let that slip my mind?"

When Ashel was just two years of age, she had developed a severe breathing problem. Doc Lynch was the only doctor within fifty miles, and he had prescribed a medication to treat her symptoms anytime she had an asthmatic attack.

Bett knew Ashel had to have the medication and after confirming she was all but out of the prescribed medicine, Bett called Misief and Ashel together and said, "We are gonna have to go back to Rock Springs tomorrow to get Ashel's medication."

Misief quickly came up with a solution and offered his mother this proposal, "There's no need in all of us going back for just a little bottle of medicine. Why I don't I ride back in to town to get it for Ashel?"

From the look on Bett's face, it was obvious she had reservations in allowing Misief to make the journey alone.

Could she trust her son?

Would he go straight to Rock Springs and come right back?

Could he stay out of trouble?

All of these questions rushed through Bett's mind as she pondered her answer.

Misief was now seventeen years old, and Bett knew the day was fast approaching when her son would want to go into town alone. She completely trusted him to go on hunting expeditions, and she had confidence he could take care of himself if he encountered any trouble. However, she had done her best to keep him away from the locals in Rock Springs, so he would not be faced with the issues related to his father. Bett knew she could not protect Misief forever and with all the chores needing to be done around the cabin, she sure did not need to lose another day's work.

So, after mulling over her options, Bett replied, "Okay, you can go get the medicine first thing in the morning. But you must promise to go straight to Doc's office and come right back home!"

****

The following morning, before the sun came up over the ridge, Bett prepared a breakfast of eggs, sausage and buttermilk biscuits. As Misief finished the last crumb on his plate, he got up from the table and kissed his mother goodbye. As Bett gave her son a hug she reminded him, "Now you be careful. I want you to go straight to Doc Lynch's office, and then come home, okay?"

Misief nodded to confirm his mother's instructions, and then said, "I will. Remember, I'm not a kid anymore."

Walking into the stable, Misief sensed a bit of freedom and excitement. This would be his first solo trip to Rock Springs, and it made him feel like a man. He wanted to prove to his mother he could be trusted. As he opened the door of the horse stable, he noticed the artwork that was etched on the back of it. The five letters he'd carved on the door six years earlier were now grayed over, but he still knew what they meant. Every time he saw the carving it reminded him of the commitment he'd made to get revenge for his father!

After saddling up Coal, Misief opened the door of the stall and made his way out of the stable. Bett waved at him through the window as he passed the side of the cabin. Misief waved back at his mother and hollered out, "I'll be back as quick as I can. Don't you worry one bit!"

Beaming with confidence, Misief was a man on a mission. He nudged Coal, and off they raced down the dusty wagon trail that would lead them to Rock Springs.

Misief had grown into a handsome young man. He had the same olive colored skin as his father, was now over six feet tall, and weighed close to two hundred pounds. Since his father's death, he'd matured in his ways and acted more like a man in his mid to late twenties than a teenage boy. The days of playing childhood games passed with his father's death. The day after his father died,

Bett immediately grew dependent on him, and he'd responded by becoming a strong, trustworthy young man.

As Misief bumped down the wagon trail at a lightning pace, he glanced down at his .38 caliber pistol strapped to his side. He peeked upward to catch a glimpse of his wide brim cowboy hat which he proudly wore on his head. This was the first time he truly felt like a man! As the dust burst skyward behind him, Misief felt freedom and the spirit of his father inside his soul.

The first half of the journey into Rock Springs was uneventful as he followed the winding path of Roberts Creek. Roberts Creek was a small stream and provided a comforting sound as the water gently rolled over the smooth rocks. It had several nice shallow places that were just perfect for horses to stop and get a drink. On the family's monthly journey into town, Bett would always pack a snack for the trip. Without exception, the family would take a break and picnic under a large Pin Oak tree that was about halfway between Rock Springs and the cabin. As Misief arrived at the familiar Pin Oak tree, he decided to pause for a moment to give Coal a break.

Watching Coal lap up the cool water, Misief reflected on how much he loved his mother and his little sister. He was determined to go to Doc Lynch's office to pick up the medicine for Ashel and head right back home without any interruptions. He desperately wanted to prove to his mother that she could trust him to go to Rock Springs alone!

After following the path along the creek for about five miles, Misief came to a fork in the old wagon trail. One fork went to the right and led over the mountain to Rock Springs. It was the quickest way to get to town and also the shortest route, but the trail going over the mountain was not designed for wagons. Misief had heard the locals talk about a gorgeous view of Rock Springs from a place at the top called Rock Pointe. He'd never been that way before, but he had always wanted to see the view from the top of the mountain.

The fork to the left went through what the locals called 'Shoots Valley'. This was the furthest route to town but was the safest and smoothest path. Misief was very familiar with this trail since it was the one they always followed when they traveled to Rock Springs in the wagon. Considering his options, he really wanted to see what was on top of the mountain, but since he'd never been that way before, he decided to stick to the familiar trail through Shoots Valley.

The final stretch leading into Rock Springs was an old dusty dirt road filled with ruts from all the wagon traffic flowing in and out of town. Misief was surprised how quickly he'd made the trip to Rock Springs. He was accustomed to the two hour journey in the wagon as it rattled along at a snail's pace, however Coal had made the entire eleven mile journey in just under an hour.

As Misief rode into town he noticed that Main Street was bustling with horse drawn wagons traveling in every direction. The sight of him riding solo on his majestic black stallion caught the eye of some of the townsfolk as he made his way past the sawmill, the feed store and the saloon. The citizens of Rock Springs were accustomed to seeing him in town, but it was always with his mother, his sister and their horse drawn wagon. Seeing Misief alone on a large black stallion seemed to make some of them feel a bit uneasy. They stared at him as he passed by. Maybe it was that he reminded them of his father, Barak. After all, he had many of the same mannerisms, the same facial characteristics and he was riding his father's horse, Coal.

Misief paid no attention to their glares and went straight to see Doc Lynch. Doc's place was on the second floor, right above the town Post Office. Doc was a gentle soul in his late 60's and was the only medical doctor within a fifty mile radius. Misief directed Coal to the old wood rail in front of Doc's office. He dismounted and stroked the horse's mane as he loosely secured him to the railing.

"Good boy, you stay right here, and I'll be right back," Misief stated as he turned to start the climb up the stairway leading to Doc's office.

On his way up the stairs, Misief spotted a teenage girl sitting alone on a bench in front of the town café. She appeared to be about sixteen or seventeen years old and was wearing a beautiful pink dress. She had long, brown curly hair and big brown eyes, which were looking right back at him.

With his focus on the gorgeous young damsel, Misief missed the upcoming step. Completely losing his balance, he fell to his knees and almost toppled back to the bottom of the stairway. Grabbing the rail with his left arm, he held on until he could get his feet back under him. He was so embarrassed he didn't dare look back to see if she'd witnessed his tumble. Regaining his composure, he quickly skipped up the remaining steps to the door of Doc's office.

Misief gently knocked on the old wooden door and instantly heard Doc's voice.

"Well, hello Misief," Doc said, as opened the door and invited him inside. "I bet you've come for Ashel's medicine."

"Yes sir," he replied. "We forgot it when we were in town yesterday."

Doc continued, "Yeah, I saw you and your family in town and thought Bett would stop by to get it. When she didn't come by I figured either she didn't have the money or you'd probably just forgotten."

Doc retrieved the medicine from a locked, glass cabinet, and Misief paid him for it. He bid Doc goodbye and quickly made his way out the door. While coming down the stairway, he scouted out the area to see if the young lady with curly brown hair was still on the bench. Sure enough, she was still sitting there reading. Even though his mother told him to go directly to Doc's office and straight back home, he wanted to take just a few minutes to find out more about this beautiful young girl.

After successfully descending the stairway, Misief was facing the café where the girl was sitting. She appeared to be completely engrossed in a book she was reading and hadn't noticed him leaving Doc's office. As he got closer to her, the sound of his footsteps caught her attention.

The young lady raised her head, brushed her long hair out of her face and made eye contact with him. As Misief stood there staring into those big, brown eyes, he completely lost his thoughts, making the situation awkward.

Finally, he collected himself and uttered, "Uh, Hi, my name is Misief."

She grinned and replied, "Hi Misief, my name is Nainsi." She giggled a little as she confessed, "I sure thought you were gonna get hurt a few minutes ago."

"Oh, you mean on the stairway? Oh, I just got my boot hung on an old broken board," he shot back with a sly smile. "I didn't get hurt. I just came to town to get some medicine from Doc Lynch for my little sister."

Misief knew that a loose board was not to blame for his fall, but it sounded reasonable. After all, he didn't want to confess that her captivating beauty caused him to nearly break his neck. He immediately changed the subject by asking, "Do you live in Rock Springs, or are you just visiting?"

"Oh, I live here," she replied. "You want to sit down?"

"Sure!" Misief proclaimed, as he took his place on the bench.

"My dad owns the local saw mill. I have two younger brothers and we live about one half mile out of town," Nainsi explained.

"I live on the other side of Roberts Mountain," Misief confessed.

"How long does it take you to get to town?" Nainsi asked.

"It's eleven miles out to our place. It takes about two hours by wagon, but I made it in less than an hour today." Misief admitted. "I rode in on my horse, Coal. That made the trip much faster," he stated, as he pointed to the beautiful black stallion that was tied up in front of Doc's office.

Then Misief asked, "So, are you waiting on someone?"

"My father," Nainsi admitted. "He's inside the café eating. It takes him forever! He knows just about everyone in town and talks almost as much as he eats. I usually just come outside and read my book while I wait for him to finish."

Trying to keep the conversation going, Misief asked, "What are you reading?"

Nainsi held out the book and said. "I'm reading this book called, 'The Album'. Have you ever read it?"

Misief shook his head and said, "No, I don't think I have."

As Misief's eyes caught the cover of the book, he did a double take. On the front cover of the book, right below the title, were three bullets. The bullets were of a very large caliber with a single blood spot on the tip of each one. The three bullets were connected with what appeared to be a leather cord, as if it were a necklace one might wear. Then Misief noticed something else—each bullet had a single initial engraved on it. The one on the far left had an 'A', the one in the middle had the letter 'M', and the one on the right had the letter 'J'. He was flabbergasted when he saw the one with the letter 'J'! That one appeared to be exactly like the bullet left by the stranger that was now attached to Coal's saddle.

Misief wondered, "Could it be that this book has information about the stranger that was in my mother's bedroom the night my father was killed?"

Misief's reading skills were marginal at best. He didn't have the luxury of attending the small one room public school in Rock Springs. Even before his father died, the only education he received was from his mother reading to him each night by the light of an oil lantern. Once his father died, he had become the man of the house, and with all the chores needing to be done, education had definitely taken a back-seat in his life. His mother had taught him to read a little bit, but he had never read an entire book. Still wondering about the bullets on the cover, Misief asked, "Is that a book about bullets?"

Nainsi giggled as she replied, "No, it's not about bullets. So you've never heard of 'The Album'?"

"Nope," he replied.

As Misief searched for what to say next, out of the café walked Nainsi's father. Her father turned to her and asked, "Are you ready to go sweetie?"

Nainsi shook her head to acknowledge her father and turned to bid Misief goodbye. Her parting words to him were, "Stop by and see me at the sawmill sometime."

Misief propped himself against a post in front of the café, as the beautiful young damsel headed down the road toward the sawmill with her father.

Once Nainsi and her father were out of sight, Misief walked the short distance back to the rail where Coal was waiting for him. He untied the horse from the rail and placed Ashel's medication in the saddle bag.

Departing Rock Springs, Misief's mind raced with questions about Nainsi and the book called, 'The Album'. Staring down at the bullet in his saddle, he could not believe her book had an exact replica of his bullet on the cover. At this moment, he had more questions than answers, but he was determined to return soon, so he could spend more time with the beautiful young girl named, Nainsi, and find out more about what might be inside this book she called, 'The Album'.

Chapter 5

"The Stranger Returns"

September 9, 1863

Three months had passed since Misief made his first solo trip to Rock Springs to retrieve the medication for his sister, Ashel. The trip proved to Bett she could trust her son to go back and forth to town on his own. Since that first trip, she'd allowed him to make two other solo journeys to Rock Springs to pick up small items that normally would have waited for the family's monthly trip in the wagon.

Misief thoroughly enjoyed going by himself to Rock Springs. Sometimes, Bett felt like he was trying to create reasons to go. However, she openly acknowledged that having him available to make a quick run into town was certainly very convenient. So far, allowing him the freedom to make the trip alone was working out well for both Misief and his mom!

On his last two trips Misief wanted so desperately to run into Nainsi again, but he had been unsuccessful in locating her. On his first follow-up trip, he'd stopped by her father's sawmill as well as the café, but she wasn't at either place. He recalled that she told him she only lived one half mile out of town, but she did not indicate which direction. On his last trip to Rock Springs, he stopped by the café, then by the sawmill, and in a last ditch effort to locate her, he roamed around town, hoping to see her in or around one of the houses that dotted the perimeter of Rock Springs. However, Nainsi was nowhere to be found.

****

Late one afternoon, while working in the horse stable, Misief heard his mother let out a blood curdling scream. Racing out of the stable, he turned the corner to see his mother lying on the ground in the garden.

"Mama, what happened?" Misief shouted as he sprinted to her.

Grimacing in pain, Bett pointed at a large rock and replied, "I was working along the fence row, trying to clean out the vines that were tangled in the fence. I stumbled over that rock and cut my leg with the axe."

The fence served to separate the vegetable garden from the area where they kept the chickens. The fence row had grown up over the years, and Bett had vowed to get it cleaned out as soon as she had the time. It appeared that while feverishly fighting with the tangled vines, she'd stepped back and stumbled over a large rock as she swung the axe. The sharp blade of the axe came across the side of her calf muscle on her right leg and split it wide open.

As Misief got closer, he saw the blood running down the side of his mother's leg and knew the cut was serious. He immediately ripped off his shirt and quickly wrapped it tightly around the open wound.

Ashel, who had been playing on a tree swing in the front yard, came running when she heard her mother scream. When she saw the blood coming from the gash on her mother's leg, Ashel burst out crying.

As she tried to calm herself, Ashel inquired, "Mama, what happened? Are you going to be okay?"

Bett opened her arms, and Ashel dove into her mother's embrace. Bett reassured her young daughter by saying, "I'm okay baby. Mama's gonna be alright."

Ashel seemed to find comfort in her mother's words.

Misief spoke up, "Ashel, I'm gonna need you to help me get Mama up to the cabin."

Misief and Ashel got on each side of their mother and helped her stand up. Leaning heavily on Misief, Bett hobbled from the garden to the front porch of the cabin where she collapsed into an old rocking chair. She asked Misief to fetch her a bucket of water from the well, and then she turned to Ashel and asked, "Sweetie, would you go get Mama some clean towels while Misief gets the water?"

Both children raced away to fulfill their mother's request. Within minutes they returned, and together the three of them cleaned the wound and tied rags around the cut to slow down the bleeding. As they secured the bandage on her leg, Bett realized the cut was much worse than what she first thought, but she kept her thoughts to herself so that she would not alarm her children.

What Bett did not know was that Misief was thinking the same thing. He spoke up and stated, "Mama, that's a very deep cut. I think I should go get Doc Lynch, so he can take a look at it."

Bett didn't want to bother the doctor and replied, "I'll be alright. There's no need to cause a fuss. Let's just get the bleeding stopped, and then you two help get me inside."

Gingerly, the two children assisted their mother inside the cabin and to her bedroom. As Bett lie stretched out on the bed with her leg elevated, Ashel began tracking down every clean rag and towel she could find. Misief stayed right by his mother's bedside, constantly applying pressure to her injured leg. There seemed to be nothing he could do to get the bleeding to stop. Still believing they needed Doc to take a look at it, Misief once again broached the subject and said, "Mama, I know you didn't want to bother Doc Lynch, but I really think I need to go get him."

Bett realized her son was probably right and feared she might need stitches to properly close the wound.

Bett nodded and said, "Okay. But it's getting dark outside, and I sure don't feel good about you going down the trail in the dark. How about you go first thing in the morning?"

Misief replied, "Mama, you have already lost a lot of blood. You need the Doc to come tonight. I will be fine. Trust me!"

Bett didn't argue the point. Deep down she knew Misief was right; she just hated to see him make the long trip to Rock Springs alone and after dark.

Misief looked at Ashel and said, "Ashel, keep applying pressure to the cut. You stay with her until I get back!"

Ashel agreed and took Misief's place at Bett's side.

Misief raced to the stable and quickly made preparations to ride into Rock Springs to fetch Doc Lynch. He stepped into Coal's stall and said, "Come on boy, we've gotta get help for mama. I sure hope you can see in the dark!"

It was as if Coal somehow understood the urgency of the situation. Normally, he would be a little cantankerous during the process of strapping on a saddle and bridle, but tonight he stood completely still and actually opened his mouth to accept the bit from the bridle. Misief put on his hat, strapped on his trusty .38 caliber pistol and hopped up on Coal. With a slight nudge from a spur and a shake of the reins, Coal burst forth out of the stable, and within seconds, the tandem was headed into the darkness in a dead run!

There was just enough moonlight to make the trail barely visible. Even in near total darkness, Misief made record time, completing the journey to Rock Springs in just forty-five minutes. A cloud of dust totally encompassed him as he abruptly brought the stallion to a halt right in front of Doc's office. Misief quickly dismounted and led Coal down to the watering trough that was in front of the local Trading Post. The horse was laboring to breathe from the eleven mile run and cherished the opportunity to drink the cool water.

Misief reached out and patted Coal on the neck and said, "Good job ole' boy, drink up. We'll be heading back home as soon as I get Doc."

Misief turned, and then sprinted up the stairway leading to Doc Lynch's office. As he cleared the last step he noticed a sign hanging on the inside of the window of the door. In the darkness he could not make out what the sign said. He knocked on Doc's door, but the doctor did not answer.

Noticing a lit lantern hanging on a post near where Coal was waiting, Misief raced back down the steps and retrieved it. From the light of the lantern, he read the sign which said, *"I am out of town for a few days. I will be back Friday, Doc."*

It was Wednesday night, and Misief desperately needed help for his mother right now. He knew that in her condition she could not wait until Friday for the doctor to return.

From his vantage point on the second floor landing, Misief turned around to see if there was anyone who could help him. All of the local businesses were closed for the day, and in the darkness he did not see anyone walking through town.

Misief turned back to the locked door and began to shake and rattle the door handle, hoping he'd simply misread the note. As he violently shook the door knob he hollered, "Doc, are you in there?"

Nothing Misief did brought a response from inside the office. Nor did it appear his hollering had caught anyone's attention in Rock Springs. It was as if he was in a ghost town, except for a little racket coming from down the street at the local saloon.

Then Misief had an idea. He began to consider the notion of breaking into Doc's office and taking what he needed to properly bandage up his mother's leg. He'd never stolen anything in his life, and his heart was racing at the thought of what he was contemplating. He knew breaking into Doc's office was against the law, but he felt like this was an emergency and merited consideration of drastic measures.

Without giving it another thought, Misief blew out the lantern and grabbed his pistol from his gun belt. Using the butt of the gun, he broke the small pane of glass that was closest to the door handle. He carefully slipped his hand inside the broken glass and unlocked the door. Peeking over his shoulder to make certain nobody was watching, he quietly opened the door and quickly stepped inside.

Doc's office didn't have any exterior windows. The glass front door was the only access for the moonlight to enter the room. It was incredibly dark in the office, and Misief struggled to find his way in the shadowy room. Soon, his eyes began to acclimate to the darkness and after three or four minutes of stumbling around, he found a cabinet filled with medical supplies. Not sure what he needed, he stuffed his trousers and jacket pockets with an assortment of ointments, bandages and tape.

As he finished ransacking the cabinet, Misief felt a cold wind blow across the back of his neck. Out of nowhere, he got this eerie feeling that someone was watching him from the back corner of the room. His heart began pounding at the thought of someone lurking around in the darkness. His first thought was to race for the door without looking in that direction. However, he felt it was imperative to know if someone had witnessed his crime.

Taking a deep breath, Misief slowly turned around to peer over his left shoulder. His knees buckled when his eyes caught a glimpse of a tall, dark figure standing in the corner of Doc's office. Misief opened his mouth to acknowledge the shadowy figure, but words did not come forth. Finally, after regaining his composure and taking a deep breath, Misief mumbled the words, "Hey, who's there?"

The strange figure did not move or respond to Misief's question. Then he noticed something—in the dim moonlight he saw a reflection coming from the stranger's boots. Whoever was standing in the darkness had on what appeared to be white boots with gold studs on them! Misief wondered if possibly these might be the same white boots that the stranger had on the night his father died!

"Hey man." Misief hollered, "Have I seen you before?"

The stranger did not verbally respond to his question. Without saying anything, the stranger began walking directly toward him. Misief froze in his tracks! He thought about grabbing his gun but really didn't want to kill anybody over a few medical supplies.

The stranger walked right up to within three feet of where Misief was standing. Even in the darkness, he was almost certain this man was the same tall stranger that he saw in his parent's bedroom six years earlier when his father was killed. This man had the same exact build, standing over six feet tall with broad shoulders. He had on the same white cowboy boots with gold studs, and this time, Misief noticed he had on a badge that, while in the darkness it was hard to be certain, appeared to be gold in color. It was a badge like a deputy or a sheriff would wear.

Staring specifically at the badge, Misief believed he saw an engraving of three bullets in the same format as the ones on the book that Nainsi was reading. The stranger said not a word, just stood there staring at the ravaged medicine cabinet and Misief's bulging pockets.

Then the stranger took several steps backwards, returning to his original position in the corner of the room. Misief reached out to close the door of the medicine cabinet but kept his eyes fixated on the stranger. Then Misief heard something fall off the top of the cabinet and land on the office floor. Glancing down, he saw a bottle of pills rolling around on the floor. He slowly knelt down to pick up the bottle and momentarily took his eyes off of the stranger.

When Misief stood back up, the stranger was gone!

He looked all around to see if maybe the man had just moved to another corner, but there was no trace of the stranger anywhere in the dark room. It was as if he had simply vanished into thin air.

Misief's body was shaking as he yelled, "Who are you, and what do you want with me? Are you the same fella who was in my mother's bedroom when they killed my father? Why the heck are you following me?"

Misief stood there trembling in the darkened silence for the next few minutes. Not a footstep could be heard. No sound of anyone breathing. It was eerily quiet in the room. He wondered if anyone outside had heard him yelling at the stranger. He stood there a moment or two, just trying to regain his composure, and quickly decided it was time to get out of Doc's office and out of town!

Misief walked to the door and peeked outside to make sure the coast was clear. With no one in sight, he snuck out of Doc's office and rushed down the stairway. Halfway down the stairway, he looked back over his shoulder just to make certain the tall, dark stranger wasn't following him. To his relief, there was nobody around, anywhere. It seemed that, for now, the stranger had vanished.

At the bottom of the steps, Misief took an immediate right turn around the corner and began walking casually toward Coal. As he walked past the Post Office, he thought about how easy it had been to just break in and take whatever he wanted from Doc's office. If not for the encounter with the stranger, the break-in would have been a piece of cake.

As Misief placed his left foot in the stirrup and prepared to ride away, he caught a glimpse of something sitting in the display window of the Trading Post. He could not believe his eyes, as he let go of Coal's reins and walked over to the glass window to get a better look.

Flickering in the light of the lanterns hanging on the posts along Main Street, Misief noticed several items that were displayed in the Trading Post window; a Remington rifle, a canteen, pieces of jewelry and several revolvers. Those items were not what caught his attention. To the left of the rifle was an old, brown leather bag. Pressing his face up against the glass, he could see an inscription on the front of the bag; the letters were 'S.F.F'. He knew this had to be the leather bag that his father lost in the infamous poker game with Lucas Benson!

There was no one inside the Trading Post, as the business had been closed for several hours. The first thing that crossed his mind was to break the glass and steal the bag, like he did at Doc's office. But the Trading Post was on Main Street and not on a side alley like Doc's office. As hard as it was, Misief decided to wait and come back at a later time to inquire about the leather bag. Remembering the severity of his mother's injury, he regained his focus and hurried back over to Coal.

****

As Misief rode out of Rock Springs, he could not get the brown leather bag or the encounter with the stranger out of his head. He wondered where the bag had been since the night when Lucas Benson left the saloon with it on his shoulder. He hoped Lucas was the one who sold it to the Trading Post, and if so, maybe the store owner could tell him where to find Lucas.

The reflections coming from the moonlight cast lengthy shadows along the trail, as Misief pushed Coal as fast as he could in the darkness. Being alone on the trail at night, along with the images of the stranger showing up in Doc's office, had his nerves on edge. His eyes kept playing tricks on him as every shadow along the trail seemed to take on the form of a person. The last thing Misief wanted was to run into the stranger along the way!

Seeing the lights of the cabin brought comfort to Misief's spirit as he pulled off the trail. After loosely tying Coal to the rail, he ran inside the cabin to find his mother agonizing in horrible pain from the cut on her leg.

Bett grimaced as she looked at Misief and asked, "Is Doc Lynch coming?"

He replied, "No mama. He's outta town and won't be back 'til Friday. But I did pick up some medical supplies for you while I was in town."

Bett was in so much pain that she didn't even ask him how or where he got the medical supplies. Since his mom did not question it, Misief offered no explanation and went right to work unwinding the bloody rags from her leg. He turned to Ashel and asked her to get him some clean water from the water jug in the kitchen. Bett moaned out loud in pain, as Misief removed the rag that had become stuck to her leg from all the dried blood. Then he took clean, warm soapy water and gently washed the bloody residue from his mother's leg. The wound was still bleeding a little, which was very concerning to him. He was not sure how much blood his mother had lost, but he knew she'd been bleeding constantly for the last three or four hours and could see that her face was getting pale.

After cleaning all the dried blood from her leg, he opened a bottle of alcohol that he'd taken from Doc's office. He warned his mother, "This is gonna sting a little bit."

Next he took a piece of white gauze bandage and dabbed it with alcohol; then he wiped it over and around the gash on Bett's leg.

Bett nearly sat straight up in the bed! She grabbed Misief's arm and whispered, "Oh, that burns!"

Misief knew it was painful, and Ashel reassured her mother by saying, "It's gonna be alright, mama. What's he's doing will make it all better."

Misief reached into the pocket of his jacket and pulled out a roll of medical tape. He tore small strips of tape and laced them across the wound, to try and pull the opening together. Then he took more gauze and placed it over the cut. Finally, he pulled a knife out of his pocket and cut a piece of cloth from a white bed sheet. He placed the cloth over the wound and covered it all with another layer of medical tape.

Misief stepped back and admired his work, as Bett continued to groan in pain. "You did a fine job son," Bett proclaimed, "But my leg is still throbbing!"

It was obvious that the cut on Bett's leg was much deeper and more serious than any of them first thought. Misief asked his mother if she thought she had cut into a muscle or maybe a nerve. Bett shrugged her shoulders but did not say anything. She was a tough woman and had endured many challenges in her life, but the pain was growing in intensity to the point that she was almost ready to break out in tears!

Misief reached into his trousers pocket and pulled out a bottle of pain pills. "Mama, take one of these," he said, as he asked Ashel to get her a glass of water.

Ashel brought her mother a cup of water from the kitchen, and Bett thanked her daughter and took the pill. Ashel then ran into the other room and quickly returned with an extra pillow from her own bed, for to her mother to place under her leg.

Misief spoke up, "Maybe that pain pill will kick in and give you some relief. I don't know anything else to do."

As Bett lay on the bed waiting for the medication to take effect, Misief realized they had completely forgotten about eating. It was already way past time for supper, but he didn't want any of them going to bed hungry.

Misief turned to his mother and said, "Mama, I am going to go into the kitchen and see what I can find for us to eat. I'll bring you something just as quick as I can."

Ashel joined Misief in the kitchen, and together they began searching for something they could prepare without much effort. He remembered there was some leftover smoked turkey from the day before, and Ashel retrieved half a loaf of bread that Bett had baked.

"Hey Sis, How about turkey sandwiches?" Misief asked.

"Sounds good to me," Ashel replied.

Together the siblings worked to prepare sandwiches for the three of them. Misief poured everyone a cup of water, while Ashel lined each plate with a couple of cookies from the cupboard.

Ashel picked up one of the plates with the sandwich and cookies and walked it into her mother's bedroom. Misief joined his sister and placed another pillow behind his mother's back, so she could sit up to eat. Once they had their mother all set, the two children went back into the kitchen and sat down at the table. After devouring one turkey sandwich, Misief realized he was still hungry and prepared himself a second sandwich.

Turning to Ashel, he asked, "You want another one?"

"No thanks," she responded, "But mama might."

Ashel stepped into her mother's bedroom to see if she wanted anything else to eat. Bett looked into the eyes of her young daughter and could see the love. She was so proud of her children. Even with the intense pain, Bett mustered up a smile and said, "No thanks honey, I've got plenty."

After eating, Misief and Ashel worked together to clean up the small mess they'd made preparing supper. Misief went into his mother's bedroom and found that Bett had drifted off to sleep. He noticed she'd only eaten a few bites from the sandwich and didn't touch the cookies at all. He blew out the flame from the oil lantern, pulled the covers up over her shoulders and gave his mother a kiss on the forehead.

Misief walked back into the kitchen and told Ashel their mother had fallen asleep. "She seems to be resting better," he stated, as he joined his sister in cleaning up the mess.

With the final dish put away, Ashel bid her brother goodnight, and she turned in for the night.

As he sat alone in the kitchen reflecting on the day, Misief remembered he'd left Coal tied up to the rail on the front porch. He picked up an oil lantern and made his way out the front door. Coal looked up at Misief as he walked toward him, and it was obvious the beautiful, black stallion was tired from the arduous journey to Rock Springs.

"You did good tonight," Misief proudly proclaimed, as he led him by the reins around the corner of the cabin.

Misief placed Coal in his stall and removed the saddle and bridle from the weary animal. As he gave Coal some oats and fresh water, his mind wandered back to the encounter with stranger in Doc's office. He was certain it was the same man he'd seen the night his father died. He wondered if this man was actually a sheriff from another territory, or maybe one of the local deputies from Rock Springs. He decided it would be worth his time to visit the local sheriff's office in Rock Springs to see if he could find clues about who this man might be.

Misief wondered how the strange man seemed to vanish into thin air.

Could it be that this was all his imagination?

He wondered if he was just having flashbacks from the night his father was killed.

Then Misief's eye caught a glimpse of the .50 caliber bullet attached to Coal's saddle. Talking out loud, Misief stated, "Well, I might be imagining that stranger, but I ain't imagining the bullet."

Coal looked at Misief in a peculiar fashion as if to ask, "Are you talking to me?"

The thought of the stranger running through his mind made him feel unsettled in the old, dark stable. Then Misief noticed his oil lantern was beginning to flicker. He walked over to check it and realized it was almost out of oil. He grabbed the lantern and wasted no time as he made a direct beeline for the door. The last thing he wanted was to get stuck out in the barn, without a lantern, on a dark night like tonight. As he stepped out of the stable, the thoughts bombarding his mind hastened the pace of his steps. With all that had happened with his mother and at Doc's office, all Misief wanted to do was to get back inside the safety of the cabin and somehow try to forget the thoughts racing through his mind.

Chapter 6

"A Note from Lucas"

September 10, 1863

Misief awoke early the next morning and immediately jumped up to check on his mother. He knocked quietly, then cracked open her bedroom door just enough to peek inside. Bett was awake, but her eyes were closed. Misief could see deep wrinkles etched into his mother's forehead, the result of the intense pain she was experiencing.

"You're still hurting bad, aren't you?" he asked.

"Yeah son, I won't lie to you, it hurts," she replied, as she opened her eyes, wincing deeply as she attempted to sit up.

Misief pulled back the quilt to take a look at her leg. He'd wrapped it the best he could before going to bed, but during the night the blood had leaked all the way through the outer layers of the bandage. Bett was bleeding so profusely that there was a large blood stain on the bed sheets.

Misief looked at his mother and said, "I've gotta go find you some help, you are still losing a ton of blood."

Grimacing, Bett asked, "Didn't you say Doc Lynch wouldn't be back until late tomorrow?"

Misief nodded and replied, "Yes ma'am. But what about Jeno or Davis? Do you think they might be able to help us?"

Since Barak's death, Jeno Stephens and Davis Williams had been available to help Bett and her children anytime they ran into problems they couldn't solve on their own. During the last few years, Jeno had come over several times to teach Misief how to vaccinate the horses and properly care for the animals. Davis spent time in the woods helping Misief perfect his hunting skills and training him on the basics of smoking meat. One of the two men usually came by at least once a month to make sure the family had plenty of food to eat, wood to burn, and to assist with any large projects that were just a little too large for them to handle on their own.

Misief turned to Ashel and asked, "Do you think you could take care of breakfast for Mama while I ride over to see if I can find Davis or Jeno?"

Ashel nodded and walked into the kitchen to begin preparing a bite to eat.

Misief kissed his mother on the forehead and said, "I'll be back in no time."

"Be careful," Bett whispered.

Misief walked out the front door and paused on the front porch for a moment. Inside his mother's bedroom, he hadn't shown how concerned he was about her leg. Looking down at the pine boards that served as the floor for the front porch, he noticed the fresh, crimson colored blood stain where his mother had lain the day before. Ironically, the blood stain was in the exact same spot where his father bled to death years earlier.

Misief purposely stepped over the blood stains and walked down the steps. As he walked into the front yard, he immediately had flashbacks of the horrible night his father died. His mind recalled the trickling blood flowing down his father's body as his life slipped away. He remembered his father mumbling these words as he died, "*If Lucas hadn't.*" Misief recalled the vow he'd made to his father to get even with Lucas. And now, as fate would dictate, his mother had bled profusely in the exact same spot where his father died.

Misief's mind then drifted back to his mom. He'd never seen his mother in such a weakened condition. Her voice was shaky, and she was as pale as anyone he'd ever seen. He knew she was seriously wounded and needed medical help beyond what he and his sister could provide. Visuals of his father dying and his mother bleeding, flipped back and forth in his mind as he directed Coal down the winding trail to where Jeno Stephens lived.

****

It took Misief a little over an hour to navigate the thirteen mile ride to Jeno's ranch. Along with his sign business, Jeno raised longhorn cattle, and Misief knew he would find him in the barn, out in the field, or in his shop working.

Sure enough, Jeno was inside the barn caring for several newborn calves. When Jeno heard Misief approaching, he stepped out of the barn, and when he saw his face, he instantly knew something was wrong.

"Is everything alright?" Jeno asked.

"It's my mama, she's hurt," Misief blurted out.

Misief, almost in tears, paused for a moment to gather his emotions before continuing. "She's in trouble Jeno; she's hurt real bad."

Misief went on to tell Jeno he'd been to Rock Springs to get Doc Lynch, but upon arriving at Doc's office, he discovered that the doctor was out of town and wouldn't be back until sometime Friday. He also told Jeno how the accident had occurred in the garden and described the details of his mother's wounded leg.

"Let's go see what we can do," Jeno stated, and he dropped everything he was doing and began saddling up his horse.

About that time, Jeno's wife, Misty Lou, came walking out to the barn. "Hello Misief," she stated as she handed Jeno a cup of coffee.

"Misief, would you like a cup? I have plenty." she asked.

Misief shook his head but said nothing.

Jeno spoke up, "Bett has cut her leg and according to Misief is hurt pretty bad. Doc is out of town, so I am going to go check on her."

"Oh my!" Misty Lou exclaimed. "Is there anything I can do?"

"I don't know," Misief replied as he shrugged his shoulders.

Jeno spoke up, "Why don't you stay with the children, and let me go with Misief to see what we can do."

Misty Lou stood in the doorway of the barn waving, as Misief and Jeno raced away.

"I'll be back as soon as I can!" Jeno shouted, as they rounded the corner of the homestead and headed down the trail.

****

Arriving at the cabin, Misief and Jeno hustled inside to find Bett quietly sleeping in her bed. Ashel was right beside her mother, sitting on a stool and gently rubbing her mother's arm in an attempt to provide comfort to her.

Pointing at a plate on the bedside table, Ashel informed them, "I couldn't get her to eat anything."

Jeno walked up to Bett, took her by the arm and gently tried to wake her. Bett turned her head toward Jeno, and in a weakened voice said, "Hi Jeno, it's so good to see you. I sure appreciate you coming."

"It's my pleasure, Bett. We'll do our best to get you fixed up in no time," Jeno calmly stated as he tried to hide his concern about Bett's condition. "Can I take a look at that cut on your leg?"

Bett nodded and Jeno lifted back the quilt from her leg to take a look at the injury. The cut was still oozing blood, and Jeno knew the outcome of this situation would hinge on the amount of blood Bett had lost and whether or not infection set in.

Turning to Misief, Jeno asked, "So tell me again, when did this happen?"

"Yesterday afternoon, about suppertime," Misief replied.

Jeno nodded and said, "We have to find a way to get this bleeding to stop. I suggest we put a tourniquet on her leg, right above the cut."

Jeno asked if they had any more clean rags or material. Misief ran quickly into the front room and returned with the white bed sheet he'd used the night before. Jeno shredded the sheet into several thin strips, and then he asked Misief to elevate Bett's leg while he secured the tourniquet tightly around it. Bett winced in pain, as Jeno worked to get the tourniquet in place.

"I'm sorry Bett," Jeno stated. "I know it hurts. We're trying to be easy with you."

With the tourniquet secured, Jeno began unwrapping the blood soaked bandages, so he could replace them with fresh clean ones. It appeared the tourniquet was working, and the bleeding was slowing down, but Jeno wondered how much blood Bett had lost.

"Mom, it's time for another pain pill," Misief stated as he gently placed his arm behind his mother's back, assisting her so she could sit up long enough to swallow the pill.

After swallowing the pill, Bett lay back on the bed, and within a few minutes she had drifted off to sleep.

Jeno gestured for Misief and Ashel to come out of the room to allow Bett time to rest. Jeno pulled the door closed, leaving just enough gap for them to keep an eye on her without disturbing her.

Ashel went to finish cleaning up the kitchen, and Jeno motioned for Misief to join him outside on the front porch.

Jeno looked directly at Misief and said, "We're gonna need to get her to Doc Lynch."

"But Doc is still out of town," Misief reminded. "How bad is she, Jeno?"

"Well, I ain't no doctor, but she looks like she's lost way too much blood," he replied. "She's in serious condition, Misief. We've gotta get her to see Doc as soon as possible."

Jeno had confirmed Misief's worst fear. His mother was in critical condition and would need professional medical attention to survive.

Jeno then told Misief that he was going to run back to his ranch to pick up additional supplies. Placing his hand on Misief's shoulder, he said, "I'll be back as fast as I can. I'm also gonna go by and get Davis. We can use his help in getting your mother to Doc's place. I'll be back before nightfall, and we'll get her to Rock Springs first thing in the morning."

Misief asked, "What can I do for her while you're gone?"

As Jeno unleashed his horse from the rail he turned back and replied, "Just make sure you or Ashel keep an eye on her at all times, and make sure she doesn't try to get up for anything. She's too weak to try to get up on her own."

Misief nodded.

"Oh, and feed the horses and make sure the wagon is in fine working order. We'll use it to take her to Doc's tomorrow," Jeno said as he mounted up.

About that time, Ashel walked through the front door and noticed Jeno was leaving. "Where are you going Jeno?" she asked in a sheepish voice.

Jeno could see the concern on little Ashel's face. He replied, "I'm just gonna go get more supplies and see if I can get Davis to come."

Ashel was fond of Davis and hearing that he might be coming satisfied her as she replied, "Ok, please hurry back."

Trying to reassure both children, Jeno stated, "Your mama will be fine until I get back."

Jeno bid the kids goodbye again, nudged his horse with his spur, and turned to head down the trail toward his place. When Jeno was completely out of sight, Misief draped his arm around Ashel and led her back inside. The worried siblings walked back into the cabin with the uncertainty of their mother's future weighing heavy on their young minds.

****

An hour or so later, Misief walked up to the bedroom door to peek in on his mother. She appeared to be sound asleep; he slipped quietly inside her bedroom and sat down beside her. Ashel followed right along behind her brother and after looking at her mother she whispered, "She doesn't look too good, Misief. I'm really scared."

Tears filled Ashel's brown eyes as she continued, "What would we ever do without mama? Misief, is she really gonna be alright?"

Misief stood up and motioned for Ashel to follow him back into the front room. He then explained the plan Jeno had in mind. "Jeno and Davis will be back tonight. First thing in the morning, we are going to load Mama up in the wagon and take her to see Doc Lynch."

Knowing that Jeno and Davis were coming, and that they were going to take Bett to Rock Springs to see Doc Lynch, gave both children a ray of hope, which allowed them to focus on the tasks needing to be done. Misief did as Jeno instructed and spent most of the day caring for the horses and making sure the wagon was ready for the trip into town. Ashel kept watch over her mother and called Misief anytime Bett would awaken or need help in any way.

****

The evening sun cast lengthy shadows across the kitchen table as Misief joined Ashel to grab a bite of supper. As they sat down, they heard horses coming down the trail. Misief jumped up, and from the front window he could see both Davis and Jeno had arrived. He met the men at the door and invited them to join them for supper.

"Sure thing," Davis stated. "But let's take a quick look at your mother before we eat."

Ashel placed two more plates on the table, while Jeno and Davis stepped into Bett's room to check on her.

Davis reached down, felt of Bett's forehead and asked, "Hello Bett, how are you feeling?"

Bett's eyes slowly opened. "Hello Davis." Cringing in pain, Bett continued, "My leg is hurting…..it feels like its burning."

Jeno spoke up, "That tourniquet might be a bit too tight, but I'm hesitant to loosen it. You can't afford to lose any more blood."

Then Jeno asked, "Bett, have you had anything to eat today? You know you need to eat something to keep up your strength."

Bett breathed deep, and then replied, "Yeah, I've eaten."

"She's only had a few small bites," Ashel interjected.

Davis clutched Bett's hand and said, "Bett, we're gonna get you to Doc Lynch first thing in the morning."

Bett faintly nodded her head as if she was saying 'thank you', but didn't utter a word. The four of them left Bett's bedroom and made their way to the kitchen. Sitting down to eat, Misief looked over at Jeno and said, "I've got the horses and the wagon all ready to go, just like you asked."

Jeno replied, "Good job, Misief, first thing in the morning we'll get started toward Rock Springs. You've saved us a lot of time and work!"

As they ate together, they discussed the strategic details of how they would get Bett to Rock Springs. They realized it would be a long, hard journey for her, but in her condition, Jeno and Davis knew it provided her the best, and maybe the only, chance to survive her injury.

****

The following morning everyone was up early getting ready for the trip to Rock Springs. Davis helped Ashel in the kitchen, and they prepared breakfast as well as a basket filled with sandwiches and hard tack. Jeno and Misief harnessed the horses to the wagon, and positioned the wagon at the front edge of the porch.

After eating a bite of breakfast, the time had come to begin the journey to Rock Springs. They lined the base of the wagon with all the blankets they could find to make a nice soft place for Bett to ride. They knew the rocky terrain along the trail would make this a tough trip for her to endure. Once the wagon was ready, Jeno and Davis helped Bett sit up in the bed. As she turned and allowed her legs to hang down over the side of the bed, blood raced into her lower extremities and created such pain that Bett let out a scream.

"You okay Bett?" Davis asked.

Breathing heavy, Bett whispered, "All the blood ran down into my legs and it felt like somebody was stabbing me!"

Bett did her best to keep anymore screams from escaping her lips because she didn't want to scare her children, but she couldn't restrain the tears from flowing down her cheeks.

"Bett, I know you are in severe pain," Davis whispered. "We will take it as easy on you as we can."

Misief, Jeno and Davis worked together to get Bett to the wagon. Misief supported his mother from behind by placing his hands under her arms. Jeno and Davis grasped each other's hands to form a human chair to carry the weight of Bett's body. The three men gently lifted her from the bed and made their way through the front room and out on the front porch of the cabin. They walked to the back of the wagon and paused to see if Bett could stand up momentarily while they climbed up to hoist her up in the wagon. But in her weakened state, Bett wasn't able.

Davis and Jeno held Bett up while Misief climbed up into the wagon. Misief reached down and gently grabbed his mother under each arm; Davis and Jeno lifted her legs, and Misief slowly pulled her into the wagon. They placed Bett on the nest of blankets with two pillows under her injured leg to keep it elevated. She seemed to be drifting in and out of consciousness and was in obvious severe pain. With Bett and all the supplies loaded on the buckboard wagon, Misief secured the cabin, and they all embarked for Rock Springs.

The previous night, while making plans for the trip, they decided that Jeno would ride along on horseback and follow the wagon. Their concern was if Bett could not endure the arduous journey to Rock Springs, one of them could ride into town and bring Doc Lynch out to them.

Davis guided the wagon with Misief and Ashel sitting in the back caring for their mother. The kids did their best to console Bett, but every time the wagon hit a bump in the trail, Bett moaned in pain. Normally, this was a two hour trip. But in Bett's condition, they knew the only way she could endure the trip would be if they took it much slower.

It was just before noon when they cleared Shoots Valley and rounded the final bend into Rock Springs. As they arrived on the outskirts of town, Jeno rode ahead to Doc Lynch's office. He wanted to make sure Doc was back from his trip and ready to treat Bett the moment the wagon arrived.

Arriving at Doc's place, Jeno tied up his horse and quickly whisked up the stairs. Stepping inside, he found the doctor busy cleaning up broken glass from an apparent break-in that had occurred while he was out of town.

"Hey Doc, what happened?" Jeno asked.

Doc Lynch turned to Jeno and replied, "Hello Jeno. Oh, I came back to find the glass in the door broken. It appears somebody broke in and stole some of my medical supplies while I was gone."

Doc didn't have a clue that Misief was responsible for the damages, but Jeno put the pieces together and surmised that Misief might have broken in out of desperation to get the supplies for his mother.

"Doc," Jeno began, "I've got Bett Stone coming in a wagon, and she's hurt real bad…we need your help."

Doc placed the broom against the wall and said, "Sure Jeno, where is she? What happened to her?"

Jeno replied, "It was an accident at her cabin. She's cut her leg bad and lost a lot of blood. Davis Williams is bringing her and the kids in the wagon and will be here any minute."

About that time, the sound of the rattling wagon was heard coming down the street. Both Doc and Jeno sprinted out to meet them at the edge of the road. Doc greeted them all as he leaped into the wagon with his black leather medical bag in hand. He took out his stethoscope and placed it against Bett's chest to hear her heartbeat. Doc then turned directly to Jeno and Davis and said, "Let's get her upstairs into my office……now!"

Jeno, Davis and Misief carted Bett up the stairs to Doc's office using the same technique that had worked when they loaded her into the wagon. Doc instructed them to take her into a small room in the back of his office. Bett was too groggy to really know what was happening around her. She spoke very little as Doc began checking her vital signs and trying to ask her questions about how she was feeling. Bett's condition made it all but impossible for Doc to glean much information from her. She intermittently cried out in pain, and Doc knew her condition was critical.

"Her vitals are very weak," Doc commented as put down his stethoscope. It was apparent to Doc that much of the pain Bett was experiencing was due to cramps in her injured leg. He knew this was not a good sign. Doc's fear was that Bett was showing signs of Tetanus.

Doc removed the tourniquet and gently unwound all the bandages on Bett's leg. He noticed the type of tape and gauze material used to bandage Bett's leg, and it occurred to him that these materials probably came from his office. He knew that no one else in town had this specific type of medical supplies. Doc didn't say anything about his suspicions since he knew his first priority was to take care of Bett's medical situation.

Upon closer inspection of Bett's leg, Doc informed them that she would need several stitches to properly close the wound. He immediately began the medical procedure as Jeno, Davis and Misief stepped outside to join Ashel who was waiting at the wagon.

"How's mama?" Ashel asked.

"She's fine," Davis replied. "Doc is going to stitch up her leg to stop the bleeding. We are going to wait out here until he gets done."

Jeno and Davis climbed into the back of the wagon to rest for a few minutes. Misief was restless and could not sit still. He began aimlessly pacing back and forth on the wooden sidewalk that lined the storefronts along Main Street. As he walked past the Post Office, he came to the Trading Post and suddenly recalled seeing a certain item in the storefront window a few days earlier. Sure enough, still sitting in the front of the showcase was the old brown leather bag.

Misief bellowed, "Hey ya'll, come here quick!"

Jeno, Davis and Ashel jumped off the wagon and ran over to where Misief was standing.

Misief pointed at the bag and exclaimed, "I think that's the bag my father lost in the poker game. Look at the initials on the front."

Jeno and Davis recognized the engraving of 'S.F.F' and looked at each other in disbelief.

Jeno knelt down and saw the initials 'B.S.' on the bottom. "Well… Would you look at that! I don't believe it!" Jeno shouted. "I think you're right, that's your father's old leather bag."

"Let's go inside and have a closer look at it," Davis said, as he held the door open for the others to enter the store.

The Trading Post was an older building that once served as an office for the land grant company. It had wooden cases with glass fronts around the entire perimeter of the store. The cases were filled with jewelry, watches, knives, and handguns. The walls were lined with shotguns, saddles, bridles and leather clothing such as chaps, boots and hats. In the back of the store sat the store owner. He was leaned back in an oak straight back chair, with his cowboy hat pulled nearly over his eyes.

Misief made a beeline to where the store owner was resting and stated, "I'm interested in that leather bag in your store window."

The store owner replied, "Be glad to help you young man." Extending his hand he introduced himself by saying, "My name is Wendell Potts."

"Hey there Mr. Potts. My name is Misief. Misief Stone. Can I ask you how long you have had the bag?"

"Um... about two weeks," Wendell replied.

"Who'd you buy it from? I mean......would you happen to remember where you got it?" Misief asked, as his heart began to pound.

Wendell removed his cowboy hat, scratched his head and said, "Yeah, I remember. I bought it from a drifter who comes through town from time to time. He's a skinny man; a well dressed fellow that sports a thin mustache. He goes by the name of Lucas."

Misief thought his heart was going to jump out of his chest when he heard Wendell say the name, 'Lucas'. Just knowing that Lucas Benson was still roaming these parts excited him.

Wendell removed the bag from the store window and handed it to Misief.

"How much do you want for it?" Misief asked.

"Two bits," replied Wendell.

Misief turned to Davis and Jeno to ask if he could borrow the money to purchase the old leather bag. Davis nodded and pulled the money from his pocket.

Both Davis and Jeno thought it would be good for Misief to have his father's bag; they believed that perhaps it would bring closure concerning his father's death. However, neither Davis nor Jeno was fully aware of Misief's deep hatred for Lucas or his burning desire for vengeance.

Wendell took the money and handed the old leather bag to Misief who immediately placed it around his neck.

Davis looked at Jeno and said, "Who does that remind you of?"

Jeno retorted, "I was just about to ask you the same thing."

Misief knelt down in front of Ashel and said, "This bag once belonged to our father. A wicked man named Lucas stole it from him."

Ashel seemed confused by the whole ordeal. She had never heard the details related to the brown leather bag, the poker game or their father's flux wire dream. Reaching out, she touched the bag and simply replied, "That's a nice bag, Misief."

****

The four of them made their way out of the Trading Post and headed back to the wagon to wait on Doc to finish stitching up Bett's leg. Knowing it would probably take Doc a little while to finish, Davis asked if the kids wanted to walk over to the café and get something to drink. Ashel and Misief had never had the opportunity to go in the café, so it was no surprise that Ashel eagerly shot up and started jumping up and down in excitement. Misief wanted to go too, but he decided he was more interested in his new prized possession. He replied, "You guys go ahead. I think I'll just wait here at the wagon and check out my leather bag."

Davis, Jeno and Ashel told Misief they would be right back and to holler if he heard anything regarding Bett. Misief promised to come get them if Doc had any news. Then he climbed into the wagon, as the three others made their way into the café.

Sitting alone in the wagon, Misief looked around to make sure no one was watching him. He wondered if perhaps the plans his father had for the flux wire might still be inside. Deep down he really didn't expect to find anything in the bag, but he hoped there might be a trace of something belonging to his father still there. He slowly unlaced the dry leather straps and lifted the flap to look inside.

Much to his surprise, inside the bag was a collection of old weathered papers. He reached his hand inside and pulled out the papers, which were very dry and brittle. With extreme care, he gently unfolded each page. Misief froze, his heart stopped, and he turned completely ashen as he read the words recorded on the top piece of paper. The message read,

Misief, I stole your father's dreams and ruined his life. You are next. I will destroy you!

Signed, L.B. - Lucas Benson

Chapter 7

"Life Alone"

September 10, 1863

Misief sat in the wagon and stared at his name on the paper, trying to figure out how Lucas could have known he would find and purchase the leather satchel owned by his father. He wondered,

Is Lucas following me?

Could Lucas actually be in Rock Springs?

His pondering was abruptly interrupted by the sound of Doc's office door opening. Misief quickly stuffed the old, worn papers back in the leather bag. Doc called down from the second floor landing and said that he was finished and they could come up and see Bett.

Still shaken by the letter he'd just read, Misief paused a moment, then turned to Doc and replied, "Okay, the others went to the café to get a drink. Let me go get them, and we will be right up."

Just as Misief began walking down the sidewalk, Jeno, Davis and Ashel came out of the café.

Misief shouted, "Doc says we can go up and see Mama."

"Did he say how she is doing?" Davis asked.

"No, he didn't say." Misief replied.

Davis nodded and led the foursome up the steps to Doc's office. Walking in, Davis and Jeno could tell by the look on Doc's face that the news regarding Bett's prognosis, was not going to be good.

Without hesitation Doc began, "She's lost a massive amount of blood. She's weak and is suffering with severe cramps. Just a few minutes ago she had a spasm in her jaw. I fear she might have Tetanus," he explained.

"She's gonna make it, right?" Misief asked in a whisper as he walked over to the door to peek in on his mother.

Doc placed his arm on Misief's shoulder and said, "I know you love your mother very much, and you and Ashel did a fine job taking care of her. But, I gotta be honest with you…she's in a fragile place right now, and we will just have to wait to see how she responds to the medication. I'm not as concerned about the blood loss as I am that she might have Tetanus."

Ashel started crying as Doc shared the news regarding Bett. Davis gently led Ashel aside to try and console her.

"So what do we do next?" Jeno asked.

Doc rubbed his forehead and replied, "I've got her leg stitched up, and I have cleaned the wound real good. She needs to keep taking this medication twice a day. All you can do is keep her resting in bed and see how her body responds."

"So we can take her home?" Misief asked.

Doc replied, "I think so; there isn't anything else I can do for her here. She's on the strongest medication I have, and the bleeding has completely stopped. Right now, she just needs to rest. I suppose being at home in her own bed might do her some good."

With that, Jeno, Misief and Davis carefully carried Bett to the wagon and gently laid her on the pallet made of quilts. They thanked Doc for his services and turned the wagon toward home.

As the wagon rattled away, Doc shouted out, "I will ride out tomorrow and check on her!"

Davis turned back and replied, "We would be much obliged! We will see you tomorrow!"

****

Nobody said much as the wagon, followed by Jeno on horseback, headed out of Rock Springs and into Shoots Valley. When they loaded up, Davis asked Misief to drive the wagon so he could ride in the back and watch over Bett. Davis found Bett's breathing to be very shallow, and her eyes remained closed most of the time. The strong medication that Doc had given her kept her heavily sedated. As Davis sat there staring at his beloved friend, he began to wonder if she would survive the trip back to the cabin.

As the wagon rattled along the trail, Misief reflected on the hundreds of times he'd been down this road with his mother and sister. Arriving at the place where the trail began to run parallel with Roberts Creek, Misief directed the wagon to the right at the fork in the road. It was only one more mile to the place where he, Bett, and Ashel always stopped when they made their monthly family journey into Rock Springs.

Nearing the familiar shade tree, it was like the horses knew this was their place to take a break, and Misief brought the team to a stop.

"We always pull in here whenever we travel home from Rock Springs," Misief explained.

Davis replied, "Sounds good to me." Turning to Ashel he asked, "Do you wanna hop down and take a short walk?"

Ashel nodded and quickly jumped up from her seat. Davis helped Ashel down from the wagon, and together they took a short walk to stretch their legs. Jeno dismounted from his horse, wrapped the reins loosely around a tree branch and joined Davis and Ashel. Misief paused a moment to take a look at his sleeping mother; then he grabbed a bucket from the back of the wagon to retrieve water from the creek for the horses. He moseyed over to the water's edge and bent down to fill up the bucket. As Misief crouched down, he heard what sounded like heavy footsteps in the woods on the other side of the creek.

The far side of Roberts's Creek was very steep and led to the top of Pinchea Mountain. It was almost impassable and was home to all sorts of native wildlife. Glancing up to see what might be causing the noise, Misief couldn't believe his eyes! Much to his surprise, there appeared to be a man walking straight toward him!

Misief immediately stood up and took two or three steps backwards. Then he froze in his tracks as his heart began beating wildly in his chest.

There he was again! The same tall stranger wearing those unmistakable white cowboy boots with gold studs! This time he stopped about twenty feet from Misief and just stared at him. Captivated, Misief made direct eye contact with the stranger.

For whatever reason, Misief wasn't afraid of the stranger and actually felt a peace settle over him as they stood there glaring at each other. From this distance, he could clearly see that the stranger had on a five point gold badge with the three bullets engraved on it.

Misief called out, "Hey there, who are you? Are you with the Sheriff's Department?"

The stranger didn't respond verbally but pointed to the brown leather bag Misief was wearing around his neck.

Misief asked, "Are you pointing at my bag?"

The stranger nodded in affirmation.

"You want my bag?" Misief asked in a puzzled voice.

The stranger nodded again.

Misief replied, "I ain't giving you my bag! This leather satchel belonged to my father and was stolen from him by a man named Lucas Benson."

Upon hearing Misief's response, the stranger turned and began hiking back up the side of Pinchea Mountain.

As the stranger was walking away, Misief called out, "Hey man, don't leave. I have questions for you, and I need some answers."

The stranger paid no attention to Misief and kept walking away.

Misief shouted out even louder, "Did you know my father, Barak Stone? Hey, come back! Do you know where I can find Lucas Benson?"

Misief continued to yell, but the stranger kept his course, didn't speak a word and never looked back in Misief's direction. In a matter of minutes the stranger had vanished into the depth of the woods.

Misief, with the bucket of water still in hand, turned toward the trail and walked back to give the horses a drink.

Jeno, Davis and Ashel soon returned from their walk, and Jeno, who had heard Misief shouting, asked, "Who were you hollering at?"

"Oh, I was just yelling at a couple of ole' beaver that were playing in the creek," Misief answered.

Misief knew he was telling Jeno a lie, but he had never mentioned the stranger to anyone. This was his third encounter with the man, and the only physical evidence Misief had to prove that the stranger was real was the .50 caliber bullet that was left on top of the wardrobe the night he first appeared. Misief feared nobody would believe his story, so he just kept his personal encounters with the stranger a secret.

Jeno laughed at his response and didn't question him any further. Davis took a quick assessment of Bett's condition as they loaded back into the wagon and prepared for the final leg of the trip to the cabin.

****

The rest of the trip to the cabin was uneventful. Occasionally, Bett would cry out in agony, but other than a few moans from a passenger that was in severe pain, it was a very quiet ride. As the wagon rattled along, the gurgle of Roberts Creek provided a bit of comfort to their troubled minds.

When they finally reached they cabin, Misief directed the wagon alongside the edge of the front porch. Davis, Jeno and Misief gently lifted Bett from the wooden bed of the wagon and soon had her settled back into her own bedroom.

Davis assembled the foursome into the main room of the cabin and said, "Guys, it's late in the day, and we are all tired and hungry. Misief, if you will take responsibility to get the horses back into the barn and fed, I will help Ashel round up a bite to eat."

Misief nodded and immediately went outside to tend to the animals, and Ashel shuffled into the kitchen to see what she could find to eat.

Davis wanted to get Misief and Ashel occupied so he could talk to Jeno in private. Motioning, he led Jeno out to the front porch. Davis spoke in whispers as he said, "I don't think Bett's gonna make it."

"She sure doesn't look good, does she?" Jeno replied.

Davis shook his head. Looking down at the planks on the porch he asked, "I don't know what these kids will do if she doesn't pull through this."

Hoping for a miracle, the two men began facing the reality that these kids might soon become orphans. As they continued talking, they contemplated what they would do with the children if Bett passed away. They felt like the best solution would be to have the children come live with one of them, but for now, they agreed to remain strong and keep their concerns regarding the future to themselves.

Davis walked back inside the cabin and found Ashel working away in the kitchen, and Jeno wandered out to the stable to help Misief finish with the animals. Fifteen minutes later, Jeno and Misief were securing the stable door and headed back to the cabin. As they walked in the back door, they found dinner was ready to eat. The four of them gathered around the table and much like the ride home from Rock Springs, the room was very quiet as each one kept their thoughts to themselves. Silently, they wondered what the upcoming night might hold.

As they finished eating, Davis spoke up, "Why don't the rest of you get some sleep, and I'll sit up to take care of Bett for a while."

They all nodded in agreement as each one placed their plate on the counter. Before heading off to bed, Misief and Ashel went into their mother's bedroom to say goodnight. At the sound of the door creaking, Bett raised her head, opened her eyes slightly and whispered, "Come on in."

Ashel took her mother by the hand and said, "Mama, I love you so much. Everything is going to be okay. We're doing our best to take good care of you."

Using every bit of strength she could muster, Bett weakly replied, "I love you too, sweetheart, and I know you are!"

Continuing to struggle for strength to communicate, Bett looked deeply into her son's eyes and whispered, "Misief, you have to know.... I am so proud of you! I love you......and.... promise me you'll always take care of your sister."

Misief leaned over his mother and kissed her on the cheek. Then he collected himself and said, "I will, I promise. I'm gonna take care of you too."

Bett communicated what was on her mind and then let her head sink back into her down-filled feather pillow.

Ashel walked closer to her mother, bent down and sweetly kissed her on the cheek. "Mama, you get some rest. I'm going to bed. I'll see you in the morning," Ashel stated in a soft voice.

The two children headed off to bed, while Jeno gathered up a few quilts and made a bed on the sofa in the front room. Davis took his place at Bett's bedside, keeping vigil as she struggled in pain.

****

Around midnight, Davis observed a change in Bett's condition. Her breathing became very laborious, much worse than any other time during the day, and Bett arched her back and grimaced in pain each time the muscles in her body would spasm. Before leaving Rock Springs, Doc Lynch had told them that severe Tetanus would cause Bett to experience major muscle spasms. As Davis watched, he feared this was what was happening to her. For the next two hours, Davis stood right by her bedside as Bett struggled to cling to life.

Then it happened. Bett took a deep breath, almost as if she was gasping, exhaled softly and then stopped breathing. Davis watched intently to see if she would take another breath, but she didn't. He placed his fingers on her wrist to check for a pulse. There was nothing—no visible sign of life.

Davis was no medical doctor, but with all his life experience, it was obvious to him that Bett had just slipped away. He bowed his head, and a single tear flowed down his sun leathered face. As he stared at what appeared to be a sleeping Bett, he became angry that they were not able to save her. Immediately he thought of Misief and Ashel and wondered how he would break the news to them. Since it was only a couple of hours until daybreak, Davis decided to wait until morning to tell Jeno and the children.

****

Jeno was the first one up, and Davis led him to the front porch to share the news of Bett's passing. Standing in the dampness of the morning fog, they discussed the best way to break the news to the children. They decided to go ahead and wake up Misief and let him know of his mothers' passing, before waking Ashel to tell her.

Jeno led the way into the room where Misief was sleeping. Tapping Misief on the shoulder, Jeno whispered, "Misief, wake up."

Misief rubbed his eyes and replied, "What's going on Jeno? Is my mother okay?"

Jeno paused a second, then stated, "I'm afraid I have bad news. Your mama didn't make it. She passed away during the night."

Misief swallowed hard, sat up in the bed and stared out the window. Jeno and Davis could tell by looking at his face that Misief wanted to burst out in tears, but he refused to allow a single tear to form.

Misief got up and walked into this mother's room to be by her side. He placed his hand in his mother's stiff, cold hand, bent down and gave her a kiss on the forehead. His jaw was clenched, but he showed no emotion as he whispered in her ear, "I love you, Mama."

Jeno and Davis dreaded telling Ashel the news but knew it was something that had to be done. While Misief was in the room with his mother, Davis and Jeno slipped in to where Ashel was sleeping. Davis sat on the edge of Ashel's bed and gently patted her cheeks. He gave her a few minutes to wake up before he spoke. "Ashel... well honey, I hate to tell you this, but your mama went to heaven last night."

Ashel was heartbroken at the news of her mother's death and in total contrast to her brother, did not hold in her emotions. She burst out in tears, clinging to Davis with a death grip. She was too young to remember her father's passing, and this was her first time to experience the death of someone close to her.

Ashel held on to Davis for five or ten minutes and then asked, "Can I see her?"

"Sure, you can see her....come with me," Davis said as he gently led Ashel by the hand.

Davis led the way to Bett's room. Ashel was tentative at first, then she let go of Davis' hand and made her way to her mother's side. She reached out and gently touched her on the face. To her surprise, her mother's face was cold and unresponsive, which was in total contrast to anything she had ever experienced. Ashel stood there and stared at her mother's lifeless body in disbelief as the tears trickled down her innocent face. "Oh Mama, what are we ever going to do without you?" she cried, as she continued stroking her mother's cheek.

Misief stood in the corner of the room and watched with a stoic look on his face as his sister openly mourned the loss of their mother. With tears dripping on her mother's body, Ashel leaned over and kissed Bett on the cheek. Ashel turned to look at Davis, who then motioned and led the children out of the bedroom to the front porch. Jeno pulled the sheets over Bett's body then gently closed her bedroom door before joining the others on the porch.

For several minutes no one said anything as they became lost in the serenity of the rising sun. Misief was first to break the silence. Blurting out he stated, "I want her buried right next to our father."

Jeno replied, "Okay, we can do that. I think that would be appropriate."

Misief said nothing else and walked around the cabin in the direction of the stable. Since his father's death, staying busy had become his coping mechanism, and it appeared that would be the way he would deal with the loss of his mother as well. Departing the stable with a shovel in hand, he walked out to the old maple tree and began to hollow out a spot about five feet away from his father's grave.

Jeno looked over at Davis and said, "I think I'll go check on Misief and see if I can help him."

Davis nodded and replied, "Why don't Ashel and I go in and see if we can round up a bite of breakfast. It's going to be a long day and we will all need our strength to get through it."

Jeno walked around the cabin and noticed Misief had already started digging. He sensed the young man was struggling emotionally and chose not to say anything to him. He decided to just let him take out his aggression on the dirt below his feet.

It wasn't long before Ashel and Davis joined them outside with breakfast. Everyone except Misief sat down by the front of the stable to eat a bite. Jeno encouraged Misief to take a break and eat, but he totally refused. After eating breakfast, Jeno and Davis joined Misief in the task of digging Bett's grave.

By lunch-time the three of them had the grave prepared and walked back to the cabin to rest. As they sat on the porch catching their breath, they saw Doc Lynch coming down the road. As Doc dismounted and tied his horse to the rail, he didn't have to ask them a single question. He knew full well the routine of the west; with dirt on their clothing and sadness written on their countenance, he knew Bett had passed away. Doc patted Ashel on the head and told her he was sorry about the loss of her mother.

"If you'd only been here, this wouldn't have happened! Isn't there anything you can do?" Ashel asked as she started crying again.

Doc paused to catch his breath. This wasn't the first time he'd heard this plea, but with it coming from a broken hearted little girl, it choked him up a little bit. "Sweetie, I did all I could—we all did," Doc replied.

Misief was stone faced as looked over at Doc and asked, "Doc, would you be willing to help us prepare Mama for burial?"

"Absolutely," Doc replied. "I'll do what I can. What exactly do you want me to do?"

Misief replied, "Mama has a favorite dress; it's blue with flowers on it. It's in the wardrobe in her bedroom. Could you clean her up and put that dress on her for us? We've already dug a grave out back."

Doc said he would be glad to help and went inside to carry out the request. He washed Bett's body, combed her hair the best he could and placed her favorite blue dress on her. An hour later they were ready to lay Bett to rest. Doc, Jeno and Davis carried Bett's body to the grave and gently laid her down. There was little fanfare as Ashel, with tear stains on her dress, placed her mother's favorite pendant in her hands and said goodbye. Davis escorted Ashel back inside the cabin, while Doc, Jeno and Misief finished burying Bett.

As he'd done for his father, Misief made a cross, and Jeno painted Bett's name on it with some old paint he found in the stable.

****

Misief and Ashel had now lost both parents, and their future was riddled with uncertainties. In addition, Misief was filled with unresolved anger from his father's death. He had specific plans of retaliation, and with every passing year, the resentment bred deeper into his heart. Oftentimes, his mother would beg him to let the anger go and to forgive those who had been involved in his father's demise, but he never accepted her request. Since his father's death, Misief did everything his mother asked of him and worked hard to help her make life at the cabin work. He tried his best to fill the shoes vacated by his father, but nobody understood the degree or depth of Misief's venomous hostility. He was a time bomb waiting to explode, and only time would tell how his mother's death would impact him emotionally.

When all the tasks associated with burying Bett were complete, they all came together inside the cabin. Doc bid them goodbye, and then journeyed back to Rock Springs. Misief felt guilty and wanted to apologize to Doc for breaking into his office, but the words never came out of his mouth.

With Doc headed back to Rock Springs, Davis sat down with Misief and Ashel to discuss their future. "Hey guys, can we talk for a minute? You know that I've known your parents since before either of you were born. We've always been like family. Well, I guess what I am trying to say is that me and my wife would like for the two of you to come live with us."

Misief had never thought about what would happen if his mother passed away. He felt like a grown man and didn't think he needed to go live with anyone. "Thanks for the offer Davis, but we'll be fine here," Misief replied.

Davis continued, "But Ashel is only eight years old, and she's gonna need someone to help take…"

Misief rudely interrupted, "She can go, but I'm not leaving the cabin."

The fury was beginning to boil up inside of Misief, and he was unable to hide his irritation at the thought of leaving the place where he had grown up. Nodding their heads, Jeno and Davis decided not to push the issue anymore. Ashel acknowledged that she wanted to go with Davis and didn't want to stay in the cabin without her mother. She pleaded with Misief to go with her, but he totally rejected the idea.

Davis offered a solution. "Why don't Ashel come stay with me and Tammy Sue for awhile and you can come by and visit her in a few days or anytime you want? Misief, it's up to you….I know your older now, but I want you to know that you will always be welcomed."

Jeno added, "Misief, remember, Misty Lou and I would love to have you stop by for supper every now and then."

Misief nodded and thanked the men for the offer, and Davis and Ashel went to pack up her belongings. Ashel didn't want to leave Misief all alone, but she also did not want to stay in the cabin without her mother. Thinking of her brother, Ashel took her favorite teddy bear, the one given to her by her mother, and placed it in the kitchen. She wanted to leave it for Misief, so he would not forget about her.

By late afternoon, they were ready for the ride home. Jeno extended his hand to Misief and told him to come see him soon.

His temper now cooled down, Misief replied, "Don't worry, I will."

Ashel ran to her brother and threw her arms around his waist. "I love you, and I will miss you, Misief," she said in her little soft voice.

"I love you too," he said, as he hugged his little sister.

The orphaned siblings embraced for several minutes. They knew their world had forever changed. Their parents deceased; they would now face the future living totally separated from each other.

Then Ashel asked, "You will come see me soon, right?"

"I promise," Misief replied.

True to the vow he made the night his father died, Misief never shed a single tear as he watched the three of them ride away.

****

For the next few hours, Misief roamed around inside the cabin like a lost puppy. Walking over to the window, he stared at the fresh dirt on his mother's grave; he walked to her bedroom door, pushed it open about ten inches, and noticed the large blood stain on her bed where her injured body had been lying. He pulled the bedroom door closed and walked into the front room to touch the quilt which was stretched out across the back of the sofa. It was a hand-made masterpiece, with every single stitch sewn by his mother. During his meanderings inside the cabin, he hoped to awaken and find that it was all just a bad dream, but the cold emptiness in the cabin solidified the truth that he was all alone.

Wanting to escape the emotional emptiness that permeated the inside of the cabin, Misief ventured out the front door and walked outside, eventually winding up at the horse stable. The stable had always served as a safe haven. It was a place filled with happy memories, the place where he'd spent the early days of childhood playing in the hay loft and learning about the horses from his father. Inside the stable, Misief walked up to Coal and said, "It's just us now—me and you—we're all alone."

At that moment, that was exactly how Misief felt. He loved Ashel very much, but he didn't feel she could understand his feelings and his need for revenge. Ashel tended to be like her mother and always saw the best in people. But Misief's nature followed the pattern of his father and couldn't let go of things so easily. He was compelled to make certain he got the last word, and always kept score so he could get even with those he perceived had done him wrong.

Oftentimes, on the occasions when Misief would let his temper show, his mother would pull him aside and warn him against following in the footsteps of his father. In Misief, Bett saw many of the exact characteristics that got her beloved Barak in so much trouble. She tried her best to get her son to forsake his desire of seeking revenge, but Misief would always say that was just not his style. His mother had often voiced her concerns to Jeno and Davis about her fear of Misief becoming another Barak Stone. Both Jeno and Davis agreed with Bett, but anytime they tried to talk to him about it, Misief would defend his position in the name of his deceased father. Misief was a good kid, until someone talked about his father or his own temperament, and then the hatred would burst out of him.

Misief spent the next several hours out in the barn brushing and feeding Coal. Over the years, a special bond had developed between him and that beautiful black stallion. He would often talk to Coal about his father or about problems he was experiencing.

Tired of brushing Coal, Misief walked a few steps and sat down on a wooden bench. He picked up the leather bag he'd purchased at the Trading Post the day before. With all the events in the last twenty-four hours, he hadn't had much time to reflect on the stranger at Pinchea Mountain or the note he found tucked in the leather bag. Reaching inside, Misief pulled the note back out to read it once again. He wanted to be certain he'd read it correctly the first time. As he unfolded the note, he felt a cool breeze sweep across the back of his neck. He slowly read the words,

Misief, I stole your father's dreams and ruined his life. You are next. I will destroy you!
Signed, L.B. - Lucas Benson

Misief dropped the note back into the brown leather bag and slung it over his shoulder. He blew out the oil lanterns and stopped by Coal's stall to say goodnight. Walking out of the stable, he allowed his fingers to rub across the name he inscribed on the back of the stable door when his father died.

"Lucas," he whispered, as he paused a few seconds to absorb the anger that was welling up inside of him.

"I'll get you!" he proclaimed as he secured the stable door behind him.

Back inside the empty cabin, Misief stretched out on his bed and laid his head on his pillow. In the darkness, his heart sank as he thought about his mother and how much he was going to miss her. Despite the loneliness, the trouble, and all of the emotional turmoil, he remained resolved to the promise to not allow a single tear to ever fall from his face. Instead of crying, he focused his attention on his pain and allowed his heart to grow harder. Gritting his teeth, the last thought flowing in his troubled young mind before he drifted off to sleep was, *"Somebody is gonna pay for all my pain. So help me, somebody is gonna have to pay. I will get my revenge!"*

Chapter 8

"A Chat with Tomar"

September 11, 1863

Early the next morning, Misief arose determined to begin his 'mission of revenge'. He made quick work of saddling up Coal and headed out on the dusty trail to Rock Springs. The sun was just peaking over the mountains in the east as he approached the fork in the road at Roberts Creek. Without exception, he had always turned left and headed through Shoots Valley. The trail through Shoots Valley was the longest but safest route to Rock Springs, and it was the only way a wagon or buggy could get there.

However, there was another way to get to Rock Springs. If you dare take the fork on the right, it would lead you on a steep, rugged trail that wound its way up and over the mountain. From the fork in the road, it was two miles to the top of the mountain. This was the quickest and shortest way to Rock Springs.

Misief's father had once told him about the magnificent view on top of the mountain at a place called Rock Pointe. According to his father, there was a massive rock that stuck out from the side of the mountain, and if you walked out on the rock, the entire valley below could be seen.

Misief paused for a moment to contemplate his options. Pulling the reins gently to the right, he decided to take the chance and go up the mountain and see if he could find the infamous rock his father had told him about.

As he reached the top of the mountain, Misief came to a small wooden sign that was engraved with the words 'Rock Pointe.' The place was just as beautiful as his father had described. The top of the mountain was flat with lush green grass. He brought Coal to a stop, dismounted and loosely tied him to a small tree.

Sure enough, to his right, about seventy-five feet off the main trail, was a rock about thirty-five feet in diameter which protruded out of the mountainside. Proceeding with caution, Misief eased his way out onto the rock as the morning breeze gently blew across the top of the mountain.

In all his life, Misief had never witnessed such breath-taking scenery. From his vantage point out on the rock, he could see the trail coming out of Shoots Valley as it wound its way into Rock Springs. He could see all the businesses on Main Street; the Post Office, the Sheriff's Office and the sawmill. To his surprise, every building in town appeared as small furniture pieces in a young girl's doll house.

Nature radiated in brilliance as the morning sun kissed each tree leaf with light and glistened off the morning dew still present in the grassy meadows. Mesmerized by the serenity of this place, Misief sat down on the rock with his back resting against the side of the mountain. For over an hour, he soaked in the solitude of this place. It was a therapeutic experience for him as he allowed his mind to dwell on the good times he had with his father, the special moments he shared with his mother and the memories of warm summer days spent playing with Ashel. For a moment, as he relaxed in solitude, the tormenting thoughts that seemed to plague most every day of his young, troubled life had subsided. He now understood why his father loved this place so much!

Like a man emerging from a coma, Misief stood up and made his way back to Coal. He was totally unaware of how long he'd laid there relaxing on the rock. Untying Coal, he mounted up and began the descent down the back side of the mountain, which lead into Rock Springs. He regained his focus on the mission ahead of him. He felt the anger return in his spirit as he carefully watched each step Coal made on the trail. To his surprise, the Rock Springs side of the mountain was much steeper than the Roberts Creek side.

Step by step, Misief meticulously guided Coal over the rocks and allowed the stallion plenty of time to wind his way along the trail. Upon reaching the bottom of the mountain, he was now only one quarter of a mile from Rock Springs. Nudging Coal in the side with his spur, he picked up the pace and soon made his way to the edge of town. His first planned stop would be the sawmill, to see if Nainsi might happen to be there.

****

The sawmill was bustling with folks moving in all directions. There were men rolling logs to be milled, horses dragging logs to designated spots and wagons being loaded with fresh cut lumber. Misief noticed one man who barked out orders to the other men and soon recognized him as Nainsi's father.

Nainsi's father didn't have much to say the day he and Misief met at the cafe, but he was sure full of words today as he directed the sawmill operations like a conductor of an orchestra. Misief wasn't sure if he should interrupt him or not, but his desire to find Nainsi outweighed his fear.

"Excuse me," Misief said.

"We're not hiring right now," her father replied.

Misief came back, "I'm not needing a job. I was looking for your daughter, Nainsi."

Her father replied, "She usually comes by around lunch-time and we go eat together."

Misief acknowledged him and decided it might not be a good idea to ask any more questions. Lunch was only a half hour or so away, so he decided to mosey over to the café and wait for her.

The café was right in the middle of town. It was next to the Post Office and was frequented by most all the citizens of Rock Springs. Misief had never had the opportunity to eat inside the café and did not go in with Ashel, Davis and Jeno the day they brought Bett to see Doc Lynch.

Misief always wondered what it would be like to dine in the café. Oftentimes he would ask his mother if they could go inside and eat, but Bett always refuted the notion. While they never went hungry, his mother always saved every penny she could and wouldn't allow them to indulge in what she considered wasteful splurges.

Bett was great at stretching a dollar and always kept a small stash hidden in the cabin for emergencies. Misief knew where his mother hid the cash and, before leaving this morning, had taken a few dollars from the emergency fund. He'd left in such a hurry that he didn't take the time to eat any breakfast. Hearing his stomach growl, Misief decided this was the perfect day to have his first meal from the town café.

Removing his hat, Misief casually strolled inside and scoped out the place. Each table was covered with a red plaid table cloth and the windows were graced with curtains made from the same red checkerboard patterned material. The scent of home cooked food reminded him of life back at the cabin with his mother. The breakfast rush was over, and the lunch crowd had not yet arrived, so he had his choice of seating.

Pondering his options, Misief chose the table in front of a large double window close to the entrance. This seat provided him the best view to see Nainsi when she arrived with her father.

Now comfortable in his seat, Misief glanced around the café but did not recognize a soul. He'd been to Rock Springs many times before, but for the first time in his life he sat there feeling totally alone. His parents were deceased; his sister had moved out, and he realized no one in town really knew much about him. Lost in his thoughts, he was interrupted by a lady in her late forties with a raspy voice.

"Hi, my name is Rachel, can I help you?" she asked.

Misief raised his head and answered, "Hi Rachel, I'd like to get something to eat."

Rachel pointed to a large board on which the menu for the day was posted and said, "There's what's on the menu today. Just tell me what you want."

Not being able to read very well, Misief couldn't determine exactly what each word on the menu said, so he replied, "Just bring me a plate of whatever you think is good and a large glass of milk to drink."

Without hesitation, Rachel spun around and went into the kitchen, which was in the back of the café. Misief had no idea what she would serve him, but he was starving, and anything would taste good right now.

While waiting for Rachel to return with his food, Misief saw an older gentleman sitting in the far corner. He was well dressed, had a slender build and sported a pencil thin mustache. The man never looked up and seemed to be dining alone.

Misief had no idea who the man sitting in the corner might be, but wondered if it was Lucas Benson. Oftentimes, as he hid in the upper loft in the stable, he would eavesdrop on his father's conversations with his buddies as they drank and reminisced about the encounter with Lucas. This man seemed to fit the description he'd heard his father give in vivid detail; it was a man with a tall slender build, a pencil thin mustache, and who was well dressed. Misief stared at the individual hoping he would look his way, but nothing he did seemed to capture the man's attention.

After five minutes of pondering the identity of the man in the corner, Rachel returned with his food. The plate was loaded down with a generous serving of pork chops, pinto beans, mashed potatoes and cornbread, along with a large glass of milk.

"You need anything else?" Rachel asked.

"Actually, yeah—Can you tell me the name of that fella in the corner?"

Pointing in the direction of the man, Rachel asked, "Oh, him? That's the local reverend, Reverend Knapp."

"Oh, okay," Misief replied.

"Anything else?" Rachel asked.

"No ma'am," Misief said as he stuffed his mouth with a big ole' bite of pork chop.

The food was some of the best he had ever tasted. It felt good to sit down and eat a hot meal like a normal person.

Shoving it in like he hadn't eaten in days, it was only minutes until Misief had devoured the entire plate of food. As he turned up the glass of milk to wash down the last bite, he heard the rusty screen door open and in strode Nainsi and her father.

Nainsi was wearing a yellow print dress with a big yellow bow in her hair. Misief caught a glimpse of the book she called 'The Album' which was tucked in her arms. Right behind Nainsi was her father, and together they sat down at a table on the opposite side of the café. Nainsi didn't notice Misief when she came in, but he definitely watched every move the young goddess made.

Smitten with her beauty, it was all he could do to resist the urge to run over to her table and plop down beside her!

Deciding it would not be polite to barge in on her lunch date with her father, Misief remained at his table and waited for them to finish eating. Resisting the urge to stare, he occasionally shifted his eyes in Nainsi's direction, capturing intermittent glimpses of her delicate charm and grace.

After placing her food order with Rachel, Nainsi glanced across the café and noticed Misief gazing at her. Misief realized he'd been caught staring and immediately dropped his head. To his surprise, Nainsi kept looking in his direction and actually winked and waved at him. Misief returned the gesture with an awkward wave; something like a beauty queen would do after she had been crowned winner of the harvest festival.

Misief sat there staring at the floor as he wondered why he seemed to do dumb stuff when Nainsi was around. The first time they met, he nearly fell down the steps and broke his neck at Doc Lynch's office. And, as if that wasn't humiliating enough, now he'd waved back at her with a goofy, feminine wave.

Feeling a mite bit embarrassed, Misief decided to leave the café and paid Rachel for his lunch with the money he brought from home. His intentions were to stroll right on out the door and wait for Nainsi outside, but like a metal object under the influence of a magnetic field, he drifted straight toward the table where Nainsi and her father were dining. The next thing he knew, he found himself standing right beside their table. As he stood there, he hoped he wouldn't say or do anything else stupid.

Nainsi's father looked up at Misief and said, "Hello son, didn't I just see you at the sawmill?"

"Yes sir, you did. Hi Nainsi," Misief nervously said.

Nainsi rolled those big brown eyes toward Misief and said, "Hello Misief, do you have time to join us?"

Nainsi sat there staring at him with her infectious smile and twirled her brunette locks in her fingers. He wanted to sit down and talk with her, but not with her father around. He was dying to know more about her book with the intriguing bullets on the cover.

After thinking about his response, he replied, "I just finished eating, so I'll wait for you outside so you can enjoy your lunch with your father."

That answer seemed to sit well with Nainsi's father.

As Misief walked out the door and took his place on the bench outside the café, he began rehearsing what he wanted to say to Nainsi when she came out.

****

It wasn't long before Misief heard the door of the café open and out walked Nainsi.

"That was quick," he said as he scooted over to make room for her.

"I wasn't that hungry," she replied.

Then Nainsi asked, "Misief, are you in town with your family today?"

Misief got quiet for a minute and lowered his head. He shared with her the news of his mother's passing and explained how Ashel had left to live with some friends of their family.

Nainsi placed her hand on his shoulder and said, "I'm so sorry to hear about your mother. How are you doing, Misief?"

He quickly replied, "I'm gonna be fine. It's time for me to make it on my own."

Misief was ready to take the conversation in a different direction, but Nainsi had one more thing to say before he could change the subject. In a sweet voice she said, "Misief, you're never alone."

He wasn't certain what Nainsi meant by that, but the words coming from her lips soothed him, and the message resonated with his spirit. Even though he barely knew her, he felt comfortable with Nainsi and believed she was going to be someone he could trust. He felt safe talking openly with her.

Misief then asked, "Nainsi, can you tell me more about the book you carry around with you all the time?"

Nainsi reached down and picked up the book lying beside her on the bench. "It's called 'The Album'. It is the story of Sheriff Adonai."

"Who is Sheriff Adonai?" he asked.

Nainsi went on to tell Misief that Sheriff Adonai was the first High Sheriff of the Western Frontier. She shared the details of how Adonai was the one who personally created everything many years earlier. She told him the book explained Sheriff Adonai's plans for the Western Frontier and how he wanted the people who lived there to live in peace and harmony. She stated her devotion and commitment to being an avid follower of Sheriff Adonai, and she shared how the writings in the book brought structure to her life and that she closely followed the teachings found inside its pages.

Misief wasn't interested in anyone telling him how to live his life. His primary interest related to the bullets on the cover of the book, since they closely resembled the bullet he received from the stranger the night his father was killed.

"Do the bullets on the cover belong to Sheriff Adonai?" he asked.

"Not really," Nainsi replied.

At that moment Nainsi's father stepped out of the café. "Are you ready to go little lady?" he asked as he rotated his toothpick in his mouth.

"Daddy, may I talk to Misief a few more minutes and then meet you at the sawmill in a little while?" she asked.

Her father nodded, told her not to be too long and headed back to the sawmill.

Nainsi continued, "Misief, I'm not an expert on this book. But I do know someone who can tell you all about it, including what the bullets represent, that is, if you wanna know more."

He replied, "Yeah, I do. Who is it?"

Nainsi went on to tell Misief he needed to go find a man by the name of Sachiel Jackson. She told him Sachiel was responsible for maintaining the main well in Rock Springs and that he was the town expert when it came to the teachings of Sheriff Adonai. She told Misief that Sachiel was an older man, short in stature with gray hair and a long, gray beard.

Misief thought he knew the person Nainsi was describing. He knew the location of the well, which was on the outskirts of town on the way to Shoots Valley. He had stopped there several times with his mother as they left town, and he seemed to remember an old man hanging around the well that matched Nainsi's description of Sachiel.

Nainsi stood up and said, "Misief, I better get back to the sawmill."

Misief nodded and then asked, "Do you eat lunch here every day?"

She replied, "Not every day, but I'm here quite often."

"Maybe I'll see you here again soon," Misief suggested.

She tipped her head just a little and said, "I'd like that."

Nainsi bid him goodbye, stepped off the porch and strode off into the noonday sun.

Misief stood up, leaned against the cedar post that held up the porch and watched as she walked down the street to the sawmill. In his heart he wanted to take off and chase after her. He'd never felt feelings like this before and wasn't sure if it was love or if he was just extremely lonely. What he did know for certain was that he thoroughly enjoyed spending time with her, so he knew he would soon be back in Rock Springs!

****

With Nainsi well out of sight, Misief walked over to Coal, put his left foot into the stirrup and threw his leg over the back of the horse. Settling into position, he glanced at the .50 caliber bullet attached to the center of Coal's saddle. While chatting with Nainsi, he got a better look at the bullets on the cover of her book, and it appeared this bullet was an exact match to one of them.

On the cover of Nainsi's book was a cluster of three bullets. Each bullet had a different initial engraved on it, with the bullet on the far right having a 'J' engraved on it. The bullet with the 'J' was exactly like the one he had on Coal's saddle. In addition, the bullets on the book cover were also an exact match to the bullets engraved on the badge worn by the stranger. Misief knew there had to be a connection between Nainsi's book, the stranger's badge and the bullet he had in his possession. He hoped this man named Sachiel would be able to help him connect the dots and solve the mystery of this bullet.

****

Misief led Coal at a slow pace through the middle of Rock Springs, paying close attention to everyone he passed. The local mercantile was buzzing with patrons who were busy buying and selling. Several deputies were going in and out of the local sheriff's office as they maintained law and order. While he didn't get too close, he was pretty sure their badges didn't have three bullets on them like the badge the stranger always wore.

Misief desperately wanted to go inside the sheriff's office to inquire and see if they might know the identity of the stranger that kept showing up in his life. However, fearful that local law enforcement might ask him about the break-in at Doc's office; he decided his questions for the town sheriff would have to wait for a later time.

At the edge of town was the local saloon. As Misief passed by, he thought about the night his father lost the brown leather bag in the poker game. From what he had gathered over the years, this was the exact building where his father lost his dream. This saloon was the place that forever changed his father's life and had a devastating effect upon the family.

The exterior of the saloon hadn't changed one bit over the years. The rusty tin sign that bore the name of the saloon was still hanging crooked by a thin wire, and the décor of wood and musty whiskey remained the same. The only thing that seemed to change was the faces of the patrons that passed through the doors each day. Some of the faces were new, as children matured into adults; other faces simply aged a little with a few more lines documenting their tough existence in the Western Frontier.

Misief glanced down to look at the carvings on his father's leather bag, which was strapped securely to Coal. His mother never allowed him to step one foot in the saloon, but now he had no one to stop him. The curiosity of going inside was tugging at his spirit like the warmth of a fire on a frigid night. He wanted to see and touch the actual table where his father sat. Without clearly thinking it through, he brought Coal to a halt, tied him to the rail and boldly headed inside the saloon.

The swinging doors brushed his shoulders as Misief strolled inside. Standing about six feet inside the saloon, he stopped to absorb each detail of the establishment. These pine board walls had witnessed all the events of that fateful night so many years ago. If only the walls could talk, they could tell him everything he so desperately wanted to know about the night that forever changed the direction of his father's life.

Across the back of the saloon was a long paneled bar which extended the entire length of the building. It appeared to be made of solid oak and was polished to a splendid shine. At the base of the bar was a gleaming brass foot rail with a row of spittoons spaced along the floor. Hanging on the ledge were towels the patrons used to wipe beer suds from their beards and mustaches.

There was a Bachmann player piano on the left side of the bar, and scattered around the center of the room were eight or ten wooden round tables which were used by gamblers as they played games of Chuck-A-Luck, Three-Card-Monte, Faro and the old house favorite, Poker. On the far right side of the room was a small stage with a sign hanging overhead advertising, *'Dancing saloon ladies every Saturday night'*.

The bartender was a well known man named Tomar Reeves. Tomar had owned the local saloon for twenty-five years, and he knew Misief's father extremely well. On numerous occasions when Barak had too much to drink, Tomar had been forced to throw him out of the saloon. Barak was known for initiating uproars, and Tomar had no problem kicking him out of the saloon whenever he got a little rowdy. Tomar was tending the bar the night Barak got tangled up with Lucas Benson, and personally witnessed the entire incident. As Misief absorbed the atmosphere of the saloon, he wondered if Tomar might know the where-abouts of Lucas.

Tomar noticed Misief and said, "Hey young man, you are Barak Stone's boy, right?"

Misief nodded.

Tomar continued, "So sorry to hear about your mother."

"How'd you know about my mother?" Misief asked.

Tomar went on to tell him that Doc Lynch had been in the saloon the night before and told him about Ms. Bett. "I hear she was a real good woman."

Misief replied, "She was the best….she took good care of me and my sister ever since my……." Misief did not finish his sentence but just looked down at the saloon floor.

Tomar had the temperament of an aggressive wolf and was accustomed to verbalizing most anything that crossed his mind. If he thought it, he usually said it. Tomar's next words were tough for Misief to hear. Opening his mouth, Tomar blurted, "Wish I could say the same about your father. There wasn't much good in that man."

Misief squirmed as the words about his father rolled off Tomar's tongue. Deep down he knew his father wasn't well liked in Rock Springs and had his share of enemies, but still, he loved his father and did not like to hear people talk badly about him. Trying to pass over the comment and change the subject, Misief replied, "Well, my father had his share of problems, I guess."

Tomar wouldn't let it go and stated, "Yeah, he had problems alright, but he brought most of 'em on himself."

Tomar could tell Misief was getting agitated so he said, "Look, I'm not trying to talk down about your father or nothing, but he'd be alive today if he hadn't been so blame greedy and hard headed."

Misief, not able to contain himself, piped up, "Lucas Benson stole his dreams from him! He stole the flux wire plans that would have made him a rich man!."

Tomar snickered, shrugged his shoulders and turned toward the back of the bar to walk away. Misief was annoyed with Tomar's attitude and was ready for a verbal fight. He continued by saying, "Tomar, my father was cheated, robbed, and nobody in this dang place would help him that night!"

This statement seemed to imply that Misief was shifting some of the responsibility to Tomar and the others present the night Lucas walked away with Barak's brown leather bag.

Tomar rotated back around and said, "Kid, you sound like your stupid father! Ole' Barak was always blaming someone else for his own mistakes. You probably don't know this, but the truth is your father stole the flux wire idea from a man who lives on the East Coast. As I understand it, your father killed that man in cold blood and then told everybody the flux wire was all his own idea. Truth is—I don't think he knew what to do with it because he wasn't smart enough to finish the testing. The Midwest Communication Network was gonna pay him for the rights, but your father was too dumb to figure it all out!"

Misief was now boiling mad and ready to engage Tomar in a fist fight. Tomar sensed Misief's anger and said, "Young man, you might not like what I just said, but it's the truth. I suggest you go on down the road and cool off a bit. I didn't intend to upset you, but don't you ever walk into my saloon and blame me for the mistakes of your father! Your father gambled away that idea because he knew he would never be able to finish the testing!"

As he left the saloon, Misief recalled the stories he'd been told regarding his father's flux wire idea. He'd always been led to believe it was his father's own idea and that his intention in gambling was to win the additional money he needed to finish testing the concept. He didn't like what Tomar had to say about his deceased father and speculated whether or not there was any truth to his story.

Could it be true that his father gambled away the plans because he knew he could never do anything with it?

Had his father really stolen the plans from someone else?

Misief was certain Tomar knew more details about the night his father got into the ruckus with Lucas. As he unhitched Coal from the rail on the porch, he was disappointed that his first trip into the saloon had not gone as he had envisioned. He knew Tomar was upset with him, and at this moment they were both too angry to discuss the encounter between Misief's father and Lucas Benson. But make no mistake—the day would come when he would return to the saloon and once again try to find out everything that Tomar could tell him.

As Misief headed off on Coal, one thing had become clear as a bell—his mother had been exactly right; there were definitely people in Rock Springs that didn't think too highly of his father!

Chapter 9

"Lucas Draws Near"

September 11, 1863

Tomar's words were still burning in Misief's ears as he rode out of Rock Springs toward the well. Their conversation, while brief in length, had raised many new questions in Misief's mind.

Had his father lied to everyone about the flux wire concept?

Did his father steal the idea from someone, like Tomar suggested?

Was his father really a murderer as Tomar claimed?

Misief wasn't sure whether to be angry with his father or with Tomar, but he could certainly feel the resentment escalating as he approached the well.

Just as Nainsi had described, standing guard by the well was an old man with a long gray beard. He appeared to be around seventy-five years old and was busy hoisting water up from the well. Misief brought Coal to a stop and got down off his horse.

"Excuse me, is your name Sachiel Jackson?" he asked.

The old man continued hoisting the water bucket from the bottom of the well and didn't immediately pay any mind to Misief's question.

Once the bucket cleared the top of the well, the old man cut his eyes toward Misief and said, "Yep, that's what they tell me. Is your horse needing some water?"

Misief replied, "Yes sir, I guess so, but that's not the main reason I stopped."

Sachiel unhooked the bucket from the rope and poured water into a trough beside the well. He gave Coal a pat on the head and said, "Drink up, boy, it's nice and cold!"

As Coal enjoyed the refreshing liquid, Misief tried to figure out how to approach the subject of 'The Album' with Sachiel. He wondered if he should just shoot straight with his questions, or start with small talk and gently work his way to what was burning in his mind.

As he stood there nervously trying to get the conversation going, Misief wondered, "Is it possible that Sachiel knows the author of the book?"

Misief stared at the old man and concluded that he sure looked old enough to have some connections with whoever wrote 'The Album'. Perhaps Sachiel could shed some light on how the bullet and the stranger got into his mother's bedroom!

As these questions circled in Misief's mind, Sachiel piped up and asked, "So, if it ain't water you're a needing, what brings you out here?"

Misief was so deep in thought that he didn't really catch Sachiel's question. "What'd you say?" was all Misief could muster from his lips.

Sachiel replied, "You said you didn't stop by the well for water. So, what are you doing out here?"

Misief cleared his throat and explained, "Well, you see, there's a girl in town. Her name is Nainsi. Her father owns the sawmill. Well, she has a book she called 'The Album', and she told me that you know a lot about that book. Is that true?"

Sachiel leaned his head back and snickered as he said, "Oh, I guess I know a little bit about it." Then he grinned to expose two gums sporting only a couple of teeth and asked, "So are you interested in her book or in her?"

Misief answered, "The book. She was reading it, and it looked interesting. She told me you would know all about it."

Sachiel was a wise old man and wasn't convinced of the young man's interest in a lengthy old book. He pushed Misief a little further by stating, "I know what Ms. Nainsi looks like……are you sure you ain't just interested in the book so that you can get a little closer to that pretty young girl?"

Misief was definitely fond of Nainsi, and he would openly proclaim that she was breathtaking to behold, but deep inside he knew he had a legitimate interest in learning as much as he could about her book.

He responded to Sachiel by saying, "Mr. Sachiel, I really wanna know about the book. I have true reasons for asking you, and it is not just to get better acquainted with Nainsi."

Sachiel slowly turned his head from the work he was doing in the well and stared straight into Misief's eyes as he spoke, "Sonny boy, you didn't stop by to talk to this old man just because you are interested in the words found inside some ole' book. I know the story contained in this book, and I ain't so certain you are all that interested in what it has to say. Why don't you tell me your real reason for being so interested in the book?"

Misief wondered what it was going to take to convince Sachiel to talk to him.

Then he got an idea. He hurried over to Coal and retrieved the .50 caliber bullet from the horse's saddle.

Holding up the bullet, Misief replied, "Mr. Sachiel, I got interested when I noticed the bullets on the cover of the book. One of the bullets on the cover looks just like the one I have."

"Where'd you get this bullet?" Sachiel asked.

Misief responded, "I'd rather not say. You probably wouldn't believe me."

"Oh, I probably would. Why don't you try me?" Sachiel insisted.

Misief hesitated at first, but finally decided to tell Sachiel the story of how he came to own the bullet. He described the details related to the night his father was killed in a shootout with the local posse. He told Sachiel about hiding in the bedroom with his mother and seeing the tall stranger in the corner of the room. He described the stranger's size, his white cowboy boots with gold studs and how the strange man left the bullet on top of the wardrobe for him.

"I guess you think I'm crazy for telling you a story like this," Misief said as he finished recounting the story to Sachiel.

"Oh no, I don't think you are crazy. I believe your story." Sachiel admitted. "Let me ask you this, did you ever happen to see that stranger again?"

"Well, yeah I......" Misief abruptly stopped talking.

Misief quickly realized that if he continued sharing the details of his second encounter with the stranger, he would admit that he was the one who broke into Doc's office. He didn't know if Sachiel was aware of the break-in, but he wasn't going to take any chances.

Sachiel persisted, "Well, have you seen the stranger again since that night in your mother's bedroom or not?"

Misief answered, "Yeah, let's just say I've seen him again a couple of times." He paused then continued, "I don't know if I'll see him again or not. I never seem to know when he will show up."

Sachiel snickered as he responded, "Oh, I'm quite sure you're gonna see him again."

"What makes you say that?" Misief asked.

Sachiel replied, "I know who the stranger is. And, if I have it figured right, he ain't done with you boy."

Misief was dumbfounded and didn't know what to say. He wondered if Sachiel, who appeared to be just some beat down old man whose lot in life was to tend to the town well, could really know the identity of the stranger.

Misief then asked, "So tell me, how do you know the stranger? Have you seen him before? Does he come by the well for water?"

Sachiel then spoke the words that totally confused Misief, "Yep, he's been by here plenty of times. Sheriff Adonai introduced me to the stranger many years ago."

Misief thought a moment, and then recalled a conversation in which Nainsi had told him about Sheriff Adonai.

Hungry for more information, he asked, "Tell me about him. Please Mr. Sachiel, will you tell me about Sheriff Adonai?"

Sachiel invited Misief to have a seat on a bench which was a few yards from the well under an old elm tree. There, Sachiel began recanting much of the same story that Nainsi had already shared with him. Sachiel validated all the stuff about the Sheriff being the one personally responsible for starting the entire Western Frontier. Sachiel told him how Sheriff Adonai wanted the West to be a place where people lived in peace. He explained the Sheriff's plans for everyone to have nice ranches with beautiful horses, green pastures full of cattle, and barns filled with hay. He told Misief that most of the locals rebelled against Sheriff Adonai, and it wasn't long before the West became a place overrun with outlaws. Sachiel finished his spill by saying only a handful of locals still follow the peaceful teachings of Sheriff Adonai.

Sachiel got up from the bench and took his handkerchief from his pocket. Wiping the sweat from his forehead he mumbled, "It would have all been good too, if it wasn't for ole' Lucas Benson."

Misief's ears perked up. He eagerly asked, "Mr. Sachiel, did I hear you right? Did you just mention the name, Lucas Benson?"

"Yep," replied Sachiel, "That man, he's trouble! If you ever run into him, get away fast as you can!"

"I'm actually on the hunt for Lucas Benson. Been looking for him for several years," Misief stated. "Do you happen to know where I can find him?"

Sachiel looked at Misief with the kindness of a grandfather as he said, "Listen to me kid...... if you know what's good for you, you'll stay clear of him. If he finds you, it won't be good! Boy, you just ain't ready to face Lucas. Believe me, I know. I also know what happened to your Pa. Much like you, he was young and full of immature ignorance, thinking he could take on Lucas Benson. Your Pa took him on alright—and lost it all!"

"How do you know about Lucas and my father?" Misief asked.

"I was there that night—at the saloon when it all happened between your Pa and Lucas," Sachiel admitted. "Your Pa's friends, Davis and Jeno, begged him not to get involved with Lucas, but he wouldn't hear of it. I watched Lucas walk away with your Pa's leather bag."

Misief ran over to Coal, retrieved the leather bag from his saddle and said, "You mean this bag?"

Sachiel's eyes were as big silver dollars, "Where'd you get that bag?" he asked.

Misief replied, "I bought it at the Trading Post a couple of days ago."

"Lucas is baiting you boy! You better watch out!"

"I ain't scared of him! I ain't scared of nobody!" Misief stated, as he put his right hand on his pistol.

Sachiel responded by saying, "You stupid kid! That gun ain't no match against Lucas Benson. You're gonna get yourself in a heap of trouble if you keep on headed down this road!"

Sachiel shook his head and walked over to a wooden box that was sitting near the well. He pulled out a copy of 'The Album' and presented it to Misief. "Son, I'm giving you a copy of this here book. What you need to do is spend time reading it. It'll explain everything you want to know about the bullet, Sheriff Adonai and the stranger that is following you."

Misief held the book in his hands like it was covered in a fungus. He wasn't sure if he could read it or not, but he was glad to get his own copy of the book and definitely wanted to thumb through the pages to see if he could find the answers to his questions. For several minutes, he stared at the three bullets on the front cover. The bullet on the far right side was exactly like the bullet on his saddle. He knew this book had to hold the answers to the mystery of his gold bullet! He thought that possibly Nainsi could help him assemble the missing pieces of the story that were burning in his mind.

Interrupting his train of thought, Sachiel said, "Son, I need to get back to work. I've gotta get more water hoisted up from the well before the Carlton men get back with their wagon."

Misief situated the book on top of the weathered papers in the leather bag and attached the bullet back to the saddle where it belonged. He bid Sachiel goodbye and told him he would stop back by soon.

As Misief rode away, Sachiel rose up and shouted, "You stay away from Lucas Benson, ya hear!"

****

As Misief made his way out of Rock Springs and into Shoots Valley, his mind had so much new information to process. This had been a day filled with mixed emotions. He thought back to his time with Nainsi at the café. Beside the fact that she was beautiful, there was something magnetic about Nainsi's demeanor. He felt comfortable around her and believed he could trust her. The time he spent with her, while brief, was the most enjoyable time he'd spent with anyone in a long time. As he thought about the wonderful traits she embodied, he wondered about the book that she always had with her, 'The Album'.

He wondered if the book was somehow connected to, or part of, the key to her wonderful spirit.

Could the book contain her secret for being so happy all the time?

Then Misief thought back to his conversation with Tomar at the saloon. He felt the anger expanding in his spirit as he replayed each detail of their volatile conversation. He had numerous doubts about Tomar's accusations, but deep down, Misief feared Tomar's stories about his father might be true.

Finally, Misief pondered his visit with the old man named Sachiel. Strange as this fellow might be, it was undeniable that he seemed to be a wealth of knowledge on anything related to 'The Album', Sheriff Adonai, and Lucas Benson. Sachiel also claimed to know the tall dark stranger but would not disclose his identity or what he might want with Misief.

More than anything else, Misief simply wanted to locate Lucas Benson. Sachiel warned him to steer clear of this man, but Misief was determined to make Lucas pay for the crimes he committed against his father. Misief visualized what he would do to Lucas when he got his hands on him. He wanted Lucas to suffer like he had suffered. He wanted him to feel the pain that had gripped his body for so many years. He wanted Lucas to know the loneliness he felt now that he was living alone in an empty cabin.

"I want him to bleed like my mother bled….I want him to die like my father died…. I wanna stand over him and watch as his life trickles out of his body like water running downstream……. I wanna be there when he breathes his last breath…..I want the last thing Lucas ever gets to see is my face….and I want to be staring into his beady eyes when they shut for the last time," Misief growled as he rode down the trail.

****

As Misief cleared Shoots Valley and approached the fork in the road at Roberts Creek, he noticed something odd up ahead. Drawing closer, he could now see that sitting right in the middle of the trail was a horse drawn wagon with a little old man crouched down beside the left rear wheel. The wagon was rickety and tattered. The side boards had grayed from years of weathering and were coming loose at the corners. The two horses hitched to the front of the wagon looked like a couple of rejects from an old traveling rodeo.

Misief couldn't tell what was being transported in the wagon, but it appeared to be loaded to maximum capacity. The wagon was draped with a large tarp, serving either to keep the cargo dry or to conceal the identity of it. Upon closer inspection, Misief understood why the wagon was standing still in the middle of the trail; the rear wheel had broken. Based on the direction the wagon was facing, it appeared the old man was headed into Rock Springs and, unfortunately, now found himself stranded.

Misief jumped down from Coal and stated the obvious, "That wheel is sure busted."

The old man responded, "Yep, I hit a rut right back there, and the blasted thing came apart."

Misief replied, "Looks like your gonna have to get a new wheel. There's no way to fix that one."

Wiping sweat from his forehead with a rag he'd retrieved from his back pocket, the old man replied, "Young man, would you be willing to help me if I was to pay you for your trouble?"

Misief paused and said, "Yeah, I reckon so. What can I do to help?"

The old man got a twinkle in his eye and said, "I gotta load of Forty Rod on this here wagon. I need someone to keep an eye on it while I go into town to get a new wheel."

"What's Forty Rod?" Misief asked.

The old man chuckled, "Forty Rod….you never heard of Forty Rod? Why that's whiskey."

"Why do you call it Forty Rod?" Misief innocently asked.

"They call it Forty Rod because it's so powerful it's been known to drop a man before he can take forty steps," the old man said laughing.

The old man continued, "I guess you're too young to know about this stuff. This wagon is filled with the best whiskey in the entire Western Frontier!"

While Misief might not have heard the term 'Forty Rod", he was well aware of the dynamics of whiskey. Numerous times he'd watched his father stagger in after a night of drinking at the saloon, and he clearly knew the impact the intoxicating potion could have on a man's life. However, not interested in bringing up his childhood, Misief just shrugged his shoulders and said, "I'll watch the wagon for you if you pay me."

The old man flipped Misief a fifty cent coin and said, "I'll give you half now and the other half when I get back with a new wagon wheel."

Misief caught the coin and nodded in agreement as the old man unhitched one of the horses and retrieved a saddle from the back of the wagon. As he mounted his horse, the old man turned back to Misief and said, "I won't be gone long. Don't you let anyone bother this wagon, you hear! Use your gun if you need to!"

Misief replied, "I won't let anyone near it….by the way, what's your name?"

"Now let's not mix social rhetoric with our business deal," the old man stated. "My name ain't important; you just guard my wagon and the whiskey, that's all you need to focus on."

Refusing to disclose his identity, the old man nudged his old mare and down the dusty trail the tandem staggered.

"I could walk faster than that old horse can gallop," Misief smirked, as he watched the old man head deeper into Shoots Valley.

Knowing he was committed to stand guard for a few hours, Misief hopped up on the wagon in search of a place to relax. Stretching out between a stack of wooden crates, he nested in and pulled his hat down over his eyes. It just a matter of minutes, he began to nod, and before he realized it, he had drifted off to sleep.

****

A cool breeze blew gently over his sleeping body as the evening sun began to slip behind Roberts Mountain. The crispness in the air roused Misief from his afternoon slumber. Rubbing his eyes and yawning a time or two, he wasn't sure how long he had napped, but he thought ample time had elapsed for the old man to get a new wagon wheel from Rock Springs and be back.

Misief stood up in the wagon and peered in the direction of Shoots Valley, but he didn't see any sign of the old man or his half dead horse. He stretched his arms outward and yawned once more as he climbed down from the wagon.

With a nap under his belt and boredom creeping into his body, Misief became increasingly curious about the load of whiskey the old man was transporting. He wondered if some of this load might be headed to Tomar's saloon in Rock Springs.

Every time Misief thought of Tomar it made him furious. As he pondered the conversation the two of them shared earlier in the day, he thought that if he knew for certain which bottles belonged to Tomar he would bust them all.

Misief looked over his shoulder to make certain the old man wasn't coming and then lifted up the tarp to examine the wooden crates filled with bottles of whiskey. Each bottle was brown in color and about nine inches tall. He gently picked up a single bottle and held it up to see if there was any writing on it. The bottle appeared to be unmarked; however he did notice some etching on the bottom of it.

Misief held the bottle up to the setting sun and couldn't believe his eyes! The insignia on the bottom of it read *'L.B.'*! He quickly turned over another bottle, then another. He scrambled over to the next crate and looked at the bottom of every bottle in that crate. He reached over to a third crate and sure enough, the same *'L.B.'* was clearly etched on the bottom of every single bottle!

Misief began to contemplate the possibilities;

>Is it possible that Lucas Benson owns this whiskey?
>
>Could this old man possibly lead me to Lucas Benson?
>
>Might it be possible that this old man actually is Lucas Benson?

Misief rushed over to his horse, jerked open the leather bag that was attached to the saddle and retrieved the note that was left for him by Lucas. He wanted to compare the insignia on the note to the insignia on the bottom of the whiskey bottles. He held the note beside the bottle, and it was undeniable! The insignia was definitely an exact match!

Misief grinned as he now believed that this broken down wagon of whiskey was going to be his connection to finally finding Lucas Benson once and for all. Excited about the possibilities, he reached down with his right hand and pulled out his revolver. He opened the chamber and pulled out one of the bullets. With the bullet in his left hand he kissed it and said, "I got something with your name on it…it's just for your Mr. Lucas….just for you!"

He cackled out loud as he loaded the bullet back in the gun and slid it back into his holster. A mighty rush of adrenaline now flowed through his veins. He savored the moment as he realized the opportunity to bring much awaited justice for his deceased father was drawing ever closer!

Chapter 10

"A Night of Fire Water"

September 11, 1863

The moon began its ascent into the night sky with no trace of the old man. It had been six or seven hours since he'd left to go get a new wagon wheel, and Misief was certain he would be back any minute. Not having anywhere in particular to be, he was determined to wait for the old man to return so he could question him further regarding his possible connection to Lucas Benson.

As Misief sat alone in the darkness, he thought he heard someone coming up the road. The moonlight was casting lengthy shadows making it hard for him to determine who it was, but he hoped it was the old man returning.

Sure enough, laboring up the road was the worn out horse carrying the old man with a used wagon wheel strapped across his back.

"It sure makes it a heap harder to travel with a big ole' wagon wheel strapped all over ya'," the old man stated as he pulled back on the reins bringing the horse to a stop.

"I reckon it would," Misief replied as he watched the man slide out of the saddle.

"You didn't let anybody bother my cargo did ya?" the old man asked.

"Nope!" Misief proudly stated. "Actually, nobody has even come by since you left."

Misief didn't want to let the old man know that he had been snooping around in the wagon, nor did he want him to know that he'd spotted the insignia on the bottom of the whiskey bottles. What he wanted to do was to somehow open the dialogue regarding the old man's identity and try to confirm the owner of the whiskey company.

The old man pulled another fifty cent piece out of his pocket and said, "Here ya go boy, thanks for watching over my wagon."

"Much obliged," Misief stated as he took the coin and stuck it deep inside his pocket for safe keeping.

The old man rolled the newly purchased wagon wheel right past Misief and leaned it against the side of the wagon. "I'm gonna have to unload most of this stuff I reckon," the old man griped as he pulled back the tarp exposing the wagon full of whiskey.

Misief knew this was the perfect opportunity to obtain the information he desperately desired. He turned toward the old man and asked, "Do you want some help unloading this stuff?"

The old man scratched his head and said, "I can't pay you anything else. I spent all I had on this used wagon wheel."

"Oh I won't charge you," Misief replied. "I don't have anywhere I need to be, and I would be glad to lend you a hand."

The old man nodded and the two of them started unloading the wagon. Each wooden crate contained four bottles of whiskey. One by one, they removed each crate from the wagon and stacked them neatly on the ground.

"I sure appreciate your help!" The old man exclaimed.

"Glad to do it!" Misief replied. "This stuff is heavy, and it would take you a long time by yourself."

By the time the wagon was about half unloaded, Misief felt like the old man was beginning to warm up to him. So far, all the dialogue between the two of them had been mindless idle talk about horses, guns and such. But Misief wanted to take the conversation a different direction and believed this was the opportune time to do so.

With a case of whiskey in his hands, Misief asked, "Did you make all this Forty Rod by yourself?"

The old man shook his head and said, "Naw, I just transport it. I ain't the one who makes this stuff."

"So who does make it?" Misief snapped back.

The old man replied, "Now there you go again! If I start telling you all my secrets, I've have to make sure to hush you up!"

Softening his voice, the old man whispered to Misief "This ain't exactly legal stuff, you know."

With the wagon empty, the old man meandered over to the edge of Roberts Creek and retrieved the largest boulder he could carry. He made a second trip to the creek and retrieved another rock, similar to the first one. He placed the rocks beside the wagon and asked Misief to stack the rocks under the axle of the wagon as soon as he had the wagon lifted up. The old man squatted under the back left edge of the wagon and lifted it using the lower portion of his back. Misief admired the tenacity of this little old man, and he quickly stacked the two large rocks under the left rear axle of the wagon.

"Ok, I got 'em under the axle," Misief hollered.

The old man released the weight, and the rickety old wagon came resting down on the stack of rocks. Misief feared the wagon might break apart as the left rear wheel dangled in the air.

Misief thought to himself, "This old wagon needs a bit more than a new wheel."

The old man removed the remnants of the busted wheel and began the task of attaching the new one. Misief continued to help by holding a lantern so the old man could see as he worked.

Misief knew this project was nearing an end, and soon the old man would be on his way. Knowing it was now or never, he decided to try once again to get the old man to talk about where he got this load of whiskey.

"So what'd you tell me your name was?" Misief asked.

"I didn't," the old man replied.

The old man didn't look up; he just kept on working.

Then the old man leaned back and proudly said, "Done! She's all ready to go. All I got left to do is get these crates of Forty Rod loaded back up."

It was obvious the old man was in a hurry to get moving and wasn't at all comfortable sitting still in the darkness with his illegal load.

"I'm way behind schedule," the old man stated as he hurried to get the crates loaded into the wagon.

Misief lent the old man a hand and helped him hoist the cargo back on the old rickety wagon. He couldn't take it any longer, and in the darkness of the night he blurted out, "Old man, can you tell me where I can find Lucas Benson?"

The old man stopped dead in his tracks and glared straight into Misief's eyes as he gave him a stern warning. "You don't find Lucas Benson boy! And you pray that he don't find you either!"

Judging from the tone in the old man's voice and the look on his face, Misief knew he should drop the subject. The old man's response led Misief to believe that he must have already had a bad encounter with Lucas.

Misief wondered if Lucas had possibly cheated him in some way.

Believing that the old man wasn't going to share any information regarding Lucas, Misief decided he would take some evidence for himself. As they took turns retrieving the crates from the ground and placing them back into the wagon, Misief quietly slipped a bottle out of a crate and hid it under a bush. He realized it wasn't a great hiding spot, but in the darkness it would be almost impossible for the old man to see it.

Misief took the crate that was now one bottle short of being full and placed it up on the wagon, while the old man was busy retrieving another crate. One by one, they continued loading the crates and soon the crate with one empty bottle was completely covered by crates sporting all four bottles. The old man was clueless that Misief had stolen a bottle of Forty Rod from him.

Misief feared he may never see the old man again. Throwing caution to the wind, he chose to give it one last shot to see if the old man would give him a hint on where to find Lucas Benson.

Misief took a deep breath, then said, "Lucas Benson cheated my father years ago, and I wanna find him so I can get even with him."

As the old man loaded the last box of whiskey on the wagon, he replied, "Boy, that's what Lucas does. He cheats you out of your life. He robs you of anything and everything you got. He don't quit until he has it all. Then he leaves you broke, busted and maybe even dead. Take my advice boy and steer clean away from Lucas Benson!"

Misief did not respond to the old man's warning.

The old man turned to Misief and asked him to help him drape the tarp back over the wagon. Then the old man loaded up his tools and his lantern and bid Misief goodbye. He thanked him for his help as he climbed up on the old wagon. With a gentle tug on the reins and a firm 'giddy up' the old horses heaved forward and the wobbly old wagon began tottering along.

Misief stood in the center of the road and watched as the wagon disappeared into the shadows of the night. When the old man was well out of sight, Misief ran to the bushes and retrieved the bottle of whiskey he'd hidden a few minutes earlier. Grabbing the bottle firmly by the neck, he quickly stashed it in his brown leather bag.

Misief was totally unaware of the irony of his actions. By placing that brand of whiskey into that leather bag, he had replicated the exact act his father had done numerous times in the past. It appeared the prophetic fears of his deceased mother might be coming to pass!

****

Misief mounted Coal and began the familiar journey back to the cabin. While he'd traveled this way many times before, he was never fond of making this trek in the dark of night. With only the moonlight to guide his way, the blackness of the trail made it difficult to see ruts and rocks. Doing the best he could to lead Coal along, it took his complete focus to make sure they did not venture off the trail. Misief soon realized Coal was doing much better than he was and allowed the horse to navigate the journey home.

In the moonlit darkness, the normal sounds along the trail seemed more pronounced than during the light of day. The gentle gurgling of the water cascading off the rocks in Roberts Creek provided comfort to his troubled mind. Occasionally, he thought he heard commotion in the woods; sounds of something stirring on the other side of the creek. He was quite sure it was just a nocturnal animal roaming around in the night, but in the back of his mind he feared a late night visit from the tall stranger.

As he listened to the rustling leaves and felt the breeze blow across his face, Misief thought to himself, "Unless that stranger can lead me to Lucas Benson, I don't wanna run into him tonight."

Feeling his anxiety increase a notch or two, Misief pulled his revolver and kept it in his right hand as he held onto the reins with his left.

As he rounded the last curve in the road, Misief placed his sidearm back into his holster. A sense of relief swept over his body with the safety of the cabin only a couple of hundred yards away.

Turning into his property, he directed Coal around the left side of the cabin and made his way to the stable. Worn out from a long day, and knowing he had several chores that demanded his attention; he wasted no time getting started. With the stable door unlatched, he walked inside and lit a couple of oil lanterns which were hanging on the wall. He led Coal to his stall, removed the bridle and saddle, and then took a fine bristled brush and gave the stallion a nice brushing. After brushing, he scooped out a bucket of oats and replenished Coal's water supply. Finally, with Coal resting in his stall, he walked over to the other two horses and made certain they had plenty of food and water. Feeling confident all of the horses were adequately cared for, he stumbled wearily into the cabin.

Walking through the front door, Misief felt the darkness encompass his entire body. It wasn't that he was scared of the dark, but this was the very first time he'd come into the cabin at night by himself. He had grown accustomed to having his mother and sister waiting for him. But tonight, with his mother's body lying cold in the ground beside the maple tree and Ashel staying with friends, the cabin was filled with dead silence reminding him that there was nary a living soul present. There was nothing simmering on the wood stove to fill the air with the comforting aroma of a home cooked meal. There were no lanterns burning to bring forth the feeling of being with those you love. In a room filled with darkness, the space around him was void of life as silence screamed in his troubled mind. On this night, the atmosphere inside the cabin was quite a volatile mixture for a young man who was filled with venomous anger and the desire for revenge.

****

Trying to get the darkened void, that consumed the place he called home, to dissipate, Misief lit a lantern in the kitchen and another one in the front room. The soft glow of the lanterns made him feel a little better about being alone. He removed the leather bag from around his neck and laid it on the kitchen table. Staring at the bag, as numerous thoughts drifted around in his mind, he reached out and unfastened the flap of the bag exposing the brown bottle of Forty Rod whiskey. He grasped the bottle in his hands and flipped it over to get a better view of the insignia, which was on the bottom of the bottle. The glow of the lantern reflected against the warm brown color of the glass bottle. He sat for about five or ten minutes just staring at the initials of Lucas Benson.

Then Misief did something that he hadn't preconceived to do at all. He pulled the cork from the bottle and poured a small amount of the clear liquid into the cup he normally used for drinking milk. He held up the cup and gently swished around the whiskey. It was impossible to know for sure what was going on in his mind, but out of nowhere, he turned up the cup and poured the liquid fire into his mouth. His eyes squeezed shut as his virgin taste buds endured the rude awakening. He'd never tasted anything so strong in all his life. His throat felt scalded, and his eyes began to water. For a moment or two, Misief actually thought he might die.

After a few minutes, the burning effects of the whiskey had subsided. What nobody knew was that moments before he turned up the cup, Misief had dedicated the first shot of whiskey to the memory of his father. After drinking that first shot, he reminisced about all the things the world had done wrong to him in his life.

Then Misief poured a second shot in memory of his mother. Repeating the same process he followed for his father; he took time to mentally torment those who he perceived were his enemies. He began to blame everyone, including Doc Lynch.

"If Doc had been available on the first day of the accident, Mama would still be alive," he whispered out loud in a rough growling voice.

Then he turned up the cup and swallowed his second shot of whiskey. Then a third; this one dedicated to his sweet sister, Ashel.

It didn't take long for his state of mind to become totally toxic and volatile. His fragile mental state, mixed with the damning effects of the whiskey was creating a combination more flammable than a Molotov cocktail.

Then Misief got an idea. He staggered into his mother's bedroom and grabbed a piece of paper. He made his way back to the kitchen table and started thinking of all those he wanted to repay. On the top of the paper he scratched out a heading in his best handwriting. It said, *'Misief's Revenge List'*. For the next hour, he sipped whiskey and scribbled the names of the people he perceived to be responsible for creating the pain he was feeling.

****

Somewhere during his drunkenness, Misief found himself on the front porch bent over the rail, as he gave back to the earth everything his stomach had consumed during the last couple of hours. The effects of the whiskey were taking its toll. His legs collapsed under him, and everything went black.

Spending the night passed out on the porch, Misief was awakened as the morning sun beamed down on his head. He rolled over to discover his face was sticky with residue from his one man party. He had a headache like nothing he'd experienced before, and his insides were extremely sore from the excruciating vomiting that had occurred during the night. The world seemed to be spinning out of control as he crawled inside the cabin and collapsed again, this time in front of the fireplace.

****

Sometime that afternoon, Davis and Ashel arrived at the cabin and knocked on the front door.

Davis rattled the door and hollered, "Hello Misief, are you here? It's Davis and Ashel."

Misief didn't answer, so Davis opened the door and walked inside. The intent of the visit was to check on Misief and to allow Ashel the opportunity to spend some time with her brother. They had no idea they'd arrived right in the middle of Misief's first drinking binge.

Davis, who knew something was not right, peeked into the kitchen and saw the open bottle of Forty Rod whiskey with the empty cup sitting beside it. Shaking his head, Davis was upset, as he had witnessed this same demonstration far too many times with Misief's father, Barak. Davis knew that Barak would drink himself blind whenever he felt sorry for himself, and it angered him to think Misief was following in his father's damning pattern.

Davis stormed over to Misief and abruptly took his left foot and nudged Misief's shoulder. He looked down at him and demanded, "Misief, what do you think you are doing?"

Lying on the floor, Misief rolled over and grunted, "What do ya'll want?"

Davis sensed the sarcasm in his voice and said, "Misief, get up. Where'd you get the whiskey? And what do you think you're doing with ….."

Misief interrupted Davis' interrogation and shouted, "I'll do whatever I want! Leave me alone!"

Ashel wasn't sure what had happened to her brother. She feared Misief was sick, so she knelt down beside him and asked, "Are you feeling alright? Do we need to get Doc Lynch to check on you?"

Davis knelt down and reassured Ashel that her brother didn't need to see a doctor. He kindly asked Ashel to go outside and check on the chickens while he talked to Misief. She obliged and left Misief and Davis alone in the cabin.

Misief clumsily pushed himself into a sitting position on the floor, as he rubbed his head. He looked rough as his hair was a mess, his face was unshaven and his eyes were bloodshot. His clothes reeked of vomit and were dirty and wrinkled from his night of sleeping on the porch.

Davis stooped down and said, "Misief, you are treading down a dangerous path. This is a similar road that I watched your father travel. I don't wanna see the same thing happen to you that happened to him."

Misief did not have all his mental faculties functioning properly and shouted, "Hey! Don't you talk bad about my father! I'm tired of people talking bad about him, and I'm gonna put a stop to it!"

Davis came back, "Misief, your father was my friend, and I loved him like a brother. I would never talk bad about him. But the truth is, your father's life changed when he lost his dream to Lucas.

He began drinking like never before, as he tried to drown his pain with whiskey; ironically with the same stuff you drank last night."

"They did him wrong Davis," Misief yelled back. "And I'm gonna get even with all of them!"

"Misief, that's exactly what your father used to say. He refused to let the past go and move on with his life. He wasted the present as he dwelt on the past. He always wanted to get even. Son, you just need to let it go," Davis pleaded.

Misief replied, "Now you're sounding like my mama. You don't know me, Davis! You don't know how I feel. I don't have anybody no more. I'm all alone!"

Davis could tell he was not getting anywhere with Misief. He knew he was an emotionally hurting young man, and he wanted to help him, but Misief was not willing to listen to anything Davis had to say.

Davis decided to try a different approach. He asked, "Misief, why don't you come and go with us back to my place for a few days? You really need to spend some time with friends who care deeply for you. You know Ashel loves you very much and could use her big brother right now."

Shaking his head Misief replied, "I'm staying here! I'm planning my revenge! Just take Ashel, and ya'll go back home. I'll be fine."

Davis realized he wasn't making any progress and was possibly making things worse. He knew this young man needed help, but he also knew Misief was old enough to make his own decisions. Davis feared the decisions Misief was making were going to lead him to more trouble and possibly even death.

Davis stepped outside and informed Ashel it was time for them to leave. Ashel ran back inside the cabin and threw her arms around her big brother. Misief didn't resist his sister's embrace, but he wasn't especially warm or cordial toward her either. Deep down he dearly loved his sister, but at the moment he felt emotionally numb. The mental pain he felt wouldn't allow him to love anyone; even someone as close to him as his own sister.

Before leaving, Davis and Ashel placed a fresh baked loaf of bread, smoked meat and an apple pie on the kitchen table. As he walked toward the front door, Davis turned to Misief and said, "Tammy Sue baked some things for you. We placed them on the kitchen table."

Misief said nothing.

Standing by the front doorway, Ashel turned back and said, "I love you, Misief."

Misief nodded but couldn't bring himself to say the word 'love'. It just wasn't in him at the time. He did respond to Ashel by saying, "I know you do. You take care of yourself, and I'll come see you soon."

"Do you promise?" Ashel asked.

"I promise," he replied.

With that final promise, Davis and Ashel proceeded to go back home. The visit didn't go anything like Davis had planned, and he was extremely worried about Misief. Since Barak's death, Davis had talked to Bett many times about the direction Misief seemed to be taking in his life. During numerous conversations with Bett, Davis mentioned how Misief shared his father's same mannerisms and temperament. Bett often confided in Davis about the hatred Misief would exhibit even as a young boy.

Now it seemed certain the recent events in Misief's life had solidified his direction toward the desire for revenge. Davis knew that Misief's current mental state, in combination with the Forty Rod whiskey, was nothing short of a disaster waiting to happen.

With Davis and Ashel far out of sight, Misief walked into the kitchen and took notice of the beautiful apple pie along with the fresh baked bread and meat they had left. He hadn't eaten a bite since his lunch the day before at the café in Rock Springs, and he was starving. He walked over to the cabinet and retrieved a fork. Then, he sat down with the pie and started eating straight from the pan. The 'revenge list', which was still lying on the kitchen table from last night, caught his eye. With a fork in one hand and a pencil in the other, he wolfed down the pie as he added additional names to his list.

After a few minutes of scribbling, Misief picked up the list and reviewed each name slowly from top to bottom.

He cracked a slight grin and, with his mouth full of pie, he laughed as he declared, "Oh yeah, I'll get you! Don't worry, I'll get all of you…..even if it is the last thing I do!"

It seemed that nothing, and no one, would be able to turn Misief around now. He was a confused and hurting young man, filled with venomous hatred over his past, and he was on a personal mission, doomed for destruction.

Chapter 11

"A Romance Blossoms"

September 29, 1863

It had been a couple of weeks since Misief's first drinking binge. Recently, he'd spent his time hanging around the cabin contemplating the notion of catching up on chores that needed to be done. Since the day his mother passed, no one had taken care of routine tasks such as, cleaning out the horse stalls, caring for the fields and completing the daily housework that a home requires.

One day Misief walked out to the stable and had every intention of cleaning out the stalls. He meandered toward Coal and basically wasted the day away thinking about his last visit into Rock Springs.

Then there was another day when Misief ventured into the garden and had solid plans to finish clearing out the fence row that his mother was working on before she died. However, the sun set that afternoon with the overgrown weeds still proclaiming their victorious stronghold on the fence.

Whenever he was inside the cabin, Misief would stare at the growing mess and declare this was the day to get started on cleaning things up. Dirty clothes were strewn around the cabin in ever growing piles; dishes were stacked on the kitchen counter with food stains that were now drier than the western soil, and the floors were covered in so much dirt you could plant a garden if you just scattered a few seeds.

Sheriff Adonai

****

A couple more days passed with much of the same lackadaisical behavior. Misief was basically spending each day lying around the cabin feeling sorry for his personal lot in life. One morning, while lazily wasting away in his bed, he remembered that he was running low on food supplies. He decided it was time to head to Rock Springs to restock his cupboards.

As Misief lay in bed mentally planning the details of his journey into town, he made of list of several things he wanted to accomplish on this particular trip. He wanted to go back by the saloon to talk with Tomar and find out more about the night his father, Barak, had the personal encounter with Lucas. And, he wanted to visit Sachiel to see if he would give him more information regarding Sheriff Adonai. Then his mind wandered to thoughts about beautiful Nainsi and his desire to spend more time with her.

While lost in his thoughts, Misief heard a noise that sounded like someone lurking in the kitchen. Jumping directly out of bed, he grabbed his pistol and craned his neck around the doorway of the bedroom to scout out the situation. To his surprise, he saw someone standing at the kitchen table with their back towards him as they seemed to be focused on something on the table. This person lurking in the kitchen seemed vaguely familiar to him, but he wasn't completely certain.

Taking cover behind an old cabinet standing outside the bedroom door, with his gun drawn, Misief shouted, "Hey, what do you think you are doing in here? You better get out before I fill you full of lead!"

The intruder didn't acknowledge Misief's presence at all and seemed to be ignoring him. There was no response to his question or threat. Instead, this person remained focused on something that was sitting on the table. Misief tried to determine what it might be that had captured the intruder's attention.

Misief knew he was going to need to get a closer look at what was going on in the kitchen and see if the intruder was alone or had an accomplice with him. Dressed only in his underwear, Misief snuck across the room on his hands and knees, and crouched behind his mother's sofa. This gave him a perfect vantage point to see what was going on in the kitchen.

As Misief studied the situation, he realized the intruder was staring at the empty bottle of Forty Rod that had been sitting on the table for the last several weeks.

Finally the intruder moved. Reaching down, he picked up the bottle and tilted it over to see the bottom. After carefully inspecting the underside of the bottle, the intruder whirled around and looked right at Misief who was still kneeling down behind the sofa.

Misief couldn't believe his eyes! It was that dang ole' same strange lawman he'd encountered before! The stranger held the whiskey bottle in his hands as he looked at Misief with eyes full of compassion. While he never spoke a single word, it seemed that the stranger was trying to convey his disappointment in finding an empty whiskey bottle in Misief's possession. The expression on the stranger's face indicated he wanted to warn this young cowboy about the damning consequences that this deadly liquid could have on his life.

After several minutes of silent communication, the stranger turned and started walking toward the front door, with the whiskey bottle still in his hands. Misief stared directly into the eyes of the stranger as he walked right past him and out the door of the cabin. Hearing the stranger walk across the porch and down the steps,

Misief hurried to the door to see which direction he went. To his surprise, the stranger was nowhere to be found.

Misief thought to himself, "He can't just disappear into thin air."

However, there simply wasn't a trace of the stranger or the brown whiskey bottle in sight. While these unscheduled encounters with this unknown lawman did startle him, for whatever reason he never felt in danger when the man appeared. It was a bit unsettling to know someone was stalking him. He wondered how the stranger got inside the cabin and how he seemed to be able to make an exit without leaving a trace. After lapping the outside of the cabin several times in his tattered underwear, he realized the stranger had simply vanished.

Misief stood on the steps leading up to the cabin and screamed at the top of his lungs, "Who are you, and what do you want with me? And bring me back my whiskey bottle!"

Misief stood silent for several minutes wanting so much to hear a response, but the air was filled with complete silence. Believing the strange lawman was gone for now, he turned and walked back into the cabin, making certain to secure the front door!

Walking into the kitchen and feeling hungry, Misief scavenged around to find himself a bite of breakfast. He sat down at the kitchen table and stared at the spot where the empty bottle once stood. On the table, right next to where the bottle had been, was his 'Revenge List'. Glancing down, he noticed the list had some new words scribbled on it, in handwriting that was not his. He picked up the 'Revenge List' to inspect it closer. On the bottom of the note someone had written these words, *"I want you to surrender."*

"I ain't surrendering to you or nobody else," he shouted as he slammed his fist down on the table.

Misief knew the stranger wore a badge and was some type of lawman. But he wondered, "Why would he want me to surrender? I ain't done anything wrong!"

While he didn't completely understand the message, the word 'surrender' only enraged him even more. He thought to himself, "Surrender, yeah right....That ain't about to happen anytime soon!"

****

After eating the last of his sugar cured bacon and nibbling on some toast, Misief made preparations to go to Rock Springs. He washed up a bit and changed into a set of clean clothes. He slid on his cowboy boots, placed his wide brim hat on his head and buckled on his holster. He slipped his 'revenge list' inside the leather bag and then draped the bag over his shoulder.

It was a perfect day for a ride into Rock Springs as the rising sun was gradually burning off the morning fog. As he casually strolled along the trail, Misief began to plot out his day. He decided the first item on his agenda would be to see if he could locate Nainsi. He wanted to tell her about his visit with Sachiel and share with her what he had learned about Sheriff Adonai. As he made his way into Shoots Valley, he passed the place where he helped the old man repair the broken wagon wheel. He thought back to the load of whiskey the old man was transporting and wondered if he might run in to him again in Rock Springs or possibly somewhere along the trail.

Misief arrived in Rock Springs as the town merchants began opening up for morning business. He directed Coal toward the sawmill, and to his delight he saw Nainsi exiting the front door. He jumped down from Coal and quickly started walking toward her.

"Hi Nainsi," he said with a smile.

"Well hello, Misief. What are you doing in town?"

"I'm in town to see you," he whipped back. "Where are you headed?"

"I'm on my way to the Rock Springs Mercantile to buy supplies for my father," she explained. "You wanna walk with me?"

"Sure thing," he replied.

After securing Coal to the rail in front of the sawmill, the two of them made their way out into the dusty road leading down the center of Rock Springs. There was something about Nainsi that just seemed to make Misief happy. On the outside, she was obviously an attractive young lady with a kind, genuine smile. But for Misief, there was something else about Nainsi that drew him to her.

Deep inside Misief's heart, he was empty and was looking for something or someone to fill the void he had experienced since the loss of his parents. Nainsi made him feel warm inside, and he noticed that his palms became sweaty every time he was around her. This young man was somewhat clueless as to what was happening to him, but Cupid had shot an arrow right through his heart. The seed of love had been sown in the soul of this hurting cowboy!

Twirling her curls Nainsi smiled and asked, "So tell me Misief, how are things going with you?"

He wanted to tell her the truth, but chose to keep his troubles to himself and simply replied by saying, "Things are going real good."

"Are you adjusting to life alone at the cabin?" she asked.

Again he provided a deceptive answer stating, "Yeah, I'm getting along better every day."

Misief wanted more than anything to be honest with Nainsi. He wanted to tell her how much he hated the feeling of being alone, and how he missed his father, mother and sister. But fearing she would not perceive him as a tough guy, he refused to show any sign of weakness or acknowledged how much he was agonizing on the inside.

They arrived at the mercantile, and Nainsi pulled out a supply list. The list read: two bars of soap, one bundle of towels, a mop and a broom. She found each item and handed them to Misief to carry while she continued shopping. He followed her around the store without saying a word. Once they had collected all the items on the list, they made their way to the front of the store and placed them on the counter.

Nainsi looked up at the store owner, who was a nice man in his mid-forties and said, "My daddy said to put these items on his bill."

The store owner replied, "Sure thing little lady, how's your father doing?"

"He's doing just fine," she replied.

The store owner responded, "Well tell him Jacob said hi."

As Jacob placed the small items in a brown bag, Nainsi replied, "I sure will Mr. Jacob."

They collected the purchased items and headed out of the store. Misief wanted to spend more time with her, so he mustered up his courage and asked, "Nainsi, do you have to go back right now, or can we go sit on the bench in front of the café for a spell?"

"I guess I have a few minutes before I have to go back," she replied.

As soon as they sat down on the bench, Misief immediately blurted out, "Nainsi, I found Sachiel and had a talk with him."

"Did he answer all of your questions?" she asked.

Sheriff Adonai

"Some of them," he replied. "He told me about Sheriff Adonai, and I understand some of what he was explaining. I told Sachiel that I was looking for Lucas Benson, and he sort of got angry with me. Sachiel told me that I should leave Lucas alone."

"Misief, who is Lucas Benson, and why are you looking for him?" Nainsi asked.

Misief paused for a moment, and then took a deep breath. "Do you promise you can keep a secret?" he asked.

"I promise," she replied.

Misief squirmed for a moment as he prepared to tell Nainsi the story. He told her that many years earlier on a Friday night, Lucas Benson and his father were playing poker. He told her the poker game took place right down the street in the Thirsty Dog Saloon. He explained how his father had invented the flux wire design and that the design was going to make his father rich. However, on that fateful night, his father gambled away the rights to the flux wire design in an attempt to raise the money he needed to complete the final testing. Misief told Nainsi that Lucas Benson cheated his father by pulling a card from under the table and basically stole his father's dream away from him.

Pulling the leather bag off of his shoulder, Misief laid the bag in Nainsi's lap and said, "This bag is the same bag that held my father's flux wire design."

"How did you get it back from Lucas?" Nainsi asked.

"I bought it!" Misief replied.

"Where'd you buy it?" she asked.

Misief pointed and said, "At the Trading Post. A few weeks ago, when my mother was ill, I was in town and spotted the bag in the front window. So, I bought it, and I've kept it with me ever since."

Misief explained to Nainsi the meaning of the letters carved in the front of the leather bag and showed her his father's initials etched on the bottom.

Curious, Nainsi asked, "Do you know how the bag got into the Trading Post?"

Misief went on and explained, "The owner of the Trading Post, Wendell Potts, told me that an old man around seventy years old brought it in a while back. He said the old man that brought the bag in goes by the name of Lucas. After I saw my father's initials on the bag, I knew it had to be Lucas Benson."

Nainsi didn't say anything but nodded her head with interest. Misief didn't want her to think he was a bad guy, so he did his best to keep from showing his anger toward Lucas. He told Nainsi that all he wanted to do was to find Lucas and ask him what happened that night at the saloon. It was extremely hard, but Misief refrained from telling her how much he hated Lucas and how he craved vengeance for all the pain that he perceived Lucas had caused him.

After Misief finished talking, Nainsi replied, "Maybe you will find him soon, and you fellows can talk."

Misief, who was now getting much more comfortable with Nainsi asked, "Can I tell you one more secret? And will you promise me that you'll never tell it to anyone?"

"Sure," Nainsi replied, as her eyes sparkled.

"You know that book, the one called 'The Album'?"

"Yeah," she answered. "Did Sachiel give you a copy?"

"Yep, he did," Misief answered. "Well, you know the bullets on the cover of the book?"

Nainsi nodded.

Misief continued, "I have one! I have a bullet just like the one on the far right. It has a 'J' on it and a small blood spot."

"That's wild, Misief!" Nainsi replied. "Where'd you get it?"

Sheriff Adonai

Misief wasn't ready to tell Nainsi about the tall stranger in white cowboy boots that kept showing up in his life. He was afraid she wouldn't believe the truth, so he fabricated a story about how he found the bullet. He said, "I found it in our cabin right after my father was shot. I believe it holds the clue to finding out the truth about how and why he died," he explained.

While his explanation wasn't the whole truth, he didn't feel like he was being totally deceptive with her. After all, he did find the bullet after his father died, and it was inside the cabin; he just withheld the part of the story about how the bullet got there. He was afraid the whole truth might scare her or make her think he was a little crazy!

Nainsi then asked him, "You never told me how your father died."

Misief clammed up and didn't say anything. Nainsi was afraid she had put him on the spot and made him feel uncomfortable.

She positioned her hand over his hand and said, "Misief, never mind. We can talk about it another time. I'm sorry I brought it up."

Misief felt his heart go all the way to the top of his throat at the touch of Nainsi's soft hand. It was the greatest feeling he'd experienced in a very long time. The tender touch of her warm, delicate skin immediately allowed her access into the locked fortress of his troubled mind.

Misief inhaled deeply and gazed into her eyes. "It's okay, I will tell you. My father was killed in a shootout one night at our cabin. We were all sitting at the table eating supper; me, my father, my mother and my little sister, Ashel. All of a sudden, we heard horses coming from all directions. It was so loud, it sounded like a storm coming from the west. Well, my mama, Ashel and I ran as fast as we could to the bedroom to take cover. Mama jerked a quilt off the bed and draped it over me and Ashel to keep us hidden. My father grabbed his rifle and went into the front room. Peeking out of a hole in the quilt, I watched the whole showdown take place. I saw my father point the rifle out the front room window and shoot at whatever or whoever was outside our cabin. I still remember the sound of his voice as he looked back into the bedroom and yelled for mama to stay down and for her to keep Ashel and me down too. Then all of a sudden, I saw my father make a mad run for the front door. As soon as his foot landed on the front porch, I heard gun fire ringing out. I'll never forget the deafening noise of all the gunshots or the eerie silence once it all stopped. If I think about it, I can still smell the scent of gunpowder that filled our cabin that night. There was smoke all inside the cabin and on the front porch. It looked like the place was on fire. I will remember every detail of that night until the day I die. Mostly, I remember how my mama's screams pierced the night skies as she ran outside and held my father's dying body in her arms."

Misief paused a moment as Nainsi sat there teary-eyed and gently rubbing the back of his hand.

Misief bit his lip, clinched his jaw and continued. "The memory of my father lying on the front porch of the cabin with blood pouring from his gunshot wounds is a picture that I can't get out of my mind. I was right there Nainsi; and I can still see my father bleeding and gasping for his last breath. I can see it just like it was yesterday. Sometimes when I am asleep, I wake up and discover that I have dreamed about it all night. I just can't seem to get it out of my mind!"

When Misief finished the story, both he and Nainsi sat quietly on the bench for a few minutes. Nainsi was not sure what to say and was shocked at what Misief had just shared with her.

He pointed to the sheriff's office and said, "They killed em, Nainsi. It was the deputies from Rock Springs that did it!"

Misief got quiet again and stared straight ahead. Nainsi sensed his pain as he vividly recounted the story of his father's death. Still not certain how to respond, in a soft voice Nainsi replied, "I'm so sorry; I shouldn't have asked you about it."

Misief didn't respond verbally, but kindness beamed from his eyes as he stared back at her. She could tell he wasn't at all upset with her, but she felt it was time to change the subject. She lifted her hand off of his hand, brushed her hair back from her face and asked, "So how is your sister doing?"

"She's doing fine," Misief replied. "She is staying with some close friends right now."

Misief's only interest at the moment was the vivacious brunette that was sharing the bench with him. He wasn't sure how Nainsi was feeling about him, but he knew for certain how he felt about her. He didn't know much about love, but he knew she made him feel really good inside, and he thoroughly enjoyed her company.

Without having a real plan or thinking it through, Misief reached over and grabbed Nainsi's small hand. It was soft and delicate to the touch. As he held her hand, he hoped she would not notice how much his palm was sweating.

He turned to Nainsi and while staring directly into those chocolate brown eyes he said, "I don't have many friends right now, and I sure like talking to you. Would you, um, would you, could we be friends?"

The proposition sure didn't come out verbally the way Misief intended, but Nainsi thought she understood the nature of what he was trying to convey.

She came back with a clarifying question, "Misief, are you asking me to be your girlfriend?"

He gripped her hand tighter and said, "Yeah, sort of, I mean, would you?"

She giggled and replied, "Yeah. I like you, Misief. I like you a lot! And, you're a very cute guy. I will be your girlfriend."

It seemed Nainsi was just as smitten with Misief as he was with her. The two of them sat on the café bench for another thirty minutes or so, talking about her father's sawmill business, her family and anything else that came into their young minds. They gazed into each other's eyes like two young love birds. Misief glanced down at their hands and paid close attention to their fingers which were intertwined together like the laces in a shoe. It felt good to physically touch another human being. It lifted his spirit to be near someone who cared about him.

The conversation between the young couple finally went full circle and landed back on her father's business. Nainsi told Misief that she had come to the sawmill this morning so she could spend the day cleaning the offices there. Then Nainsi remembered the cleaning supplies lying beside the bench. She jumped up and said, "Misief, I better get back to the mill before my daddy comes looking for me."

Misief helped Nainsi gather up the supplies, and the two strolled together down the dirt road right through the middle of Rock Springs. As they arrived at the sawmill, Misief turned to Nainsi and asked, "Can I come see you again soon?"

"You better," Nainsi replied in a flash. Then she leaned in and kissed him lightly on the cheek.

"You take care of yourself cowboy," she said in a soft flirtatious voice.

As Nainsi twirled around to walk inside, Misief grinned from ear to ear and replied, "I will! Goodbye Nainsi. I'll see you soon!"

"Bye now," she said, as she winked at him.

With a spring in his step, Misief started walking back down the middle of Rock Springs. He wasn't sure where he was going next, but he knew the trail would lead him back to this young lady; his beautiful new girlfriend that went by the name, Nainsi!

Chapter 12

"A Pocket Full of Money"

October 4, 1863

After saying goodbye to Nainsi, Misief headed directly for the Trading Post. He was curious to see if Lucas had been back in the past few weeks. He tied Coal to the rail and stepped up on the old wooden boards that served as a sidewalk for the store. Peering into the store window, he noticed Wendell hadn't filled the space in the showcase that once served as the home for his leather bag.

As Misief entered through the door he called out, "Hey Wendell, do you remember me?"

Wendell responded, "Oh yeah, you're that young fella that bought that leather bag awhile back. I see you got it around your neck!"

"Yeah that's me," Misief acknowledged. "I always keep this bag with me!" Misief paused for a second and then asked, "By the way, has that Lucas fella been back in here?"

Wendell looked up at the ceiling, like the answer to Misief's question might be written up there, and said, "Yeah, as a matter of fact he has been back. He was in here the other day. He dropped in and wanted to pawn an old knife. He's always pawning stuff but never comes back to get it."

Curious, Misief asked, "Which knife did he pawn? Do you still have it?"

"I think so," Wendell replied in a not so certain voice. "I think it's still on pawn, so it would be in the back room. Let me go see if I can find it, and I will show it to you."

Wendell disappeared behind an old brown curtain hanging between the front show room and the storage room.

While Wendell was busy searching for the knife, Misief scouted out the store and noticed a young man about his age standing in front of the jewelry counter. He thought this guy looked familiar and walked over to get a better look at his face. Sure enough it was a young man by the name of Billin Macdo.

Billin was a short and stocky guy with thick curly brown hair. He had on old, wet, cowboy boots, which were caked in mud and looked like he'd just walked through a swamp. His appearance was rough to say the least; with his face unshaven and his hair sticking out from all sides of his cowboy hat, it was obvious he wasn't spending much time in front of the mirror!

Then Misief put the entire picture together in his mind as he remembered that Billin's father was the local blacksmith. Misief and his father had visited Billin father's shop several times across the years.

Misief tapped him on the shoulder and asked, "Your Billin, right?"

"Yeah, that's me," Billin verified. "I recognize your face, but I don't recall your name."

"Misief, Misief Stone," he responded.

"Hello Misief, good to see you again. So are you buying or selling today?" Billin asked.

"Aw, just mostly looking," Misief said. "What about you?"

"I want that watch," Billin stated as he pointed to a beautiful gold pocket watch displayed in the case.

"Whew, that thing sure looks expensive," replied Misief.

Billin drew himself closer to Misief, lowered his voice and asked, "Hey, do you wanna help me?"

"Help you do what?" Misief asked.

Billin replied, "Help me get this watch. When the old man comes back out, why don't you get his attention on something else, so I can get that watch?"

Misief replied, "Wendell's in the back looking for a knife for me. I'll be talking to him about it when he comes out. You just do what you have to do."

Billin nodded, and Misief walked back over to the counter. In just a few seconds, Wendell came walking out of the back room. He laid the knife on the counter and said, "This knife actually comes off pawn today. I'm gonna be putting it in the display case for sale."

Misief picked up the knife and opened the blade. It was a single blade knife with a handle that looked like it was made out of some type of animal bone. It wasn't anything special, and he wasn't all that interested in the knife, until he looked at the base of the open blade. Engraved on the blade were the initials, 'L.B.'!

That was all Misief needed to see, to know that he had to own this knife! "I'll take it," Misief blurted out.

"It will cost you one dollar," Wendell informed him.

Misief reached into his pocket and pulled out the money. He gave it to Wendell and then placed the knife into his leather bag. Like a treasure chest, the leather bag now contained several clues regarding Lucas Benson: the signed note he found in the bag when he bought it; his personal copy of 'The Album', given to him by Sachiel; and now the knife with the initials 'L.B.' on the blade. Proud of his new trinket, Misief turned and bid Wendell goodbye.

Sheriff Adonai

On his way out of the Trading Post, he paused, then turned back to Wendell and asked, "Hey Mr. Wendell, would you be willing to do me a favor?"

Wendell replied, "I might, depends on what you are gonna ask me."

Misief posed the question, "If I were to write that Lucas guy a note, would you give it to him the next time he comes in?"

Wendell thought it over a minute and said, "I reckon so. There's a piece a paper on the counter. Write down your message, and I'll see that he gets it next time he drops by here."

Misief took a small piece of paper and began to write a short note as best he could. The note read,

Lucas,
I would like to talk to you about the night you played poker with my father, Barak Stone. Please tell Mr. Wendell a time when we can meet.
Signed, Misief Stone

Misief folded the note and handed it to Wendell. He thanked Wendell for his willingness to help him and told him he would check back with him in a couple of weeks. Wendell tucked the note under the edge of the counter and sat back in his chair as Misief walked out the door.

****

Outside the Trading Post, Billin stood grinning like an opossum, waiting for Misief to exit the store.

"I got it! Thanks, for your help ole' buddy," he stated.

In a shaming tone, Misief replied, "Wendell's a nice ole' man. You should have paid him for that watch instead of stealing it."

Billin wasn't interested in any speech or reprimand. He motioned for Misief to mount up and follow him. Once they were at a safe distance, Billin stopped, reached into his front pocket, and pulled out the beautiful gold pocket watch. Misief took the watch and admired the detailed engraving encompassing the entire watch case.

"What are you gonna do with such a fancy watch?" Misief asked.

"I don't know, it just looked pretty and I wanted it. Besides, I paid nothing for it," Billin bragged.

"Why are you so interested in that old knife you got from Wendell?" Billin asked.

Misief pulled the knife from the leather bag and showed it to Billin. "Look close—do you see those initials carved in the bottom?"

Billin nodded.

"Well, those initials belong to Lucas Benson. He is the man that I am looking for," Misief said in a calm but determined voice. He then shared with Billin his plans to find Lucas and settle the score.

The two young men continued chatting as they rode their horses down the middle of Rock Springs, and in just a few minutes, they arrived at the blacksmith shop owned by Billin's father.

As they dismounted, Billin replied, "Well, I sure hope you find that Lucas guy and settle the score with him."

Misief walked Coal to the front of the blacksmith shop and stated, "I'll get him!"

Sheriff Adonai

Billin's father walked outside to greet the two young men, and they followed him into the blacksmith shop where he was in the process of forming a new set of horseshoes.

Misief turned to Billin's father and asked, "How much does it cost to get a new set of horseshoes?"

"Does your horse need new ones?"

Misief pointed at Coal's hooves and said, "Yeah, it's been awhile."

Billin's father walked over to Coal to get a closer inspection of the situation. After checking out each hoof, he spoke up and said, "Misief, if you will help me around the shop today, I will make you a new set for free."

"That sounds like a deal," Misief replied.

The rest of the day Billin and Misief help clean up around the blacksmith shop and worked to form a new set of horseshoes for Coal. Billin was accustomed to helping his father and showed Misief how to use the pincers to remove the old shoes. Then he took a hoof knife and nippers to shape Coal's hooves for the new shoes. Billin's father placed each shoe in a forge, and once the metal was red hot, he shaped each shoe using a hammer and anvil. In just a little while, Coal was sporting a brand new pair of horseshoes. Misief thanked Billin's father for his willingness to help him.

Realizing it was getting rather late, Misief knew it was probably time to head back to the cabin. He thanked them both, bid them goodbye and headed out the door of the blacksmith shop.

Billin followed Misief outside and whispered, "Hey Misief, you wanna go down to the saloon for a little while before you head home?"

Misief shrugged his shoulders and said, "I reckon. There's nobody at the cabin waiting for me anyway."

Billin grinned big and said, "It's Saturday you know. The saloon ladies will be dancing tonight."

"Oh really?" Misief said with his interest perked. "Is it worth the trip?"

"Oh yeah!" Billin replied. "Have you ever seen them?"

Misief shook his head.

"Then you don't have a clue about what you are missing!" Billin proclaimed. "Come on, let's go."

The two young cowboys mounted up and headed down the dusty road to the saloon on the edge of town. They tied their horses to the hitching post and meandered inside. The Saturday night crowd was just beginning to assemble as they strolled past the card tables and up to the bar. Behind the bar stood the saloon owner, Tomar Reeves. Tomar didn't say anything, just stared at Misief as he took a seat on a stool at the end of the bar. Billin picked the stool next to Misief and sat down. Then they both ordered a shot of Forty Rod Whiskey.

Out of the corner of his eye, Misief caught a glimpse of the brown bottle as Tomar tipped it up and poured whiskey into each glass. This bottle looked just like the ones the old man had on the wagon that was broken down on the trail just a few weeks earlier. Misief wanted to get a look at bottom of the bottle, but Tomar wasn't close enough to allow him to determine if Lucas' initials were on it or not.

Tomar placed the shots of whiskey on the counter, and Billin picked up his glass and downed it in a single gulp. Misief, not wanting to be outdone, turned up the whiskey and swallowed it right away. Not a fan of the taste, Misief drank it thinking it was part of the expected journey that accompanied manhood. While Misief tried to regain his composure from ingesting the 'gasoline like' beverage, Billin placed more coins on the bar and ordered a second shot for each of them. Tomar obliged, and before you could blink, those two shots followed the same path as the first ones.

As they gazed at the crowd, Misief noticed a peculiar group of men sitting in the corner of the saloon. He had never seen these men in Rock Springs before. They were dressed in the finest leather chaps and wore black studded cowboy hats. They all had on black and white vests made of untanned cow hide.

Misief pointed his finger in their direction, turned to Billin, and asked, "Who are those fellas in the corner over there?"

Billin grabbed Misief's finger and pushed his hand down. "Stop pointing! Those guys are part of the Marshall gang. They're bad news—nothing but trouble. It's best to leave them alone, and stay out of their way," Billin warned, as if he'd interacted with them before.

Misief continued, "So what do they do?"

Billin shared how the Marshall gang roamed the western territory raising a ruckus almost everywhere they stopped. "They claim to be cattle ranchers," Billin explained, "But my father says they just use that as a cover for their criminal activity. They've stopped by the blacksmith shop several times needing horseshoes."

Tomar was eavesdropping on the two of them and chimed in on the conversation. "Billin's right, leave them alone. If you mess with one of them, you'll have to fight all of them. Most of the time, they'd just as soon kill you as look at you."

"I ain't going to bother them," Misief stated as he sarcastically rolled his eyes at Tomar. "We didn't come to start any trouble; we came to see the ladies, right Billin?"

"That's right! Bring out the women," Billin shouted, as his voice echoed around in the saloon.

The rest of the patrons began parroting Billin, and immediately the saloon was filled with men stomping their feet and chanting, "Bring out the women! Bring out the women!"

Tomar climbed up on a stool behind the bar and shouted, "Now calm down, one of the ladies will be out in just a jiffy. She's in the back getting all 'dolled up' for you fellas."

Billin and Misief ordered a third shot of whiskey; this time Misief paid Tomar for the round of drinks. The two young men parked themselves on their stools and tried to wait patiently for the show to start. Misief wasn't sure what to expect, but his male hormones, along with the whiskey, had him geared up and ready to party.

It suddenly got quiet in the saloon as a man walked out from the back and took a seat at the piano. He began playing a melody which went on for several minutes. Misief wasn't certain what was about to happen, but he assumed the man was playing long enough to give the men in the saloon time to get seated and to finish up the card games they were playing.

Then the piano man picked up the pace of the music, as out of a back room exploded a young lady strolling across the floor in a long pink dress. Her name was Rhoda, and she looked to be in her twenties. Her pink velvet dress was adorned with red feathers which matched her hat. The men in the saloon whistled and cheered as Rhoda strutted up to the bar. With the help of a couple of young men, she climbed up on the bar smack-dab in front of Misief and Billin. Gazing right at Misief, Rhoda blew him a kiss and winked. Misief hadn't seen such red lips on a lady in all his life and was spellbound as she seductively performed less than eighteen inches from his face.

Rhoda charmed the men by dancing in erotic rhythm with the music provided by the piano man. She danced high upon the bar for five or ten minutes, utilizing the entire length of it as her stage.

Then, the same two men that gently lifted Rhoda up on the bar returned to help her down. She began to sing with the voice of a dark angel as she roamed between the tables and across the saloon floor. Some of the rowdy, drunken patrons tried to touch Rhoda as she provocatively passed by their table, but they were quickly dealt with by the men who were assigned to protect her. The alcohol the male patrons had ingested, along with the visual seduction filling their eyes, was a toxic combination. It wasn't long until Rhoda had worked the crowd into a frenzy. With each enthralling move she made, catcalls and vulgar offers could be heard all over the saloon. Misief got caught up in the moment and seemed to be hypnotized by his first taste of the dark side of sexual night life.

After a thirty minute performance, Rhoda returned to the back room of the saloon to the wild applause of the men. By the time Rhoda had finished singing and dancing, the majority of her costume lie scattered all over the saloon floor. The same two men who helped her up on the bar went around and collected the articles of clothing from those who were trying to keep the lace covered pieces as souvenirs.

After Rhoda left, the men in the saloon resumed drinking and playing poker. By now, both Billin and Misief were intoxicated to the point that they were having trouble maintaining their balance on their bar stools. Misief roared in laughter at everything Billin said, even if it wasn't funny. The more Misief laughed, the more Billin tried to be funny. These two young men were now making so much noise that the other patrons in the bar took notice of them.

A gentleman in his early forties walked over and said, "Boys, its okay to have a good time, but you might want to tone it down a bit. The Marshall gang is in here tonight, and they don't take kindly to your silliness."

Billin spoke up, "It's a free country, and we'll laugh all we wanna."

Misief laughed hysterically at Billin's response and in a drunken slur said, "Yeah, we ain't scared of the Marshall gang."

The gentleman nodded and walked away knowing he'd warned them. Both Billin and Misief continued acting crazy, laughing and hollering at everyone in the bar. Tomar, who had been in the back room, walked out and saw the ruckus Billin and Misief were causing. He marched straight over to them and said, "Fellas, I'm warning you both. You need to tone it down."

Billin made some type of joke about 'toning it down' which caused Misief to laugh so hard he fell off his bar stool. As Misief fell backwards, he inadvertently bumped into a man who was carrying three beers. The man fell over a table and was sprawled out on the floor. The man that Misief fell into was not just any ole' Rock Springs local; he was one of the members of the Marshall gang; a man who went by the name, Brazen.

As Brazen collected himself, he realized the three beers had spilled on the floor and all over his clothes. Brazen rose to his knees and glared at Misief who was still trying to get up off the floor.

Brazen spoke up in a gruff voice and said, "Hey kid, you owe me three beers."

Misief replied, "I don't owe you nothing, you just need to watch where you're going."

Both Brazen and Misief climbed to their feet without taking their eyes off each other.

Brazen got up in Misief's face and said, "Boy, you best go ahead and get three beers ordered and sent to that table over there in the corner, or I'm gonna clean this mess up with your face."

Before Brazen could say anything else, Misief picked up an empty whiskey bottle that was sitting on the table next to him, and without thinking it through, took a swing at Brazen. The bottle smashed right above Brazen's ear, crashing into pieces as it impacted his head. Brazen collapsed to the saloon floor as blood spurted from the gash on his temple.

The rest of the Marshall gang quickly got wind of what had just happened to Brazen and jumped up from their table to defend him. Immediately, the entire bar broke out into an all-out brawl. Fists were flying in all directions, chairs were being used as weapons and men were fighting each other with no real clue of who was fighting whom.

Misief knew he had to hightail it out of the saloon to keep from getting killed. Frantically, he began looking around the saloon for Billin. Crawling around the outside wall, he made his way to the front entrance. He stood up one last time to see if he could locate Billin, but didn't see him anywhere. He did see that Brazen was beginning to regain consciousness from his wallop on the head and was trying to stand up. Misief was somewhat relieved to know he hadn't killed the man, but he sure didn't want to be around when Brazen regained all his senses.

All of a sudden, Misief heard someone whisper his name from behind him. He peeked over his shoulder and saw Billin had escaped the ruckus and was already outside the saloon untying both of their horses.

"Let's get outta here," Billin mouthed.

Misief didn't need coercing and immediately backed his way out of the saloon doors and onto the wooden sidewalk. In a single fluid motion, he grabbed Coal's reins, mounted up and gave a nudge as the stallion raced away from the saloon. Billin took the lead and glanced back at Misief as he instructed, "Follow me; I wanna show you something."

Billin led Misief about a mile outside the edge of Rock Springs to a location just past the old well. There they came upon an old abandoned shack that once served proudly as the office of a local gold mining company. Feeling they were a safe distance away from the saloon, they sat on their horses and burst out laughing at what had just happened. "I thought you were a dead man," Billin acknowledged.

"Whew, I did too," Misief admitted as he hooted at the situation.

Rubbing his head he continued, "I guess I had too much to drink tonight.....by the way, where did you go during all of that commotion? I couldn't find you anywhere!"

Billin opened his coat and exposed a stack of bills. Then he explained, "While everybody was busy fighting, I snuck behind the bar and took us a little cash to tide us over. Here, have some. You earned it."

"How did Tomar not see you?" Misief asked.

Billin explained, "Tomar was so busy trying to get everyone to quit fighting and to stop breaking his furniture, that he wasn't paying attention to the bar."

Billin handed Misief at least half of the stolen bills. Misief thought about refusing the money, but he took it and placed it in his trusty brown leather bag.

Misief looked at Billin and said, "I guess I better get going home before they come looking for us."

Billin agreed, "Probably so, let's do it again sometime."

Both of them cackled out loud, feeling no remorse for their actions. Misief told Billin he would connect with him the next time he was in town. Billin nodded and the two young men parted ways.

****

As Misief rode off into the dark of the night, his mind reflected on all the things that had happened that day. He smiled as he thought about his new girlfriend Nainsi. He remembered the touch of her skin as he held her hand. He thought about how much he enjoyed her companionship and the look in her eyes as they talked about their lives.

Coming to Roberts Creek, he followed the trail to the right and shifted his mind to the knife he'd bought earlier from Wendell at the Trading Post. He snickered when he thought about how Billin had stolen the pocket watch. His smile quickly vanished as Misief wondered how and when he would finally find Lucas. He hoped it wouldn't be too long before Lucas returned to the Trading Post to get the note he'd left for him. Riding alone in the darkness, he painted a detailed mental picture of the moment he would take a bottle and smash Lucas over the head just like he'd done to Brazen.

Thinking of situation with Brazen, Misief allowed his mind to reflect on the last few hours at the saloon. He replayed each tantalizing move of the voluptuous lady who danced at the saloon. He didn't realize the impact the visualization was having on his young male mind. Her dancing stirred up erotic thoughts and sexual emotions that he'd never experienced in his young life.

After a mile or two of reliving the night of visual female exploitation, Misief drifted back to thoughts of his altercation with Brazen. Sobering up a bit as he traveled toward home, he became a little concerned. He hoped the Marshall gang was on their way out of Rock Springs and that he never ran into them again.

Making the final turn toward the cabin, Misief decided it might be best if he stayed out of town for a few days, just in case the Marshall gang decided to hang around town to get even with him.

Ironically, he'd left home this morning completely innocent. Now, just twelve hours later, the influence of his associate had led him to a day filled with poor choices and a future that would be spent paying for his actions.

Chapter 13

"Locked Up"

October 5, 1863

Misief's night of drunken slumber was interrupted by the sound of someone banging on the front door of the cabin. Rubbing sleep from his eyes, he peeked out the back window to see the sun barely rising over the trees. He wondered who would be knocking at the door so early in the morning. The knocking persisted and was followed by someone shouting at the top of their lungs. The banging on the door, the shouting, and the glare of the rising sun did nothing but aggravate the hangover that was pounding in his head.

"Misief Stone, we need to talk to you," rang clearly from someone with a rough, deep voice that penetrated the stillness of the morning air.

The first thing that crossed Misief's mind was that it might be the Marshall gang. He grabbed his gun and holster from the crate beside his bed and fastened it around his waist. At this point, he didn't even have his pants on, and he was still in somewhat of a mental fog from the previous night of drinking and partying.

Making his way to the front room, he pushed back the curtains just enough to see who wanted to talk to him. Standing on the front porch were two uniformed men; both of them appeared to be wearing badges, and each of them had a sidearm strapped around their waist. Misief quietly tiptoed across the wooden floor and placed his back against the front door.

"Who are you, and what do you want?" he asked.

"We are deputies from Rock Springs. We need to talk to you Misief Stone. Now open the door!" bellowed one of the men.

"I ain't done anything wrong," he retorted, refusing to open the door.

The men immediately replied, "We didn't say that you are guilty of anything. We just need to talk to you!"

Misief stepped back and unlocked the door. He cracked it open a few inches and realized both men had badges identifying them as lawmen from the Rock Springs Sheriff's office.

Misief reluctantly opened the door, as one of the deputies stated, "Misief, my name is Deputy Gore, and this is Deputy Zeke. We're investigating a theft that occurred last night at the saloon. Would you mind answering a few questions?"

The deputies could immediately ascertain that Misief was suffering from a hangover and had probably passed out after a night of drinking. Deputy Gore commented, "Mr. Stone, you look a little rough this morning. Are you alright?"

"I'm fine," Misief replied, as he rubbed his head.

Deputy Gore was a tall, younger man with a slender build. It was hard to understand exactly what he was saying due to the wad of chewing tobacco rolling around in his mouth. He face bore brown trails clearly indicating the path the tobacco juice had followed as it journeyed down the side of his chin.

Deputy Zeke was a bit shorter than Deputy Gore and had a much heavier build. He appeared to be in his mid to late forties and continued the questioning by asking, "Misief, there was a sizable amount of money that came up missing from the saloon last night. Do you know anything about it?"

Misief shook his head and declared, "I don't know anything about any missing money. I didn't steal it!"

Deputy Zeke responded, "Nobody is saying you did. But, there was an altercation at the saloon last night, and when it was all said and done, somebody had stolen a stack of money that Tomar kept behind the bar. You were identified as being at the saloon and as being the instigator of the fight. We are just investigating what happened."

"The other guy started it," Misief replied. "That gang would have killed me if I hadn't protected myself."

Deputy Gore stepped forward and shifted the tobacco to the side of his mouth so he could speak. "Misief, we ain't here to talk about no fight. We're trying to find out who stole a large amount of money from Tomar."

"I done told you once, I didn't steal anything," Misief stated, as he took a step or two forward.

Misief kept slowly walking toward the edge of the porch to keep the deputies away from the front door of the cabin. He wasn't sure how much money Billin had given him, and he was afraid the deputies might want to come inside the cabin to execute a search of the place.

"Who were you with last night?" Deputy Gore asked, as he spit off the porch.

"I wasn't with anybody," Misief replied. "I was all alone!"

Deputy Gore continued by asking, "You sure you weren't with a young man named, Billin Macdo?"

"I know who Billin is, but I wasn't with him," Misief argued.

"Somebody saw you and Billin drinking together," Deputy Gore stated.

"I might have sat beside him at the bar," Misief admitted. "But I didn't steal any money."

"Did Billin take the money?" Deputy Gore asked.

"You will have to talk to him about that. But I can tell you that I didn't steal any money," Misief replied.

As Deputy Gore continued with his questions, Deputy Zeke peered through the open front door. He noticed Misief's hat and boots lying on the floor, and he presumed that Misief had just thrown them off as soon as he arrived home last night.

Deputy Zeke then noticed the brown leather bag lying on the other side of the room. Beside the leather bag was a jacket and a pair of pants. Deputy Zeke wanted to get inside the cabin to search the pants to see if the stolen money might be in the pockets. It was a long shot, but the veteran lawman knew that drunken criminals were often very careless, and he believed he might just get lucky and find the missing money.

Deputy Zeke interrupted the conversation between Misief and Deputy Gore and asked, "Misief, do you mind if we go inside and look around?"

Misief replied, "I'm telling you both the truth, I ain't stolen any money."

Deputy Zeke came back, "Okay, if you didn't do anything then you wouldn't mind if we go inside and have a look around would you?"

The two lawmen made their way inside the cabin. Deputy Zeke made a beeline for the pair of pants lying on the floor. He placed his hand in the pockets, pulling them inside out as he searched for the stolen money. One pocket had a few coins in it, another one had three dollars inside, but the stolen money was not in the pants.

Misief watched closely as the two lawmen rummaged through the cabin looking for clues. Deputy Zeke snooped around in the kitchen as Deputy Gore searched the bedrooms. After fifteen minutes or so, both lawmen came back to the front room empty handed.

Misief thought they were about to leave when Deputy Zeke looked at Deputy Gore and asked, "Did you check that leather bag over there in the floor?"

"Nope, I didn't check that."

Deputy Zeke reached down to pick up the bag as Misief dove down and grabbed it. "You can't look in there. This was my father's private bag!"

The two lawmen pounced on Misief and quickly wrestled the leather bag away. On any other day, Misief could have put up a much better fight, but this morning he was still feeling the effects from a night of heaving drinking and was not able to outwrestle the two lawmen. Deputy Zeke opened the bag and pulled out a stack of bills.

"Well, well, what have we here?" Deputy Zeke asked with a smirky grin on his face. "Looks like you have been lying to us boy."

"I tell you, I didn't steal this money," Misief retorted.

Deputy Gore grabbed Misief by the left arm and yanked it behind his back. "You're in a whole heap of trouble, sonny," he stated, as he place him in a pair of rusty handcuffs.

Deputy Gore continued, "Misief Stone, we are placing you under arrest for the theft of the money from the saloon. You're gonna take a little trip with us to the jail."

Before leaving the cabin, the deputies allowed Misief to put on his pants, his boots and a jacket. They removed his gun and placed it in the saddlebag on their horse. They confiscated the leather bag and said, "Everything in this bag is evidence, so we'll be taking it too."

Deputy Gore led Misief outside while Deputy Zeke went to the stable to retrieve Coal. They hoisted Misief up on top of Coal and tied his hands to the saddle. Then they took his feet and shackled them together beneath Coal's belly. Deputy Zeke closed the cabin door, and Deputy Gore grabbed Coal's reins and led him away.

****

The eleven mile ride to Rock Springs was quiet and uneventful. However, it was an arduous journey as Misief did his best to maintain his balance while traveling with his hands bound and his feet tied together. beneath his horse's belly. Because Misief was still battling a hangover, each step Coal took echoed in his head like a cluster of ringing church bells on Sunday morning. In his mind, he was trying to figure out what he would say to defend himself when he faced the judge. He knew he did not steal the money, but since the deputies found it in his bag, he knew it did not look good for him.

As they cleared Shoots Valley and began the final stretch into town, Misief began thinking about the embarrassment of being paraded through the middle of Rock Springs in this condition. What would the locals think of him, as they glared at this young man who was shackled, both hand and foot, being lead like an animal to jail?

Misief didn't want anyone to see him in this situation, so he hollered at the deputies and asked, "Hey deputy, would you take off these handcuffs if I agree to ride in peacefully on my own?"

Deputy Gore spoke up, as tobacco juice dripped down his face, "You must be funning me boy! We ain't untying you until we get you behind bars."

Misief then asked, "Well, what about taking the back way into town?"

In an agitated voice Deputy Gore replied, "Nope! We are going down Main Street!"

Sheriff Adonai

To his dismay, the deputies led Misief right through the middle of Rock Springs. As they approached the sawmill, he hoped Nainsi wouldn't be anywhere around. He did not want her to see him being led through town in shackles, fearing it might destroy the one thing that seemed to be going well in his life.

Trying his best to hide, Misief bent his head down, and it appeared he got his wish, as the mill seemed to be temporarily deserted. Neither Nainsi nor her father were anywhere in sight. He breathed a sigh of relief and silently prayed that he would get this legal matter resolved without Nainsi ever finding out.

Within a few minutes of passing the sawmill, the long journey came to an end as the lawmen got down off their horses and tied them to the hitching post in front of the Sheriff's Office. Once their horses were secure, the deputies unshackled Misief and helped him down off of his horse.

Misief asked, "What are you gonna do with Coal?"

Deputy Gore explained, "We'll take him down to the livery, and they'll watch him for a spell. You're gonna need to get somebody to come get him."

Misief replied, "I have a good friend; his name is Davis Williams. Can somebody contact him to see if he'll take care of Coal for me?"

Deputy Gore assured Misief by saying, "Sure, we can get a message sent to him. Don't you worry, the horse will be waiting for you when you get out—that is if you ever get out!"

****

The Rock Springs Sheriff's Office was a small, two-story building with two offices and a courtroom on the first floor and several jail cells upstairs. The front door led to the first office which was used for booking prisoners. The walls of this office were lined with oak file cabinets; above the file cabinets were pictures of all the men who had bravely served as Sheriff of Rock Springs. In the corner of the room was a wooden desk.

The deputies grabbed Misief by the arm and led him in front of the wooden desk. As he stood there in handcuffs and leg shackles, he meticulously reviewed each photo hanging on the wall. He wanted to see if he could spot a picture of Sheriff Samuel Anderson, who was serving as sheriff when his father was killed. As he stared at the pictures of the lawmen, he saw a photo that sparked his interest. It was not a photo of Sheriff Anderson; it was a photograph of a sheriff who had a strong face with chiseled features. But it wasn't the picture of the man that caught his eye, it was the name etched in gold below the picture. The gold plate read, 'Sheriff Adonai, First High Sheriff of the Western Territory'. Both Nainsi and Sachiel had told him all about Sheriff Adonai, but Misief was not aware that his picture was hanging in the local Sheriff's Office.

The deputies interrupted Misief's meanderings as they began the booking process. Deputy Gore took a seat at the desk and began filling out the paperwork. He asked Misief various questions about the events that had occurred the previous night at the saloon. Deputy Zeke took the money and the brown leather bag and locked them both in a safe located in the corner of the room. Misief feared someone might steal his leather bag and his treasures that were hidden away inside. The leather bag and its contents were his most prized possessions.

Concerned, Misief asked, "Are you sure nobody will take my bag?"

Deputy Zeke shook his head and said, "It will be here waiting for you."

As the deputies continued methodically carrying out each step in the booking process, another lawman that stood about six foot, two inches tall came in through the front door.

Deputy Zeke acknowledged the lawman and said, "Good news Sheriff, we found him; and we also found part of the stolen money. This boy was sleeping at his cabin when we arrived. We searched the place and found the stolen money stuffed inside a leather bag."

This lawman's name was Sheriff Tim Martin. Sheriff Martin appeared to be in his late forties and was the current High Sheriff of Rock Springs. He had dirty blonde hair, sported a pearl white revolver and wore boots made of black bear skin. He took off his hat and hung it on the hook outside his office, which was behind the booking room.

The High Sheriff did not say anything to Misief but looked at him with disgust. Turning to Deputy Zeke, Sheriff Martin asked, "You guys got the other one too, right?"

Deputy Zeke nodded his head and said, "Yeah, we got 'em both."

Sheriff Martin approached Misief and said, "Looks like you are in a little trouble, young man. Now we do things fair around here, and you'll get a chance to defend yourself in a few days. Judge Frye will be coming through, and he'll preside over your trial. Until then, you are gonna be locked up."

Misief responded, "But Sheriff, I didn't steal any money."

Sheriff Martin walked over to the safe and looked at the leather bag and the stack of money lying inside it. Then the sheriff turned to him and asked, "Son, did the deputies find this bag and this stash of money in your cabin?"

Misief replied, "Yes sir."

Sheriff Martin continued, "Was there anybody else there at the cabin with you last night?"

Misief looked down at the floor and shook his head, "No sir."

"Well I don't know what it looks like from your side of the room, but I sure wouldn't want to be in your shoes," Sheriff Martin stated as he stared directly at Misief.

Sheriff Martin then asked, "Is there anybody you want us to contact to let them know you are here?"

The High Sheriff knew the story of Misief's father all too well, but he was not going to mention it at this time. He also knew that Misief's mother had just recently passed away.

Misief took a deep breath and said, "If anyone goes out by Davis Williams' place, would you mind telling him that I am here, and ask him to take care of things around the cabin until I get back? I also asked the deputies to send a message out to Davis asking him to take Coal home, and keep him until I get out."

Sheriff Martin reassured Misief that he would send a deputy out to inform Davis of his whereabouts later that afternoon. Then Sheriff Martin instructed Deputy Zeke and Deputy Gore to place Misief in the cell area as soon as they were finished with the paperwork.

Walking toward his office, Sheriff Martin turned back and gave one last instruction, "Keep the two of them apart—separate cells!"

****

Deputy Gore and Deputy Zeke led Misief up the stairway to the second floor. The upstairs of the building had several old rusty cells that appeared to be leftovers from an old European dungeon. Three walls of each cell were made of iron, with the back wall and the top made of rough cut wood. In addition to the cells, there was a room in the corner where the deputies took turns sleeping while on duty. The second floor was dimly lit and was filled with the pungent aroma of dirty manhood. It was apparent the men locked up in the Rock Springs jail were not afforded much opportunity to partake in personal hygiene.

The back wall and the ceiling of each cell were littered with carvings, sketches and messages from those who had previously inhabited these rooms of incarceration. The only furnishings in each cell were a set of wooden bunks and a couple of old blankets. Other than that, it was a totally empty space. Entering the cell, Misief glanced across the hallway and caught a glimpse of Billin. Based on the conversation downstairs between Sheriff Martin and the two deputies, Misief assumed Billin had been picked up.

As soon as Billin saw Misief, he blurted out, "So they got you too. You ain't confessed to nothing, have you?"

Misief looked at Billin sarcastically, but didn't respond at all. Everything Billin said last night at the saloon was comical, but there was nothing funny about what was happening now. After removing the handcuffs and leg shackles, the deputies secured the door to Misief's cell and went downstairs.

Billin again asked in a loud voice, "You ain't ratted on me, have you partner?"

"I ain't anybody's 'partner'!" Misief replied.

Billin continued, "You didn't mention me at all, did you?"

"I ain't told anybody anything. How'd they find out about me anyway?" Misief asked in a hushed voice.

Billin stated, "I don't know yet. Somebody must have seen something, but I just don't know who it could have been."

Misief looked over at Billin and said, "They have my part of the money. They found it in my leather bag when they searched my cabin."

Billin shook his head in disgust, "How stupid, Misief. Why didn't you hide it when you got home?"

Misief mumbled, "Can't say I remember getting home."

Billin laughed out loud, but Misief wasn't amused in the least bit. He was already wishing he'd never met the likes of 'Billin Macdo'.

Misief stared at Billin and thought silently, "I just met this guy yesterday, and he's already got me locked up in jail!"

For the next several hours, Misief sat alone in the dirt infested cell, while Billin kept calling over to him, trying to spark a conversation. Misief was in no mood to talk to Billin, but that did not keep Billin quiet.

"Hey partner, talk to me!" Billin shouted over and over.

Finally disgusted, Misief replied, "I done told you, I ain't your partner, and I ain't interested in talking to you!"

Billin just kept on talking to anyone who would listen, and Misief did his best to ignore everything that Billin was doing and saying. He sat there in disbelief and wondered how he had allowed himself to get involved with someone as obnoxious and misguided as Billin Macdo.

****

Later that afternoon, the door to the stairway opened, and Deputy Zeke entered carrying a single tray in his arms. On the tray were plates of food and several tin cups filled with spring water. The deputy placed the plates on the floor and pushed them into the cells with his foot. He then handed each prisoner a cup of water through the cell bars.

As he turned to walk out, the deputy said, "I'll be back in a few minutes to collect the plates and cups. Eat up men."

Misief looked down at the plate of food that was lying on the floor. He could not clearly identify what was on the plate, but it looked like oatmeal or grits with a piece of cornbread on the side. The food didn't look the least bit appetizing, but he hadn't eaten a bite all day, so he decided to give it a try.

Misief picked up the spoon that was embedded in the mush and took a bite. Whatever it was, the food had the consistency of sticky paste and appeared to be a blend of several grains such as oats, barley and grits. The taste was rather bland, but before he knew it, most of it had disappeared from the plate. The cornbread was the best part of the meal, and Misief saved it until last. After washing down the last bite of cornbread, Misief pushed the plate and cup back under the cell door.

After a while, Deputy Zeke came back upstairs. "Was it good?" the deputy asked in a sarcastic voice as he collected the empty dishes.

Misief didn't respond to the deputy's snide question. He acted as if he didn't hear him and simply wandered over to the corner of the cell.

Still tired from the long night of partying, Misief decided to take a rest on the wooden bunk. He rolled up the old blanket that was lying on the bed and placed it under his head. Staring straight up at the wooden ceiling in the cell, he admired the artwork left by the inmates that had graced this space before him. As he read each name, each slang phrase, and each set of personal initials, Misief pondered the journey that had gotten him into such a mess. Glancing across the ceiling, then moving his eyes down the back wall, he noticed someone had carved 'R.I.P.' on the cell wall, and he thought to himself, "I sure don't wanna die in this place."

****

As evening shadows faded into the shimmer of darkness, Misief's eyes began to get heavy. He was moments from drifting off to sleep when he caught a glimpse of a familiar inscription on the ceiling, right above the door. He hadn't noticed it earlier that afternoon when he was admiring the artwork that donned the cell walls. He jumped up to get a better look, and sure enough, etched deep into the fibers of the wood were the initials *'L.B.'*!

Now wide awake, Misief placed his finger on each letter as he pondered the thought of Lucas Benson actually being locked up in this cell. As his finger rounded the top of the letter 'B', he thought back to all the damage brought upon his life by Lucas. He desperately wished he could locate this elusive man. After several minutes of hypnotic focus on the initials, he turned and walked back to the wooden bunk. Lying down, he rotated his head to get one last glimpse of the initials.

Although Misief was totally exhausted and needed to rest, sleep completely evaded him on his first night in jail. Consumed with the thoughts of Lucas and the uncertainty of his future, he wrestled in the darkness. Endless thoughts flowed through his mind like the water cascading over the rocks in Roberts Creek.

Misief Stone began the previous day as a young man bound only by his refusal to let go of the brokenness of his past. Now matters had become drastically worse, as he found himself alone in the darkness, held captive by the rusty bars of an old jail cell!

Chapter 14

"Guilty"

October 12, 1863

Seven long days had passed since Misief's arrest for allegedly stealing money from Tomar Reeves after a wild night of carousing at the saloon. He remained locked in a dirty cell waiting on the arrival of Judge Frye to hear his case and pronounce a verdict.

Misief was completely miserable in jail. He hadn't slept more than an hour or two per night since he arrived, and the only food he'd eaten was the mush-like substance the deputies religiously served the inmates three times a day. Billin was still in the cell across from him, and his constant nonsense was wearing on Misief's nerves. More than anything else, Misief simply wanted to make it all go away and for the authorities to let him go back home to his cabin. He missed the time he spent with Nainsi; he missed his own bed; he missed his beloved horse, Coal; and most of all he missed his freedom. He didn't like being locked up, nor did he like to be told what to do and when to do it. His incarceration felt like he was nothing more than a wild animal in a cage!

To add insult to injury, Misief's once private cell was now occupied by two other men. The first was a man by the name of Jack Drew. He was brought in during the middle of the night three days after Misief was locked up. Jack was supposedly wanted for attempted bank robbery in another town and was picked up by the Rock Springs deputies. He didn't talk much and spent most of his time sitting quietly in the corner. The second man was brought in a day later; his name was Clive Black.

Mr. Black was an older gentleman with a patch over one eye. He had a thick mustache that extended down over his lower lip. He wore leather chaps with fringe down both sides of the legs and a black ten gallon hat. Misief wasn't sure what Clive was accused of, but he found him quite amusing. Clive was an awesome storyteller and was always sharing the details of his life's adventures. Misief wasn't sure all of Clive's stories were true; nevertheless, it was far better than the nonsense Billin kept spouting from his cell across the hall.

Right before lunch, Deputy Gore came up the stairway and opened the door leading to the cells. He got everyone's attention and announced, "Judge Frye's in town. He's headed to the café to get a bite of lunch. Once he's done eating, he'll be holding court. Misief, Billin, you boys get ready because you will be his first case."

This was the announcement Misief had been waiting to hear for the last week. He wanted his chance to plead his innocence in front of the judge. He desperately wanted to prove to everyone that he didn't steal the money. But most of all, he wanted to get out of this dark, smelly jail cell!

Deputy Gore and Deputy Zeke soon returned with two sets of leg irons, two pair of handcuffs and a large, round rusty key ring that held the keys to all the locks in the jail.

Deputy Gore spoke up and ordered, "Billin, turn around and face the back of the cell. Place both hands above your head with your fingers laced together. Now, spread your feet apart, and do not move."

Billin complied with Deputy Gore's instructions. Deputy Zeke unlocked Billin's cell, and both lawmen walked inside. Deputy

Zeke grabbed Billin's right hand and twisted it behind his back. He snapped a handcuff on his right wrist and then grabbed his left arm to fasten the second cuff on his left wrist. You could hear the teeth on the ratchet click as the deputy squeezed each cuff to ensure they were securely fastened.

Deputy Zeke then prepared to attach the leg irons while Deputy Gore stood watch to make sure Billin did not resist. Bending down, the deputy placed the irons around each of Billin's ankles and then led him out of the cell. They placed Billin with his back against the wall and instructed him to stand perfectly still and say nothing while they removed Misief from his cell.

The two deputies prepared to enter the cell holding Misief, Jack and Clive. Deputy Gore instructed Jack and Clive to step away from the door and take a position against the back wall. He told the two inmates to face the wall and place their hands on their heads. Deputy Gore then instructed Misief to sit on the floor with his back to the cell door. Once the three inmates were positioned to the deputies' satisfaction, Deputy Gore unlocked the cell door.

Deputy Zeke gripped Misief from behind and said, "Get up slowly and walk backwards."

Misief didn't open his mouth and did exactly as he was told. Deputy Zeke backed him out of the cell one step at a time until they were both clear of the cell door. Now standing outside the cell, Deputy Gore quickly locked the cell door to ensure Clive and Jack would not hinder this process.

Misief was led across the hallway to the empty cell where Billin had been staying. Inside the secured cell, Deputy Zeke applied the handcuffs and the leg irons to Misief in the same manner they had used on Billin. Once both Misief and Billin were tethered in chains, the deputies led them toward the door leading to the stairway.

The walk down the stairway was painstakingly slow and difficult. With both legs fastened with leg irons, Billin and Misief did their best to maneuver each step. Arriving safely at the bottom, the lawmen led the two accused young men into the courtroom to face the judge.

The walls of the courtroom were completely covered with dark oak panels, and there was an oak railing separating the spectators from those who were actual participants in the courtroom proceedings. On each side of the room there was a table with four or five chairs, reserved for members of the prosecution and defense. Beyond the oak railing was a series of wooden benches which were filled with locals from Rock Springs who came to witness the trial.

Front and center in the room was an elevated platform with a desk for the presiding judge. To the left of the judge's bench was a row of chairs dedicated for potential jurors. On the right side of the judge's bench was a place earmarked for the deputies to stand guard to ensure each trial could proceed without disruption.

Deputy Gore and Deputy Zeke led Misief and Billin to the table on the left side of the courtroom facing the judge's bench. The onlookers were silent as the accused shuffled into the courtroom with their feet bound. The only sound was the rattling of the chains that served to keep the young men from running out of the building in search of instant freedom. Once Misief and Billin were seated, the deputies took their place standing to the right of the judge's bench.

Misief glanced over his shoulder and caught a glimpse of a couple of faces he recognized. Seated on the second row were Davis Williams and Misief's sister, Ashel. Misief didn't verbally respond but nodded his head to acknowledge their presence. Davis waved back to let him know he was there to support him.

One row behind Davis sat Tomar who had come to witness justice take place. He was not fond of Misief before all this occurred, and now he was bent on seeing these boys pay dearly for their crime.

Then Misief's heart sank as he scanned to the rear of the courtroom and noticed who was sitting on the very back row. It was his girlfriend, Nainsi. He'd hoped to keep his arrest a secret from her, but apparently word of his incarceration had spread throughout Rock Springs rather quickly.

Trying to mentally get away from the reality of what was happening, Misief thought back a few days earlier, when he sat on the bench in front of the café and held Nainsi's hand. He remembered the warmth of her touch and the feeling he felt in his heart as he courted her. He hadn't yet told her that he loved her, but he knew something special was blossoming between them. As he sat there in utter shame, bound up in iron shackles, Misief wondered how life had so quickly gone wrong. In this moment of disgrace, he didn't acknowledge Nainsi's presence in the courtroom and acted as though he hadn't noticed her at all.

Misief's interest in those who were seated in the courtroom galley came to an abrupt end when a man in his late fifties with thinning hair entered the room wearing a black robe. The man was about as wide as he was tall and wore a pair of wire rim glasses with very thick lenses.

Deputy Gore moved forward and announced, "All rise."

At that moment everyone in the courtroom stood to their feet. Misief watched as the man, whom he assumed was the judge, took a seat behind the oak desk.

Deputy Gore then announced, "Court is now in session, Honorable Judge Frye presiding."

Deputy Gore stepped back, and everybody in the courtroom was seated. The judge took a moment to organize the paperwork on his desk. Then he peered out over his glasses and called out, "Billin Macdo, are you present?"

Billin replied, "Yes sir judge, right here."

Judge Frye looked at Deputy Gore and said, "Deputy, would you kindly lead Mr. Macdo to the bench."

Deputy Gore took Billin by the arm and led him to the judge's desk.

Judge Frye began, "Mr. Macdo, as I read over the report, you have been charged with stealing money from Mr. Tomar Reeves at the saloon. I also understand your father has come forward to report the crime and has turned in your share of the stolen money."

Billin was totally unaware that his father had found the cash and turned it over to the authorities. He thought it was safely hidden where nobody would ever find it. His countenance changed as he realized he was in real trouble and might not be able to weasel his way out of this situation.

Judge Frye continued, "Mr. Macdo, how do you plead to the charge of stealing money from Mr. Reeves?"

Billin paused for a moment as the wheels turned in his head. Until now, he felt he could beat the charges against him since the lawmen did not find the money on him, and they did not have any witnesses who could prove his guilt. Billin was completely caught off guard when the judge announced his own father had led the authorities to him.

With this in mind, Billin responded, "Guilty, sir."

Judge Frye pronounced, "I sentence you to nine months in the Rock Springs Jail. In addition, you must pay back Mr. Reeves double what you stole from him."

The judge picked up his gavel and with a swift motion, he pounded it down on the wooden desk and stated, "Case closed. Take him back to jail to serve out his sentence."

Deputy Zeke led Billin out of the courtroom and back to his cell. Misief was blown away at how fast all this was happening. He had entered the courtroom with hopes of convincing the judge that he didn't steal the money, but he didn't have any tangible proof that Billin was the actual thief.

Before he could fully gather his thoughts, he heard Judge Frye call out, "Misief Stone are you present?"

Misief stood to his feet and said, "Here, sir."

Deputy Gore led Misief to the front of the judge's desk just like he'd done for Billin. The judge pulled out the documents and said, "Mr. Stone, this report states that you were in cahoots with Mr. Macdo. You both were in the saloon when the money was stolen from Mr. Reeves. The report also indicates the deputies discovered some of Mr. Reeves' money in your bag when they came to your cabin the next morning. Is this true?"

Misief took a deep breath and replied, "No sir, judge, ah, that ain't exactly how it happened. You see, I didn't steal any money. Billin, uh… well, Mr. Macdo stole the money during the fight that broke out at the saloon. I met up with him after the brawl, and he showed the money to me. He gave me some of the money to hold for him, but I didn't steal it, honest I didn't."

Judge Frye paused, and then repositioned his glasses before he spoke, "Young man, do you think this is the first time I've ever been in a courtroom?"

Misief replied, "No sir."

Judge Frye was getting annoyed and had no tolerance for what he perceived was a young man trying to lie his way out of trouble.

"Mr. Stone, if you didn't steal the money, why did you take it from Mr. Macdo when he offered it to you?"

"I don't know. I guess I shouldn't have," he replied.

Judge Frye inquired further, "Do you have any proof or witnesses to back up your story, Mr. Stone?"

"No sir, I don't. It was the two of us that was there that night. You just gotta believe me. I didn't steal the money."

Judge Frye paused again as he combed over the details of the report. While the judge was silently reading, Misief caught a glimpse of someone standing in the corner of the courtroom. He couldn't believe what he was seeing as his eyes locked on the mysterious, but familiar stranger. This lawman appeared out of thin air and had on the same white cowboy boots Misief had witnessed on previous occasions. The stranger didn't budge or utter a sound. He just watched the courtroom proceedings like an interested spectator. Misief looked at the others in the courtroom to see if anyone else noticed the stranger, but no one else seemed to see him standing there.

"Is this lawman just a figment of my imagination?" Misief wondered. "Am I just imagining this stranger, or is he real?"

Continuing to keep his eyes locked on the stranger, Misief thought, "But the bullet on Coal's saddle—I didn't imagine that! I know that's real, so this stranger must be real too!"

Questions regarding the stranger bombarded his mind as Judge Frye contemplated his decision. Misief wondered why this stranger continued to show up at all the critical moments in his life. He began to replay each occurrence with the stranger one by one;

"I saw the stranger the night my father was killed."

"Then, I saw him in Doc Lynch's office the night I broke in and stole the medical supplies for my mother."

"The third time I ran into him was on the way back to the cabin right before my mother died."

"He was in my kitchen the morning after I drank all that whiskey."

"And now he's right here in the courtroom. I wonder what he wants and why he keeps bothering me."

Misief quickly shifted his attention to the matter at hand when Judge Frye cleared his throat and said, "Mr. Stone, quite frankly I believe you were a willing participant with Mr. Macdo in the theft of the money from Mr. Reeves. Maybe you were not the one, who actually took the money, but you admitted to being involved in the fight at the saloon the night the money was taken, and witnesses saw you there with Mr. Macdo. The fight certainly could have been a diversion so that Mr. Macdo could take the money without being caught. The report indicates you were the instigator of the altercation in the saloon. If you had been innocent, I would have expected you to take your part of the money back to Mr. Reeves that night or at least have been forthcoming with the deputies when they questioned you about the missing money. But you didn't take it back, and you didn't tell them about the money until they discovered it in your leather bag. Whether you actually took the money or not, is irrelevant. Based on the evidence, I find you were an accomplice to stealing the money from Mr. Reeves. Therefore, I find you guilty. Your sentence will be the same as that of Mr. Macdo, nine months in the Rock Springs Jail, and you must pay back Mr. Reeves double what you stole from him."

With that proclamation, Judge Frye brought down the gavel against the wooden desk. That sound of the gavel smacking the desk echoed in Misief's stunned mind as he realized he was headed back to jail.

Judge Frye offered one more bit of advice before Misief was escorted out of the courtroom. "Mr. Stone, if by chance you are actually innocent as you say, let this be a lesson to you to do a better job of selecting your friends. Associating with the wrong people will always get you in trouble and take you down a road to destruction."

Misief nodded in agreement but didn't say anything in response to the judge. He dropped his head and stared at the floor in disbelief at what had just happened. Out of the corner of his eye, Misief saw the stranger still standing in the room. The stranger stared back at him with tender and compassionate eyes, and somehow Misief felt the stranger believed his claim of being innocent of stealing the money. Then, all of a sudden, the stranger turned, took one step forward and vanished as quickly as he'd appeared.

As Misief shuffled slowly across the floor, he looked around and realized that Davis and Ashel were still in the courtroom. His eyes scanned the back of the room for Nainsi, but he could not find her. He wondered when she left.

Did she leave when she heard the judge's verdict?

Was she present to hear him explain his version of the story and proclaim his innocence?

Would she ever give him another chance?

Misief wondered if he would ever see Nainsi again. He feared his poor choices might have forever ruined his relationship with her.

He was only a couple of steps from being completely out of the courtroom when Davis and Ashel caught up with him. Deputy Gore paused for just a moment allowing Davis the opportunity to speak, "Misief, we will come see you while you here."

Misief responded, "Thanks Davis. Will you go by the livery stable, and get Coal for me? Will you take him with you, and take care of him and things at the cabin until I get out?"

"Sure thing," Davis replied. "The deputies already told me to pick Coal up for you while I was in town. He'll be waiting for you when you get out."

"Misief went on, "And…make sure you take care of her too," he stated as he winked at Ashel. Ashel winked back at her big brother as a tear strolled down her face.

Deputy Gore told Misief it was time to go and directed him up the stairway to the cell that would become his home for the next nine months.

With each eight inch rise in the stairway; with each clank of the leg irons; Misief felt the weight of his decisions come crashing down on him. He had not mentally prepared himself for the possibility of being found guilty. He was fully confident his innocence would win out. He was now extremely angry with Billin for dragging him into this mess. He wondered why Billin didn't take responsibility for stealing the money, and tell the truth to the judge.

Deputy Gore led Misief to the top of the stairs and met Deputy Zeke who was standing outside the cell waiting for them. Billin was already locked away inside his cell, and he watched in curiosity as Misief returned from the courtroom and appeared to be headed back to his own cell.

The deputies separated Misief's legs as wide as the chains would allow. Then Deputy Zeke reached down and unlocked the leg irons. With Misief's legs free, Deputy Gore unlocked the cell door and instructed him to walk inside. Next, Deputy Zeke instructed Misief to turn around so he could unlock his handcuffs. .

Now that Misief was free of restraints, the deputies told him to stand in the far corner and face the wall.

Misief stood perfectly still in the corner, while the deputies began the methodical process of securing leg irons and handcuffs on Jack and Clive who were sharing the cell with Misief. It was now their turn to go before Judge Frye and face the charges that were levied against them.

Misief spoke up and said, "I sure hope you fellas have better luck than I did."

Clive turned back and asked, "What happened, kid?"

Misief replied, "The judge didn't believe my story. He didn't believe I was innocent."

Clive laughed and said, "Well heck fire boy, you know we're all innocent! There ain't any of us guilty!"

Misief was not in the mood for Clive's humor and sat down on the bunk as the deputies took Clive and Jack downstairs to face Judge Frye.

Once the deputies were out of sight, Misief hollered over at Billin and asked, "Why didn't you tell Judge Frye that I didn't have anything to do with stealing that money?"

Billin snickered and replied, "Why Misief, I couldn't have done it without you! You helped me steal the money just like you helped me get that watch from the Trading Post. You are the best at creating a distraction, so I can get what I need. Don't you see—we are a team!"

Misief became furious! He could feel his blood boiling. With eyes projecting darts of hatred and anger, he yelled, "I didn't help you steal that watch, and I didn't have anything to do with stealing that money, and you know it!"

Billin just laughed and said, "You're my partner Misief, we are in this business together!"

Misief exploded and began beating the cell bars with his fists and screaming like a mad man. "I hate you Billin Macdo! We are not in anything together! And I ain't your partner! You better thank your lucky stars that I can't get my hands on your right now! If I could, I'd choke you 'til you died! You sorry, good for nothing, worthless piece of horse crap!"

Misief paused a moment and walked to the edge of the cell and stared right at Billin. With demonic contempt, his voice shifted to a growl as he methodically stated, "Billin, you can mark it down—when I get out of here, I'm gonna make you wish you were never born!"

Misief turned and began pacing back and forth in his cell as he continued screaming obscenities at Billin. His rage blew into a full blown tantrum as he started kicking the cell doors and the walls. His outburst became so loud that it interrupted the proceedings going on in the courtroom below.

Deputy Gore stormed in through the door and shouted, "You better hush up, boy! This is your home for the next nine months! You better get used to it, and learn to control yourself!"

Misief calmed down a bit as Deputy Gore provided this final warning, "Boy, don't make me come back up here. I promise it won't be good for you if I have to come back!"

Misief nodded at the deputy and sat down on the bunk. With his face blood red, he stared at Billin with demonic hatred beaming from his eyes. At that moment, Misief mentally added the name, 'Billin Macdo', to his revenge list.

Misief spent the rest of the afternoon sitting in his cell boiling mad at the world. Somehow, someway, someday—all of those on his revenge list, including Billin, would regret the day they ever messed with him. The baggage in Misief's life was increasing; the choices he was making were taking him deeper into trouble; and his refusal to let go of the pain of his past was flowing through his veins like the venom of a timber rattler. Misief knew he might have to wait nine months to execute justice, but there was definitely a day of reckoning in store for all those on his list!

Chapter 15

"Life Behind Bars"

October 19, 1863

Misief took a pencil he'd found and walked over to the back wall of the cell. He placed a vertical line beside the other marks he'd made on each of the previous six days. This mark on the wall represented the seventh day of his two hundred and seventy-four day sentence.

Turning toward Clive, Misief proclaimed, "One week down and only two hundred and sixty seven days to go!"

Clive Black was found guilty the same day as Misief and was sentenced to one year in jail. Jack Drew had been transferred to another town to stand trial for additional charges, so Misief and Clive had spent the last week locked up in the cell together.

Misief spent the last few days simply trying to adjust to his new life behind bars. His days were now an endless cycle of playing cards with Clive, thinking about his girlfriend Nainsi, and pacing back and forth inside the cell. He'd completely resisted engaging in any type of dialogue with Billin, but that hadn't stopped Billin from trying to talk to him. Luckily for Misief, two new inmates had been brought in by the deputies and were placed in the cell with Billin. This gave Billin someone else to focus on, which was a welcomed relief to Misief.

A day or two later, Misief and Clive were following their normal daily routine and were engrossed in a game of poker when all of a sudden the door to the stairway opened. Deputy Gore and

Deputy Zeke walked in escorting a middle aged man who was bound in leg irons and handcuffs. The deputies led the man to the front of the cell and instructed Clive and Misief to stand and face the back wall with their hands up high over their head. Clive and Misief immediately placed their cards on the floor and obliged the instructions of the deputies, and with the cell secure, Deputy Gore walked the man inside and unshackled him as Deputy Zeke stood guard.

Deputy Gore slammed the iron door shut and said, "Okay boys, the show's over, you fellows can go back to what you were doing."

Misief and Clive turned around to get their first glimpse of their new cell mate. The man was a bit timid and was standing in the far corner, looking a bit dazed about what had just happened. For several minutes none of them said a word and just stared at each other.

Misief broke the awkward silence and introduced himself to the man. "My name's Misief Stone," he said, offering to shake his hand.

The man hesitated at first, but then reached out and shook Misief's hand and said, "Hello son. My name is Jamison, Jamison Hunt."

"Hello Mr. Hunt," Misief replied.

Jamison was about five feet, four inches tall and couldn't have weighed more than one hundred and thirty-five pounds. His eyes were crystal blue, and his hair had prematurely turned a dark shade of gray. His long beard covered most of the wrinkles in his tired, weathered face. He was wearing mismatched clothes that were tattered and old, and a couple of toes on his left foot extended through a hole in his worn out boot. Based on Jamison's appearance, Misief guessed his age to be near sixty, but later would discover that Jamison was only forty three years old. It was obvious this was Jamison's first time in jail, and he was clueless as to what he was supposed to do next.

The three inmates spent the next few minutes getting to know each other with high level conversation. Clive and Misief did most of the talking while Jamison just nodded and listened. Misief offered to let Jamison take his lower bunk since Jamison wasn't the tallest man he'd ever met, and seemed to be a bit frail. Jamison accepted Misief's generosity and walked over to lie down on the bunk.

Misief didn't intend to gawk at Jamison, but he couldn't help but wonder what in the world this man could have done to end up in jail. Jamison didn't look like a criminal or appear to have the ability to hurt anyone. He was polite and spoke with a gentlemen's charm. He looked like a typical father that, instead of being locked up, should be at home with his family telling bedtime stories to his children.

While Jamison napped on the bunk, Misief and Clive went back to playing cards. Trying to keep his voice down, Misief whispered, "What do you think he's in for?"

Clive dealt the cards and laughed, "Misief, I already told you—we're all innocent! He ain't done anything wrong!"

Misief replied, "Oh Clive, I ain't kidding. Look at him—he doesn't look like a criminal to me."

Clive retorted, "You can't go by looks Misief. We criminals come in all shapes, sizes and colors!"

After a brief twenty minute nap, Jamison woke up. He yawned once, rubbed his eyes and then stood up to stretch.

Clive looked over at Jamison and asked, "Mr. Hunt, you sure didn't sleep very long. Do you wanna join us in a game of cards?"

Jamison stroked his long beard, looked at Clive and Misief with his warm blue eyes and said, "Boys, you don't have to call me Mr. Hunt. You can just call me, Jamison."

Clive replied, "Ok, Jamison, do you wanna join us for a game of poker?"

Jamison responded, "Oh, I don't know. I never learned how to play cards. You boys go ahead, and I'll watch you."

Clive nodded, and the poker game continued without interruption. But, the curiosity regarding Jamison's past was driving Misief insane! He desperately wanted to know what crime Jamison committed to land himself in jail.

Another hour or so passed as Jamison quietly watched Clive and Misief play poker. Misief was waiting for the right opportunity to ask Jamison about his past, but he couldn't figure out how to ask him without seeming nosey.

His curiosity finally got the best of him and Misief stated, "Well, I get out in two hundred and sixty five more days. Those liars accused me of stealing money from Tomar Reeves at the saloon, but I didn't do it."

Jamison didn't take Misief's bait. He nodded to acknowledge Misief's statement, then just sat quietly and watched as the two men played cards.

Misief spoke up, "Jamison, I get out in two hundred and sixty five more days."

Jamison looked at Misief and then posed this question, "So tell me young man, have you learned anything to keep you from coming back to jail?"

This was not the response that Misief wanted. He didn't want to dig into his own background; he wanted to find out more about Jamison.

Misief pointed across the hallway at Billin and replied, "Yeah, I did Jamison. I learned to stay away from that low-life."

Jamison simply nodded, but did not offer any additional information.

"Clive's in here for pulling a gun on a stage coach driver," Misief stated as he looked over at Clive.

Clive added, "But I didn't pull the trigger."

Clive and Misief chuckled together, but Jamison didn't even crack a smile. It seemed he had something very serious on his mind.

Finally Misief boldly blurted out, "So tell us Jamison, what crime did you commit to get locked up?"

Jamison lowered his head when he heard Misief's question. Shame overwhelmed him as he mumbled, "Let's just say I did something bad," Jamison replied, "Real bad! And leave it at that!"

Based on his obvious remorse and broken spirit, Misief thought Jamison must have committed a violent crime like murder. He then asked, "Did you kill somebody?"

Jamison stared at the cracks in the wooden floor of the cell and didn't initially respond. It was obvious he was in emotional pain and didn't want to talk about the details related to his incarceration. Finally, Jamison shook his head and said, "I didn't kill anyone, but I might as well of killed all three of them."

Tears began to trickle down the wrinkles on Jamison's weathered face and into his long beard. Misief could see Jamison was emotionally broken and didn't ask him anymore questions. Misief had never witnessed a grown man cry before in all his life. His father had always taught him that real men don't cry or show their feelings, and he felt a little uncomfortable as Jamison openly exposed his inner emotions. Without a clue as to what crime

Jamison had committed, Misief could tell this man was truly sorry for his actions.

As evening gave way to the blackness of night, Misief could hear Jamison crying in the darkness. Jamison was a broken and remorseful man—struggling to break free from the sins of his past.

****

Early the following morning the deputies delivered breakfast, which was the usual 'mush-like' oatmeal substance, to all of the inmates. Misief continued his normal routine of taking the pencil and making another tic mark on the wall. "Two hundred and sixty four days to go," he announced to anyone who was listening.

Since the day Misief first discovered 'L.B.' carved in the cell, he'd wanted to ask the deputies if they knew anything about the carvings. As Misief tracked the date on the wall, he got the attention of Deputy Zeke and asked, "Hey Deputy, can I ask you a question?"

"What is it?" Deputy Zeke asked.

Misief pointed to the initials on the cell wall and said, "I noticed 'L.B.' carved in the wall. Do you know if these initials might belong to a man named Lucas Benson?"

"Oh yeah, I'm sure they do. I know Lucas well," the deputy replied, "He's is in and out of jail all the time. It's hard to keep him away. Sometimes I think he does things just to get locked up!"

Deputy Zeke headed back downstairs while Misief continued staring at the 'L.B.' etched into the grain of the wood.

"I sure wish Lucas would show up while I'm here," Misief mumbled.

Jamison peered up from eating his breakfast and said, "Young man, if you know what's good for you, you'll steer clear of Lucas Benson!"

"What's that?" Misief asked.

Jamison paused for a moment, took a bite of oatmeal and then replied, "Listen to a man who has been tricked by Lucas one time too many. Leave him alone!"

Misief replied, "How did Lucas trick you?"

Jamison shook his head and stated, "That ain't important. Just take my advice, and leave him alone!"

In youthful arrogance, Misief responded, "Just tell me what Lucas did to you, and I will get him back! Lucas ruined my father's life, and I'm searching for him. And, when I find him, I'm gonna make him pay for what he has done to my family!"

Jamison reached his hand out to Misief and said, "Son, your foolishness is gonna get you killed. If you only knew what I've been through, you'd listen to me, and leave that crazy man alone."

"You can save your breath! I ain't giving up until I get him!" Misief declared.

Jamison was unaware of Misief's deep seeded desire for vengeance. He didn't know that this young man had spent most every waking moment of the past six years dreaming of the day when he would get even with Lucas Benson. It had become the essence of his broken existence. This misguided endeavor had robbed Misief of any hope of peace in his life. In his twisted way of thinking, he held to the belief that he would not experience real peace until judgment had been delivered to all those who brought pain into his life.

Realizing his plea was falling on deaf ears, Jamison gave up talking to Misief about Lucas. Broken from his traumatic experience, Jamison crouched down on the floor in the corner of the cell and began crying. Misief could hear Jamison mumbling something as he sobbed but was not sure what he was saying.

Trying not to be obvious, Misief slowly moved a little closer to Jamison to see if he could make out what he was saying. Now standing only eighteen inches away, Misief heard Jamison mumbling, "If only I'd listened to Sheriff Adonai... If only I'd listened to Sheriff Adonai........" Over and over Jamison repeated the same phrase as tears rolled down his face. "If only I'd listened to Sheriff Adonai."

Misief slid down the wall and sat down beside Jamison and asked, "Jamison, do you know Sheriff Adonai?"

Jamison wiped his face, took a deep breath and nodded his head. "Yeah, I know all about Sheriff Adonai. But I was too stupid to listen whenever anyone tried to talk to me about following him."

Misief replied, "I've got a few friends that seem to know about Sheriff Adonai. My girlfriend Nainsi has a book called 'The Album'. It has stuff about Sheriff Adonai written inside. And, I met a man named Sachiel Jackson who works at the town well. I think he knows a lot about him too."

Jamison spoke up, "You know Sachiel?"

Misief replied, "Yeah, one day when I was asking Nainsi about Sheriff Adonai, she told me that Sachiel was the one I needed to talk to. I didn't get to spend much time with Sachiel, but he did say Sheriff Adonai was responsible for starting the entire Western Frontier."

"He told you right," Jamison stated. "It was Sheriff Adonai's plan for the west to be the best place in the world. Many years ago, you didn't have all the chaos you have today. When Sheriff Adonai started the Western Frontier, all the plains were filled with beautiful green pastures. Long horn cattle roamed everywhere without the need for barbed wire fences. Watering holes flowed with crystal clear water, and everybody had plenty to eat. The land was peaceful, and the coyotes roamed wherever they wanted, with the little children walking right beside them."

"It's sure not that way anymore! What changed?" Misief asked.

"Lucas Benson—that's what changed everything!" Jamison replied.

With a puzzled look on his face Misief asked, "Everybody keeps warning me about Lucas Benson and telling me stories about how he tricked them out of their possessions and ruined their lives. Tell me how I find this Lucas fella, so I can put a stop to it!"

Jamison shook his head from side to side and said, "Boy, Lucas has already found you. He's the one responsible for you being in this ole' jail cell."

Jamison sighed and said, "Heck, its Lucas that is responsible for me being in this nasty ole' jail!"

Jamison placed his head between his knees and once again starting singing his remorseful song, "If I'd only listened to Sheriff Adonai.....If I'd only listened to Sheriff Adonai."

Misief tried to squeeze more information from Jamison, but his mind was focused on his failures. He knew he would be locked in the same cell with Jamison for several more months. With that in mind, he decided to let the issue go for the night and wait for another day to glean more facts from Jamison about Sheriff Adonai.

****

November 18, 1863

It was the middle of the afternoon on a chilly November day when Deputy Zeke came through the stairway door with a visitor walking behind him. To Misief's surprise, tagging along with

Deputy Zeke was Davis Williams. Davis had come into town specifically to check in and see how things were going.

"Misief, this man is here to see you," Deputy Zeke announced.

Davis walked up to the cell and through the bars, shook Misief's hand.

"How are you doing?" Davis asked.

"I'm doing okay," Misief answered. "The food ain't too good, but I'm gonna make it. How is Ashel doing?"

Davis replied, "Considering everything, I think she is doing alright. She's trying to adjust to life without her mother and without you. I won't lie; it's been hard on her. Some days she cries a lot, and other days she seems to be doing better. We try to keep her busy, to keep mind off everything that has happened."

Feeling responsible for Ashel's pain, Misief looked down and said, "Davis, she's sure been through a lot for a little girl. It just doesn't seem fair does it?"

"No, I guess it doesn't," Davis said as he leaned back on the wall across from the cell. "Sometimes we just have to make the best of the cards we're dealt. Tammy and I will be there for her. And she's gonna need you too, Misief."

Misief nodded in agreement, "I know that. There ain't much I can do for her as long as I'm locked up in this jail cell. Will you tell her that I promise to come see her as soon as I get out?"

"I sure will," Davis replied.

For the next fifteen minutes Davis and Misief talked about hunting, the cabin, life in jail and Misief's horse, Coal. Davis reassured him by telling him that he had taken Coal to his place the day of the trial and that the stallion was in good condition.

"I think that horse misses you," Davis joked.

"I miss him too!" Misief proclaimed. "That horse is my best friend in the world!"

Misief motioned for Davis to move closer to him and through the bars he whispered, "Davis, it's important to me that you know that I did not steal that money. I was with Billin the night it was stolen, but I didn't take it!"

"I believe you Misief," Davis replied. "Let's just learn a lesson this time, and be real careful when selecting our associates!"

Misief nodded in agreement.

About that time Deputy Zeke came back through the door and said, "Your time to visit is up Mr. Williams."

Davis stared straight at Misief, winked and whispered, "You take care of yourself!"

"I will," Misief replied.

As Davis followed Deputy Zeke through the door, Misief hollered, "Davis, give Ashel a hug for me?"

Davis shouted back, "You got it!"

Misief moseyed over to the corner of the cell and slid down the wall to the floor. He crossed his arms and placed them on his knees, burying his head in his arms. For the next hour or so, he remained slumped in the floor torturing himself over all the mistakes he'd made in his life. An overwhelming rush of guilt swept through his entire being as recalled all his broken promises.

He thought about the promise he'd made to his dying mother, reassuring her before she died that he'd watch out for and take good care of Ashel. A promise filled with well meaning intentions—but the reality was that he'd hardly seen his sister since his mother passed away. His mind screamed accusations and filled his countenance with condemnation, as he remembered every detail of his past failures. He longed to close his eyes and make all his pain go away, but no amount of dreaming was going to change the fact that he would remain locked in this cell for several more months.

January 21, 1864

The holiday season had come and gone; being alone in jail during Christmas had been extremely hard for Misief. It had been over two months since Davis had stopped by to visit with him. Every day seem to be just like the one before; it started with mushy oatmeal and water, then a combination of playing cards, talking to the other inmates until there was nothing left to say, dreaming of loved ones and longing for the day when he would finally leave this nasty place. Each morning Misief took the broken pencil and etched another mark on the wall. One hundred and seventy six more days to go and he would be a free man!

As Misief swallowed the last bite of breakfast, the door leading up from downstairs opened and to his surprise, there stood High Sheriff Tim Martin and right behind him was Misief's girlfriend, Nainsi!

Sheriff Martin began, "We normally don't allow women folk in here, but she's been insisting to come see you, and her father said it was alright. I'm gonna leave this stairway door open, and I will be back in just a few minutes."

As Sheriff Martin turned to walk downstairs, Nainsi took off her coat and walked sheepishly toward the cell where Misief was housed. She'd never been inside the sheriff's office and definitely never experienced the deplorable conditions of the cell area. The whole jail scene was unsettling to her. The inmates in the cell across the hall began to whistle and make off colored vulgar comments. Nainsi tried to ignore their crude language as she focused her eyes on Misief. It broke her heart to see him locked up in jail. She had grown so fond of him, but this situation had caused her to question the possibility of them having a future together.

Coming closer to his cell, Nainsi asked, "How are you doing, Misief?"

"I'm doing okay. A little over six more months and I'll get outta here," he exclaimed.

"I wanted to visit you sooner, but they wouldn't let me," she admitted.

Nainsi took a deep breath and then said. "Misief, I've been wondering about all the things I heard during the trial. All of this has been troubling my mind, and I just don't understand why…..I mean…I thought you were a good guy, and I felt like we had such a great time on the bench outside the café. Then the next day I heard you'd been arrested. I came to the trial believing that there was no way you had done what they had accused you of doing, but then the judge found you guilty. I just don't know what to think….."

Misief took Nainsi's hand. At first he did not say anything; he just reminisced as he felt the warmth of her soft skin.

Clearing his throat, he began by whispering, "Nainsi, you gotta believe me, I didn't steal the money. Do you remember that day on the bench at the café?"

Nainsi nodded.

Misief continued, "After you went back to the mill, I stayed in town for a while longer. Shortly after you left, I met a guy by the name of Billin Macdo. Don't look, but he's in the cell across the hall. Well, Billin and I spent the day together, and at first he seemed like a nice guy. Later that night, we ended up at the saloon. A fight broke out, and he stole the money from behind the bar while everybody was fighting. We both left the saloon on horseback about the same time. When we got to the edge of town he stopped, and that's when he passed off half of the money to me. I shouldn't have taken the money from Billin, but I'd been drinking and wasn't thinking clearly, so I took the money home with me that night. The next morning the deputies found the money in my leather bag when they came to my cabin. I promise I didn't steal the money."

Nainsi replied, "Why were you in the saloon?"

"I made a mistake Nainsi," Misief pleaded, "I'm sorry. You gotta forgive me, Please!"

"Misief," Nainsi said with her head bent down, "I didn't wanna bring it up, but when we first met, everybody warned me about you. They told me about your father, and they told me you would end up just like him. They all said that I should stay away from you. But, I told them you were different. I told them you were a caring, kind and sweet man. Now everyone, including my father, wants me to stay away from you. I had to beg him to let me come to the jail to talk to you today."

Misief wasn't sure how to respond or what to say. For a few minutes he just stood there looking at her, searching for the right words. He wished they were in a more private setting, so he could talk openly with her. But Misief knew he better plead his case before Nainsi turned and walked out of his life forever!

Finally Misief responded, "Nainsi, I am a good person, you gotta believe me. I care so much about you and would never do anything to hurt you. I just made a bad choice. I am begging you to give me a second chance. Please?"

Nainsi grabbed Misief's hands and standing face to face, with only the bars separating them, she replied, "Misief Stone, I'm gonna give you a second chance! But you have to promise me that you'll never go back in the saloon or hang out with that Billin fellow anymore."

"Oh, I promise!" Misief agreed.

Misief and Nainsi stood there staring into each other's eyes and caressing hands until Sheriff Martin came up to tell her it was time to leave. Misief feared this might be the last time he would see her until his release, which was six more months away.

"Come here," Misief whispered. He cupped his hands around her face and whispered, "Nainsi, I love you."

Nainsi's smile stretched from ear to ear as she whispered, "I love you too."

Misief didn't want to let go of Nainsi's hands. As the vivacious brunette backed away from the cell, his heart felt like it was going to break. The sound of her footsteps walking down the stairway brought a renewed sense of regret for his foolish behavior. He closed his eyes and tried his best to capture a mental image of her long curly hair, those big chocolate brown eyes and the mint green dress she was wearing. He inhaled a deep breath in, in an attempt to smell the fragrance of her perfume as it lingered in the air. He wanted to forever remember her and was hoping they could soon pick back up where they left off, before all this 'jail stuff' had happened.

This cold January morning began with him believing his relationship with Nainsi was as frigid as the outside air; but her visit had warmed his spirit and given him a renewed sense of hope.

Chapter 16

"An Innocent Man Murdered"

July 12, 1864

Nine months had passed since Judge Frye threw down the gavel and announced the verdict, "Guilty! You are sentenced to serve every single day of your time in the Rock Springs Jail!"

On that brisk October afternoon, when the cell door slammed closed behind him, Misief began counting the days until he would be a free man again. He started each day by taking a pencil and making a single line on the wall of his cell. Each pencil mark represented a day served and was a constant reminder of how close he was to freedom.

This final day would begin the same way; however if everything went according to plan, this day would end very differently than all the others! This was the day he'd dreamed of since they'd locked him away last fall!

"This is my last day! I get out of this joint in just a few more hours!" Misief proclaimed enthusiastically.

"What are you gonna do first?" Clive asked.

"Just breathe man, just breathe in the fresh air," Misief replied, as he took a deep breath and patted his chest, showing his cellmates how he'd inhale the fresh air once he got outside.

"After I get my fill of fresh air, I'm gonna go find Nainsi and see if she will go out on a date with me," Misief stated.

Misief jabbered non-stop! He talked about wanting to check on Ashel, and he spoke of his excitement to see his beloved Coal—

talking about him as if the horse was actually human. Jamison listened intently as Misief carried on all morning about what he was going to do once he was released.

Once Misief finished rambling, Jamison pointed his bony finger at him and said, "Just be careful boy. Don't do something stupid and end up back in jail with me and Clive."

Misief bragged, "Don't worry—you won't see me back here ever again!"

****

As the morning faded away and lunch was complete, Misief knew it was drawing close to his time of release. Over the last few months, he'd grown close to Jamison, but he could not get him to open up about the nature of his crime, or talk about Sheriff Adonai. Misief felt like Jamison knew more than he was sharing and desperately wanted to get as much information from him before his opportunity was over. He decided to try one last time.

Hoping to catch Jamison in a good mood, Misief walked over, sat down beside him and said, "Jamison, as you know I'm leaving in a little while. You and I have become good friends during our time here. I sure would like to know more about Sheriff Adonai before I leave. I didn't know if you might be willing to tell me more about him before I go?"

Since the first day when Jamison talked openly to Misief about Sheriff Adonai, Jamison had been very hesitant to discuss the subject. But now, Jamison knew Misief would be leaving soon, and he thought it was time to share with him the story of the great High Sheriff.

Jamison nodded his head and said, "Okay, I'll tell you whatever you wanna know."

Misief exclaimed, "I wanna know everything—everything about Sheriff Adonai that you can tell me."

Jamison sat on the edge of his bunk and asked, "Misief, when the deputies brought you in, did you happen to notice the picture of Sheriff Adonai hanging on the wall downstairs in the front office?"

Misief nodded and said, "Yep, I did."

"Did you see the picture below it?" Jamison asked.

"If I did, I don't remember it," Misief replied.

"When they release you today, they will take you through the front office. As you walk through, pay close attention to the picture hanging right below the one of Sheriff Adonai. Hanging directly below the picture of Sheriff Adonai is a picture of Sheriff Edgar Manuel," explained Jamison.

"Okay, I'll stop and take a look at it. Now tell me everything, I'm all ears," Misief said as he leaned closer to Jamison, not wanting to miss a word.

Jamison took a deep breath and began to share a very strange story with Misief. The story went like this:

A very long time ago, Sheriff Adonai created the entire western frontier with his own hands! It was a spectacular place filled with budding flowers and emerald green trees. The valley floor was filled with all types of cattle, buffalo, sheep and chickens; with all the animals coexisting in perfect harmony.

The first family that settled here was selected by Sheriff Adonai, and let me tell you, they had it made! Sheriff Adonai promised that their lives would be perfect if they remained obedient to his ways and followed his laws. Life for this first family was incredible! They didn't ever get tired; they did not have to work for a living, and anything they wanted was right at their fingertips! Life was good!

However, it wasn't too long until the first family disobeyed Sheriff Adonai by eating something that had been forbidden. Not too long after this first act of disobedience, the land experienced its first murder. As time passed, the Western Frontier became populated with more and more settlers. These settlers had no regard for Sheriff Adonai and completely stopped following the laws he had set in place. Wickedness became the normal way of life. Outlaws started roaming the entire prairie, robbing and killing innocent folk. Men started fighting over the land and stealing each other's cattle. Saloons popped up in every town, filled with scantily clad ladies who enticed the men to come in to drink whiskey and engage in shameful acts with them. Sheriff Adonai was upset with how things were going on the Western Frontier, so he sent a lawman named, Sheriff Edgar Manuel, from the main office to the frontier, to enforce the law and to teach the people how to live right!

Here is how Sheriff Edgar Manuel arrived on the Western Frontier; it was a beautiful moonlit night when a very pregnant young girl was traveling through the wilderness with her husband. Her husband, a carpenter by trade, walked alongside his wife as she rode on the back of an ole' mule. The couple was headed to his hometown so he could check in with the local officials and register as part of an ongoing census.

Along the way, this young girl gave birth to a baby boy in a stranger's barn. She named her son Edgar Manuel, a name given to her from Sheriff Adonai. Edgar Manuel grew up and took on the role of High Sheriff. In so many ways, he was just like Sheriff Adonai!

Sheriff Manuel did his best to teach the people the laws as outlined by Sheriff Adonai. He spent his time doing good deeds and always helped the hurting people. He was a caring man and always had time for those who were in need. The sad thing was that only a few folks seemed to care about what Sheriff Manuel had to say.

Sheriff Manuel tried to explain to the people that he had been sent by Sheriff Adonai and that he was authorized to speak on Sheriff Adonai's behalf. Most of the folks did not believe him, and soon many people wanted him dead!

Jamison paused and shook his head, as a tear dripped down his face.

"What's wrong Jamison?" Misief asked. "What happened to Sheriff Manuel?"

Jamison continued:

Sheriff Manuel was in the town of Stone Ridge, which is about fifty miles north of Rock Springs. He rode into town on his horse, and some of the local folks lined both sides of the road and waved at him as he rode into town. Several of them were ecstatic that the High Sheriff had come to visit their little community. But, there were those who opposed everything Sheriff Manuel stood for—these people were under the evil influence of Lucas Benson.

"LUCAS BENSON!" Misief shouted, as his heart rate elevated. "Did you say Lucas Benson?"

"Yep, that's what I said. Now hold on, let me finish," Jamison scolded.

"Yes sir," Misief replied.

Jamison cleared his throat and continued:

Ole' Lucas Benson wanted Sheriff Manuel killed and tried several times to lure him into his trap. Sheriff Manuel was too wise and crafty to fall for any tricky temptation of ole' Lucas. So, one day Lucas decided to try a different approach. He began making his case with the local authorities, trying to convince them that Sheriff Manuel was a trouble maker.

Misief asked. "How did Lucas do it?"
Jamison raised his eyebrows and explained:

Lucas Benson is crafty serpent! He can talk a man into doing almost anything! Lucas persuaded the local people and the authorities in Stone Ridge that Sheriff Manuel was claiming to be Sheriff Adonai himself. Well, let me tell you, that didn't sit well with many of the folks in the territory, especially the ones who still followed the teachings of Sheriff Adonai and held him in high regard.

The local authorities decided to set an ambush to capture Sheriff Manuel. They wanted to bring him in for questioning about these outlandish accusations of him saying he was Sheriff Adonai. But Sherriff Manuel blended in with the crowd and snuck away.

"Whoa—that's smart," Misief said.
Jamison nodded his head and said, "Hang on Misief! I'm not finished."

One day the unthinkable happened when one of Sheriff Manuel's own deputies ratted him out. For thirty silver coins, the turncoat, back-stabbing deputy provided the government officials with inside information of the whereabouts of Sheriff

Manuel. Later that night, they found and arrested the sheriff and drug him in to be interrogated.

When the authorities asked Sheriff Manuel if he was claiming to be Sheriff Adonai, he looked them straight in the eye and said that he and Sheriff Adonai were 'one in the same.' When Sheriff Manuel made that statement, they all got enraged. They considered it a crime unto death to claim to be Sheriff Adonai.

Misief squirmed a little and asked, "But Sheriff Adonai sent Sheriff Manuel to the Western Frontier, right?"

Jamison shook his head and continued. "You're exactly right. But the folks in Stone Ridge didn't believe Sheriff Adonai had sent Sheriff Manuel. They accused the sheriff of false impersonation and started screaming for him to be executed."

"Executed? I thought Sheriff Manuel was trying to help the people. Why would they want to kill him?" Misief asked as became more engrossed in the story.

Jamison stood up and began pacing back and forth in the cell as he continued.

Sheriff Manuel was helping the folks. He made the sick ones feel better and fed those who were hungry. But his actions just didn't sit well with some of the higher ups who claimed to be followers of Sheriff Adonai. A local lawyer was fuming mad about all this, so he contacted a shady judge who set up a mock trial around midnight.

"Midnight!" Misief exclaimed. "I didn't know they hold court at midnight!"

Jamison replied, "They don't. Not unless they are trying to pull some funny business. In the dark of night, with very few in the room, the crooked judge grilled Sheriff Manuel extensively, demanding that he renounce his claim to be one with Sheriff Adonai."

"Did Sheriff Manuel change his statement?" Misief asked.

"Nope!" Jamison replied. "Sheriff Manuel stood strong and wouldn't change his claim of being one with Sheriff Adonai."

Misief asked, "What happened then?"

Jamison hesitated and then said:

The judge demanded they give Sheriff Manuel a severe beating to see if they could 'knock some sense' into his head! They stripped most all of the sheriff's clothes from his body and took him out behind the livery stable. After tying him to the fence so that he could not get away, they beat the sheriff with a horse whip until the blood from his back puddle in the dusty western soil.

Misief couldn't help but interrupt again. "That ain't right," he said.

Jamison replied:

No, it ain't right. Misief, they beat the sheriff until they almost killed him, but there was nothing those blood thirsty animals could do to make Sheriff Manuel waiver. He knew who he was and what he was sent to do! He knew he was 'Sheriff Adonai' in the flesh. He knew that he had been sent to the Western Frontier to bring a new sense of peace to the prairie.

Later that night, they paraded Sheriff Manuel around in his underclothes, trying to humiliate him. Half naked, they forced a hat made of briars on his head. The men present shouted out, 'look at the High Sheriff' as they spit tobacco juice in his face. Black and blue from head to toe, nasty chewing tobacco spit all over his face and drenched in blood, they forced Sheriff Manuel back into the courtroom. The judge then asked the sheriff again if he still claimed to be one with Sheriff Adonai. Sheriff Manuel did not respond at first, but then nodded that he still claimed to be one with Sheriff Adonai.

The spineless judge spoke up with the verdict and said, "Sheriff Manuel will be put to death, 'Stone Ridge' style.

Misief sat there on the cell floor and whispered, "That just don't seem right." Looking up at Jamison, he asked, "Did they kill him?"

Jamison nodded and continued telling the gruesome story:

Early the next morning, they made Sheriff Manuel climb all the way up Possum Hill, which was a mile or so outside Stone Ridge. They tied the sheriff to a pole with his feet stacked one on top of the other, bound tightly together. There was a wooden cross beam towards the top of the pole, and the men stretched the sheriff's arms out each way, tightly securing his arms by placing a rope around each wrist.

The executioner was dressed in black, from his black cowboy hat to his shiny black boots. He walked up to Sheriff Manuel and revealed to him the .50 caliber weapon he planned to use to enforce the judge's verdict. Sheriff Manuel showed no fear; he wasn't even mad at the executioner who was about to pull the trigger and bring an end to his life. Some of those who were standing by, actually heard Sheriff Manuel whisper a prayer of forgiveness for the executioner before he ever fired the first shot!

Misief butted in, "Wait a minute! Did you say the executioner had a .50 caliber weapon?"

Jamison replied, "Yep, that's what he used."

Misief sat in silent contemplation as Jamison continued:

The executioner circled Sheriff Manuel and scoffed with the local outlaws that had gathered to watch the killing. Enjoying the sight of a lawman dying, the outlaws shouted out in a sadistic tone encouraging the executioner to hurry up and fire the first shot. In a barbaric fashion of killing, the executioner aimed the barrel of the gun at Sheriff Manuel's head for several minutes. The crowd, which was growing by the minute, cheered even louder for the executioner to fire the weapon, and kill Sheriff Manuel.

The executioner lowered the weapon from Sheriff Manuel's head and pointed it toward his feet. Then a blast echoed in all directions, as the executioner fired the first shot through the feet of Sheriff Manuel. The sheriff grimaced, his eyes closed, as intense pain shot through every fiber of his body. The bullet ripped through his flesh, shredded muscle into stringy pieces of threads, exposed nerve endings and blew the bones of his feet into tiny shrapnel. Blood gushed out of the gaping hole in his feet and poured out onto the dusty ground.

Jamison could no longer control his emotions and had to take a break. Tears flowed down both sides of his face as he tried to recount the details of the brutal execution of Sheriff Manuel.

"Don't stop now," Misief said as he moved closer to where Jamison was standing.

Jamison inhaled several deep breaths, and then continued by saying:

> *The executioner stalled a few minutes as he taunted and laughed at Sheriff Manuel's agony. Then the executioner walked up to the bleeding sheriff and, in a cruel joking manner, asked him if his feet were hurting. The sheriff did not speak a single word. The crowd cheered the actions of the executioner, treating him as if he were their hero. Everyone knew that Sheriff Manuel had to be in excruciating pain, but no one showed any remorse.*
>
> *Ready to get the show moving forward, the executioner aimed the mighty .50 caliber weapon at the inside palm of the sheriff's right hand and squeezed the trigger. The gun discharged with a thundering blast. Once again, Sheriff Manuel hollered out in agony and just about passed out from the pain! His hand had a hole blown clean through the center of it, so big you could see daylight from both sides. His blood ran out of the open wound, dripping onto the ground below.*

Jamison paused for a moment, ran his fingers through his hair and resumed the story:

> *Sheriff Manuel was in intense pain, but the executioner wasn't about to quit yet. He set his target on Sheriff Manuel's left hand and let out a blood curdling laugh as though he was enjoying delivering the deadly punishment. With a grin on his face, he blasted a third shot which blew a gaping hole through the left hand of the sheriff. The executioner strutted six steps*

forward, and then twisted around to admire his work. Heartless, he yelled, "Who is going to save you now, Sheriff?" The crowd roared in laughter as the executioner continued to verbally banter the dying sheriff.

Sheriff Manuel was an innocent man. He wasn't guilty of anything. Through all the torture and pain, he offered forgiveness to the executioner; to the judge; and even to the insulting crowd. He knew death was closing in on his body. The life giving blood was pouring out of his body like an overflowing creek in a spring rain storm. Soon his life on this earth would be over, but in his heart Sheriff Manuel knew he'd fulfilled his purpose and completed the job he'd been sent to do by Sheriff Adonai. He remained compassionate to the people of the Western Frontier, and his love for them never wavered.

"It just doesn't seem right," Misief said in a low voice.

"It wasn't right. But as I understand it, this was all part of Sheriff Adonai's plan," Jamison explained.

"So that day Sheriff Manuel died?" Misief asked.

Jamison nodded and continued:

The sun beamed down from above as the executioner yanked out a twelve inch knife from his belt. He held the blade over his head to catch the reflection of the sun, and then he turned it from side to side until the glare was reflecting directly into the eyes of Sheriff Manuel. With his hands wounded and bound to the wooden beam, there was nothing Sheriff Manuel could do to protect his eyes from the blinding beams of light. It was just another sick way the executioner found to torment the dying sheriff.

Sheriff Manuel's breathing became shallow as his life slowly faded away. About that time, the heavens were filled with the blackest clouds the world had ever seen. It became eerie outside as the entire Western Frontier went completely dark, right in the middle of the day. Only moments from death, in a final act, Sheriff Manuel raised his head and looked up into the western sky. With strength that was motivated by his love for the people, the sheriff looked upward and yelled out, "Sheriff Adonai, I have done what you sent me to do. My work here is finished."

As soon as the words left the lips of the dying sheriff, his head fell forward, and his body collapsed. The bleeding from his feet and hands subsided as his precious heart beat for the final time. The executioner charged over to the sheriff's body with his twelve inch knife clutched in hand. He plunged the knife into Sheriff Manuel's side, shredding it wide open. All his innards and blood gushed out of the gigantic opening. As the bodily fluid splashed on the executioner's boots, he hooted and hollered, "We won Lucas! We won!

"So the executioner worked for Lucas Benson?" Misief asked. Jamison explained:

I'm not exactly sure, but based on what I understand, he either worked for Lucas Benson or was operating under the influence of Lucas. Either way, it cost the sheriff his life. Right after the executioner cut him with his knife, the crowd began celebrating by shooting their rifles and pistols in the air! For about fifteen minutes it was as if all of hell was rejoicing, as they had successfully killed the one who was sent to the Western Frontier to save them.

Then it all went completely quiet as the whole earth shook! Lighting flashed in all directions as the agent of death swept over Possum Hill. The sound of their celebration was annihilated as fear swept over the mountain and through the valley. Some even considered the possibility that Sheriff E. Manuel might have been telling the truth. But it was too late—the sheriff was dead!

They left Sheriff Manuel's lifeless body tied to the post for several hours. Now that the killing was over, the crowd lost interest and started leaving. One by one, they journeyed back to their homes and places of business.

Misief broke in and asked, "Didn't Sheriff Manuel have any friends at the execution?"

"Not many," Jamison confessed. Then he continued:

But there were a handful of people there who dearly loved him. His mother stayed right by his side through it all. Watching all of this happen to her son just tore her heart to shreds. The sheriff also had a few deputies that believed in what he was trying to do, but they weren't man enough to stand up against the local authorities. They just stood by and watched as he was brutally murdered.

Around sundown, a couple of Sheriff Manuel's supporters, who wanted to give him a proper burial, proceeded to the office of a local official and asked for permission to take the sheriff's body down off the pole. The official agreed, so they retrieved his body and cleaned off some of the dried blood before burying him in a grave that had been dug for somebody else. They found a large river rock and placed it at the head of the grave. On the rock they wrote,

"Sheriff E. Manuel.
High Sheriff of the Western Frontier"

Jamison was overcome with emotion and bowed his head, crying uncontrollably like a child who had unintentionally disappointed his parents. In Jamison's mind, he knew the killing of Sheriff Manuel was nothing more than a cold blooded murder. He was certain they had killed a man who was only trying to teach the people how to live honorable lives. But evil schemes had won, bringing an end to the sheriff's life. Most of all, it broke Jamison's heart when he thought of the actions of his own life and the impact his actions had on Sheriff Adonai and what he was trying to accomplish for the people of the Western Frontier.

Misief knew Jamison was emotionally drained from recalling the story of the murder of Sheriff E. Manuel. He suspected the tale did not end with the burial of the sheriff, and he desperately wanted to find out if there was more to the story. He wondered if there might be some clue that would assist him in his quest to find Lucas Benson. He gave Jamison a moment to gather himself and then asked, "Okay, so his friends buried him in somebody else's grave. What happened after that?"

Jamison lifted his head. His eyes began to sparkle as he proclaimed:

Before Sheriff Manuel's death, he told those closest to him that if he was ever killed not to worry one bit because he was going to rise from the dead! He made this statement on several occasions, and even the local authorities in Stone Ridge heard about his claim that he would rise from the dead. The authorities feared that the sheriff's friends might sneak out to the grave at night and steal his body to make it appear as though he did come back to life. So, to make sure that didn't happen, the authorities ordered armed guards to stand watch over the grave, day and night!

On the morning of the third day, some of Sheriff Manuel's friends went to the grave to pay their last respects. The guards were still on duty watching over the grave, but to everyone's surprise, the grave was completely empty! The dirt was sunk in, and the sheriff's body was gone! There was nothing left but a three-by-six foot hole in the ground!

Jamison paused again and immediately Misief asked, "So somebody did steal his body?"

Jamison shook his head and said, "Oh no, nobody stole his body. The guards never left their post. Just like Sheriff Manuel promised, he came back to life! Over five hundred folks claimed to have seen Sheriff Manuel alive after that day. Some people ate with him, and a few even touched him to prove that he wasn't a ghost! Believe me; Sheriff E. Manuel came back to life! And he's still alive……even today."

Misief leaned his head against the wall as he contemplated the viability of this tale. Jamison knew Misief had his doubts about whether this was a factual story or just another western myth. He knew Misief would have to determine for himself if he believed Sheriff E. Manuel was a real living person or just a fabled super hero.

Misief didn't want to insult Jamison, but at face value it did seem like a far-fetched story coming from a broken man. He thought the story seemed somewhat plausible, until Jamison got to the part about Sheriff Manuel coming back to life.

Pondering it all, Misief asked, "Jamison, if Sheriff Manuel is alive, where is he right now?"

Jamison answered, "He's with Sheriff Adonai. He promised to come back to the Western Frontier one day, and when he does return, it will forever change things around here."

Misief did not know what else to ask. Jamison had obliged him by telling him the story of Sheriff Adonai and Sheriff Manuel. Whether he chose to believe the story or not would be something he would have to determine on his own.

Jamison tapped Misief on the shoulder and said, "Son, just stay open about all of this. There is so much going on in your life that you can't see or touch or even explain. But promise me that when you get out, you'll think about what I've told you."

Misief replied, "I promise."

Jamison continued, "You also told me that you have a copy of 'The Album'. Promise me that you will at least read it for yourself. Don't take my word for it; read it, and see if I ain't telling you the truth. That book has the entire story and much more!"

Misief promised Jamison he would read The Album and then reached out and shook hands with him. He thanked Jamison for sharing the story, even though at the moment it didn't make too much sense. Misief still wondered why Sheriff Manuel would be so nice to those who killed him. He couldn't grasp why the sheriff loved the people so much—people who did not return the love back to him. Being raised by a hardnosed father, this type of forgiving behavior was certainly not the way he had been taught. At this moment, he had no intentions of forgiving anyone and was determined to get vengeance on those who had brought pain into his life!

About that time, Deputy Gore walked in and asked, "Misief Stone, are you about ready to get outta here?"

Misief leapt to his feet and replied, "You bet I am!"

"Alright, let's go," the deputy stated.

Misief gathered up the few belongings he had in the cell. Then he walked over to Clive and gave him a hug as he bid him goodbye. Clive had been a good friend and always had a tale that made Misief laugh. Clive had sure assisted in making the time in jail pass by much quicker.

Then Misief turned his attention to Jamison; this man had almost become a father figure to him. Jamison was nonjudgmental and always encouraged Misief to straighten out his life. As the two men drew near to each other, Jamison through open his arms and embraced Misief with tears streaming down his cheeks. Whispering into Misief's ear, Jamison said, "Misief, I've completely ruined by my life. I'm afraid Sheriff Adonai will never forgive me for the horrible things that I have done. But you, you are still young, and your crime is nothing more than petty theft. I beg you; make your peace with Sheriff Adonai soon. Don't end up a dumb old fool like me!"

As Misief turned to walk out of the cell, he actually wished he had more time to better understand what Jamison was trying to convey. He wondered what Jamison had done that had created such a bad relationship between himself and Sheriff Adonai.

Deputy Gore unlocked the cell door, and Misief walked through a free man. As he made his way down the stairs to the lower floor of the sheriff's office, his mind flashed back to all the events of the last nine months. He could hardly believe the nightmare was finally over.

Downstairs, the deputies had all of Misief's possessions waiting for him in the front room. As he walked toward the door, Sheriff Tim Martin spoke up and warned, "Keep yourself outta trouble son. I don't wanna see you back in here any time soon."

Misief answered, "Yes sir, I will."

Before exiting the office, Misief took a moment to glance at the pictures of all the previous lawmen that lined the walls. Just like Jamison had said, right below the picture of Sheriff Adonai was a picture of Sheriff E. Manuel. As he stared at the picture, he thought back to the story Jamison had just shared with him regarding the cruel murder of Sheriff Manuel.

Grabbing the doorknob, Misief turned back and said, "You guys take good care of Jamison!"

Deputy Gore replied, "You obviously don't know what he's locked up for do you?"

"No, he wouldn't tell me," Misief replied.

"Well, Jamison ain't as nice as guy as you seem to think. He's done some awful bad things, and he finally got caught," the deputy explained.

Misief was curious and asked, "What'd he do?"

"You just wait; his story will eventually come out," was all Deputy Gore would say.

Misief walked out the front door of the jail still perplexed as to the nature of Jamison's crimes. On the surface Jamison appeared to be harmless, but apparently there was far more to the story than he was willing to share. All Misief knew for certain, was that Jamison cried a lot, and seemed to be truly longing for forgiveness!

Now free of iron bars and shackles, Misief felt like skipping down the center of the main street! He made a beeline for the livery stable to reunite with his beloved horse, Coal. As he walked down the road there were numerous thoughts roaming around in his head. He wondered where he might find Sheriff Adonai, so he could tell him how sorry Jamison was for the things he'd done wrong. He wasn't certain how long Jamison would be in jail, but based on the deputies comments, Misief assumed Jamison would have to spend the rest of his life paying for his offense.

Wandering down the road, Misief absorbed the fresh air and paused to allow the gentle breeze to blow through his hair. Freedom felt good to his dirty, dry skin. In his mind he began to prioritize all the things he wanted to do now that he was free. First on the list would be to find Lucas Benson; followed by visiting his sister Ashel, as he had promised. Then he wanted to see Nainsi and spend time with her. But first things first, it was time to retrieve Coal from the livery stable and get back out to the cabin to see if he could restart his life!

Chapter 17

"Freedom"

July 12, 1864

The livery stable was just a couple of buildings down from the Rock Springs jail and was managed by a young man named Lopez.

Lopez was of Spanish descent and had thick, black, curly hair which was bundled up on his head with a red-plaid cotton rag. The cotton rag bulged on all sides, but did its best to keep the large volume of hair pulled back out of his face, as Lopez tended to the animals.

Misief walked inside the stable and noticed Lopez standing inside the first stall beside a beautiful Palomino stallion. It appeared he had just finished bathing the animal and was now brushing down its velvet coat.

"Excuse me," Misief interrupted.

Lopez stopped brushing, whirled around and replied, "Yes, sir. My name is Lopez. What can I do for you?"

Misief replied, "Hello Lopez, I'm Misief Stone. I just got outta jail and my friend, Davis, was supposed to drop my horse by here earlier this week. He's a black stallion that goes by the name of Coal."

"Oh yeah, he's here. He's a good looking horse. I've got him in the back," Lopez stated in his Spanish accent.

As they walked through the stable, Misief quickly spotted Coal and ran ahead of Lopez to greet his old friend. He leapt up on the fence and made his way to Coal's side. "Hey buddy, did you miss me?" Misief asked as he gave the horse a big hug.

After settling up with Lopez, Misief placed his belongings in his saddle bag and mounted up. He directed Coal out of the livery stable and rode slowly through the middle of Rock Springs, paying close attention to the sidewalk and storefronts, in hopes that he might catch a glimpse of Nainsi.

Passing the last building, Misief was disappointed that he did not see the young damsel anywhere in town. She was not sitting on the bench that graced the front of the café, nor did he see her as he peered through the office windows of her father's sawmill. He thought about stopping in at the mill, but decided to wait until he could find out for certain if Nainsi's father was comfortable with him being around her.

When Misief cleared the town of Rock Springs, he gave Coal a light nudge and immediately the stallion responded. His powerful legs exploded into a mighty sprint as Misief held on with all his might. While Coal couldn't verbally converse, it was obvious the horse was excited to once again be reunited with his owner.

Each thunderous hoof slapped the ground below, and dust flew everywhere as the pair quickly faded out of Rock Springs and into the unknown future. Pondering the decision for only a few seconds, Misief decided to take the shortcut over the mountain instead of traveling the long way around, through Shoots Valley. Not only would this be the quickest way home, but it also afforded him the opportunity to spend a few minutes on top of the mountain at a place he loved, called 'Rock Pointe'.

As the pair reached the base of the mountain, Misief slowed Coal to a walking pace, and he carefully guided the stallion along the rocky trail that led to the top. Fifteen minutes after they began the ascent up the mountain, they arrived at Rock Pointe. He brought Coal to a halt and loosely tied the reins around a small dogwood tree that stood along the edge of the trail. With Coal secured, Misief walked out on the large boulder that extended out of the face of the mountain. From his vantage point high above the valley floor, he looked down at the town of Rock Springs, paying close attention to the small building that had served as his home for the past two hundred and seventy days. The jailhouse building was easy to discern from the other buildings that ran up and down Main Street, and as he stared at the jail, he vowed to never again make the mistake of crossing the gray line between right and wrong.

"I don't ever want to spend another night in there," Misief mumbled, as he searched for a place to rest.

The glow of the setting sun cast lengthy shadows throughout the valley as Misief laid back on the rock. It was a therapeutic experience to simply feel the warmth of the sun on his skin. As he soaked in the ambiance of the afternoon, he thought about how he'd always taken the little things of life for granted, and how amazing it was to just relax and enjoy the serenity of nature as the gentle breeze blew across his face. For the next fifteen to twenty minutes the young cowboy paused to soak in his new found freedom!

Before long, the evening shadows began to invade. Not wanting to finish the journey home in total darkness, Misief knew he needed to get moving. Stretching a time or two as he yawned, he moseyed back over to the place where he had secured his horse. As he untied Coal's reins, he thought he saw a trace of a smile on the horse's face.

"Are you ready to go home, boy?" he chuckled, as he put his left foot into the stirrup.

Misief placed his hat on his head and repositioned the leather bag around his neck. Before departing the top of the mountain, he paused for a moment to make certain all his valuables were still in his possession. Opening the top flap he peered inside the bag to see the knife he'd purchased from Mr. Reeves at the Pawn Shop. He ran his finger across the initials of Lucas Benson which were inscribed on the handle. Below the knife was the wrinkled note—filled with Lucas' threatening words. The note served to remind Misief that Lucas was out to get him and that he better keep one eye looking over his shoulder.

In the very bottom of the leather bag was his copy of 'The Album', given to him by Sachiel the day he visited with him at the town well. Misief was relieved to know the deputies hadn't taken these items from him. Knowing all his treasures were safe in his leather bag, he nudged Coal, and the two made their way down the back side of the mountain.

With the last sliver of daylight dangling at the base of the horizon, Misief arrived home at his cabin. The first thing he noticed was how abandoned the property appeared. After the death of his mother, he had no interest in maintaining the cabin or the property. Now that he had been incarcerated for nine months, the landscape in front of the cabin was overgrown and snaky. The weeds had completely overtaken the garden and the fence rows. It was obvious the homestead was in desperate need of attention. As he led Coal around the cabin toward the stable, he knew he needed to get started working first thing in the morning.

Inside the stable, Misief patted Coal on the back and said, "Its sure is good to be home boy!"

After removing Coal's saddle, bridle and reins, Misief found some oats and filled the water bucket with fresh water.

"This will hold you until morning," he stated, as he secured the stable and headed for the cabin.

Misief paused, took a deep breath, and then went inside. At first glance, it appeared everything was just like he'd left it the morning the deputies escorted him to jail. His dirty clothes were still lying on the floor; the furniture was blanketed in a layer of dust; and the entire cabin had a musty scent from being closed up and empty for the better part of a year.

Misief lit several lanterns and checked out each room, one by one. After a full audit of the cabin, he was relieved to find that no one had ransacked the place while he was away.

His first challenge was finding something to eat. The kitchen cupboards were all but bare. He hadn't purchased, harvested or captured anything to eat since his mother's death, and before his arrest, he'd decimated the surplus of food that had filled the shelves in the kitchen. Scavenging every corner of the kitchen, he was able to scrape up a small portion of smoked meat and quart jar of corn. It wouldn't be a feast, but it would be much better than the daily plate of mush he'd endured while in jail!

Misief walked out behind the cabin, gathered up an armload of wood to fire up the cook stove and then retrieved a pail of water from the well. Once the fire was burning, he placed an iron skillet on the hot stove and sliced off several pieces of meat. The aroma of the simmering beef replaced the musty smell that had consumed the cabin. In another pot, he poured the jar of corn. With the food warming on the stove, he walked into the front room and opened the door to allow fresh air to circulate through the cabin.

Stepping out on the front porch, Misief noticed the gray plume spiraling skyward from the smoke stack in the kitchen and the warm glow of the lanterns shining brightly through the cabin windows. Even though his mother and sister were not with him, it felt so good to be home. While a couple of slices of smoked beef and a jar corn were a far cry from delicacies worthy of a banquet, just being free from the confines of the iron jail cell was reason enough to declare this evening a night of celebration!

****

The morning sun streaked through Misief's bedroom window waking him from a much needed night of rest. For the last nine months, his bed had been nothing more than an old wooden slab with a thin blanket serving as a mattress.

"Man, I slept great!" He declared as he rubbed his eyes a time or too. "It felt so good to sleep in my own bed!"

Pushing the covers off his body, Misief rubbed his eyes and stumbled through the cabin to the kitchen. The fire in the wood stove was still smoldering a bit, so he quickly split up a few pieces of wood for kindling and placed them on the orange embers. Next, he filled an old metal coffee pot with water from the well and placed it on top of the stove.

As he pottered around in the kitchen searching for the coffee, Misief noticed a teddy bear lying in the corner on the cabinet. Knowing the cuddly bear was out of its normal place, he picked up the stuffed animal and soon realized it belonged to his beloved sister, Ashel. With all his trips into the kitchen, he'd never noticed the toy animal and was completely clueless that his sister had purposefully placed it there the night she left to go live with Davis and Tammy Sue.

Misief picked up the bear and placed it against his nose. He closed his eyes and took in a deep breath as he thought of his little sister. He reminisced about all the good times they had at the cabin when they were younger. He remembered what a hard and devoted worker she was, as she did her part to help out by baking and cleaning. As he clutched the bear, he wondered how Ashel was doing with her new living arrangements. He recalled the promise he'd made to his mother before she died. Believing the bear was a sign, Misief was convinced that this was not the day to focus on the needs inside the cabin or outside on the property. Today, the most important thing was to honor the promise he'd made to his mother; it was time to go check on his little sister, Ashel!

****

It was midmorning when Misief arrived at the Williams homestead. Tammy Sue was outside hanging clothes on a cotton rope that was stretched between two maple trees. She was a cheerful, spirited lady, and her influence was a critical component in getting her husband, Davis, to focus his life in a positive direction. Peering over the clothes line, Tammy Sue was the first one to see Misief as he came riding up the road.

Tammy Sue greeted him saying, "Hello Misief! It's so good to see you! How are you doing?"

Misief replied, "I'm doing good Tammy Sue. How's Ashel?"

About that time, Ashel burst through the front door and raced toward her big brother. The two siblings embraced as tears streamed down Ashel's little face. Ashel was ecstatic to see her brother and refused to let go as she gripped him with both arms so tight!

Then Davis, who was busy working in his shop behind the house, came out to join in the reunion celebration. The scene in the front yard of the Williams home resembled a family homecoming as the four of them stood there reminiscing.

Once the time of greeting concluded, Tammy Sue stated, "Let me hang up this last pair of trousers, and then we can all go inside."

Turning to Misief, Tammy Sue asked, "Have you had breakfast yet?"

Misief hem hawed around and then said, "Well, I had some left-over meat last night."

"Let me fix you something to eat. Would you like to have some eggs, bacon and biscuits?" Tammy Sue asked.

Misief's mind drifted back to the stale bread and thick, cold mush served during his time at the jail. His mouth began watering as he thought about warm, homemade biscuits.

"Oh, yes ma'am, that would be great," Misief replied.

Davis, Ashel and Misief gathered in the front room and began catching up on all that had happened in the last nine months.

During the conversation, Davis asked, "So, how does it feel to be outta jail?"

Misief replied, "Man—you have no idea! It feels so good to be outta there."

Davis followed that question by asking, "Have you thought about what are you are gonna do with your life since you're out?"

Misief quickly responded, "Sorta...I met a man by the name of Jamison while I was locked up. I need to help him take care of something. Then, I've got to get started cleaning up the cabin. The weeds have taken over the place, and the stable is in bad shape too. The whole farm has gone down since mom's death. I was gonna get started today, but I walked into the kitchen this morning and found Ashel's bear on the counter. Well, finding the bear brought back memories, and I knew I needed to come see Ashel."

Ashel's smile lit up the room. "You found my bear?"

"Yep," Misief replied.

Pulling the bear out of his coat, he replied, "Here it is, I brought it for you!"

Ashel, who was sitting beside her brother, gave him another big hug as she took the bear from him. It was obvious Ashel missed her brother very much. Maybe it was the fact he was the only living family member she had left, or maybe she missed the times they spent together as siblings, but nevertheless, she never took her eyes off him or let go of him as they talked.

The aroma of sizzling bacon filled the entire Williams home as Tammy Sue labored away in the kitchen. The smell of breakfast cooking took Misief back to a time in his life when his mother, Bett, was still alive. Most every morning, Misief and Ashel's day began with a large meal prepared by their mother. Ashel would set the table while Misief went outside and tended to the critical early morning needs of the animals in the stable. Once his mother had breakfast all ready, Ashel would open the back door and call for him to come inside. Those were good days; past days; days that were forever etched into the fiber of his memories.

While Misief was momentarily lost in his daydreaming, Tammy Sue walked in and placed a plate on the table beside him.

"Thank you so much!" Misief stated as he eyed the hot plate of breakfast delicacies.

"Would you like some coffee?" Tammy Sue asked.

"That would be great," Misief replied.

"I'll get it!" Ashel declared.

Misief devoured the eggs, bacon and biscuits as the four of them continued catching up on all the news that had occurred during the last year. Misief was excited to hear that Davis had taught Ashel how to swim and that he had taken her on a couple of hunting trips. While Ashel stayed close to his side, Misief could tell his sister had adapted very well to her new life as a part of the

Williams household. It was comforting to know that his sister was living in a safe environment with people who truly loved her.

After spending several hours inside and enjoying lunch together, Davis, Ashel and Misief went outside and wandered around the farm. Ashel showed Misief the horse that she had learned to ride. It was a four year old buckskin mare that Davis had raised since birth. The horses' name was Shelly, and it was obvious that Ashel and Shelly had bonded.

"Do you wanna see me ride her?" Ashel asked.

"Sure!" Misief replied.

Like a veteran, Ashel demonstrated no fear as she displayed her equestrian skills, leading Shelly through several maneuvers including right hand turns, left hand turns and trotting.

After an impressive demonstration, Ashel excused herself to go inside and wash up. While she was away, Davis invited Misief to join him in the building where Davis had his scale shop. The two of them spent the next hour or so working together on a couple of broken scales that belonged to a local rancher. As they finished up, Davis looked at Misief and said, "Misief, my scale business is real good right now. I could sure use some help here at the shop if you would be willing to come work with me."

Misief was a caught off guard by Davis' offer. He thought about it for a moment, and then replied, "Uh, okay, thanks Davis. I'll keep that in mind. As you know, I have a lot that I need to do at the cabin. I don't think I would have time to come work with you right now."

Davis didn't push the issue. He simply responded by saying, "I understand, but if you change your mind, just let me know."

Davis knew Misief needed a positive start to his life, but he realized it was something the young man would need to do on his own. He knew that pushing Misief into this decision would not be possible or wise.

Misief again acknowledged Davis' offer and told him he would think about it. Davis felt like that was at least a step in the right direction. If Misief was willing to consider the idea, he thought he might be able to approach him again at a later time.

It had been a wonderful day! After a nice evening meal, Misief told them he needed to head back home. Before he left, Tammy Sue packed a large bag full of fresh fruit, meats, eggs and some cheese. As Misief walked to the front door with the bag of supplies in his arms, Ashel grabbed him and gave him the tightest hug she could muster. She reached up and kissed him on the cheek and told him she loved him. Misief placed the bag on the floor, and picking Ashel up, he hugged her tightly as he told her he loved her too. It wasn't easy for him to show his emotions, and only Nainsi and Ashel had the ability to pull out his softer side. After promising Ashel he would return soon, and thanking Davis and Tammy Sue for their hospitality, he mounted up on Coal and headed down the road back to the empty cabin.

****

In the days following his visit with Ashel, Misief stayed busy working. On the first day he labored from sunrise to sunset inside the cabin, washing clothes, sweeping floors and straightening up the kitchen. With the inside of the cabin in apple pie order, the following morning he took a Kaiser blade and cleared away all the weeds that were growing closest to the cabin. Once that task was complete, he proceeded to clear a three foot wide path from the front of the cabin to the road. Not stopping there, he went to the back of the cabin and cleared a path from the kitchen door to the front of the stable. Next, he walked over to the maple tree where his parents were buried and cleaned up the area around their graves. With energy still remaining, Misief went inside the stable and began cleaning out the stalls.

As the sun began to set behind the mountain, Misief walked into Coal's stall and asked, "What do you think? Does it look better in here to you?"

Not expecting the animal to answer him, Misief commented, "Well, I think it looks better! Let me get you some more hay and oats before I go!"

With the stable clean and Coal fed, Misief decided it was time to call it a day. As he left the stable, he noticed the engraving on the inside of the door. The etching had graced the stable door since his father's death. Each time Misief saw the artwork it reminded him of his promise to his father. A flood of emotions swept over his soul, as his eyes focused on each detail of the engraving. With negative emotions flowing freely through every fiber of his body, Misief reached out and began retracing the letters with his finger.

He began by tracing the vertical line of the first letter from the top to the bottom. At the bottom of the vertical line he moved his finger to the right to follow the short horizontal line.

Next was the second letter; like the first letter, he traced the 'U' shaped form from beginning to end.

Letter three; Misief placed his finger in the big round letter that was almost a complete circle.

Then he moved his finger to the fourth letter, tracing the two vertical lines that touched at the top and separated as they flowed downward. He slowly fingered the crossbar that connected the two vertical lines in the middle.

Finally, he moved his finger to the letter at the far right. This letter was in the shape of a serpent and was the final letter in the engraving. Misief called this letter 'the wicked letter" and felt it best represented the true character of the enemy named in the etching.

Misief drew out his knife and scored a line on the 'serpent shaped letter' as if he was cutting the head off of a snake. He hesitated there in silence as he continued to emulate cutting the snake into pieces. The longer he stared at the etching, the more the emotions inside his body began to boil. His blood pressure elevated; his face turned beet red; and his countenance went from calm to intense rage. He could feel his body tremble as he focused on the inscription. The person named in this carving brought out all the suppressed anger of his past.

All of a sudden, the silence was broken as he screamed out at the top of his lungs, "Someday! Someday, I'll get you Lucas Benson!"

While Misief unleashed his anger inside the stable, he was totally clueless there was someone willing to take away all the pain of his past and replace it with peace. He didn't know the answer to the brokenness of his life was within his grasp, etched in the pages of 'The Album'. Sadly, he'd never taken the time to even open the book. Instead, he continued to wallow in resentment, living each day tormented by the unforgiveness that had become a permanent resident in his young mind.

Working himself into a violent froth, Misief slammed the stable door shut and cursed as he made his way toward the cabin. Along the way, he paused beside his father's grave and breathed one final vow, "Someday, I'll get him for you! That I promise you Pa!"

Chapter 18

"Two Secrets"

July 15, 1864

With the cabin, the stable and the surrounding property back in operating order, Misief decided it was time to go to Rock Springs to see if he could locate Nainsi. The last contact he had with her was the day she visited him while he was in jail. For the last six months he'd kept a detailed image of that day in his mind, remembering her mint green dress, her long brown curly hair and the twinkle of her big brown eyes. He thought often about the touch of her soft, delicate skin as they held hands through the cold, steel bars of the cell door.

Just before Nainsi left the jail they'd declared their love for each other, as they each whispered, "I love you." Misief hoped Nainsi's feelings for him hadn't waned, but until he got a chance to talk to her again, he wouldn't know for sure. After all, it had been six long months since he'd last spoken to her.

During the ride from the cabin to Rock Springs, Misief rehearsed, over and over, what he wanted to say to Nainsi once he located her. This young damsel had overtaken his heart, and he wanted to explain what happened that night at the saloon and apologize for hurting her. Provided she would give him the chance to bear his soul, he wanted to come completely clean and share all the details surrounding how the money was stolen from the saloon.

Guiding Coal along the trail, Misief pondered another potential challenge; Nainsi's father. This man was well aware of Misief's conviction and the time he'd spent in jail. He wanted to get the opportunity to talk directly with him to see if he could straighten things out between them. He knew that if things were not square with Nainsi's father, it would have a devastating impact on his ability to continue courting her.

Yellow, arrowleaf balsamroot flowers dotted the floor of the meadow as Misief passed through Shoots Valley. The melting of the heavy winter snowfall provided the moisture necessary to keep the blossoms in full bloom all summer. Focusing on the beautiful colors bursting forth from the warm soil, his heart beat in double time, and his hands began to sweat. For unknown reasons, he feared Nainsi might reject him; after all, she had not come back to the jail to see him since her first visit in January. He thought to himself, "Maybe she decided to move on with her life, and find someone else; someone who could stay out of trouble."

As Misief approached the sawmill, he noticed Nainsi's father standing on the front porch talking to one of the hired hands. He surmised that since her father was already outside, he might as well go ahead and face the music and see where he stood with him.

Nainsi's father caught a glimpse of the young cowboy out of the corner of his eye. What Misief didn't know was that Nainsi's father was in hopes that he would forget about dating Nainsi. Her dad had approved Nainsi's visit to the jail to see him, but he was dead set against their relationship going any further. Seeing Misief approaching on his stallion sent an angry wave of emotion through Nainsi's father's body. Hoping Misief would ride on down the road, he was angered a mite when he realized the perceived trouble maker was headed his way.

Misief dismounted, took off his hat and asked, "Sir, I wonder if I could talk to you for a minute?"

"I see they let you outta jail," her father sarcastically stated.

"Yes sir, I've been out several days now," Misief replied. "Sir, for what it's worth….and whether you choose to believe me or not is up to you…… but, I promise I didn't steal that money from Mr. Tomar Reeves!"

"That's not what the judge said," her father snapped.

Misief replied, "I understand, but I was at the saloon that night, and I know the whole truth." He continued, "I'm not a bad guy. I was going through a tough place in my life. I know that's not an excuse, but I made a bad choice. I was at the wrong place at the wrong time. I know that I shouldn't have been at the saloon at all. Sir, I really do care about your daughter, and I would never do anything to hurt her."

Nainsi's father tightened his jaw and warned, "Young man, let me tell you something…….if I ever hear of you doing anything to hurt her, I will come looking for you, and when I find you it won't be good!"

"I promise you, I'll never harm a hair on her head as long as I live!" Misief replied.

Her father paused a moment, rubbed his head and stated, "Son, I'll shoot straight. I ain't too fond of you. I'm thinking you will probably turn out just like your father. But, Nainsi has taken a liking to you. She has been begging me for several months to let her visit with you. So far, I've not allowed it. It goes against my better judgment, but I am going to take you at your word and give you one more chance."

"Thank you, sir!" Misief replied. "I appreciate you giving me a second chance with her. Is Nainsi here now?"

Her father nodded and confessed, "Yes, she's inside. I reckon you can go inside and see her."

Misief knew the best thing to do was to drop the debate of his guilt or innocence and simply accept Nainsi's father's offer to give him a second chance. Not saying another word, Misief went inside the mill.

Inside the front office sat the love of his life! She was sitting with her back to the door and had not heard a word of his conversation with her father, nor did she hear him enter through the front door. His hands became increasingly sweaty as a lump formed in his throat. Stuttering a bit, he spoke softly and said, "Hello Nainsi."

Turning around, her eyes opened wide with excitement as she replied, "Misief! I didn't hear you come in. It's so good to see you!"

Nainsi stood up and softly asked, "Does my father know you're here?"

Misief shook his head and calmly stated, "Yeah, he does. I spoke to him before I came inside. He told me that I could come in and talk to you. Do you have time to go for a walk?"

"Sure," Nainsi replied. "As long as my father says it's alright."

Misief opened the front door and politely asked, "Sir, would it be alright if Nainsi and I went for a short walk? We will not be gone long."

Her father nodded. He didn't say a single word but glared at him as they strolled by. Misief knew Nainsi's father wasn't thrilled at the idea of them being together, but as long as Nainsi was allowed to go walking with him, he wasn't going to say a single word!

Once the couple cleared the corner of the sawmill property, they turned left and walked down the wooden sidewalks that flanked the storefronts of Main Street. Misief was still uncertain exactly where he stood with Nainsi, but he could tell by her countenance that she was glad to see him. There might be a few things left to discuss, but he was extremely pleased with how the day had unfolded to this point.

Misief began by saying, "Nainsi, I wanted to tell you again how sorry I am for everything that has happened. As I told you the day you visited me in jail—I want you to know for a certainty that I didn't steal any money."

"Then why did they find you guilty?" Nainsi asked.

Misief knew he had shared part of the story with Nainsi the day she visited him in jail. Feeling she wanted a more detailed explanation, he took a deep breath and shared the entire episode; "It happened like this—I was at the saloon with Billin. We'd been drinking, and before I knew it a fight broke out. During the fight, I crawled out of the saloon to keep from getting killed! I met up with Billin on the outskirts of town, and he showed me this large stack of money. He's the one who stole the money, not me! Anyway, while we were sitting there in the darkness, he reached out and gave me half of the money. Not thinking, I took the money home with me. I don't know why I did that. I guess I was a little drunk at the time and not thinking straight. The next morning, before I had a chance to wake up and think about what had happened, two Rock Springs deputies were knocking on my door. They found the money, handcuffed me, and took me to jail. I know that I shouldn't have accepted the money from Billin. I promise you, I didn't steal any money. He took it, not me."

Nainsi listened to his explanation, and then the couple walked in silence as she meditated on his story. Then Nainsi stopped and took Misief by the hand.

"Misief," she said as she looked into his eyes, "I believe you. I believed you when you told Judge Frye that you were innocent; and I believed you that day in the jail. But, you have to promise me that you will stay away from the saloon, and steer clear of Billin Macdo!"

Misief quickly replied, "Okay, I will. I promise you that I will stay away from the saloon and Billin. So, what about your father? What's it gonna take to get him to like me again?"

Nainsi sighed, "I'll be honest with you. Everyone seems to know all about the story of what happened with your father. He developed quite a reputation in Rock Springs, especially with the saloon patrons and outlaws. I think my father fears you'll grow up to be just like him. He believes you'll always be in trouble, out drinking and running with the wrong crowd. My father just doesn't want me to get mixed up with anyone that's gonna be bad for me."

Misief dropped his head in shame. He did not like what Nainsi was saying, but he knew she spoke the truth. He knew her father was only looking out for what he believed would be in his daughter's best interest.

Nainsi continued, "Misief, you seem to carry around a lot of baggage from your past. Oftentimes you talk about getting even with all those who did your father wrong. It seems to weigh you down. No disrespect intended, but your father has been dead for several years. Time has passed. Can't you just forgive and forget?"

Misief replied, "Nainsi, it's not that simple. You just don't understand. Right before my father died, I made a promise to get even with those who did him wrong. They need to pay for what they did to him. Especially Lucas Benson! He's the one who stole the plans my father had for his life. That night, Lucas cheated my father out of his dreams. My father never recovered and ultimately paid dearly for it—in my opinion, it cost my father his life!"

Nainsi asked, "So are you willing to let all this from the past ruin your life, too?"

Misief did not respond.

She continued, "Misief, you wear your father's leather bag around your neck all the time. I know it reminds you of your mission to get revenge, but I think it is driving you in the wrong direction. I sure wish you could just let it go."

Misief replied, "I can't Nainsi…..I can't let it go. It's all I think about…..it haunts me when I am alone……it is on my mind all day long…….it's in my dreams when I sleep. I don't think I will rest until I get the revenge I promised to him."

Nainsi then asked, "Misief, while you were in jail, did you spend any time reading from 'The Album'?"

"Not much, why?" he asked.

She replied, "Because it could help you with all of this. 'The Album' tells us that we should forgive those who do bad things to us. It warns us that if we keep anger bottled up inside and refuse to forgive, it can do great harm. It does not really hurt the one who is the focus of your anger, but it only hurts you. Unresolved anger will lock you into your own personal prison! I think that is what has happened to you."

Misief jokingly replied, "Well, I ain't in prison! I was locked up, but I am free now!"

Nainsi replied, "That's not what I mean!"

Misief stopped and sat down on the wooden sidewalk in front of the local emporium. Shaking his head, he responded by saying, "Nainsi, I'm just so confused. I have so many questions in my mind."

Nainsi responded by asking, "So what are you confused about?"

Misief didn't respond at first. Shrugging his shoulders, he sat there silently.

After a few minutes of contemplation, he looked up at Nainsi and said, "There was this one thing that happened while I was in jail. A fellow inmate by the name of Jamison told me this wild story about a man by the name of Sheriff Manuel. I actually saw Sheriff Manuel's picture on the wall of the sheriff's office a few days ago. Anyway, have you ever heard of Sheriff Manuel?"

"Oh sure," Nainsi replied. "Everything he did is all written in 'The Album'."

Curious, Misief asked, "So tell me, did Lucas Benson kill Sheriff Manuel?"

Nainsi replied, "Not directly, but he influenced those who were responsible for his killing. As I understand the story, Sheriff Manuel was sent to the Western Frontier by Sheriff Adonai. Sheriff Manuel came to bring peace and to teach us how to live. I know that Sheriff Manuel would want you to forgive those who did you wrong. Did Jamison tell you how Sheriff Manuel died?"

Misief nodded, "Yep, he told me the whole story."

Nainsi then added, "So you know that Sheriff Manuel came back to life three days after they killed him?"

Nodding, Misief confessed, "That's what Jamison said. I'm not so sure about that part of the story. That confused me!"

Nainsi continued, "Well, then you probably also know that as Sheriff Manuel was dying, someone heard him offer forgiveness to those who opposed him, and he forgave the madman who pulled the trigger and shot him."

"That's what Jamison said too," Misief replied.

Misief listened intently to everything Nainsi shared with him regarding Sheriff Manuel. In the back of his mind he considered the possibility that what she was saying might be the truth.

About that time, they caught each other staring at the leather satchel hanging around Misief's neck.

"I made a promise, Nainsi. I promised my father I would get even. The revenge is not for me, it's for him," Misief whispered as he embraced the leather bag.

"Are you sure about that?" Nainsi asked, with a twinge of doubt in her voice.

Nainsi continued. "I fear that satchel is gonna get you in more trouble! And you know, if you end up back in jail, I'm certain my father will never let me see you again."

With her point clearly expressed, Nainsi didn't push the issue any further. The two young spirits spent the rest of the day enjoying each other's company and were noticed by many Rock Spring residents holding hands as they leisurely strolled in and out of the local businesses. As the day came to a close, Misief believed his life was back on track—however, Nainsi feared the leather bag around Misief's neck might become the one thing that could destroy their relationship!

****

October 17, 1864

The leaves gave up their deep green color opting for the orange, brown and golden hues of autumn; the evenings drew cooler and winter approached. Over the past several months, Misief seemed to be walking the straight and narrow path. At least that's what everyone thought!

He spent the majority of his time working around the cabin and sprucing up the property. He had also remained faithful in his promise to Ashel. At least once a week, he journeyed to the Williams' place and would spend the entire day with his baby sister.

If Misief wasn't at the cabin working or with his sister, you could bet he was in town with Nainsi. Nary a week passed that he didn't make the journey into Rock Springs for a social call. Oftentimes, Nainsi would spend time reading to him. Sitting shoulder to shoulder, with fingers intertwined, she would read, and he would follow along. To his surprise, his reading skills had greatly improved as she read him the incredible adventures recorded inside the pages of 'The Album'.

Every one of his visits to Rock Springs always ended the same way. He would walk Nainsi back to the sawmill and ask her father if she could come to the cabin for a picnic. The protective father always responded by saying, "I don't think that would be a good idea."

Misief never let her father's declination preclude him from asking again next time! He believed that he would wear him down, and someday her father would reply, "Yes, she can go with you!"

Although Misief and Nainsi were growing closer with each weekly visit, there were a couple of secrets he was keeping from her.

The first secret that Misief was keeping from Nainsi was related to the stranger that appeared from time to time. The last time he ran into the stranger was one night while he was working in the stable. He was alone and had just finished caring for Coal. As he prepared to turn out the lanterns and head to the cabin, he sensed he was no longer the only one in the stable. Turning slowly, he caught a glimpse of a silhouette. Sure enough, there was someone standing in the far corner of the stall. Startled, he quickly drew his weapon as he hollered out, "Hey what are you doing in here?"

When Misief recognized that this was the same stranger that he'd seen many times before, he slipped his sidearm back into its holster. As usual, the stranger was wearing white cowboy boots with gold studs, and pinned to his shirt, positioned right above his heart, was a five point star with three bullets on it. The strange lawman never said a single word, but just stared at the leather bag Misief had draped across his shoulder. Misief was clueless as to why the stranger seemed to be so interested in his leather bag, but on this night in the stable, he responded as always, "I've told you before, you ain't getting my leather bag! I don't know what you want with me, but get outta here, and leave me alone!"

With that, the stranger vanished.

Misief wanted to tell Nainsi about these encounters, but feared she would not believe him and might even think he was crazy!

The second secret Misief was keeping from her was far more serious and had the potential to destroy their relationship. This secret pertained to the saloon.

Unbeknownst to most everyone close to him, the exception being the saloon patrons, Misief had developed a weekly habit of sneaking into Rock Springs. Most every Saturday night, he would quietly slide into town and slip into the saloon. Once inside, he'd find his regular place at the bar and order a drink or two. The alcohol was not necessarily the problem; his real challenge was that he had become obsessed with watching the saloon ladies as they caroused through the smoky bar singing for the patrons, and rubbing up against the men.

These women of the night were decked out in brightly colored ruffled dresses. Under their bell shaped skirts they sported colorful petticoats that barely reached their kid boots. Their arms and shoulders were bare, and they wore their bodices extremely low cut and revealing. Lacy stockings encased their long, shapely legs and were held up at thigh level with solid white garters.

Misief had become enamored with staring at these scantily clad women. He would sit for hours at the bar drinking, while lost in his own mental fantasy. Over and over, images of the painted ladies strolled carelessly through his intoxicated mind.

Misief watched and wondered, as in the late hours of the night the ladies would entice the men to join them in the privacy of rented rooms on the second floor of the saloon. In the shadows of darkness, what little was left to the imagination became available for purchase, as the men engaged in sexual activity with these morally loose females.

Misief watched every step each couple took, as the drunken men walked hand in hand with the half dressed ladies, until they disappeared into the blackness of the darkened balcony.

To this point, Misief had not given in to the temptation of physical engagement with any of the women. However, each week it seemed his ability to resist was weakening. He was totally unaware of the addiction that was firmly grasping him in its clutches. He had not forgotten his promise to Nainsi, to never go back to the saloon, but the demons inside his mind made it all but impossible for him to resist the temptation.

This problem began several months earlier and had become a sick ritual. Without exception, every Saturday began the same; he would get up in the morning and vow that he was not going back to the saloon. Like clockwork, around 5:00 in the afternoon, the spirit of addiction would come knocking on his door, and before he knew what was happening, he would find himself on his horse sneaking into town. After a night of drinking himself crazy and filling his mind with vulgar images, he would stagger out of the saloon and go back home to sleep off the effects of the alcohol. Every Sunday morning, with a head throbbing with a hangover, Misief would once again proclaim that he was never going back to the saloon. His intentions were pure; his motives were honest; but the enticement had developed into an addictive habit that was more than he could conquer on his own!

Not only was Misief dealing with a sexually driven pornographic addiction, but each time he became intoxicated it seemed to re-energize his passion for revenge with Lucas Benson. Most every Saturday night, as he lingered in the saloon waiting for the women to take the stage, his mind drifted back to thoughts of his father and his broken past. One minute Misief would find himself straddling a bar stool as he drew mental images of illicit women. The next moment his mind shifted to thoughts of what it would feel like to put a bullet between the eyes of ole' Lucas. The combination of sexual imagery and revenge flowed together like a lethal cocktail. This poison was deadlier than any compound a drug store doctor could conjure up!

Misief knew full well that if Nainsi caught wind of his saloon activity, it would be the end of their relationship. He loved that young lady more than anything in the world; well, that was what he would tell everybody. But the risk of forever losing his relationship with his soul mate was not enough to keep him from his secret weekend trips.

Deep down, Misief knew he would probably get caught someday. And getting caught would bring additional pain into his life; it might even be the infamous nail in his own emotional coffin! Even so, this addiction had gripped its slimy clutches so deep into his life that he felt powerless to break free!

Chapter 19

"The Picnic"

March 30, 1865

The winter thaw was almost complete as the warm, spring air forced old man winter back into hibernation for another year. The pasture out behind the stable was dotted with clusters of daises that had vibrant yellow centers surrounded by brilliant white petals.

Since his release from jail last July, Misief had developed a routine, which he followed meticulously week after week. The vast majority of his time was spent alone at the cabin, as he focused on regular maintenance as well as taking on repairs that had been neglected since his mother's death.

His greatest accomplishment was tackling a spot of ground that had been completely useless in the past. Mostly filled with weeds and saplings, Misief spent many days during the cold winter months cutting down the trees and filling in the low spots with topsoil. He capped off this endeavor with a brand new barbed wire fence, which fully surrounded this plot of ground. With the seed already purchased and waiting in the loft, he planned to establish this new spot as a pasture dedicated to a few head of cattle that he hoped to get established by the end of the summer.

In addition to working around the homestead from sunrise to sunset, occasionally Misief would journey out to the Williams' place to visit with his sister. While Ashel always begged her brother to come more often, it seemed something always came up that prohibited him from getting there as regularly as he should.

And let's not forget the young lady in Rock Springs; even the cold, blustery winter weather could do nothing to prohibit him from trekking to Rock Springs once or twice each week to spend time with Nainsi.

His relationship with Nainsi was going extremely well. Up to this point, he had been successful in keeping his secrets from her. However, now that many in the community were beginning to see them as a 'couple', he feared that somebody from the saloon, either in idle conversation or with intentions of hurting him, might tell her about his Saturday night encounters with the painted ladies.

He was still not allowed to officially date Nainsi, but her father would permit them to walk around town together, go inside the café to grab a bite to eat, and sit on the bench and talk. It wasn't exactly what Misief had in mind, but he was grateful for the time he got to spend with her. While Nainsi's father hadn't completely warmed up to him, he did think the old man was softening a bit.

Without exception, at the end of each day spent with Nainsi, Misief would bravely go inside the sawmill, locate her father, and ask him if she could go on a picnic at the cabin with him. The response was always an emphatic—No! But, he refused to let her father's response discourage him at all.

Just a few days earlier, Misief was escorting Nainsi back to the sawmill when he proclaimed, "Nainsi, I've got a feeling—I believe that very soon, possibly even this spring, your father is going to finally say yes and allow us to go on a picnic together."

Nainsi snickered and replied, "I don't know about that! What makes you think he is softening his position?"

Misief replied, "Well, when I first started asking your father for permission, he would snort a little, raise his eyebrows, curse a time or two, then say a loud—No! But now, he's stopped snorting! He just shakes his head back and forth while he stares at me with that evil stare!"

Nainsi giggled and replied, "My father doesn't snort!"

Misief cracked a smile and stated, "Well, I don't know what else to call it. It sounds like a snort to me!"

"And my father does not curse!" she proclaimed.

"Oh, I don't know," Misief responded. "All I know for certain is that he always mumbles something before he tells me, No! Maybe he is not cursing, but I don't think he is saying a blessing over me, or telling me how much he loves me!"

Regardless of what Nainsi believed, Misief was certain that it would not be long until her father gave in and allowed him the opportunity to escort her out to his cabin. He was patiently waiting for that day to occur!

****
April 26, 1865

It was an unseasonably warm April morning when Misief mounted Coal and headed into Rock Springs to spend another day with Nainsi. Following his normal routine, his first stop was the sawmill to see if she was inside the business or at her home, which was a short distance outside of town.

Misief quickly dismounted and tied Coal to the hitching post which ran along the front of the building. As he stepped up on the front porch, he met Nainsi's father, who was on his way out of the office. Her father never had much to say, but on this particular spring morning, he walked through the doorway and with a smile on his face, he greeted Misief and said, "Hello, young man! It's a fine day, just a fine day!"

Sheriff Adonai

Misief was stunned. Outside of their brief conversation last summer when Misief first got out of jail, Nainsi's father hadn't said two words to him in the last six months. But on this morning, he was smiling and whistling, and he greeted Misief with something far better than a grunt!

Misief quickly replied, "Yes it is! It is a beautiful spring day!"

Nainsi's father continued, "Yes sir, it sure is! It's the best day I've had in a long time!"

Misief was not certain what to say next, but he believed that if Nainsi's father was willing to carry on a conversation with him, he should do his part to keep the dialogue going.

"I take it something really good has happened for you this morning?" Misief asked.

"It sure has!" Nainsi's father answered. "I was just awarded the contract for the largest tract of timber west of the Mississippi River! I've been working on this deal for over a year, and this morning the telegram arrived stating that my company will get to harvest the timber for the entire parcel. Oh yes, this is a big deal for us!"

Extending his hand, Misief replied, "Congratulations sir! You deserve it!"

Nainsi's father accepted Misief's handshake and said, "Thank you!"

As he walked toward the edge of the sidewalk, Nainsi's father continued by saying, "Well, I'm going over to the café and share the news with the fellas over a bite of breakfast. You and Nainsi have a good day!"

Misief believed this was his moment! He thought that since her father was in such a good mood, why not take this opportunity and ask him if Nainsi could go with him today to his cabin.

Nainsi's father was now well on his way toward the café. Turning from the front door, Misief crossed his fingers and asked the question, "Sir, excuse me just a moment. As you said, this is such a beautiful spring day, and you know, for several months I've wanted to take your daughter to my place for a picnic. I know that so far you have been against it. I promise I will take good care of her and be a perfect gentleman. Nainsi is a fine young lady, and I would just like to show her where I live and take her on a picnic down by the creek that runs behind my property."

Her father stopped.

Misief inhaled.

Neither man spoke.

Misief waited as Nainsi's father seemed to be contemplating the idea. At a minimum, he had not barked out an immediate refusal of the notion.

"Well, I tell you what," her father began. "I'm in a real good mood today. If you promise me that you will take good care of her, and have her back home before sundown; then I reckon she can go with you."

"I promise!" Misief replied, as a grin stretched across his face.

"Now remember, if anything happens to her, then I will come looking for you!" Nainsi's father warned.

"I will treat her like an angel and guard her with my life!" Misief declared.

Misief was ecstatic and raced inside the sawmill to share the news with Nainsi.

"Nainsi, Nainsi, guess what just happened!" Your father said you can go with me on a picnic at the cabin!"

Nainsi replied, "You gotta be kidding!"

"No, I ain't kidding! I just asked him…..I met him as he was walking out the door headed to the café. He was in a good mood…some land deal got approved…..and so I thought I would just go ahead and ask him first thing this morning while he was in such high spirits. And, the next thing I knew, he said okay!"

"Did he say when I can go?" Nainsi inquired.

"Today!" Misief proclaimed. "We can go today!"

Nainsi jumped up and said, "Let me finish what I'm doing, and we'll get going!"

Nainsi quickly wrapped up what she was working on and slipped into the back room to slide on a pair of leather breeches under her skirt. When she was ready, walking hand in hand, the two of them made their way out into the beautiful spring sunshine.

As Misief untied Coal from the railing, Nainsi asked, "Are you sure my father said it was alright for me to go today?"

"I'm sure!" Misief replied.

Misief could tell Nainsi was a bit apprehensive about leaving Rock Springs with him since she had not heard the approval come from her father. Wanting her to be able to relax and enjoy the day, Misief suggested, "Why don't we walk over to the café, and you can hear it directly from him."

Nainsi nodded. She knew it would ease her mind to hear her father say that he was okay with her going.

Within minutes the pair exited the café. Her father still approved of the couple traveling to Misief's cabin for a picnic. On his way out, Misief once again promised her father that he would take good care of her and have her home by sundown. In addition, Misief shook her father's hand and thanked him for giving him this opportunity.

Once outside, Misief placed his left foot into the stirrup and threw his right leg over Coal's saddle. Steadying himself by placing one hand on the saddle horn, he reached down and gently helped Nainsi up on the stallion. She placed her hands around his waist, and the lovebirds headed slowly down the dusty road which led out of Rock Springs toward Shoots Valley.

Once they were a mile or so out of town, Nainsi snuggled up closer to Misief and drew her arms tighter around him. The horse trotted at a slow pace as the couple enjoyed the warmth of the spring breeze and the views of the budding trees which filled the valley floor.

Clearing Shoots Valley, they soon approached Roberts Creek. Not in any particular hurry, Misief directed Coal toward the edge of the trail and then pulled back on the reins bringing the horse to a stop.

Glancing over his shoulder, Misief asked, "You want to stop, and take a break?"

"Sure!" Nainsi replied.

Misief assisted Nainsi down off the horse and led her to the edge of the creek. Running along the creek, about four feet from the water's edge was a fallen oak tree. Misief wiped off a spot to make it clean for her, and she sat down beside him on the log.

Misief reached out with his left hand and took Nainsi's right hand. Intertwining his rugged fingers with hers, he spoke up and said, "This is the place my mama and sister and I would always stop on our way into town."

"Oh really," Nainsi replied, as she swept her brunette locks out of her face.

"Yeah, this is the place. Coal knows this spot so well I don't even have to tell him what to do." Pointing to the stallion, he said, "See, he gets a drink without me even saying a word!"

Nainsi giggled, and then asked, "So tell me, how is Ashel doing?"

"She's doing good," Misief stated. "She's really growing up fast. She actually came home with me a few days ago and spent the night. It was good having her around, but I know that living with the Williams is the best for her."

Nainsi replied, "I'm sure they can give her a mother and father role model in her life. But never forget, you are her brother, her only living blood kin, and she needs you too!"

The young couple sat on the log for twenty to thirty minutes talking about everything and nothing in particular; but they never stopped talking. It was obvious they were falling deeper in love with each passing moment. All they really wanted was to be with each other, and they didn't need anything else.

Tuning to Nainsi, Misief asked, "Are you ready to head out?"

"Sure," she replied.

****

The final stretch to the cabin was a short ride following the trail which ran parallel with Roberts Creek. The mid-morning sun peeked through the trees, ushering in new life to the budding foliage. Passing through direct sunlight to areas with lengthy shadows, they causally made their way toward the cabin.

Pulling the reins slightly to the left, Misief directed Coal onto the property and proclaimed, "Well, we are here! This is my cabin!"

Misief was the perfect gentlemen and assisted Nainsi down off the mighty stallion.

"I like it!" Nainsi admitted. "It has such a homey feeling, nestled among all these trees."

Before escorting Nainsi inside, Misief gave her a quick tour of the outside of the property. "This is the well house. I helped my father build the stone wall around it!" Misief bragged.

"That's nice work!" Nainsi winked and replied. "I might get you to build something for me someday!"

Misief reached for Nainsi and declared, "I'd build you anything you want! Anything, you just name it!"

Passing the well house, they walked in the direction of the stable. Misief paused as they approached the maple tree which marked the location where his parents were buried. Pointing at their graves, he recounted the story of his mother's passing.

Next, Misief took Nainsi inside the stable and showed her the loft where he played as a young boy. He shared with her the stories of his father teaching him how to ride a horse, shoot a gun and become a tough cowboy. Even though Nainsi had heard horrible things about Misief's father, it was clear that the man Misief loved and remembered was a hero to him.

"Let me show you one more thing, and then we will go inside," Misief stated as he led Nainsi by the hand. "This is the new field I've been telling you about! In the past six months, I've cleared away all the saplings and filled in several low spots with top soil. The fence wire is all brand new, and once I get it reseeded, I can start placing cattle inside."

"That is awesome! I am so proud of you!" Nainsi responded.

Misief added, "I'm gonna make it bigger. But for now, this is enough to get me started in the cattle business."

With the outside tour complete, it was time to go inside. Misief opened the front door, and like a perfect gentlemen, allowed Nainsi to enter first. Placing his hat on the nail beside the door, he suggested, "Nainsi, why don't you make yourself at home while I go in the kitchen and fix us a picnic lunch. You can sit on the sofa or look around in the bedrooms. Whatever you want to do is fine with me."

Nainsi shook her head and replied, "Okay, but I would be glad to help you."

"I got it!" Misief said. "Just give me a few minutes."

While Misief worked in the kitchen, Nainsi roamed around inside the cabin checking out every room. After completing a self guided tour, she poked her head inside the kitchen and stated, "Misief Stone, I am impressed. You keep this place in perfect order! I wasn't expecting to find your cabin so neat."

"What were you expecting?" Misief asked, as he sliced off pieces of meat.

"I don't know. I guess I thought this place would be a disaster!" she admitted.

Misief laughed and replied, "My mother taught me to keep things neat. After she died, I admit, it did get out of order for a spell. But, over the last few months, I've worked hard to get it back into shape and even put my own touches on a few things."

With a twinkle in her eye, Nainsi responded, "Well, I am very impressed!"

Soon Misief entered the room carrying a basket filled with goodies. Lifting the basket up, he said, "I've got it all ready! Are you in the mood for a picnic?"

"Sure," she replied. "Where did you get such a nice basket?"

"It belonged to my mother," Misief answered. "She would stuff it full of food every time we went into Rock Springs."

"Are we going to stay around here or go someplace?" Nainsi asked.

Misief replied, "I know a great place just a short distance from here. Roberts Creek runs along the back of the property, right at the base of the mountain. Do you want to walk, or shall I get Coal?"

"How far is it?"

"Only a half mile or so," he replied.

"Then I'm fine with walking," Nainsi stated.

Picking up a blanket to sit on and with basket in tow, the couple walked through the front door and headed toward the back of the property. The young lovers laughed and talked as they leisurely strolled across the pasture and through a thicket of woods.

As soon as they exited the woods, it opened up into a beautiful meadow. Roberts Creek rumbled in the background, as the stream cascaded along the base of the mountain, creating the perfect backdrop for a spring picnic.

"What about right here?" Misief asked, as he placed the basket on the ground.

"This is perfect!" Nainsi replied.

Misief spread out the quilted blanket on the ground and treated Nainsi to a lunch of sliced beef, bread, and apple pie. The pie was actually backed by Tammy Sue Williams and was given to him a couple of days earlier when he visited with Ashel.

After lunch, the couple took a walk partway up the mountain, spent time wadding in the creek, and even stretched out on the blanket to grab a quick nap as they soaked up the spring sunshine. As promised, Misief was the perfect gentlemen and treated Nainsi as if she was royalty!

Before either of them could believe it, the day had slipped away and the evening sun was casting lazy shadows across the meadow. Not wanting to upset her father at all, Misief knew it was time to begin the journey back to Rock Springs. If he was one minute late, he was certain he would never get the opportunity to bring Nainsi back to his cabin again.

As they approached the front porch of the cabin, Misief slid the blanket and picnic basket inside the cabin and suggested, "Why don't you wait here on the porch while I go get Coal from the stable."

The gentle breeze blew through Nainsi's hair as the evening sun cast beautiful highlights across her face. As Misief rounded the corner of the cabin, he was smitten with her radiant glow. To him, she was a goddess! She was the most incredible woman he had ever seen!

Misief climbed down from Coal and asked, "Are you ready to head back?"

Standing up, Nainsi replied, "I guess we better! We don't want to be late!"

Misief reached out his hand, and Nainsi gently placed her delicate hand in his. He paused for a moment and stared directly into her chocolate brown eyes. In his spirit, he sensed her warmth and before contemplating the consequences, he placed his hands on Nainsi's hips, drew her close and pressed his lips to hers. There wasn't a single trace of resistance from Nainsi as the two young lovers embraced and shared their first kiss!

As he held her close, he whispered in her ear, "I love you, Nainsi."

She leaned up and whispered to him, "I love you too, Misief Stone."

Misief's heart skipped several beats as the young goddess batted her dazzling eyes and smiled at him. Misief didn't want this tender moment to end, but he also didn't want to jeopardize her getting to come back in the future. Staring into her eyes and dreaming, Misief took his index finger and while holding her close, traced the outline of her lips.

Exhaling, he whispered, "Come on, brown eyes, we better get going."

As Misief loosen his grip on Nainsi and turned to walk toward Coal, she grabbed his arm and said, "Wait a minute!"

"What is it?" Misief asked.

"I haven't thanked you for today. I want you to know that this has been one of the best days of my life! You are a good guy Misief, and I am so glad we are sharing our lives together!"

Nainsi then pulled the rugged cowboy close and kissed him again.

"I just wanted to say thanks..." she whispered as she winked at him.

Misief and Nainsi climbed up on Coal and began the eleven mile journey back to Rock Springs. Along the way, the couple talked non-stop as Nainsi wrapped her arms around Misief and hugged him tight.

As they approached the fork in the road which went through Shoots Valley, Misief turned around and asked Nainsi if she was alright with taking the fork to the right, which led over the mountain. He wanted to take her by Rock Pointe, and he believed they had enough time to make it up the mountain and back down to Rock Springs well before sundown. She shook her head in agreement, and he told her to hold on tight as they began their ascent on the twisting, turning path that led up the mountain.

Soon they arrived at the summit. Misief led Nainsi out onto the large rock that extended from the side of the mountain. This was Nainsi's inaugural visit to Rock Pointe, and she was enamored with the view from high above the valley floor. Standing arm in arm, Misief pointed out all the buildings in Rock Springs, including her father's sawmill.

"This is one of my favorite places!" Misief admitted.

"I can see why," Nainsi replied. "With you up here, it is one of my favorite spots too!"

After sharing their third kiss of the day, the couple climbed back on Coal and began the descent down the mountain. As he meticulously guided the stallion down the slippery trail, Misief turned around to Nainsi and said, "I'll take you on a picnic at Rock Pointe someday soon."

"I'd love that!" Nainsi responded.

****

Soon the couple found themselves on the outskirts of Rock Springs. Knowing it was well past business hours, Misief didn't even stop by the sawmill, opting instead to take Nainsi directly to her home.

Nainsi's parent's house was located about one half mile from the center of Rock Springs. It was a charming, white, cottage style home, with several chimneys dotting the roof line. There was a large porch which extended all the way across the front. Seated on the porch in a handmade cane rocker was Nainsi's father, who waved as the couple rode into the yard.

Looking up at the sun that still had about one-fourth of a sliver visible over the mountain, Misief said, "I got her home before sunset!"

Nainsi's father nodded and said, "You sure did! Just barely, but you did get her home before dark!"

Misief helped Nainsi down off the stallion. Twirling her curls with her fingers she sweetly said, "Misief, I had an amazing time today!"

"I'm glad you did. I know that I won't ever forget it!" he replied.

Misief thanked Nainsi's father for allowing his daughter to go to the cabin with him. He climbed back on his horse and headed down the road toward Rock Springs. He kept his eyes glued on Nainsi until he was so far out of sight that he could no longer see her. Once she'd disappeared from sight, he nudged Coal, and the pair disappeared into the evening sunset.

All the way home, Misief replayed the events of the day. He knew it had been one of the best days of his life. In the darkness, with Roberts Creek flanking his side, he declared that he had to find a way to break his addictions. The vivacious young damsel had stolen his heart, and he was determined not to jeopardize losing what was happening between them!

Chapter 20

"I'll Do It My Way!"

May 16, 1865

The April picnic with Nainsi had rejuvenated Misief's desire to do the things necessary to keep their relationship strong. Everything was now going well in his life. All the damage from his time in jail seemed to be in the past, and his future appeared to be filled with hope. However, in the back of his mind, he knew there was one thing that, if brought into the light of day, could destroy everything he had worked so hard to establish.

It was only three weeks ago, on his return trip to the cabin after a marvelous day spent with Nainsi, that he vowed it would never happen again. Just the prior evening, as he sat on the front porch watching the stars, he'd solidified his commitment to ensuring this awful habit was forever left in the dusty trails of the past.

But temptation trumped intentions, as on this particular Saturday afternoon the demons in Misief's mind were working overtime. He'd secretly continued making the journey to Rock Springs every Saturday night, possessed by the sexual imagery of the saloon ladies. Misief was unaware of the influential force of the damned, and the spirits refused to let him make lifestyle changes without an eternal fight for his soul. What confused him the most was that Monday through Friday his willpower seemed to be stronger than his weakness, but when Saturday came, he was at the mercy of his addiction.

Something about this particular Saturday seemed even worse than any of the others. It was as if the regular horde of demons had arrived early and brought reinforcements to raise the intensity of temptation to its highest level yet. From the moment his head lifted from his pillow and his feet hit the floor, all Misief thought about was the painted ladies and their bodies as they danced half naked around the saloon. He tried to focus on the chores he needed to complete around the cabin, but visions of their soft, delicate, flesh completely bombarded his infected mind. With every task he tried to complete, his eyes twisted the normal view of nature and tools hanging on the walls of the stable into sexual visions of the curves of their shapely bodies.

Shaking his head in an attempt to clear the images from his mind, Misief wondered how he'd ended up with such a crippling sexual obsession to live pornographic imagery. Struggling to get through the day, he wondered who or what could deliver him from his addiction to watching the young ladies at the saloon.

Misief battled the temptation all day, doing everything in his mortal power to resist. One minute he vowed he was never going back to the saloon; the next moment he was mentally planning his trip. Back and forth he drifted between the conflicting options, like a rubber ball being passed around between two young children on a playground.

Around sundown, the ball bounced for the final time as the Saturday night ritual began to unfold. First, a bath from water he'd drawn from the well, then a clean change of clothes and quicker than you could imagine, he was ready to fulfill the desires of his perverted mind.

After placing his hat on his head and securing the front door, Misief walked off the porch and turned to head toward the stable. To his surprise he noticed someone rumbling through the garden.

The sun was casting lengthy shadows making it difficult to determine their identity. Misief pulled his gun and darted behind an oak tree for cover. Keeping his body shielded by the large trunk of the tree, he peered around the edge and realized this person was headed straight toward him.

Misief pulled the hammer back on his pistol and yelled, "Hold it right there Mister, or I'll blow your head clean off your shoulders."

The intruder stopped.

Misief waited to see what the man might do next.

The intruder held up both hands as if he was surrendering. Misief realized this person appeared to pose no immediate threat and wasn't looking for a confrontation.

The intruder turned left and started walking toward the stable. Misief watched intently as the man stopped in front of the stable doors.

As the setting sun illuminated the man's face, Misief immediately realized the man standing in front of the stable was the tall stranger in the white boots!

"Not you again! What do you want?" Misief screamed.

The stranger spoke not a word. He just stood in front of the stable doors, raised his hand with a single finger pointing up, and shook his hand back and forth. It appeared he was trying to warn Misief against going to Rock Springs.

"You get out of my way!" Misief demanded. "I'm going to Rock Springs tonight, and you ain't gonna stop me!"

Then the stranger slowly reached out his left hand toward the leather satchel Misief had around his neck. Motioning with his fingers, the stranger once again asked for Misief's leather bag.

"I've told you before, you can't have my leather bag," Misief firmly stated. "I don't know who you are or why you keep bothering me, but please leave me alone and get outta my way! I'm headed to Rock Springs tonight, and that's final!"

The stranger stood his ground and once again shook his head back and forth as if to try and warn Misief of impending danger. But Misief was in no mood for his antics and shouted, "I said get outta here, and leave me alone! Now go!"

Quicker than the blink of the eye, the stranger disappeared, vanishing into thin air!

Misief looked in all directions, but there was not a trace of the stranger anywhere. Just like before, the stranger came from out of nowhere and vanished in the same manner. Each encounter with the stranger unnerved Misief, and he wished the stranger would just stay away and leave him alone.

Believing the stranger was gone for now, Misief walked inside the stable and prepared Coal for the ride. As he laced Coal's saddle, he wondered why the stranger was so interested in his leather bag. This was the second or third time the stranger had gestured for his satchel. Misief feared the stranger might somehow be connected to Lucas Benson, but he was not sure.

Trying to put the vision of the stranger behind him, Misief continued to prepare for his Saturday night trip to Rock Springs. For a brief few minutes, he did give serious thought to canceling the trip and just spending the evening at home. But those notions quickly faded like the smoke of a match, as the demonic horde ambushed his mind with visions of females dancing and twisting. Within minutes, the warning given by the stranger was forgotten; it was nothing more than a passing memory.

"It's time for some Saturday night female action!" Misief stated, as a devilish grin slid across his face.

****

Misief arrived at the outskirts of Rock Springs just after sunset. The cover of darkness promised to hide the unmentionable acts that were about to unfold inside the saloon. Saturday night was the wildest night at the local tavern, as the ladies were at full staff and perfectly willing to do most anything to fulfill the desires of the drunken cowboys. The men had pockets full of money from a hard week's work, and the ladies knew exactly what was required to transfer that income into their possession. This was their opportunity to make bank, and as soon as the alcohol began flowing across the counter, the fair skin of their delicate, shapely, feminine bodies began creeping out from under their colorful costumes. Make no mistake, there was not an ounce of true love present in the establishment; this was a calculated procedure for these ladies to glean cash from a herd of hormone driven fools.

With Coal secured to the post behind the saloon, Misief quietly slid through the double doors and mingled in with the crowd that was rapidly growing. After taking a seat on the last stool on the right, he instructed Tomar, the owner of the saloon, to pour him his usual, a shot of Forty Rod whiskey followed by a large beer with foam lapping over the edges. And with that, Misief's night was off and running.

Misief did not engage in conversation with anyone. Nor was he interested in playing any of the card games that were taking place throughout the saloon. He had come to the saloon for one reason and only one reason! He waited patiently on his bar stool, sipping his beer, as he contemplated what was about to begin, and it wasn't long before the night's exotic entertainment took center stage.

As advertised, one young, blonde haired, damsel kicked off the activities by singing while the pianist tapped the ivory keys of the Bachman piano. As the melody flowed across her rose colored lips, articles of her clothing fell from her body like the golden leaves of a maple tree in autumn. Her act was followed by a chorus of ladies who began parading throughout the saloon, gyrating to the beat of the music. Their moves were just as intoxicating as the alcohol, and Misief's addictive desires were once again ignited with the poison that seemed to temporarily medicate him.

In was right after midnight when Misief finally stumbled out of the saloon. His mind was completely consumed with the visions of the scantily dressed females, and his body was drugged by the altering effects of the alcohol. He staggered off the front porch and using the side wall of the building as a support, worked his way around to the back where Coal was waiting for him. Rounding the corner of the building, Misief noticed one of the dancing ladies standing behind the saloon.

"Well hello pretty thing! What are you doing back here?" Misief asked in a slurred tone.

The young lady pretended not to hear Misief and tried her best to just ignore him, hoping he would get on his horse and ride away.

Once again Misief asked, "What are you doing back here? You gonna do a dance just for me?"

The young lady shook her head to let Misief know she was not interested in him, and in his altered state of mind, he didn't notice she had tears streaming down her cheeks. It would have been obvious for a sober person to discern that something had just occurred that had upset this young lady; but in his drunken condition, Misief only thought of his own lustful desires.

He walked closer to her and said, "Come here, darling, and give this cowboy a hug."

Misief reached out and forcefully placed his arms around her; immediately she began to resist. He pressed his body against hers, and she fought to free herself from his tremendous grip. The young lady screamed as Misief continued his physical advances toward her. Irritated at her refusal to perform, Misief gripped, and then jerked down on the front of her bodice, trying to remove it to expose her body. Frightened, she continued to scream as loud as she could as Misief continued his sexual assault on her.

About that time, two men came out of the back of the saloon and heard her screams. They rushed over and quickly pulled Misief off of the young lady. Gathering herself, the young lady raced into the darkness with what little clothes she had been wearing, torn loose from her body.

Then the two men decided to teach Misief a lesson; with one man holding Misief's hands behind his back, the other man began punching him in the face. Defenseless, the drunken young lad absorbed several severe hits, the last being a punch in the gut which brought him to the ground. Severely beaten, Misief was left laying in the darkness. For the next several hours, he remained on the ground bleeding as he drifted in and out of consciousness.

Early on Sunday morning, as the sun began to break over the horizon, Misief began to stir. His head was throbbing, and he could taste the dried blood pasted on his busted lip. His eyes were swelled shut and would barely open. His stomach ached, feeling like it was about to explode. He could barely remember what had happened, but he did recall the encounter with the saloon lady. Everything after that was a blur, and he was clueless as to who had beaten him.

Moving at the pace of an elderly man, Misief managed to get up to his hands and knees, and then he slowly made his way up to his feet. Stiff and incredibly sore, he hobbled over to Coal who was still tied up to the rail behind the saloon. With all the energy he could muster, he crawled on the back of the stallion and sheepishly made his way out of town.

Misief rode about a mile and realized he was in no shape to make it all the way to his cabin. Pondering his options, he decided to ride to the old mining shack that was on the edge of town. This was the same shack he and Billin had hid behind the night Billin stole the money from the saloon. He limped up to the front door and peered inside the broken glass. Inside, he noticed an old desk and chair completely covered with dust. It was obvious nobody had used this shack in many years. He pushed open the door and barely made it inside before his knees buckled causing him to collapse on the dirt covered floor.

Lying on the dusty planks, Misief wondered if he was just bruised up, or did he actually have broken bones. It hurt to stand; it hurt to walk; and it hurt to breathe! Uncertain of the severity of his wounds, he simply wanted to lie on the floor and see if the pain might soon subside.

Noon came and went, and as the afternoon rolled on, Misief began to feel a bit better. His hangover had subsided, and his eyes were now opening a little better. However, his rib cage felt like he'd been kicked by a mule, and he wondered if his ribs might be broken. His lips were dry and busted; and the salty taste of blood crept into his taste buds every time his tongue moved in his mouth.

****

It was now about an hour before sundown, and Misief felt like he might have the strength to ride back to the town well to get some water. Slowly rising to his feet, he took a moment to make sure his legs would support him. He then noticed an old mirror hanging on the wall. Curious as to the damage to his face, he walked over to the mirror to survey the situation. Wiping the dust from the reflective surface of the mirror, he could see his left eye was black and his lip was busted in two places. He had dried blood caked all over his chin and down his neck. Shaking his head back and forth, he mumbled, "What a mess!"

Misief began walking back and forth in the shack to test the stability of his legs. Twisting, bending, stretching, he moved in all directions trying to free his muscles from the frozen effects of his body's overall soreness.

"I feel like I've been run over by a train!" Misief whispered as he continued working to get his body functioning enough to endure the short ride to the well.

He ventured outside and stared at Coal knowing it would be a challenge just to get on the tall stallion. Looking at Coal, who was staring back at him, Misief stated, "What are you looking at? Somehow I got on you last night, so I know I can get back on you now!"

Moving at the speed of cold molasses, Misief made his way into the saddle and gave Coal the command to get moving. With each step the stallion made, Misief felt pain deep inside his abdomen. The sucker punches hurled to his stomach left him so sore he could barely breathe as the horse trotted down the trail. Pulling back on the reins, he slowed Coal down to a walk trying to minimize the jolts to his body.

After fifteen minutes or so, Misief finally reached the well. Peering in all directions, there was no one in sight. Slowly dismounting, he began the process of drawing a bucket of water from the well. He lowered the bucket down the shaft to the water below using the wooden crank handle on the side of the well.

Hearing the bucket make contact with the water, Misief began to turn the handle in the opposite direction to bring the water to the surface. Within moments, the bucket appeared out of the darkness and was overflowing with nice, cold water. Forming a cup with his hands, he began drinking and washing his face. The cool liquid felt like medicine to his battered body. Next, he poured some water into a trough beside the well for Coal to drink.

"Drink up boy," he instructed, as he eased down on the bench beside the well. Misief stared at the sun setting in the west and thought back to the previous afternoon at the cabin when the stranger tried to stop him from going to the saloon.

"I sure wish I'd listened to that man wearing the white boots," Misief whispered, as he did his best to sip the water with a busted lip.

As he rested, he wondered if the young lady at the saloon or the two men had reported the incident to the local authorities. He contemplated the notion that the Rock Springs deputies might be out looking for him, and that he potentially could be facing another stretch in jail if convicted of this crime.

With hunger pains gnawing on his spine, Misief wanted to venture into town to get something to eat, but not knowing if he was a 'wanted' man or not, he convinced himself that it was probably best to maintain a low profile for another day or so.

Standing to his feet Misief mumbled, "There is one thing worse than being hungry, and that is being locked up."

With a belly full of water, and most of the dirt and blood washed from his face, he re-filled his canteen and returned to Coal. Slowly climbing into the saddle, he directed the horse toward the old mining shack. He believed that one more night spent at the shack would provide him enough time to heal so he could make the journey to his cabin.

Back inside the shack, with Coal secured outside, Misief began exploring the remnants of the once occupied building. In the far corner, on a small wooden table, was a stub of a candle about four inches in length. Misief took a match from his satchel, and soon a dim glow filled the inside of the room. As he placed the matches back inside the leather bag, his eyes glanced down at the binding of the book that was inside his bag. The flickering light from the candle danced like a serpents tongue as it reflected off the gold letters of the title of the book.

"The Album," Misief whispered, as he ran his index finger across the bold letters. While he always carried the book with him, he only read it when he was with Nainsi. But this evening, in the serenity of the candlelit room, he felt compelled to remove the book from the bag.

Hesitant at first, he removed the book from his leather satchel and placed it on the table, right beside the candle. He thumbed through the pages, and soon an underlined passage caught his attention. The words leapt off the page as Misief held the candle in his hand and read:

> *Follow Sheriff Adonai's example in everything you do, because you are his dear children. Live a life filled with love for others, following the example of Sheriff Manuel, who loved you and gave himself as a sacrifice to take away the punishment for all the crimes you've ever committed. And remember, Sheriff Adonai was pleased with the sacrifice of Sheriff Manuel.*
>
> *Get rid of all sexual and immoral behavior from your life. Stop telling obscene stories and dirty jokes – these are not good for you. Instead, let your life be filled with thankfulness to Sheriff Manuel. Remember, nobody who participates in an evil lifestyle will inherit all the goodness that Sheriff Manuel has for you. Once you were living an evil life, but now you have the light of Sheriff Manuel to guide your life. For the light of Sheriff Manuel can live*

within you, and when it does, it will produce a life that is good, right and true.

As Misief momentarily closed the book, he reflected on the words he'd just read. He was not exactly sure what the passage meant, but it was clear that Sheriff Adonai and Sheriff Manual wanted people to live their lives focused on loving others. In addition, it was unmistakable that these sheriffs encouraged people to live their lives free from many of the evil activities that had become a normal part of his young life.

The confusing part of the passage was the reference to 'the sacrifice of Sheriff Manuel'. As Misief sat at the desk, he recalled the story Jamison told to him about how Sheriff Manuel voluntarily died for the people of the Western Frontier. Misief wondered if the killing of Sheriff Manuel was related to this particular passage. He was perplexed why anyone would be willing to voluntarily give up his life for people he did not know. With that thought in mind, he flipped open the book and read these words:

When the people of the Western Frontier were utterly helpless and acting like dang fools, filling their lives with nights of drinking, swearing, fighting and committing evil acts of all kinds, Sheriff Manuel came to the Western Frontier and died for them. Nobody would be willing to die for a bad person; however somebody might be willing to die for a person who was especially good. But Sheriff Adonai showed us how much he loved us by sending Sheriff Manuel to die for us while we were still wicked, corrupt, gun slinging people.

Misief was about to close the book when he decided to read one last passage. He thumbed toward the back of the book and saw these words underlined:

> *If any of you want to be a follower of Sheriff Adonai, you must put aside your own selfish ambition, surrender to me and follow my teachings. If you try to keep going down the selfish road you are traveling, you will ultimately lose your life. But if you surrender to Sheriff Adonai you will find true meaning and happiness in life.*

"I ain't surrendering to nobody," Misief snorted as he slung the book to the floor. "I've gotta get even with Lucas Benson before I do anything else."

With darkness enveloping the entire Western Frontier, Misief decided to call it a day. Blowing out the candle, he made a pallet on the floor out of a couple of old quilts. As he lay there in the stillness of the night, he contemplated the words he'd just read from 'The Album'. While he despised the concept of surrendering his life to anyone, he sure was tired of the life he was living! He wanted to change his ways, but he seemed powerless to do it on his own.

As Misief closed his eyes and drifted off to sleep, he quietly whispered these words, "Sheriff Adonai, if you are real and can bring happiness to my life I sure would appreciate it. I just don't know if I believe........."

****

The sun had been shining for a couple of hours before Misief opened his eyes. Enjoying a dozen or more hours of rest, he woke up Monday morning feeling much better than the day before. As he stood up and stretched a few times, he realized the soreness in his rib cage was much better. Moseying over to the dusty mirror, he noticed the swelling in his face had subsided, and other than a scab on his busted lip, he was beginning to look like his old self again. It had now been over thirty six hours since his last meal, and he decided it was worth the risk to slide into Rock Springs and grab a bite to eat at the café.

Within minutes, he'd collected his belongs and was walking through the front door of the old shack. As he stepped outside, he realized the ground was damp from the rain that occurred during the night.

"Boy, did you get wet?" Misief asked with a smile on his face as he secured his bags on Coal.

As Misief slowly rode toward town, he glanced at the mountain peaks in the distance. He sensed freshness in the air and hoped the rain shower was a sign of the beginning of a new day in his life.

****

It was close to 9:00 AM when Misief rode into Rock Springs via the back road. Still concerned that the local deputies might be looking for him, he tied Coal up behind the livery stable.

"Coal, you wait right here, and I'll be right back," he whispered, as he surveyed his surroundings.

Cautiously maneuvering from building to building in the direction of the café, Misief was pleased to see that the majority of the morning traffic had dissipated, and the café was relatively empty.

Spotting a table in the back corner, he slid into the seat without anyone paying any attention to him. Within minutes, Rachel, the waitress, approached him and asked, "Hello Misief, what can I get you to eat?"

"How about some eggs, bacon, pancakes and coffee," he replied.

Rachel recorded his order, turned and walked back into the kitchen. He didn't think she noticed his busted lip, and she didn't seem to act suspicious when she talked with him. He wondered if it was possible that the saloon girl hadn't told anyone about what had happened out behind the saloon on Saturday night. Uncertain of who knew what, he kept an eye focused on the front door as he patiently waited for his breakfast.

Soon Rachel returned with four scrambled eggs, a generous serving of bacon, a stack of pancakes and a large cup of coffee. Misief thanked Rachel for the food, and within minutes, he had inhaled every morsel. There was not a crumb left on his plate!

Settling up with Rachel, he walked out of the café and immediately felt his energy level rising. The food was exactly what his body needed!

Rounding the corner of the cafe, Misief walked toward the back of the building making certain to maintain a low profile. While he did his best not to act suspiciously guilty, it was difficult not to be somewhat paranoid of anyone who looked his direction.

"Just blend in and act normal," he thought, as he kept his eyes focused straight ahead.

Within minutes Misief worked his way to the back of the livery stable where Coal was patiently waiting for him. Quickly mounting up, he nudged the stallion and they took off on the back road that led out of Rock Springs.

As he passed by the rear of the saloon, Misief noticed a group of men gathered near the back door of the building. He wasn't certain what they were doing, but it appeared to be some sort of business transaction that was taking place. He was trying his best to pass by undetected, but the men noticed him the minute he came out from behind the livery stable!

Unbeknownst to Misief, the group he had interrupted was the infamous Marshall gang. As fate would have it, he'd shown up right in the middle of an illegal business transaction between the Marshall gang and a few local businessmen from Rock Springs. The last thing they wanted was a witness who could report them to the authorities.

One of the members of the Marshall gang hollered, "Hey, what are you doing back here?"

Misief replied, "I'm just headed home! You fellas have a good day," he said as he attempted to get away.

To his dismay, one of the men recognized him, and Misief immediately realized he was staring right into the eyes of Brazen, the man he'd clobbered with a beer bottle the night Billin stole the money from the saloon. Brazen stood up, pulled his weapon, and appeared to be eager to settle the score.

All Misief had wanted was to quietly slip in for a bite of breakfast and get back out of town without being seen. Now his day had taken a serious turn in the wrong direction.

If the situation wasn't bad enough, it immediately got worse! At the same moment he locked eyes with Brazen, Misief heard several horses approaching. Looking back over his shoulder, he shook his head in disbelief, as deputies from the Rock Springs Sheriff's Office were closing in on the situation.

Acting upon a tip from a local citizen, the deputies were aware of the illegal transaction that was going down behind the saloon. Misief now found himself caught in a precarious and potentially deadly situation!

"Let's get out of here!" one of the Marshall Gang members hollered!

"Stop right there! You're all under arrest!" rang out from one of the deputies!

Immediately, horses and humans dispersed in all directions! Gunshots followed as the sounds of ricocheting bullets filled the air. Misief ducked his head, jerked the reins and kicked Coal as he shouted, "Giddy up, boy!"

What began as a calm sundrenched Monday morning had quickly turned into a hailstorm of lead, and now Misief's only objective was to save his own life!

Chapter 21

"Surrender!"

May 18, 1865

Misief immediately made a right hand turn and followed the road beside the saloon. Reaching the corner of the building, he directed Coal to turn again, and raced down the middle of Main Street. Approaching the sawmill, he made another quick turn and ducked in behind the building to contemplate his next move.

With his gun drawn, Misief remained motionless expecting the arrival of a member of the Marshall gang or one of the local Rock Springs deputies at any moment. As he paused in the stillness, he thought it sounded as if the majority of the commotion had shifted to the far end of town. Knowing that he could not hide out behind the sawmill forever, and wanting desperately to get home to the safety of his cabin, Misief made the decision to make a mad dash out of town.

Misief knew Coal was as fast as lightning, and his speed could not be matched by any other horse in Rock Springs. All he needed was a legitimate head start, and he was confident nobody would catch him. Even with that knowledge, there was a voice in his head that screamed words of caution. This voice of reason reminded him that if he made just one little mistake, it could lead to a member of the Marshall gang putting a lead slug in his head or a local lawman placing a set of cuffs on his wrists. Neither option seemed very appealing at the moment!

Speaking to Coal as if he was a human accomplice, Misief whispered, "Coal, we're gonna slip down the edge of this building, so I can take a peak down the road. As soon as I determine the coast is clear, I want you to run like you've never run before! Okay?"

With his instructions communicated to the stallion, Misief slowly led Coal toward Main Street. Arriving at the corner of the building, Misief rose up and look left, then right; the coast was clear. While in the distance he could still hear men hollering, the gunfire had momentarily subsided. The loud voices seemed to be coming from behind a building on the other end of town, and Misief believed this was his opportunity to make a run for the cabin!

Misief gave the black stallion a definitive nudge in the ribs and with a shake of the reins, yelled, "Giddy up boy."

Coal shot off like a bullet out of a rifle barrel. As the stallion raced at a blistering pace, Misief held on for dear life! The mighty animal ran as if it knew its owner's life was in peril!

Within moments, they arrived at the fork in the road. Wanting to get to the safety of his cabin as soon as possible, Misief decided to go up the Rock Springs side of Roberts Mountain. He knew this route would be much faster than going the long way around through Shoots Valley.

Even though he had slipped out of town undetected, severe paranoia began to set in. Misief believed he was being pursued and on occasions thought he heard the rhythmic sound of horses' hooves as they closed in on him. His heart was now racing so fast he thought it was going to explode right out of his chest. However, a quick glance over his right shoulder confirmed that he was alone on the trail.

"Maybe I'm just hearing things," he thought.

Misief gained his composure and focused on the next priority: getting to the safety of Roberts Mountain. He knew that if he found himself in a gunfight, the rugged mountain landscape would provide places to hide or at least a place to take cover. Out in the open plains he was a sitting duck, but once inside the canopy of the forest, he knew he would be in a better position in the event of a confrontation.

Pushing Coal as hard as he could, he knew he was only minutes from the base of the mountain. As the stallion continued to make a beeline for safety, Misief pondered how he ended up in this precarious position. In his mind, all his actions were based on defendable emotions; however, he wondered how he'd slipped up and was once again running from the law!

On the exterior, Misief seemed to have it all together, but on the inside, he was an absolute mess! At times, he felt as though he was destined to bring pain to those who really loved him, and over the last few months, he felt like he was always trying to stay one step ahead of those who wanted to do him harm. While he talked of hunting down Lucas Benson, he was actually a young man trying to run away from his past! Pursued by horrific images from days gone by, he continued making decisions that extinguished the rays of hope that promised of a bright future. His downward spiral was fueled by resentment and an unwillingness to forgive. His addictions now controlled him like a master puppeteer controls each move of a toy puppet. His heart ached when he thought of his mother; he felt shame when he thought of how he had failed his sister; and guilt swept over his body each time he lied to Nainsi.

He stayed on the run all the time! If you were to ask him where he was headed, Misief would proudly proclaim that he was searching for Lucas Benson, to bring honor to his father's name. But in reality, Misief Stone was running from himself!

Finally reaching the base of the mountain, Misief knew the winding trail to the top would require him to slow down. While he was in a hurry and wanted to stay ahead of those who might be pursuing him, he didn't want to do anything that would cause Coal to slip while going up the steep, rocky, mountain trail. Glancing back over his shoulder, he checked one last time before beginning the ascent up the mountain. While he did not see a soul stirring, he firmly believed someone would be coming sooner or later.

The rain shower that had occurred during the night left a small amount of moisture on the mountainous trail. The thin coat of moss that covered the rocks was extremely slick, causing Coal's hooves to slip from time to time. With his own adrenaline level extremely elevated, it was difficult for Misief to be patient and allow Coal the time needed to naturally pick his way through each slippery obstacle.

Plodding along at a steady pace, they soon approached the halfway point up Roberts Mountain. Misief gently pulled back on the reins and gave Coal a quick break. He used the opportunity to settle his own nerves and took several deep breaths as he kept a keen eye on the trail leading up the mountain. After a final deep breath, Misief closed his eyes a moment, sat perfectly still and listened.

Nothing! The entire mountain seemed to be completely quiet; almost eerily quiet. The only sounds that could be heard were the gentle breeze as it slithered carelessly through the leaves above him and the sound of a horse and his rider catching their breath!

Calmed a bit, Misief nudged Coal and the tandem continued their journey up the last section of the mountain. Working together, they made great time, and soon Misief found himself approaching the grassy clearing that carpeted the top of the mountain. With the infamous ledge known as Rock Pointe on his left, he paused to survey the beauty of the open meadow and the majestic stone formation that protruded out of the mountain.

Then the unthinkable occurred! About the moment Misief began to relax in the serenity of the mountain summit, he caught a glimpse of someone standing in the center of the trail that led down the back side of the mountain. He estimated the individual to be about 100 yards away, and he was not sure if the man had spotted him or not.

Quietly, he slid down off of Coal and led the stallion away from the main trail into the edge of the woods nearest Rock Pointe. Finding a cluster of dogwoods, he secured Coal to one of the small saplings and hoped the remaining trees would provide cover for the animal.

"Stay right here boy, while I mosey up a little closer and see who's out there," Misief stated as he gently patted Coal on the head.

Rock Pointe was about fifty yards ahead and was about halfway between the spot where Misief had secured Coal and the location where the person was standing on the trail.

"I need to get to Rock Pointe," Misief whispered, as he untied his leather satchel from Coal's saddle. "The rock will provide me with cover!"

After placing his favorite leather bag around his neck and loading his rifle, he headed out in the direction of the massive rock structure. Moving meticulously from tree to tree, he paused occasionally to check the movement of the individual and to carefully plan his next move. Without exception, each time Misief slipped his head out from behind a tree to check, this individual was in the same place, standing perfectly still right in the middle of the trail!

Misief was about halfway between his horse and Rock Pointe when this thought crossed his mind, "What if the person standing in the trail is one of the members of the Marshall gang? Could it be that they had doubled around through Shoots Valley and come up the back side of the mountain?"

"That's impossible," Misief whispered. "As fast as I pushed Coal, there is not a horse alive that could have traveled all the way through Shoots Valley and beat us to the top of the mountain!"

Moving parallel with the main trail, and using the mountain foliage as cover, Misief kept inching towards Rock Pointe as he contemplated the possibilities of the identity of the individual.

After fifteen minutes of crawling, tip-toeing and careful maneuvering, Misief reached his destination. Stepping onto the rocky surface of the landmark, he glanced to his left to catch a quick glimpse of the valley floor below.

A cracking noise in the distance immediately shifted Misief's focus from the spectacular view of Rock Springs to the situation at hand.

"That sounded like a breaking branch." Misief thought.

Misief was not at all prepared for what happened next. While crouched on the massive rock with his back against a sycamore tree, he heard a voice cry out, "Misief."

Misief's heart skipped a beat! He didn't recognize the voice at all and wondered, "Who in the world would be wandering around in the woods that would know my name?"

His initial thought was that it had to be one of the deputies from the sheriff's department. Most all of the lawmen in Rock Springs knew him personally from his nine month visit in their facility. He immediately thought to himself, "I ain't going back to jail without a fight!"

Carefully rising from a crouched position to standing, he kept his back firmly planted against the large sycamore tree. He held his rifle parallel with his body and listened for any possible sound. He heard nothing!

Misief continued standing in that position for what seemed like an eternity, but it was probably more like three or four minutes. During that time, not a soul stirred, and the deafening sound of silence was all that filled the air. There were no footsteps rustling through the foliage scattered on the forest floor. There were no voices carried by the gentle breeze that softly fluttered the leaves on the trees.

Then Misief began to wonder if his paranoid state of mind was to blame.

Was it possible that his brain was playing tricks on him?

Had he simply imagined that someone was calling his name?

Could the stress of the situation and the fear of capture be to blame?

It only took a moment to answer the questions swirling in his head, as once again he clearly heard someone shout, "Misief!"

This time it was unmistakable! This calling out for him was far louder and much clearer than the first time, and it sounded like the person had somehow maneuvered in much closer to Misief's current location. He knew he couldn't just stand there behind the tree and allow whoever it was to move in on him.

"I've got to turn around and get a visual on them," Misief whispered.

While keeping his body shielded by the tree, Misief turned one hundred and eighty degrees and now had his face plastered against the bark. Raising his rifle, he slid his head out from behind the tree to scan the forest.

Misief saw nothing!

He brought his head back to center and slowly leaned to the left.

Still not a person in sight!

"Where is he hiding?" Misief wondered.

Then he noticed an oak tree about fifty feet in front of him. While the trunk of the oak tree was not as wide as the sycamore, he knew it would provide a better vantage point to locate and possibly identify this person. Without giving it a second thought, Misief stepped out from behind the large sycamore and raced for the oak tree.

"I made it," Misief whispered, as he pressed his back against the tree for safety. As he stood there trying to calm his breathing, he was certainly not prepared for what he heard!

"Misief Stone," rang a voice that echoed through the woods like a clap of thunder from a storm!

"Misief Stone, where are you?" asked the voice that sounded as if it was right in front of him, standing behind him, and in the tree above him, all at the same time!

Absolutely coming apart at the seams emotionally, Misief totally disregarded his safety and began scanning in all directions.

He looked west, nothing!

He glanced to the south, nothing!

Misief made two complete revolutions and still, nothing! He even scanned the treetops thinking maybe they had shimmied up a tree...but there was not a person stirring anywhere!

Perplexed, stunned, and void of any idea of what to do next, Misief stood still with his back against the tree.

Then, without thinking through the potential consequences, he screamed at the top of his lungs and asked, "Who are you, and what do you want with me?"

Misief waited and wondered if he would get a response.

And then, out of the distance came a deep, authoritative voice. The voice stated, "Misief Stone, I've come one last time to ask you to surrender!"

"Surrender for what?" Misief screamed.

There was no immediate response.

Once again Misief shouted out, "I ain't done anything wrong—and I ain't surrendering!"

Suddenly, Misief noticed movement in his peripheral vision. Without a doubt, there was someone about forty to fifty yards ahead that was moving in his direction. Fearing the oak tree did not provide adequate cover, he sprinted back to the safety of Rock Pointe and the larger sycamore tree.

Then another passionate plea rang through the forest. "Misief Stone, stop running! It's time to surrender!"

Beads of sweat began to form on Misief's forehead as he contemplated his options. With the idea of surrender being low on his list, he screamed, "Dang it, I ain't surrendering! Turn around now, and leave me be!"

Back at the safety of the sycamore tree, Misief sensed the aggressive nature of this person. He realized a showdown was imminent. He believed that if he was to get off this mountain alive, he was going to have to engage this person and potentially use deadly force.

Now lying flat on the ground, Misief pointed his rifle in the direction of the last known location of the aggressive intruder. He was determined not to surrender and had made up his mind to shoot anyone or anything that moved toward him.

As he tried to calm down and catch his breath, Misief caught his first real glimpse of the person walking through the woods. It was obvious they were headed directly toward him. And, to his surprise, it appeared they were unarmed.

Now even more puzzled about the situation, Misief's eyes shifted to the feet of the approaching stranger. To his dismay, this person was wearing a pair of white cowboy boots!

Misief shook his head in disbelief and said, "Oh no, it ain't that dang stranger again, is it?"

Sure enough, as the man grew ever closer, Misief could clearly see the gold studs on the side of the pearl white cowboy boots. The white boots were all the confirmation Misief needed, to know this was the same stranger who had appeared to him so many times in the his life.

As he watched intently, Misief wondered why the stranger was now calling out his name and talking to him. This was different from any other interaction Misief had experienced in the past, when all the stranger would do was stare and motion as he asked him to give up his leather satchel.

With the stranger only seventy five feet from his location on the rock, Misief took aim at the five point star that was fastened to his shirt, right over his heart.

Pulling back the hammer, Misief yelled, "Stop right there! Don't make me kill you!"

A smile came to the stranger's face as he replied, "Son, your bullets have no impact on me! You just need to put down your weapon and surrender!"

"You think I believe that?" Misief snorted. "I'll blow your head clean off your shoulders, and we'll see what kind of impact it has on you!"

The stranger wasn't fazed by Misief's threat and continued to walk directly toward him.

The distance between Misief and the stranger was now only twenty five feet. Misief was about to make a life changing decision. With his finger on the trigger he mulled over his three options:

"If I pull the trigger and kill this lawman, I will automatically become an outlaw and be on the run for the rest of my life."

"If I pull the trigger and the authorities catch me, I will hang."

"If I don't pull the trigger and I surrender, I will probably lose Nainsi as she will not tolerate another jail sentence."

Believing it was now time to take action, Misief made the decision that he was not going back to jail. Without giving it another thought, he pulled the trigger and the rifle discharged a bullet headed directly for the heart of the stranger.

To Misief's surprise, the stranger didn't flinch at the gunshot, and it appeared as though the bullet either missed him or just went right though him.

Misief cursed and quickly fired a series of shots as the stranger kept walking straight toward him. With each shot, the bullets just glanced right through the stranger without doing any harm.

Misief continued cursing the stranger as he fired shot after shot, until the rifle clicked, indicating it was completely out of ammunition.

With the stranger standing three or feet in front of him, Misief trembled as he screamed, "Who are you, and why are you always following me? Are you a ghost? Have you been sent to haunt me?"

The stranger cracked a smile, shook his head and replied, "I'm no ghost, Misief."

The stranger's voice was full of compassion as he began to answer the questions that had burned in Misief's mind for many years. "Misief, my name is Sheriff Jachin. I've been following you since you were a little boy. It's time for you to surrender."

"Surrender for what?" Misief asked in a sarcastic tone.

"Misief, I want you to surrender your past; surrender your anger, your desire for revenge, your rage, and most of all, surrender yourself," Sheriff Jachin replied.

Misief looked totally puzzled at Sheriff Jachin's response, and asked, "What territory is your jurisdiction?"

"I have jurisdiction over the entire Western Frontier," Sheriff Jachin answered.

"I ain't done anything to you, so why don't you just leave me alone?" Misief asked in protest.

Sheriff Jachin responded, "Your right, son. However, you were born needing to surrender."

Sheriff Jachin reached into his pocket, pulled out a .50 caliber bullet and pitched it to Misief. From his crouched position on the rock, Misief caught the bullet in his left hand. He realized it was exactly like the bullet he'd found on the wardrobe in his mother's bedroom, after his father's death.

Misief then asked, "Okay, so we know you were the stranger in the bedroom the night my father was killed. Did you kill him?"

"No, I didn't have anything to do with the death of your father," Sheriff Jachin replied. "Like I've done with you, I actually tried many times to get your father to surrender to me, but he always refused."

Sheriff Jachin continued to explain, "You see, I'm with Sheriff Adonai. He's the one who sent me to talk to you. Sheriff Adonai wants you to give up your old life, and surrender to him."

Misief asked, "So you work for Sheriff Adonai?"

"I guess that's one way to look at it," Sheriff Jachin replied as he nodded.

Misief, still not understanding, asked, "I've heard of Sheriff Adonai and Sheriff Manuel. I saw their pictures on the wall in the sheriff's office when I was in jail. Are you the same as Sheriff Manuel who was sent by Sheriff Adonai?"

"Not exactly; Sheriff Manuel is the son of Sheriff Adonai and was sent by him for a specific purpose. Sheriff Adonai needed Sheriff Manuel to sacrifice his life for the people of the Western Frontier," Sheriff Jachin explained.

Misief questioned him further, "Are you a son of Sheriff Adonai like Sheriff Manuel?"

Sheriff Jachin clarified as he said, "No, Sheriff Adonai only has one son, and that is Sheriff Manuel. I am the spirit of Sheriff Adonai. My role is to be a personal helper to every man and woman who surrenders their life to Sheriff Adonai. I help them live morally upright lives and live peacefully with their fellow man. Misief, I can help you too if you will just surrender."

Then it all started to make sense. "So.....you're the 'J bullet' on the cover of 'The Album' book?" Misief asked.

"Yes," Sheriff Jachin replied.

"Sheriff Adonai is the father; Sheriff Manuel is his son, and I am the spirit of Sheriff Adonai. We are three in one, each with a separate job in helping the people of the Western Frontier. 'The Album' explains each of our roles and purposes. The bullets on the cover of the book are engraved with an initial representing each of us."

Sheriff Jachin continued, "Misief, look at that old leather bag you have around your neck. It's weighing you down. You're busy focusing on the issues of your past, and your past is bringing pain into your present life. You're obsession with finding Lucas Benson has opened you up to feelings and actions that are detrimental to your well-being. Your 'revenge list' needs to be handed over to me so that I can deal with those who have hurt you. You need to let me fight your battles."

Sheriff Adonai

Misief responded, "But I wanna get even with Lucas Benson. He did my father wrong."

Sheriff Jachin answered, "I know you do, son. I do understand your anger, but let me fight Lucas Benson for you. I promise I will get him."

Sheriff Jachin then unveiled a brand new leather bag.

"What is that?" Misief asked.

Sheriff Jachin explained, "This new bag is an exact match of the old leather bag of your father's that you've carried around for years."

Sheriff Jachin held out the new bag and said, "Misief, I'd like to offer to trade your old worn-out bag for this new one. You've spent your life carrying around the baggage of your father's past. There is nothing but pain and broken memories associated with your old bag."

Sheriff Jachin kept going, "Misief, this new leather bag has seven letters on it. The letters are, 'T.P.S.A.H.F.M.' and the letters represent, *'The Plans Sheriff Adonai Has For Misief'*. You see son, before you were born, Sheriff Adonai developed a plan for your life. It is a good plan, custom designed for you. But you've been following your own plan. You've been wandering along on a path headed for personal destruction. There is a better path for you! The plans personally developed by Sheriff Adonai for you are contained in this new leather bag."

Sheriff Jachin continued talking as Misief pondered the offer, "Misief, Sheriff Manuel came to the Western Frontier to show the people how to treat each other. The locals refused to listen to him because they were under the influence of Lucas Benson. That is why they shot and killed Sheriff Manuel. At any point in the killing, Sheriff Adonai could have sent forces to rescue Sheriff Manuel, but Sheriff Manuel willfully surrendered his life, and

Sheriff Adonai chose to allow his son to die, to set you free. All you have to do is accept the sacrifice of Sheriff Manuel, and from that point forward, I will be with you to help you in every aspect of your life. Misief, I want to release you from the prison of your past. I want to help you break the addictions that have you bound. With me helping you, you can break the addictions!!! But it's your choice! You must be willing to accept forgiveness, and to offer forgiveness to those who have harmed you. You need to believe that Sheriff Adonai has a plan for your life. I promise you, it is a good plan, and all you need to do is simply surrender and allow him to take over."

Sheriff Jachin walked over to Misief and sat down beside him. Misief offered no resistance and just sat there not sure what to say or do.

Sheriff Jachin looked straight into Misief's eyes and asked, "Misief, I know you've had a rough life. You've watched both of your parents die. You've had so many bad influences in your life, and now you're all alone. The poor choices you've made have you on the run. Aren't you exhausted? Don't you want peace and deliverance from all the chaos in your life? Wouldn't you like for your life to have purpose and meaning?"

Misief dropped his head, looked at the ground and nodded. Sheriff Jachin gently placed his hand under Misief's chin and with the love of an endearing grandfather, lifted up his head.

"Misief," Sheriff Jachin began, "Your eyes are bruised; your lip is busted, and your ribs are sore. You just got out of a nine month stretch in jail. Is this madness worth all the pain?"

Sheriff Jachin reached out with the new leather bag. "Swap bags with me, Misief. Let go of the past, and accept the new life Sheriff Adonai has for you. I promise, I will always be with you to help you, and I will never leave you!"

Misief looked up at Sheriff Jachin and asked, "How can you help me all the time?"

Sheriff Jachin answered, "Misief, I am a spirit; the very spirit of Sheriff Adonai. If you swap leather bags with me and accept the sacrifice Sheriff Manuel made for you, I will live inside of you. There is nothing we can't do together! I have an unlimited supply of strength available for you. I will be in you, and I will help you make the changes you so desperately want to make in your life. I know your thoughts, and I know that you want to change. You want to be free from the addictions that grip you. But, I don't force my way on anyone. Misief, the choice to surrender-to swap leather bags with me, is totally up to you."

Misief reached down and stared at the leather bag that was hanging around his neck. He gently removed the old bag and pulled it to his chest. He opened the flap and slowly pulled out his revenge list, the knife that once belonged to Lucas Benson, the handwritten note from Lucas, and his copy of 'The Album' given to him by Sachiel. It was obvious Misief was carefully weighing his options as he held the mementos in his hands.

After several minutes of careful contemplation, Misief began placing each artifact back into his leather bag and closed it. Without any additional coercing from Sheriff Jachin, Misief reached out and handed over the leather bag to the sheriff.

Sheriff Jachin immediately took the old leather bag which was filled with representations of bitterness, pain, anger and feelings of revenge that had tormented Misief throughout his entire life. Then Sheriff Jachin smiled as he handed Misief the brand new leather bag that contained the personalized plans Sheriff Adonai had for his life.

Clutching the new leather bag close to his chest, something occurred that had not happened since the night Misief's father died.

As Misief's old self began to die and a new spirit began its residency, he felt the warmth of a single tear form in his eye. This single tear was followed by another, then another. Soon tears began to flow down his cheeks and onto his shirt. Sitting on the massive rock, Misief released all the anger that had embodied him for so many years. He felt the warmth of forgiveness as his heart had been set free from the hatred that had gripped him all his life.

Misief closed his eyes and savored the breeze of freedom as his mind was now liberated and could focus on love and forgiveness. There at the top of Roberts Mountain, at a place called Rock Pointe, Misief Stone surrendered his old life and became a brand new man!

When Misief opened his eyes, he was surprised to see Sheriff Jachin wasn't sitting beside him anymore. He stood up and yelled, "Sheriff Jachin, Sheriff Jachin, where are you?"

There was no answer.

Misief sat back down on the rock and placed his hands on his heart. He closed his eyes and breathed the words, "You are inside me Sheriff Jachin! I feel your spirit within me!"

Misief immediately opened the new leather bag. Inside the bag he found a brand new copy of 'The Album' with his name engraved in bold letters. He ran his fingers across his name, 'Misief Stone'. Placing the book down by his side, he peered back into the bag and noticed a letter. The letter was written in crimson blood on beautiful gold paper and was personally addressed to him. The letter read:

Misief Stone,

I, Sheriff Adonai love the people of the Western Frontier so much that I sent my only son, Sheriff Manuel to die for every man, woman, boy and girl. Now that you have accepted the sacrifice of Sheriff Manuel, I've authorized Sheriff Jachin to live in your heart. He will be your friend, your guide, and your strength. He will never leave you and will always be with you. At this very moment, Sheriff Jachin lives in you, and you can talk to him anytime you need to.

My son, you are now a free man. You have been set free from the pain that had you bound for so many years. You are forever free, and you are forgiven for all the evil things you've done in your life. Celebrate your freedom!

Misief, someday Sheriff Manuel will return to the Western Frontier. I'll tell you all about that and all about the wonderful plans I have for your life in your brand new personalized copy of 'The Album'.

Welcome to the family, son!

High Sheriff Adonai
Creator of the Western Frontier

PS. The next time you see Jamison, please tell him that Sheriff Adonai still loves him!

Misief stood up and surveyed the valley below. The trees, the grass and the flowers had never seemed more vibrant and alive! Glancing upward, an eagle soared overhead against a cobalt blue sky! The warm summer breeze felt like a personal massage upon his face. His heart was light, and his mind had been set free. The anger from his past had dissipated, and his soul no longer cried out for revenge. He had experienced the mighty force of forgiveness, and every fiber of his being wanted to make amends for all the pain he'd caused to those he loved!

Misief was ecstatic and wanted to tell somebody about his encounter with Sheriff Jachin. He looked in every direction but realized he was alone on top of the mountain. Then, it occurred to him that Coal was still tied up in the cluster of dogwood trees.

As Misief approached Coal, he immediately noticed something was missing. The .50 caliber bullet that he had attached to Coal's saddle was gone. In the place normally occupied by the bullet, was a brand new leather necklace. He picked up the necklace and saw there were three bullets hanging on it. The first bullet was engraved with the letter 'A'; the middle bullet had an 'M', and the third bullet bore the letter 'J" for Sheriff Jachin! There was a note attached to the necklace which read:

Misief,
Please accept this necklace as a gift from us to you. You are now on our team! Wear it with pride!
Signed, Sheriff's Adonai, Sheriff Manuel & Sheriff Jachin

Tears flowed down his face as he fastened the necklace in place. It was his honor to be counted as a member of the Sheriff Adonai family. He was grateful for the sacrifice of Sheriff Manuel, and he was comforted knowing that Sheriff Jachin would be living within him for the rest of his life!

As Misief untied Coal from the tree, he gave his stallion a kiss right on the mouth! "Sorry boy, don't know what got into me. I'm just feeling happier than I have ever been in my entire life."

Coal was clueless, but seemed to sense that his master had experienced a life-changing transformation!

Misief climbed up on Coal with his new leather bag around his shoulder and his necklace dangling from his neck. He felt so much relief now that the bondage of the past had been lifted from him.

No longer did he feel responsible for the sins of his father. He was free to live the life Sheriff Adonai had personally customized for him.

"Come on Coal, it's time to get started living," Misief declared as he settled into the saddle.

Instead of traveling to the cabin to hide, Misief turned around and decided to head back to Rock Springs. The first thing he wanted to do was to find Nainsi and tell her about his personal encounter with Sheriff Jachin. He also wanted to go by the jail and let Jamison know that Sheriff Adonai still loved him and was willing to forgive him if he would only ask.

Before the stallion took a step, Misief paused for just a moment. He realized his life would still have some tough moments and times of temptation, but somehow he felt a new level of confidence with Sheriff Jachin living inside him to help him. He'd never had a constant companion, and this new feeling of intimacy with his creator was the most amazing thing he'd ever experienced.

With one hand on Coal's reins, Misief clutched his new three bullet necklace with his other hand and prayed;

"Sheriff Adonai, Sheriff Manuel, and Sheriff Jachin, thank you for being patient with me on those days when I was so bad! Thank you for forgiving me! Thank you for loving a sinful young man like me. Please be with me as I start my new life! I cannot do it alone; but I know you will be there for me! Most of all, thank you for your peace! I've never felt like this in all my life! Amen."

There at Rock Pointe, with the noonday sun beaming overhead, Misief Stone prayed the first prayer of his brand new life!

As Misief made his way down the trail, he was grateful that he had been given a fresh start. He now had an opportunity to build an honest relationship with the love of his life, Nainsi. He had a renewed chance to fulfill the promise he made to his mom to take care of Ashel. He knew it was time to become a man who was not afraid to stand up for what was right and to live a life committed to following the teachings of Sheriff Adonai!

As Misief approached the bottom of Roberts Mountain, he thought about the irony of his entire life. Up until this encounter, he had refused to surrender and was always determined to do things his way. However, the thing he feared the most, to simply surrender, turned out to be what actually set him free!

Epilogue

The Bible tells us, "In the beginning, God Almighty (*Sheriff Adonai*) created the heavens and the earth (*the Western Frontier*)." He created the planets, the stars, the sun and all living things, including plants, animals and human life. God created a man named Adam and a woman named Eve as the first people.

Adam and Eve lived in a beautiful place called the Garden of Eden. Life in the Garden of Eden was perfect; until one day, Satan *(Lucas Benson)* slithered into the garden and persuaded Adam and Eve to disobey God. When Adam and Eve succumbed to the temptation of Satan, sin entered into the heart of mankind, and as a result, all of humanity inherited a sinful heart that separates us from God.

But God had a remedy for this sin problem. 2,000 years ago, in the town of Bethlehem, God Almighty sent His Son, Jesus Christ *(Sheriff Manuel)* to be born to the Virgin Mary. His name was Emmanuel, which means, 'God with Us'.

Jesus Christ was God in the flesh. He came to earth to teach us how to live and how to love. He also came to pay the final sacrifice for sin so that we could have a personal, intimate relationship with God.

When Jesus was just a young man in his early thirties, he was falsely accused of blasphemy and sentenced to death. His execution was ordered by Pilate and carried out by Roman soldiers. The soldiers beat Jesus with a whip, spit upon Him, and then forced Him to personally carry His own cross before ultimately nailing Him to it by His hands and feet.

Around midday, Jesus died, and the entire world went dark. A massive earthquake ensued which shook the whole earth, and the veil in the Holy Temple ripped from the top to the bottom. Jesus was then buried in a borrowed tomb that was heavily guarded by Roman soldiers. On the morning of the third day after His crucifixion, Jesus Christ rose from the dead in a display of His power over death, hell and the grave!

Shortly after rising from the dead, Jesus ascended back to Heaven to be with God the Father. But He didn't leave us alone, He sent us His Spirit (*Sheriff Jachin*). Just as Sheriff Jachin promised to be with Misief, the Holy Spirit lives in the hearts of all God's children. The Holy Spirit of God is our strength, our guide, and our constant companion.

God Almighty still loves the people of this world. He loves you! God is calling out and asking you to surrender your life to Him and accept the sacrifice He paid for you. God wants to take away the brokenness of your past and give you a brand new purpose, a new outlook and a new heart!

Just like Misief, God reaches out to us and speaks to us through the Holy Spirit. Maybe the Holy Spirit is speaking to you right now. When you hear His voice, will you consider surrendering your life to Him?

Are you tired of running?

Are you tired of harboring the pain, anger and brokenness of your past?

God sent His Son to die so you could be set free from this bondage. But, the choice is yours! Follow Misief's example and surrender!

To surrender your life to God Almighty and accept the sacrifice that His Son, Jesus Christ, made on your behalf, you just need to repent of your sins and ask for His forgiveness. He promised us that if we ask, He will cleanse us from all of our sins and adopt us into His eternal family!

If you need additional spiritual guidance or would like to know more about Jesus Christ, I encourage you to speak to your local pastor or spiritual leader. I'm sure they would be excited to talk with you about this important decision. If you do not have anyone available to talk with you, feel free to contact me at SheriffAdonai@gmail.com.

May God bless you as you walk down the dusty trail of life with Him!

D. Keith Jones

Other Books from D. Keith Jones

Sheriff Adonai, The Search for Havenwood, is the second book in the Sheriff Adonai series. The saga continues, as Bracken and his new found friends embark upon a journey to find love that has slipped through their fingers. However, Lucas Benson and his cohorts are determined to ensure their mission ends in failure.

This story is filled with adventure, suspense, love, and mystery. You will laugh, you will cry, and you might even find yourself trembling in fear; but ultimately you will have to ask yourself the question, "Are you on the trail to Havenwood?"

Order Your Copy Today at SheriffAdonai.com!

Other Books from D. Keith Jones

What does it mean to live a life blessed by God? The world has so many definitions regarding the blessings of God. Some bible teachers say it is all about tangible items such as money, cars, homes and good jobs. Is that the meaning of a life blessed by God? Others will tell you to give everything away to the poor to find God's blessing. Is this the right approach? *"Relinquish Control"*, is an easy to read book that will walk you through the biblical truths on how to position yourself to be blessed by God. God wants to bless His children more than you will ever know!

Order Your Copy Today at SheriffAdonai.com!